**Forge Books by
Larry Bond and Jim DeFelice**

Larry Bond's First Team
Larry Bond's First Team: Angels of Wrath
Larry Bond's First Team: Fires of War
Larry Bond's First Team: Soul of the Assassin*

*Forthcoming

LARRY BOND'S FIRST TEAM

FIRES OF WAR

LARRY BOND AND JIM DEFELICE

FORGE®

A TOM DOHERTY ASSOCIATES BOOK
NEW YORK

This is a work of fiction. All of the characters, organizations, and events
portrayed in this novel are either products of the authors' imagination or are
used fictitiously.

LARRY BOND'S FIRST TEAM: FIRES OF WAR

Copyright © 2006 by Larry Bond and Jim DeFelice

All rights reserved, including the right to reproduce this book, or portions
thereof, in any form.

A Forge Book
Published by Tom Doherty Associates, LLC
175 Fifth Avenue
New York, NY 10010

www.tor-forge.com

Forge® is a registered trademark of Tom Doherty Associates, LLC.

ISBN-13: 978-0-7653-4640-7
ISBN-10: 0-7653-4640-0

First Edition: November 2006
First Mass Market Edition: December 2007

Printed in the United States of America

0 9 8 7 6 5 4 3 2 1

Author's Note

The First Team and the Joint Services Special Demands Project Office are entirely fictional.

Although the author has relied upon his research into the operations of certain actual nuclear facilities and related entities, the commercial entities, nuclear facilities, and waste sites described in this book are a product of the author's imagination.

Dramatis Personae

FIRST TEAM

Bob "Ferg" Ferguson
Sgt. Stephen "Skip" Rankin, U.S. Army
Sgt. Jack "Guns" Young, U.S. Marines
Thera Majed

SUPPORT PERSONNEL

Col. Charles Van Buren, commander, 777th Special Forces
Jack Corrigan, mission coordinator
Lauren DiCapri, mission coordinator

WASHINGTON

Corrine Alston, counsel to the president
Jonathon McCarthy, president of the United States
Thomas Parnelles, CIA director
Daniel Slott, deputy director, CIA
Josh Franklin, assistant secretary of defense
Senator Gordon Tewilliger
James Hannigan, legislative assistant to Sen. Tewilliger

SOUTH KOREA

Park Jin Tae, businessman

NORTH KOREA

General Namgung il-Tan, commander First Armed Forces
Dr. Tak Ch'o, scientist, Peoples' Waste Site 1

ACT 1

Heartless time floats,
    A dream, on and on . . .

—from "The Seventh Princess," traditional
    Korean song for the dead

1

SICILY

"Dance?"

The blonde took a step backward, clutching at the collar of her blouse as if it had been wide open.

"I don't *think* so," she said.

"Come on. You look like you could use a dance." Bob Ferguson gestured to the side of the open piazza, where a small jazz band was playing. "They're playing our song."

"This isn't dance music," said the woman stiffly, "and you're very forward."

"Usually I'm not," Ferguson turned to the woman's companion and pleaded his case, "but I'm here on holiday. Tell your friend she should dance with me."

"I don't know."

Ferguson laughed and turned back to the blonde. "I'm not going to bite. You're British, right?"

"I am from Sweden."

"Coulda fooled me."

"You're Irish?"

"As sure as the sun rises." He stuck out his hand. "Dance?"

The woman didn't take his hand.

"How about you?" Ferguson asked, turning to the other woman.

"I'm Greek."

"No, I meant, would you dance?"

Thera Majed hesitated but only for a moment. Then, shrugging to her companion, she stepped over to Ferguson, who immediately put his hand on her hip and waltzed her into the open space near the tables.

"Hello, Cinderella," whispered Ferguson. "How are you doing?"

"I'm fine. What's going on?"

"I felt like dancing."

"I'll bet. What would you have done if Julie accepted your offer?"

"I would have enjoyed two dances."

Ferguson whisked her out of the way of a hurrying waiter.

"There's no one else dancing, you know," said Thera.

"Really? *'But I only have eyes, for you.'*" Ferguson sang the last words, grabbing a snatch of a song.

"Why are you contacting me?"

"Itinerary's changed," he said, spinning her around.

"What's up?" she asked as she came back to him.

"Everything's being moved forward. Some sort of push by the UN. You're leaving for Korea in the morning."

Ferguson danced her around, improvising a stride slightly quicker than a standard foxtrot to swing with the jazz beat. He'd learned to dance as a teenager in prep school—the only useful subject he picked up there, according to his father.

"We're not going to have time to get security people on your team," he whispered, pulling her back.

He felt her arms stiffen and started another twirl.

"You all right, Cinderella?" he asked her, reeling her back in.

"Of course," said Thera.

"We'll have people standing by. Relief caches will go in while you're down South, exactly where we'd said they'd be. Plan's the same; you're just not going to have anyone on the IAEA inspection team with you." He stopped and looked at her. "You cool with that?"

The IAEA was the International Atomic Energy

Agency. After two months of training, Thera had been planted on the agency as a technical secretary; her team had just finished an inspection in Libya.

"I'm OK, Ferg. We shouldn't make this too obvious, do you think?"

"Hey, I'm having fun," he said, leaning her over.

He glanced toward the Swedish scientist, who was watching them with an expression somewhere between bewilderment and outrage. Ferguson gave the blonde a smile and pulled Thera back up.

"If you want to bail, call home. We'll grab you."

"I'm OK, Ferg. I can do it."

"Slap me."

"Huh?"

"Slap me, because I just told you how desperately I want to take you to bed."

"I—"

" 'I only have eyes, for you . . .' "

"I won't," said Thera loudly. She took a step back and put her hands on her hips. "No."

"Come on," said Ferguson. "We're obviously meant for each other."

Thera told him in Greek that he was an animal and a pig. The first words sputtered. She imagined herself to be the technical secretary she was portraying, not the skilled CIA paramilitary looking for violations of the new Korean nuclear nonproliferation treaty.

And she imagined Ferguson not to be her boss and the man who had saved her neck just a few months before but a snake and a rogue and a thief, roles he was well accustomed to playing.

Though he was a handsome rogue, truth be told.

"Go away," she said in English. Her cheeks were warm. "Go!"

"Should I take that as a no?" Ferguson asked.

Thera turned and stomped to her table.

She seemed to take that well," said Stephen Rankin sarcastically when Ferguson got back to the table. "What'd you do, kick her in her shins?"

"I tried to, but she wouldn't stand still." Ferguson sipped from the drink, a Sicilian concoction made entirely from local liquor. It tasted like sweet but slightly turned orange juice and burned the throat going down, which summed up Sicily fairly well.

"You think she's gonna bail?" Rankin asked.

"Nah. Why do you think that?"

"I don't think that. I'm asking if *you* think that."

Ferguson watched Thera talking with the Swedish female scientist. He could still smell the light scent of her perfume and feel the sway of her body against his.

She wasn't going to quit, but she was afraid. He'd sensed it, dancing with her. But fear wasn't the enemy most people thought. In some cases, for some people, fear made them sharper, smarter, and better.

Ferguson thought Thera was that kind of person; she'd certainly done well in Syria, and there was as much reason to be afraid then as there would be in North Korea.

He jumped to his feet to chase the thought away. "Let's get going, Skippy."

"One of these days I'm going to sock you for calling me Skippy."

"I wish you'd try. Let's get out to the airport."

2

"Ms. Alston? Ma'am?"

Corrine looked up from her computer to see Jess Northrup, poking his head in the doorway.

"President was wondering if you could wander into his office in about five minutes," said Northrup, who as an assistant to the chief of staff was the president's schedule keeper. "Senator Tewilliger's in there."

"Thanks, Jess." Corrine hit the Save button and stood up. "How's the car?"

Northrup's face, which had been so serious his cheeks looked as if they were marble, brightened immediately. "Paint job over the weekend," he said. "Assuming matters of state don't interfere."

"You promised me a ride with the top down."

"Soon as it's done."

Northrup's car was a 1966 Mustang convertible he'd started rebuilding soon after Jonathon McCarthy won re-election as senator nearly four years before. McCarthy was now president, but Northrup's car still lacked key items, among them an engine.

"Do you have a fresh yellow pad?" she asked her secretary, Teri Gatins, in the outer office.

"Wandering into the Oval Office?" said Gatins.

Corrine returned the assistant's smirk. Having an aide "spontaneously" interrupt him was a favorite McCarthy tactic for cutting short visits from people like Gordon Tewilliger, who were too important and dangerous to blow off but too dense to take all but the most obvious hint that it was time to leave.

"You have that appointment with Director Parnelles at Langley on Special Demands this afternoon," said Gatins as Corrine took the notebook. "Should I get you a sandwich?"

"I'm not really hungry. It's only eleven."

"I'll get corned beef," said the secretary, picking up the phone.

The president's office was only a few feet down the hall, but in that distance Corrine transformed herself, consciously changing her stride and stare. Senator Gordon Tewilliger was not, technically speaking, an enemy, but he was far from a friend.

Very far. Though he was a member of McCarthy's own party, there were strong rumors that he was thinking about launching a primary fight against him. The election was a good three years away, and Tewilliger had steadfastly denied that he was interested in the job, but even the newspeople thought he was testing the water.

Corrine winked at Northrup, knocked once on the door, and pushed inside.

"Well, now, if I didn't know any better, Gordon," said McCarthy, eyes fixed on Tewilliger, "I might think one or two of those projects there smelled of pork."

"Pork?"

"*Pork* might not be the proper word in this context." McCarthy came by his South Carolina accent honestly— his forebears, as he liked to call them, had been in the state since before the revolution—but sometimes it was *more* honest than others. At the moment it was honest in the extreme.

"I expect that many of those programs are important programs in their own right," added McCarthy. "One or two of those highway patrol elements, I believe, should be funded through Transportation. And in a case or two of high priority relating to homeland defense, those items might be added by our budget director, working in close relation with your staff, of course."

Senator Tewilliger, who for a moment had felt as if he'd been punched in the stomach, now felt like a man pulled from the ocean. He knew it was partly, perhaps mostly, a game—he'd seen McCarthy operating in the Senate and was well aware how smooth he could be—but still, in that instant he felt grateful, even flattered, that the president was going to help him.

Then he felt something else: the absolute conviction that he, Gordon Tewilliger, deserved to be the next president of the United States. McCarthy couldn't be trusted with power like this.

Corrine cleared her throat. "I didn't realize you were in the middle of something."

"Well, now, Miss Alston, I am always in the middle of something," said McCarthy. "Isn't that right, Senator?"

"Yes. Corrine, how are you?" Tewilliger nodded in Corrine's direction.

"Senator Tewilliger and I were just discussing how important the security of Indiana is. He has been doing quite a bit of work to ensure that we do not forget the state in the upcoming homeland defense bill."

"Just keeping the home fires burning," said the senator.

It occurred to Corrine that, had McCarthy lost his bid for president, she could well be working for Tewilliger right now, as counsel to the Senate Armed Services Committee; he had inherited the chairmanship when McCarthy left.

Then again, she and Tewilliger had clashed in the past, and it was much more likely that he would have fired her. He liked his aides and staffers to be people he could push around.

Tewilliger got up to leave; McCarthy got up as well, extending his hand. "It occurs to me, Gordon, that you haven't declared which way you will vote on the Korean nonproliferation treaty."

"No, I haven't," said Tewilliger.

"Well, now, I hope you will explain your views to me on any possible objection you have."

"I'm not sure I have any objections."

McCarthy continued to grip the senator's hand. "You're worried about verification of the treaty?"

"We all have concerns."

"That is a difficult section of the entire document, I must give you that." McCarthy glanced toward Corrine. "Have you had a chance to finish your review, Miss Alston?"

"I have looked at it, yes, sir," said Corrine. The president made it sound offhand, but in fact Corrine had reviewed several drafts of the treaty and spent countless hours with State Department lawyers refining some of the language.

"And what do you think?" said McCarthy.

"At first blush, the language appears solid. The difficulty is making sure North Korea complies with it."

"Now that is the first time I think in the history of the Union, perhaps in the history of *mankind,* that a lawyer has admitted there is something of importance beyond the letter and face of the law," said McCarthy. He turned back to Senator Tewilliger. "I have some concerns about verification, but ultimately our question should be: Is the treaty better than nothing?"

"I've always taken a hard line with North Korea," said Tewilliger. "We have to be tough with them. We need assurances."

"What sort of assurance would be sufficient, Senator?" asked Corrine. "We have their six warheads under constant surveillance. Their launch vehicles have been dismantled. The International Atomic Energy Agency will inspect all military and nuclear facilities on the peninsula and Japan. Beyond that, we have the satellites and—"

"That's another thing that bothers me," said Tewilliger. "South Korea is being treated like a pariah here."

"Well, now, Gordon, I have to say the South Koreans are the least part of the problem," said McCarthy. "They have less to hide than the preacher's wife."

"I didn't say they were a problem, just that they have to be treated fairly."

"True, true," said the president. "Perhaps you could give the verification matter additional thought. Maybe someone from State could go over and brief your committee."

"Yes. Of course." Tewilliger decided it was time to leave. "I better let you get back to work."

"Always a pleasure talking to you, Gordon," said McCarthy, walking with him to the door.

"South Korea's being treated unfairly?" said Corrine after the senator was gone. "Where did that come from?"

The president pulled his chair out and sat down. He had known Corrine literally all of her life; her father was one of his best friends, and he had visited the family at the hospital the day after she was born. She'd worked for him since high school, first as a volunteer, then as a lawyer.

"Well, dear. What the senator just told us is very interesting," explained McCarthy. His thick Southern drawl not only made "dear" sound like "deah"; it removed any hint of condescension. "I would wager a good part of the back forty that some of Senator Tewilliger's Korean-American constituents are feeling that North Korea is getting all of the attention."

"The South Koreans pushed for the deal."

"South Korea did, yes. We are not talking about South Korea. We're talking about the senator's constituents. Very different."

McCarthy leaned back in his seat. Against his wishes, the disarmament treaty had become an important centerpiece of his foreign-policy strategy, an important test not only of his plans to limit the growth of nuclear weapons—Iran was his next target—but of his influence with Congress. Lose the vote, and Congress would feel emboldened to block any number of initiatives.

"And how precisely *are* we doing on verification?" he asked Corrine.

"The mission is proceeding. The IAEA just changed its

inspection plans, pushing things up. The First Team should get there in—"

McCarthy put up his hand. He didn't want to know the specifics, just that Corrine had it under control.

"You know, Parnelles is not in favor of the treaty," said Corrine, referring to CIA Director Thomas Parnelles.

"As I recall he said he is not *opposed* to the treaty," said McCarthy.

"Same thing, if you read between the lines."

"Not precisely. Mr. Parnelles is very careful with his words, very, very careful. There are no lines to read between."

McCarthy folded his arms. He admired Parnelles a great deal, but having a strong man in charge of the CIA presented certain problems. Appointing Corrine as his "liaison" to Special Demands and its so-called First Team of CIA paramilitary officers and Special Forces soldiers was one of several steps he'd taken to keep some control over the agency without pulling the reins too tight.

"Like many of the people who work for him at the CIA," continued the president, "Tom Parnelles does not trust the North Koreans to tell him whether the sun is shining on a cloudless day."

"Do you?"

"Of course not." McCarthy laughed. "That's why your people are there."

Corrine wasn't particularly comfortable calling the First Team "her people," but she let the remark pass.

"Anything else, Jon?"

"No. Thank you, dear. I believe I should release you back to your regular chores."

"I'll have that briefing paper on the requests from the Senate ready for you first thing in the morning, so you can read it on your way up to Pennsylvania."

"Very good." McCarthy was heading off on a nine-day, twelve-state swing across the country in the morning. "By the way, Miss Alston, I spoke to your daddy last evening. He asked me to send his regards."

"Oh?"

"He was concerned that you are not getting enough time off. He saw a picture of you on the television the other day and said you looked rather ragged."

"I hope you took full blame for that."

"I did, I did. And I gave orders to the press secretary to keep you off camera from now on."

"I'm in favor of that."

"Call him a little more, would you, dear?" said McCarthy as she got up to leave.

"I call him once a week."

"That's not very much to a father. Trust me."

"Yes, Mr. President."

ROME

Ferguson and Rankin caught a commercial flight from Sicily to Rome's Da Vinci airport, where they were supposed to be met by a specially chartered Gulf Stream and flown to Korea. But the plane had been delayed leaving the States and wouldn't arrive for several hours; it would need at least one on the ground to refuel.

Rather than hanging out in the terminal, Ferguson decided they should go into the city. He could check the latest intelligence at the embassy, then maybe find a decent dinner and an espresso. Ferguson had always liked Rome; when he was a kid, his father had come over every few weeks from Egypt and Ferguson had occasionally tagged along.

He realized now that his father had probably been running a spy here or sending back material he'd gathered in

Cairo—most likely both—but at the time it seemed like a vacation.

"Rome's cool when you're a kid," he told Rankin in the cab. "I used to play hide-and-seek in the Forum ruins and chase cats in the Coliseum."

"I wouldn't mind seeing the Coliseum," said Rankin. "And St. Peter's."

"St. Peter's? The cathedral?"

"Why not?"

The taxi driver looked over his shoulder and told them that the cathedral would be closed for tours in an hour and, if he wanted to see it, he'd better go there first.

"All right, you go over to the church. I'll meet you there when I'm done," Ferguson told Rankin.

Rankin could never tell with Ferguson whether he had another agenda or not—usually he had three or four going at a time and would share only one and a half—but finally he decided Ferguson was just trying to be nice.

Uncharacteristically nice, as far as Rankin was concerned, but what the hell.

"Thanks," he told Ferguson. "I appreciate it."

"Any time, Skippy."

Rankin felt his face burn red but kept his mouth shut.

Ferguson's first order of business in the embassy's secure communications center was to check in with the mission coordinator back home in what was affectionately known as "The Cube." Nothing more than a high-tech communications center—albeit one located in a bugproof concrete bunker—The Cube was located beneath a nondescript building in a ho-hum industrial park in Virginia. Mission coordinators manned the Cube around the clock, providing Ferguson and other team members with whatever they needed. A small group of researchers and analysts were also housed at the facility, assigned to support current operations.

"Hey, Ferg," said Jack Corrigan, the mission coordinator on duty. "Sorry about the plane."

"Not a problem, Jack. Gave Rankin a chance to connect with his inner tourist."

"Van wants you to check in with him."

"He's my next call."

"How was Thera?"

"Crazy legs? She's just fantastic."

"Huh?"

"Long story, Jack. She's fine. Looking forward to it. Promised to send postcards."

"IAEA just told their staff."

"Good for them. Can you get me Van?"

"On it."

A few minutes later, Colonel Charles Van Buren's voice snapped onto the line.

"Hey, Ferg," said the colonel, speaking from Osan military base in South Korea. "Where are you?"

"On my way. What's going on? You sound tired."

"Playing basketball. Gettin' my ass whooped."

"We set?"

"Everything's planned out. We have an unexpected bonus from the navy: amphibious warship we can use as an emergency base in the Yellow Sea."

"Oh that's discreet. No one will look for us there."

"It'll be two hundred and fifty miles offshore."

"Long way to swim."

"Only for an emergency, Ferg. Don't worry."

"All right. We'll be out there soon. Keep your elbows to yourself."

His phone calls done, Ferguson went over to one of the computers that could be used to access the Internet without being traced. He sat down at the machine, put his hands together, and then spread his fingers backward, cracking his knuckles on both hands the way his piano teacher had when he was six or seven. He smiled wryly, remembering the smells of stale cigarettes and staler sherry that had drifted from Mr. Cog when they sat down to practice. Ferg had had four years of lessons, on and off, and besides a mean "Chopsticks" and half a Beethoven sonata, the knuckle cracking was all he'd retained.

Ferguson called up Microsoft Internet Explorer and used it to find the main page of a small telephone company in Maine that offered high-speed Internet connections and e-mail boxes back in the States. From there he entered an account name and password and checked his personal e-mail. There was only one piece of correspondence in the file, and in fact he'd read it twice already, but it was what he had come to look at. The file popped open in the mail reader, narrow black letters on a ghost-white screen.

FERG: Well, you've always said play it straight, so here goes . . .

Ferguson scrolled through the numbers that followed, which had been taken from a medical test a week ago. The most important numbers measured the amount of radiation in his body following his ingestion of a rock-sized piece of iodine. They indicated that his thyroid cancer was spreading to areas well beyond the neck area, including his pancreas and liver.

This was the third time he'd looked at the e-mail, and he knew the numbers by heart now. It was the message in layman's terms from the doctor that he wanted to read . . . or not.

As you can see, there are cells there that we don't want. A lot of them. We've discussed the feasibility of further radiation treatments; obviously, that's your decision. As I said, I can recommend some clinicians who are pursuing other avenues of inquiry. Let me know . . .
—Dr. Zeist

The conversation about radiation therapy—the only effective, tested treatment after removal of the thyroid—

had taken place before the test. The doctor had repeated what Ferguson himself had already read in the medical papers regarding his thyroid cancer: In essence, further radiation treatments wouldn't do any good.

"Other avenues of inquiry" were trial programs for untested therapies, aka wild shots in the dark, uncomfortable shots in the dark, most of them.

Ferguson folded his arms. His cancer had always seemed theoretical, even when they'd taken out his thyroid. His body was screwed up and out of whack, to be sure: He had to take synthetic thyroid hormones twice a day, or he turned into Mr. Hyde within twenty-four hours, the sharp corners of the world closing in around him and his head exploding. But he didn't feel like he was going to *die*, to really die.

Thyroid cancer was supposed to be the easiest cancer to beat, like the flu, or measles. The little glowing dots on the doctors' screens and the long reports of scan results didn't match up with who he was. He wasn't going to die, not from cancer for cryin' out loud.

A part of him had always suspected that he was a prisoner of fate, that in the end he'd have no more power over his future than a housefly trapped in a spider's web. But not *this*.

"Ah, screw this horseshit," Ferguson said out loud.

He hit the button to delete the e-mail.

Rankin took another step to the side, admiring Michelangelo's *Pietà*. The statue loomed over the space of the side altar, the folds in the marble so supple they seemed to be floating on the wind. Working the stone required not only artistry but physical strength and finesse, hitting it with enough force to shape the marble yet not quite enough to turn it into dust.

Rankin was so absorbed in the statue that he didn't hear Ferguson sneaking up behind him.

"I didn't know you were such an art lover."

Rankin just barely kept himself from jumping.

"There's a lot about me you don't know, Ferg." He turned to leave.

"Hey, take your time. Plane's not even at the airport yet."

"I'm done," said Rankin, walking away. "Let's get something to eat."

Ferguson looked up at the face of Mary, her agony crowded into elongated, blank eyes. Her lips were parted, as if she were about to say something, and yet the marble rendered her forever mute.

Once, on a visit with his dad when he was seven or eight, Ferguson thought he heard the statue whisper something to him about saying his prayers. Convinced, he did so for the next two weeks without fail, easily his longest streak, not counting the lead-up to Christmas.

That was back in the days when religion was easier, when a person was a good Catholic simply if he or she went to mass. Now going to mass made him feel just the opposite.

Ferguson stared at the statue. He could hear some of the tourists whispering nearby; undoubtedly that was what he had heard when he was a kid, but he winked at her anyway, preferring to keep the fantasy alive.

4

**SOUTH CHUNGCHONG PROVINCE,
SOUTH KOREA**

Roughly forty-eight hours after Bob Ferguson took her into his arms in Sicily, Thera Majed stepped out of a white SUV at the Blessed Peak South Korean Nuclear Waste Disposal and Holding Station thirty miles northwest of Daejeon. A gust of wind caught her by surprise and sent a cold shiver through her body. It was unusually cold for early November, but as Thera zipped her heavy parka closed, she thought of how much colder it would be when she reached North Korea.

Cold and alone, though surrounded by people.

Most of whom would hate her.

Thera glanced at one of the security guards, then pushed herself forward, joining the others queuing to go into the administration building near the front gate. Their guides waited in front of the main door in their shirt-sleeves, smiling stoically.

"Thera? Where are you?"

Though he had been born in Kenya, Dr. Jamari Norkelus spoke with a very proper English accent, direct from Cambridge, his alma mater. He also tended to be more than a little brusque and came off like everyone's most annoying spinster aunt. Norkelus ran the inspection team as if it were a church group, with curfews and daily reminders to wear proper attire. He even checked on the junior staff people to make sure they were in their rooms at night. He claimed it was because the UN had issued a directive against bad publicity, but Thera suspected he was simply an uptight voyeur.

"You will need to record the director's remarks," Norkelus told her. "Please take notes."

Thera reached into her bag for her pad as she made her way to Norkelus's side.

"Just the gist," added Norkelus in a stage whisper when she reached him. "To show we think he's important."

"OK."

Thera had been surprised to see in Libya how much of the inspection visits were devoted to diplomacy and protocol. Much of this morning's tour, for example, was completely unnecessary. Not only had the team members already studied the waste plant's layout, but several had been consultants during its design. The scientists and engineers on the team knew the function of most of the machinery and instruments better than the people handling them, but simply rolling up their sleeves and going to work was considered rude. And besides, the inspections had to be carried out according to an elaborate and lengthy set of protocols hashed out over months by negotiators after the basic Korean nonproliferation treaty was signed.

The agreement called for reciprocal inspections of nuclear facilities on both sides of the Korean border and in Japan. For every North Korean facility inspected, a South Korean facility would be checked; inspections in Japan, which had considerably more sites, were to be conducted on a more complicated schedule, though roughly in proportion with those in Korea. Different teams of inspectors would look at everything from nuclear-energy plants to waste facilities; Thera's team was concerned with the latter. The inspections in Japan and South Korea were formalities added to the treaty as a face-saving gesture for the North Koreans, but the team members would strictly observe all of the protocols nonetheless.

In this case, the inspection of the waste facilities was truly reciprocal: The Blessed Peak Waste Disposal and Holding Station happened to be an almost exact twin of the facility in North Korea's P'yŏngan-puko, or northern P'yŏnpan Province, where the team would go next. Both had been designed and built by a French firm within the last two years; the funding for the North Korean plant had come from the earlier framework agreement that had set the stage for the final disarmament pact.

High-tech monitors and robot train cars played prominent roles at the facilities. All of the waste that arrived at the South Korean facility was sealed in an appropriate containment vessel; even so, no human came within fifty yards of it, at least not under normal circumstances.

Things in North Korea were not quite as automated nor as strict—the containment "vessels" in some cases amounted to simple metal barrels, moved from trucks by forklift to the train cars—but they were nonetheless a significant improvement over the procedures followed just a few years before, when waste was dumped into open pits by workers using shovels, rakes, and in some cases their bare hands.

Most of the waste that came to both plants was low-grade radioactive substances left from medical testing and industrial testing, or the by-products of their production. But the plants also contained temporary storage facilities for spent nuclear fuel. These were the areas that the IAEA had come to look at. For only the fuel from nuclear reactors could be processed into weapons.

A typical nuclear reactor was fueled by uranium or plutonium pellets no larger than the average man's thumb. The pellets were loaded and sealed into long metal tubes called rods, which were then inserted into the reactor. The controlled nuclear reaction that resulted generated electricity for a number of years, depending on the plant's design.

As the reaction proceeded, the fuel became "spent," changed by the reaction into material that could no longer fuel the reactor. But the spent fuel represented only about three percent of the pellet. Once removed through "reprocessing," the unused material could be used in another reactor.

Reprocessing was not, however, an easy task. The rods were very hot and highly radioactive when first removed from the reactor. To prepare them for reprocessing, they had to be cooled, which in some circumstances could take as long as ten years. They were then encased in lead and steel–lined cement canisters that looked like large barbells. The containment vessels allowed the fuel to be safely transported without danger of leakage.

Like much else connected with the nuclear industry, the shipping and reprocessing of fuel was an expensive operation, performed only by special plants. It was also highly regulated, for it was relatively easy to extract weapons'-grade material during the process. This was especially true for rods from plutonium-fueled plants such as those built by North Korea.

At Blessed Peak, spent nuclear fuel was collected from two research reactors in the western part of the country and stored until it could be shipped with waste from other Korean and Japanese plants for reprocessing in Great Britain, something which generally happened every one or two years. In North Korea, the waste was collected from the country's sole operating nuclear power plant for shipment to Russia for reprocessing every eighteen months.

Blessed Peak's *wonjon nim,* or director, explained all this with the help of an elaborate PowerPoint presentation in the administration building's small auditorium. At nearly six eight, he was the tallest Korean Thera had seen since she arrived. He was also the palest; his skin seemed almost translucent. But he was an energetic man, bouncing across the stage as his slides appeared, talking in both Korean and fluent English. His silver-and-black hair occasionally blended into the background of the slides, leaving his brown suit hurtling back and forth to the nuances of tracking shipments and protecting against catastrophe.

Thera took notes during the director's presentation, but her mind was on her *real* job: planting miniature monitoring devices known as "tags" at the North Korean site. Because Blessed Peak was so similar, she would plant another set here to compare the North Korean results when the tags were collected again in three months.

Less than a half-inch square, the detectors were hidden inside fake radiation buttons, the warning indicators worn by the inspection team to detect accidental exposures to radiation. Thera had memorized a list of twenty-five possible spots to plant the devices; she was aiming to plant between six and eight at each site.

The tags were designed to detect radiation from plutonium-239. Exploiting recently developed nanotechnology, the tags were extremely sensitive gamma-ray spectrometers, or, in layman's terms, they were "tuned" to detect radiation produced by the bomb material. Tests had shown they could reliably detect about .03 grams of the material at 10 meters, a vast improvement over the most commonly used sensors, which could detect perhaps a third of a gram at the same distance.

Besides providing a check on the IAEA's tests, the First Team operation would show if materials from illegal reprocessing were being shunted into the secondary and low-level waste area, something the North was suspected of having done with its earlier extraction program.

The tags had gold-colored ends, which had to be upright. The gold turned red if the tag made a detection. While a full analysis of the tag would provide additional data about the exposure, the simple indicator would make it relatively easy to check on the site. Another IAEA inspection was tentatively scheduled in three months.

The director came to his last slide, and the scientists applauded politely before filing out of the room. They toured the monitoring station down the hall, where technicians controlled the machines that received and moved waste containers. The setup reminded Thera of an elaborate toy-train layout one of her cousins used to have in his basement that used a wireless remote to run the engines. The trains here were full sized, and they worked in conjunction with large cranes and automated lifting gear.

Radio devices permanently attached to the containment vessels showed where the recyclable power waste was at all times. No terrorist could steal the potentially dangerous waste, the director boasted, at least not without the entire world knowing.

Security around the perimeter of the plant and in the area where the recyclable fuel was kept was relatively strong; cameras with overlapping views covered a double fence, which was patrolled by guards at irregular intervals. But the security system left the rest of the facility relatively open, making Thera's job simple, assuming she could drift away from the pack.

That part wasn't going to be easy today, though.

Norkelus kept prodding her to stay close to their host, reminding her in pantomime that she should be jotting things down.

The director led them into the reception building, a large shedlike structure whose ribbed walls were made of steel. Every truck or trainload of waste entering Blessed Peak came to the large building first, where it was recorded, classified, and then prepared for storage. A large overhead crane, similar to that used to load containers onto and off of ships, sat near the middle of the building. The crane could swivel 360 degrees, setting containment vessels and waste "casks"—essentially smaller vessels with less serious waste—onto the special railroad cars.

"No people," said the director, waving his hand, "except the truck driver. All is controlled from the administration station, with the aid of the cameras."

He pointed overhead, where a pair of video cameras in the ceiling observed everything in the building.

The cameras made it impractical to plant the tags inside, but Thera wouldn't have to; the metal ribs that ran upward from the ground to the roof on the outside would make easy hiding places near the door.

As the group left the building, Thera pulled out a pack of Marlboros and broke off from the rest of the group. She lit up, then leaned against the side of the building.

It was a perfect cover: She could slide a sensor right into the metal seam while pretending to light a cigarette.

Why not do it now?

She slid her hand inside her pocket, flicking off the exterior casing of the tag and sliding the detector between her fingers.

One-two-three, easy as pie.

"Miss?"

Thera looked up in surprise. A man in a lab coat was staring at her a few feet away.

"Um, cigarette," she said, holding the cigarette up guiltily.

"You will come with me," said the man. "Come."

"But I was just having a smoke."

The man grabbed her arm. It took enormous willpower not to throw him down to the ground and even more not to flee.

5

DELAWARE COUNTY AIRPORT, INDIANA

Senator Gordon Tewilliger pulled himself into the limo and shut the door. The weather had turned nasty and his plane from Washington, D.C., had been delayed nearly an hour from landing at Delaware County Airport, just outside of Muncie, Indiana. That meant he was even further behind schedule than usual.

"State Elks dinner begins with cocktails at six." Jack Long, his district coordinator, leaned back from the front seat. "Your speech is scheduled for about eight thirty. You can just blow in, do the speech, then skip out. Which will get you over to the hospital before ten."

"That's still not going to help us, Jack."

"You cut the ribbon at the Senior Center at six. We go from there directly to the Delaware County reception. You spend fifteen minutes there, then we swing over to the Boy Scout assembly to give out the Eagle badges."

The door to the limo opened, and Tewilliger's deputy assistant, James Hannigan, slipped in. Though his title seemed to indicate that Hannigan was number three in the hierarchy of his aides, in actual fact he was the senator's alter ego and had been with him since Gordon Tewilliger had first run for state assembly. Hannigan, a short, wiry man, put his head down and ran his fingers through his hair, trying to rub off some of the rain. Once the aide was inside, the driver locked the doors and put the car in gear. The windshield wipers slapped furiously, as if they were mad that the rain had the audacity to fall.

"Finish the Eagle badges no later than seven-ten," continued Long, "then stop by the reception at the Iron Workers Union. If things run late, we can cut that. Then—"

"You don't want to cut the Iron Workers," said Hannigan.

"Gordon could stand on his head, and they won't endorse him," said Long.

"Sure, but Harry Mangjeol from Yongduro is going to be there, and he wants to say hello."

"He wants more than that," said the senator. "He's going to harangue me about the nuclear disarmament treaty again. 'South Korea get raw deal.'" Tewilliger mimicked Mangjeol's heavily accented English.

"He and his friends are supplying the airplane to New Hampshire tomorrow," said Hannigan. "It wouldn't be politick to tell him to screw off."

"No, I supposed it wouldn't," said Tewilliger.

Mangjeol was a first-generation Korean-American who owned an electronics factory halfway between Muncie and Daleville. Though a rich man in his own right, Mangjeol was more important politically as the representative of a number of Korean-American businessmen with deep ties to South Korea.

The Americans were always complaining that the North was getting away with something. Oddly, at least to Tewilliger, in the next breath they would say how much they hoped the peninsula would be reunified, as if getting the two Koreas back together wouldn't require a great deal of compromise and understanding.

"McCarthy's not budging on the disarmament agreement," said Tewilliger. "He won't change a word."

"A powerful argument to Mangjeol in favor of backing you for president," said Hannigan.

"Here we go, Senator," said Long.

Tewilliger looked up, surprised to find that they were driving up to the senior center already.

"Mayor's name is Sue Bayhern. Serious lightweight, but she gets eighty percent of the vote," said Long, feeding the senator the information he'd need to navigate the reception. "The place cost six point seven million dollars; the federal grant covered all but two hundred thousand."

"*Our* grant, Jack. They're always *our* grants," said Tewilliger, opening the car door.

SOUTH CHUNGCHONG PROVINCE, SOUTH KOREA

Thera's right knee threatened to buckle as she walked with the man in the lab coat toward the administration building near the gate. She wasn't sure what the fuss was all about. She'd never gotten the tag out of her pocket.

Had they somehow figured out she was a spy?

"What's going on?" she asked in Greek and English, but the man didn't answer. Four guards ran from the building.

The man in the lab coat yelled at them in Korean, "She must be detained." The men immediately began escorting them.

Thera had studied Korean for over two months, and had become proficient enough to hold uncomplicated conversations but couldn't understand everything the man told the guards. When they reached the building, she stopped and demanded to know what was going on.

"*Jal moreugesseoyo,*" she said. "I don't understand."

The man in the lab coat told her to go inside.

"Why?"

He pointed at her fist, where her half-smoked cigarette continued to burn.

"This?" She held up the cigarette. "This is what you're upset about?"

"Very important law for all. No exceptions."

"I'll put it out. God. It's not a big deal."

The man in the lab coat responded by slapping her across the mouth. Stunned, Thera dropped the cigarette. Once again, it took all of her willpower to respond the way the mousy secretary would: Rather than decking him she let herself be led inside, then down a hallway to a part of the building she hadn't seen on the tour. A door was opened, and Thera was shoved inside. The man in the lab coat ordered her to strip.

"Like hell I will," said Thera. The mousy act had its limits.

"You will do as I say," repeated the man. He approached her with his hand out, threatening to strike.

"I am *not* taking my clothes off. I want to see the director. I want Dr. Norkelus. I was only having a cigarette."

The man swung his hand. Thera ducked quickly out of the way. Her body poised to strike back, she yelled for Dr. Norkelus.

Thera's speed and poise surprised the Korean. He caught hold of himself, realizing he had gone too far.

"Empty your pockets," he told her in English.

"I want Dr. Norkelus."

"Empty your pockets."

"Where? There's no table or anything."

He said something to her in Korean that she didn't catch, then turned and left. The others remained in the room.

"It's just cigarettes, see?" Thera reached into her pocket and took out the pack. She showed it to the soldiers. One of the men shrugged; the others were immobile. She couldn't tell if they spoke English or not. "I was just grabbing a smoke. Nicotine fit."

Thera shoved her hand back into her pocket, slipping

her fingers around the sensor she'd opened and trying to return it to the case. It wouldn't quite snap together. Finally she took the pieces from her pocket, grasping them in her palm so that only the top part was visible.

One of the soldiers was watching.

"It's just a sensor. See? Like yours?" She pointed to the somewhat larger clip-on devices on their uniform shirts. "To make sure no one's poisoned. I have the spares. And a lighter." She put the tag into her other hand, pushing it closed in the process. Then she took out the lighter. "See? Cigarettes. I'm addicted."

The man smiled nervously but said nothing. Thera pulled out the rest of the tags, showing them to the men. Then she took out her pocket change and some crumpled *won* notes.

"See? Nothing. You think I have a gun?" She turned to the guard who had smiled. "You smoke, too, yes? I can't say it in Korean. Smoke?"

"Dambae," said the man. "Cigarette."

"That's it. *Dambae.*"

"No, no, no," said the man, wagging his finger as if she were a child.

The door opened. A short, squat woman in a lab coat entered, scolding the men in Korean and telling them to leave. Then, still speaking Korean, she told Thera she was going to be searched.

Thera feigned ignorance.

"You must be searched," said the woman in English. "Take off your coat."

"I have cigarettes, a lighter, not even lipstick."

"You must be searched."

"Because I had a cigarette?"

"Cigarette smoking is forbidden inside the compound. Very dangerous. Any violation . . . this is taken very seriously. We have strict procedures. It is the country's law, not ours."

"I guess."

"Please take off your coat."

An hour later, Dr. Norkelus appeared with the facility director. He was carrying Thera's belongings in a clear plastic bag. The extra radiation sensors were at the bottom, along with her cigarettes.

"I have to apologize for the way you were treated," said Dr. Norkelus, "but smoking is forbidden. Strictly forbidden."

"Yeah," said Thera. She snatched back the bag.

Norkelus stiffened. She wasn't acting like the mousy secretary, and he didn't like that. He needed to feel superior, in charge.

"I'm sorry," said Thera, trying to get back into character. "I was just having a cigarette. They made me strip."

"Outrageous," said Norkelus, his protective instincts kicking in. "The Koreans . . . they are very careful about their rules; they do not have the best attitude toward people breaking them."

Especially when they're women, Thera realized. She decided she wouldn't mention the slap; it would only complicate things further.

"I'm sorry about the cigarettes. It won't happen again."

"Yes. That would not be good."

Thera left her things in the plastic bag until she got to the hotel. When her roommate Lada Rahn went to dinner, she poured everything out on the table. The fact that she wasn't allowed to smoke inside the complex took away her easiest cover for planting the bugs. Hopefully they wouldn't be as strict or as health conscious in North Korea.

The dummy cases were intact; it didn't seem as if any had been opened. Thera decided she would examine them anyway. She slipped her fingernail beneath the tab of the first unit, pushing gently. The top popped off and shot across the table to the floor.

As she got up to get it, she heard her roommate putting her card key into the door. Thera scooped everything into her pocket just as the door hit against the sliding dead bolt Thera had secured to keep her out.

"Sorry, I locked it," said Thera, going over. "I was just going to take a shower."

The roommate was a chronic giggler and reacted with one now. Thera let her in, then retreated to the bathroom to sort things out. As she was replacing the device she'd opened, she noticed that the edge of the chip had turned red.

As had all of the others.

DAEJEON, SOUTH KOREA

Ferguson had just taken a seat at the restaurant when his satellite phone rang. He smiled at the waitress, who was handing him a menu, then took out the phone, expecting it to be Jack Corrigan, the mission coordinator back at The Cube, whose timing was impeccable when it came to interruptions. But instead he heard Thera's hushed voice tell him that she needed to talk to him.

"Cinderella, why are you calling?" Ferguson glanced up at the waitress who was approaching with a bottle of sake.

"I need to talk to you," repeated Thera.

"You need out?"

"I need you to meet me."

"Where and when?"

wo hours later, Ferguson walked into the lobby of
the Daejeon Best Western carrying a suitcase. He
went up to the reservation desk and checked in as a German businessman, carefully starting his conversation
with a small amount of German—nearly all he knew—
before switching to a pigeon English. When the clerk
took his credit card, he turned and looked around the
marble-encased lobby. The balcony above was empty.
Aside from the doorman, the place seemed empty, which,
Ferguson hoped, it wasn't.

The clerk returned his card and gave him a key. The
room was right down the hall.

"Actually, I'd like something on an upper floor.
Above," added Ferguson. He put his thumb up.

"Above?"

"As high as you got."

Perplexed, the clerk started to explain that he had
given the gentleman one of the best rooms in the hotel.

"It's not the best if it's not what I want," said Ferguson.

The clerk conceded and found him a room on the
twenty-third floor. Ferguson thanked him very much, assured him that he could carry his own bag, and headed for
the elevator. The car arrived instantly and began to glide
upward.

It stopped on the third floor. Ferguson took a step back
as the door opened. Thera stepped inside, practically out
of breath. Neither of them spoke until the door closed and
the car began moving upward.

"What's going on?"

"The sensors found plutonium at the waste site today. I
don't know where."

"Is that all?"

"Ferg, this is serious. All of the tags were red. I was
only there for a few hours. There is a *lot* of material
there."

She handed him a small manila envelope.

"All of them?"

"All of the ones I had with me. They're all red."

"Maybe there's a leak in the recycling storage area," said Ferguson.

"No."

Thera explained what had happened.

"The tags were put in a plastic bag along with the rest of my stuff. They were taken out to Norkelus, who was over by the rail cars at the time. He came straight to the administrative building. They never got near the stored rods."

The elevator stopped. Thera stepped back against the wall, eyeing the short American who came into the car. He gave her a goofy smile, then turned and poked the button for twelve.

Ferguson stared at the bald spot on the back of the man's head, trying to will some sort of identity out of his brain. Finally as the car started upward, he asked if the man knew where the party was.

"Party?" The man turned around. "What sort?"

"I'm sorry. I thought you were Alsop, Yank friend of mine." He shoved his hand out toward the man and introduced himself as Bob Jenkins, an Australian in the city on business. "Alsop's around some place, sniffing out the party."

The shorter man shrugged.

"Alsop, Mr. Party," said Ferguson. "You one of the teachers?"

"Teacher?"

"The English-language teachers. Convention down the street."

"No, I'm just a technician for a machinery company," said the man. He started to explain that he'd come to Korea from the States to check on an instrument the company had sold the Koreans some months before.

"Software has to be tweaked every few weeks," said the man as the door opened. "Gets old real fast, I'll tell you."

"If I find the party, I'll let you know," promised Ferguson.

The door closed.

"Seemed legit," Thera said.

"Probably." Ferguson leaned against the back of the elevator. This was the one contingency they hadn't planned for: finding nuclear material in *South* Korea.

"What are we going to do?"

"Did you leave a set?"

"No."

"Do it tomorrow," said Ferguson.

"All right. I'll leave them overnight, then pick them up on our last day. How will I get them to you?"

"Leave them under your mattress when you get back and go out for dinner. We'll get them. If something goes wrong, send an e-mail to your mother back in Greece and tell her you're having a lovely time."

"OK."

"Don't call, Thera. And do *not* come looking for me."

"This was important."

"Yeah, I know. Listen, this could just be a screw-up in the gadgets. They all went red? Sounds like a mistake."

"You really think that, Ferg?"

Ferguson shrugged.

The door opened. Ferguson picked up his bag. Thera put her hand out to stop him.

"What if I have to talk to you again?"

"Don't."

Thera took the elevator back to the fourth floor. As the doors opened she took a breath, then plunged out into the hallway, walking quickly to the stairs a few steps away. Five minutes later, she was back on the street, wending her way to the bar where she was to meet Julie Svenson and some of the others from the inspection team.

"There you are!" said Julie as she slipped into the

booth near the back. "We called your room, and Lada said you had gone out. That was an hour ago."

"I got a little confused on the street," said Thera. "Then I asked for directions."

"Your first mistake," said one of the scientists.

"True," said Thera. "Very true."

DAEJEON, SOUTH KOREA

"Where've you been?" Rankin asked when Ferguson slid in next to him at the bar.

"Visiting the temples. I'm thinking of becoming a Buddhist."

"You'd have to give up meat. And booze." Rankin took a sip of his Coke. "Corrigan was looking for you. You didn't answer his call."

"Oh, gee. Must've forgotten to turn the phone on again. *Tsk, tsk.*"

Rankin smirked. He liked Corrigan even less than Ferguson did.

"There's a complication," said Ferguson.

The bartender came over. Ferguson leaned on the bar, eyeing the bottles of Western liquor. "Scotch," he said finally. "Let's try the Dewar's, on the rocks."

"He doesn't speak English, Ferg."

"Dewar's," said Ferguson. "That's Korean."

"So what's going on?" asked Rankin.

"The sensors say there's plutonium somewhere in the waste site."

"What, here?"

"Maybe it's a screwup, maybe not."

Ferguson glanced across the bar. There were about a dozen other people, all Japanese businessmen, gathered in different knots, all stooped over their drinks and conversations.

"So what do we do?" Rankin asked.

"Hang tight. Thera's planting some more tags. She'll pick them up day after tomorrow; we'll get them from the hotel and fly them home."

"You tell Corrigan?"

"No sense telling him yet."

"Why not?"

"We don't want to be wrong on this. Washington'll freak."

"That's it?"

"Uh-huh."

Thera had let the tags get out of her possession. Because of that, the results were automatically suspicious; she really had no way of knowing where they had gone. If he told The Cube, Ferguson would have to explain what had happened. It wasn't a major screwup, given the circumstances, but he didn't trust Corrine or the CIA's deputy director of operations, Dan Slott, to know that. Corrine especially.

The bartender brought over a glass and the bottle of Scotch. Ferguson took the glass and handed it to Rankin.

"What's this for?"

"In Korea, you always fill the other guy's glass."

"I don't like Scotch."

"You should've thought of that before I ordered it."

9

The Korean security guards accompanying the inspectors called Thera "Cigarette Queen," snickering among themselves as she tagged along behind a group of technicians setting up monitoring equipment at the reception building. She acted like she didn't understand the jokes, helping the techies lug the gear over and unpack it. It was gofer work, but it suited her just fine.

On her third trip back to the truck, she veered in the direction of the embedded rail line used to ferry material to the recycling holding area. Thera slipped her hand in her pocket and took one of the tags from the shielded envelope she'd hidden there. Then she got down on one knee and pretended to tie her shoe. As she did, she slid the thin tag into the narrow furrow next to the rail.

Thera took a breath, then started to rise. All of a sudden she had a premonition: *The guards were about to arrest her.*

She sensed—she *knew*—that they were right behind her and that in the next second would grab her. The sensation was as strong as anything she had ever felt in her life. Thera held her breath, but nothing happened.

She took a step. Nothing. Another step. Nearly trembling, she continued on her way to the truck.

It'll get easier as it goes, she told herself, walking back with the bag she'd been sent to retrieve. She made a show of being cold, stamping her feet and rubbing her hands. One of the engineers took the hint.

"You ought to go over to the administration building and warm up in the lounge," he suggested.

"Good idea."

Thera had always despised the helpless-female routine, but the role came in handy now; her shivers were so convincing she almost fooled herself. She did the shoelace trick again, this time with the other foot, planting a tag in another track, then presented herself at the door of the administration building, where the two young guards were happy to let her inside.

Yesterday she'd been a prisoner, now she was a princess; the male engineers in the monitoring station practically tripped over themselves as they rushed to show her to the lounge. They found tea and some cookies, telling her in halting English that it was unusual to have such beauty in a person so intelligent. They thought she was one of the scientists; Thera didn't correct the mistake.

She was just getting up to go back outside when one of the guards from the day before appeared in the doorway to the lounge. With a stern face, he beckoned her out into the hallway, then smiled, opening his palm to reveal a pack of cigarettes. He gave them to her, then motioned with his head for her to follow him outside.

Thera sensed a trap.

"Gomapjiman sayanghalkkeyo," she told him. "No thank you. I really can't; we'll get in trouble."

"No trouble. *Sssssh,*" said the man, putting his finger to his lips.

Trust him or not?

Fear swept over her again. Thera forced herself to nod, forced herself to go with him.

The guard practically bounced his way outside, leading her around the corner of the building and out toward the yard, where some empty train cars were parked.

"Here," he said, sliding a cigarette into her hand. He cupped one as well.

Thera waited until he lit up, then did so herself, puffing with her hands hiding her face.

The spot was perfect, out of range of any of the surveillance cameras but strategically located. She had no trouble planting a tag as they finished their cigarettes, partners in crime.

And so it went. By the time the inspection team broke for lunch—a catered affair in the administration building—Thera had planted all of the sensors. She spent the rest of the day doing odd jobs for different members of the team, trying to get a feel for the plant's routine so that she would have no trouble picking up the tabs tomorrow.

The ride back to the hotel was unusually quiet, the scientists and engineers feeling the effects of jet lag. Thera stared out the window, going back over the site's layout in her mind, comparing it to North Korea's. There'd be more guards there, but the video coverage would undoubtedly be poorer.

The cigarette trick would work.

What if it didn't?

She needed a new gimmick.

"You must be thinking of a statue," said Neto Evora, leaning forward from the seat behind her. Evora headed the ground sampling team; he and his crew had spent the day in the recycling area shoveling random half-kilogram piles of dirt into boxes.

"Why a statue?" said Thera.

"Because your eyes seem to see beauty," explained the Portuguese scientist.

"Thank you."

"Maybe you'll have dinner with us."

"Sure."

"We're going into Daejeon and get real food," Evora added. "We deserve a little reward for all our hard work."

"I didn't work very hard."

"But you deserve a reward anyway," said Evora, his eyes twinkling.

The reward Evora had in mind was himself. A half-dozen members of the inspection team went to a *no-raebang* or Korean karaoke joint, a bar with small soundproof rooms and karaoke machines where groups could sing, party, and dance.

Thera was one of two women with the group, and she found herself the focus of most of the attention. Evora kept pouring her drinks and urging her to sing. Six foot two, he had curly black hair and eyes that seemed to tunnel into hers when he spoke. He had a handsome face and wonderful shoulders, and moved reasonably well on the dance floor. Not as good as Ferguson had but almost.

Thera found herself debating whether she should take him to bed. She decided not to, but later, back in her room listening to her roommate's snores, she fantasized about the Portuguese scientist, wondering what his arms would have felt like around her, imagining his finger brushing her breast.

Sex was an accepted part of spycraft if you were a guy. Someone like Ferg probably had sex all the time when working undercover.

Not that she knew that for a fact.

Things were somewhat more ambiguous for women. Someone like Slott would certainly not approve . . . Then again he wouldn't ask, as long as you provided the results.

Evora wasn't interesting enough to keep her attention, and Thera started visualizing herself retrieving the tags from the site. She began seeing guards everywhere, watching her.

Her mind began to race, unable to stop the permutations of fear multiplying in her brain.

They'd seen her, filmed her already, were waiting to spring it on her tomorrow.

Norkelus knew she was lying about the cigarettes.

She'd be caught in North Korea. She'd be tortured and locked away forever.

Thera tossed and turned in her bed, the sheets and covers wrapped around her, squeezing sweat from her pores. And then the phone was ringing with their wakeup call, and it was time to get up.

10

With the president and some of his key advisors away, the West Wing of the White House where Corrine had her office was relatively quiet. This meant fewer interruptions for Corrine, and by four o'clock she was actually caught up on her work or at least as caught up as she ever was. She called over to The Cube to check on the First Team's Korean operation.

"This is Lauren," said Lauren DiCapri, the on-duty mission coordinator. "Who's this?"

The phone system in The Cube would have already identified Corrine, but she told her anyway. "So what's going on?"

"Nothing. We're good."

There was a strong note of resentment in Lauren's voice; she belonged to the camp that resented Corrine as an outsider and impediment to their jobs.

It was a big camp, and included Ferguson and CIA Deputy Director of Operations Daniel Slott. The arrangement itself was part of the problem. The lines of authority were somewhat hazy and had been so even before Corrine's arrival. The CIA people who worked with Special Demands answered to Slott for administrative purposes and had to work with him on mission details. The Special Operations people assigned to the First Team—like Rankin and Guns—had two masters, the military and Special Demands, while the Special Forces detachment and its assorted support units had their own colonel, Charles Van Buren.

Until Corrine's appointment as the president's *con-*

science—McCarthy's term for her job as his designated representative—Special Demands had basically been run by Ferguson, who, after getting a directive from Slott, worked things out on his own.

Or so it appeared. Corrine had had a devilish time figuring out exactly how the chain of command really did run, and her efforts to insert more oversight, while they had had some impact, probably hadn't changed things all that much. Ferguson and his people still had incredible leeway once given a mission.

She didn't want to second-guess them, much less hamstring them, but she did want them to stay within the bounds set by the president. Finding the right balance was incredibly difficult, especially when the people she was supposed to supervise resented her.

"Thera's still in South Korea?" Corrine asked.

"Yes," said Lauren tersely.

"Well, let me know if anything comes up."

"Absolutely."

"I'm not the enemy," snapped Corrine. But it was too late; Lauren had already hung up.

SOUTH CHUNGCHONG PROVINCE, SOUTH KOREA

Thera got up and went into the shower, not wanting to have to wait for her roommate. She let the hot water pummel her face, then backed off the heat until the water sent shivers through her body, shaking away the fear and paranoia she'd stewed in all night. She saw the tags in her hand, saw herself slipping them under the mattress, moving on. It was going to be easy, easiest thing she'd ever done, a piece of cake.

She'd have to take her roommate to dinner, make sure she was out of the way.

Bring her to karaoke with Evora.

Ugh, if she could stand it. Thera's head was OK, but her stomach felt as if it had been pushed up into her chest. Too much kimchi.

Done with her shower, Thera dressed and headed downstairs to the coffee shop, where the team gathered for breakfast before assembling in one of the hotel conference rooms and starting out. As she stuck her cup under the spout of the coffee urn, Dr. Norkelus tapped her on the shoulder.

"A word, please."

Thera finished filling her cup, then took a teaspoon and a small amount of sugar, stirring meticulously before placing the cup on a saucer. Norkelus stared at her the whole time, his expression similar to the look a vice principal might give when calling a student out of study hall for cutting up. Finally he tilted his long nose downward, then swung around and walked toward the exit.

Thera followed, sure she was going to be scolded, though she wasn't exactly sure why. Had someone seen her smoking with the guard? Or was last night the problem? Norkelus had a puritanical streak. He walked with a gait so stiff it reminded her of some of the Greek Orthodox priests who'd taught her religion when she was young, righteous, sanctimonious old bastards who once made a girl spit out her bubblegum and stick it on her head for chewing in class.

Norkelus went into an empty conference room. Thera nearly bumped into him just inside the door.

"Tony is sick. I'll need you to compile the logs and e-mail them to New York and the Hague," he told her.

"Tony's sick?" Thera managed, caught off guard.

"The UN secretary general wants the briefings. Here are my notes."

He handed her a small flash-memory card, used by the team's voice recorders.

"OK, sure," said Thera. "I'll get to work on it as soon as I get back."

"It has to go out by noon, our time."

"Noon?"

Norkelus tilted his head slightly. He didn't comprehend her question, or rather why she was asking it. The secretaries weren't needed on the inspections for anything more than running errands; here was real work that needed to be done.

And besides, she was a secretary; he was the boss.

"It has to be out of here by noon, or they have to get it by noon their time?" asked Thera.

"Our time."

"In New York, it'll be, say ten at night."

"You have an objection?"

"No, of course not."

"When you're done, you can help make sure everything is ready for the trip North. We should be back by three."

"I can go out to the site to help break down the equipment."

"Unnecessary," said Norkelus. "Thank you, though."

Thera tried to think of an excuse, any excuse, to get out to the site, but nothing would come.

"Is there a problem?" asked Norkelus in his coldest you-better-not voice.

"It's only that it may not be enough time," said Thera. "To have the report done by noon."

"I'm afraid it will have to be."

12

Ferguson spread the Asian edition of the *Wall Street Journal* out on the table in the Korean Palace Hotel's restaurant and opened to the editorial page. The editors had decided to denounce the nonproliferation treaty with North Korea, claiming that it was a "poorly worded document more dangerous than hopeful. The fact that inspections have already begun shows how utterly worthless it is; the North Koreans only agreed because they know it has no teeth."

The editorial writer made a few valid points about the limits of the testing protocols, though it was clear from his overall tone that, in his opinion, nuking North Korea was the only viable way to deal with the country.

Ferg's sat phone began to ring as he turned the page.

"Batman speaking," he said, hitting the talk button.

"Ferg, something's up," said Jack Corrigan, the desk man on duty in The Cube. "Can you talk?"

"I can always talk, Robin. The question is whether anyone listens."

"We got a problem, Ferg. Our friend just sent an e-mail to her grandmother telling her she has to stay inside today and work."

"That's it?"

"More or less."

"Don't tell me more or less," snapped Ferguson. "Read me the message, Corrigan."

"But—"

"Read me the message."

"You want it in Greek or English?"

"Now you tell me, Jack, do I speak Greek?"

"I don't know what you speak some days," said Corrigan. "Gram: Hope you're well. Having a challenging and exciting time in new job. Going to all sorts of places and getting plenty of exercise—I think I've lost all the weight your chicken soup put on. Yesterday I got to go out, but today it's desk work. Even though the sun is shining, I'll be in all day. Lots of unfinished business. Then there's a frowny face."

"Cute. What else?"

"That's it. What do you think—"

"We're on it."

Ferguson slapped off the phone and got up, leaving the newspaper spread out on the table.

"Gotta go," he told the approaching waiter. He unfolded a five-thousand-won note from his pocket and let it flutter to the table. *"Tto bwayo."*

Ferguson had just hailed a taxi when his sat phone rang again. It was Rankin.

"Something's up. Thera didn't get in the trucks with the rest of the team at the hotel," said Rankin.

"Yeah, something's goin' on," said Ferguson, stepping onto the curb as a cab veered across traffic to pick him up.

"You want me to go in?"

"No, hang back. She's OK. Where's Guns?"

"Sleepin'. He watched her hotel all night."

"All right. I'm pickin' you up. We'll be there in twenty minutes."

The typically thick city traffic made it more like fifty. Rankin, who'd been watching Thera's hotel from a parking garage across the street, had been standing outside the whole time and felt like a penguin with frostbite. When he grabbed the taxi's door his finger nearly froze to the metal.

"Cold, huh?" said Ferguson as he slid in.

"No, it's fuckin' July."

"Get warm soon," said the driver helpfully from the front. "This unusual weather."

Rankin frowned at him. He hated nosey taxi drivers.

Ferguson leaned across him and bent over the front seat. "Driver, take us to Hard Rock Café. Yes?"

"Hard Rock, yes," said the man. "Good place for party."

"That's what I like."

Ferguson tucked a thick wad of won notes in the driver's hand when they got to the restaurant. Both men walked silently to the right of the entrance, ducked down a set of stairs they had scoped out the day before, and crossed to the back of the building. Five minutes later they were standing at the counter of a rental car agency three blocks away, reserving a Hyundai.

"You gonna tell me what's going on?" Rankin said as they walked to the car.

"I didn't think you were interested."

"Don't be a prick, Ferg. I didn't want to ask questions while people were around."

"Thera can't pick up the tags. Her work assignment must've changed. You and I are going to go take a closer look at the site and figure out what we're going to do."

"We're going in? How?"

"See, that's the problem with explaining things to you, Skip. Every time I do, you ask more questions. Sooner or later I'm going to run out of answers."

G enerally the best and easiest way to get into a highly secure facility was through the front gate. But Ferguson decided that wasn't going to work in this case. The South Koreans had upped their security to impress the IAEA inspection team, and any work crew, especially one with an out-of-place Caucasian or two, would draw close scrutiny. Presenting themselves as members of the inspection team wouldn't work, either;

that was too easily checked, and, besides, they didn't want to do anything to draw any suspicion to the inspectors.

The next best option was to come in from the extreme northern perimeter, which bordered a nature preserve and was guarded only by razor wire and infrared cameras. It was a long way around: Rankin estimated that simply getting to the perimeter fence from the entrance to the nature reserve would take two hours, and it would take another hour and a half to hike from the perimeter fence into the compound.

"There's another problem," said Ferguson as they scouted the fence line from the park. "The security cameras overlap pretty well. I don't think we can get over without blinding them."

Rankin took Ferguson's binoculars, peering over the crest of the hill toward the fence. The cameras were well hidden; he only knew where to look because they had prepared a map of the security layout for the mission. An infrared image taken just after sunset had been used to pinpoint the cameras; their housings dissipated heat more quickly than the surrounding rocks and brush.

"Hit 'em with a fog machine," said Rankin finally.

"Too suspicious unless the weather warms up," said Ferguson. "Besides, that's a hell of a lot of fog."

"Take them a long time to respond to a blackout," suggested Rankin. "We just cut the power. We're inside by the time they get up here. We throw a fader on another unit, so we don't have to go out the same way."

A "fader" was a device that interfered with the camera's ability to scan by disrupting its power circuitry, in effect "fading" the image so that it appeared to be a random malfunction. While difficult to detect, the device had to be placed inside the camera to work.

Ferguson abruptly slid down the hill and started back in the direction of the car. Rankin scrambled to follow.

"You figured it out?" said Rankin.

"You did," said Ferguson. "You just don't know it yet."

13

SOUTH CHUNGCHONG PROVINCE, SOUTH KOREA

Since tomorrow was a travel day, Norkelus ordered the entire inspection team to have dinner at the hotel and refrain from "partying." While his decree drew snickers from the senior scientists, junior technical members and staff were shuffled upstairs immediately after dinner to pack "and get a head start on sleep."

Evora winked at Thera, signaling that she should sneak out and join him and the others, but she decided it was better to avoid temptation and went upstairs. After packing, she and her roommate flipped through the channels for a while without finding anything interesting in English. Thera started to read; within a half hour, her eyes were drooping. She put down the book and turned off the light, falling asleep within a few minutes.

C ome on, Cinderella, your pumpkin's waiting."
Thera woke with a jerk, only to feel herself pushed back down into the bed. She tried to scream, but a hand was clamped firmly on her mouth.

"It's me," whispered Ferguson, standing over her. "Come on. Before Rankin climbs into bed with your roommate."

Rankin was standing on the other side of the bed, holding a small mask over Thera's roommate's face. A squeeze bulb was connected to the mask; he'd just finished spraying a mild sedative to make sure she remained sleeping.

"What's going on?" Thera whispered.

"*Sshh,*" replied Ferguson.

Thera slipped out of bed, grabbing for her clothes on the nearby chair.

"You don't have to get dressed," Ferguson told her. "We're not going very far."

Suddenly self-conscious, Thera pulled on her jeans over her pajamas and grabbed for her sweater.

"No feet?" Ferguson pointed at the pajama bottoms, which were covered with miniature ducks.

"Very funny."

"I always figured you for teddy bears."

"They didn't have my size." Thera sat at the edge of the bed. "We can't go out in the hall. They may see us."

"We're not going in the hall." Ferguson pointed to a sliding door at the other side of the room. "We're in the room above. Come on. This won't take long."

A rope dangled at the side of the balcony. Thera leaned over, making sure no one was on the nearby terraces, then hoisted herself up to the next floor. Guns—Jack Young, the other member of the team in Korea—was waiting on the balcony. He helped her over the railing.

Ferguson came up next, followed by Rankin.

"Have a seat," he told her, gesturing at the bed. Ferguson stared for a brief, brief moment at her black curls and green eyes, thinking she really was Cinderella, or the next best thing. Even with a baggy sweater and jeans, she was hard to resist.

"I need a map of the spots where you put the sensors," he told her. He reached over the wastebasket, where he'd stashed a notebook and pencil earlier.

"I have twenty minutes. Then I turn back into a mouse," he added, "Rankin turns into a cockroach. You don't want to see that."

"I'll go with you."

"No way. If you're caught, the whole mission collapses. Besides, you're leaving for North Korea first thing in the morning. It may take us a while to get back."

"I can do it, Ferg."

"Come on, Cinderella, the map. I'm already getting a hankering for cheese."

Thera took the pad and began sketching the general outline of the base.

"They're taking attendance downstairs," said Guns, who was watching a feed from the wireless video cam they'd placed in one of the lighting fixtures. It showed Norkelus walking down the hall, knocking on the doors. He was two rooms away from Thera's.

"Get Cinderella back to the ball," Ferguson told the others, pulling off his black cap and sweater. "Bring her back up once the coast is clear."

"Never going to make it."

"She'll make it," Ferguson told him running to the door.

The tenor's song, drunken but perfectly on key, exploded from the elevator as the door opened.

" 'And it's no, nay, never, no nay never no more, will I play the wild rover, no never, no more.' "

Ferguson kicked the volume up a notch as he stepped out into the eighth-floor hallway. The rogue's lament captured Norkelus's attention just as he knocked on Thera's door. Ferguson stopped walking but not singing, belting out the chorus as he put both hands on his fake glasses and pulled them from his nose, as if trying to get the hallway into focus. Then he started walking again, holding them in front of his face as he approached the bewildered scientist. When he got to within three feet, Ferguson stopped singing and concentrated on angling the glasses to get a proper perspective of the scientist.

"Who are you looking for?" demanded the scientist.

" 'Tain't but lookin' for a soul," said Ferguson, slurring his words into a drunken Irish brogue. "But I am lookin' for me room. And if you could point it out to me, laddie, I'd be much obliged."

"You're on the wrong floor."

" 'Tis nine," said Ferguson.

"Eight."

"Nine."

"Eight."

Ferguson staggered back a step. "This is nine," he insisted.

"Please go to your room, or I will call security," said Norkelus.

"You're a man who knows his numbers. I can see that."

Thera's door opened and her face appeared in the crack. She was back in her pajamas. "What's going on out here?"

"Nothing," said Norkelus. "Go back inside."

"Is this eight or nine?" said Ferguson, bending so that he was eye level with her.

"The is the eighth floor," she said. And then she added something in Greek, which he didn't understand, though he guessed the drift: Go back to bed, you dumb lout.

"Eight, not nine. A thousand pardons, miss. And sir."

Ferguson bowed, then turned and went back to the elevator. While he waited, he decided the night needed a triumphant air and began singing "Finnegan's Wake."

R ankin, back pressed against the side of the building as he stood on the narrow balcony, listened as Thera told Norkelus that her roommate was "dead out." The scientist grunted but apparently didn't believe her; the light flicked on, and Rankin saw the curtains flutter. He grabbed hold of the rope and put his foot on the building, ready to climb if he had to.

"Yes, then, good. I will see you in the morning," said Norkelus gruffly. The light flipped off; Thera appeared.

"Wait," whispered Rankin.

"Why?"

"Case he comes back."

"He won't."

"Wait."

Thera scowled but then disappeared. Rankin squatted, waiting. He'd heard a bit of Ferguson's act through the door. It was vintage Ferguson. The CIA officer had a gift for bullshit; he'd seen him talk his way into and out of dozens of tight places, blustering and cajoling and always ladling on the crap.

It was part of the game, a tool, but it left Rankin vaguely uneasy. One of the things about Special Forces was that the people you worked with didn't bullshit.

Except for officers. Officers were always full of it.

Guns stuck his head over the railing above and whistled, signaling that the coast was clear.

"Come on, Thera," whispered Rankin. "Let's get this done."

14

SOUTH CHUNGCHONG PROVINCE, SOUTH KOREA

Three hours later, armed with Thera's hand-drawn map, Ferguson and Rankin stepped toward the rear door of an Air Force C-130 Hercules.

"Ready, Rankin?" Ferguson said, yelling over the rush of the wind in the rear of the plane.

"If you are."

"Hey, piece of cake," said Ferguson, clamping the oxygen mask against his face.

A night jump into a black hole from thirty thousand feet was not exactly Rankin's idea of a piece of cake, but he still felt a certain elation as he stepped out of the

Herky Bird into the cold night air. Airborne training had been one of Rankin's favorite "schools" in the army, an absolute blast from the let's-get-acquainted-with-gravity first jump to the hairiest night dive into the raging ocean. Even now, after maybe five hundred jumps—most recreational and from a considerably lower altitude—he loved the smack of the wind against his body and the loud rush that filled his ears as he spread his arms and began to fly rather than fall.

He was still more brick than airplane, if truth be told, since he was in fact plummeting at a good rate, documented by the dial altimeter on his left wrist. A global positioning satellite (GPS) device was strapped to his right; there was very little starlight and no moon, and he'd need to rely on it rather than his sight to get down to the target area.

A few meters to the right, Ferguson tucked his right side slightly to keep himself on course as he fell. The cold, thin air pressed through his jumpsuit, icy hands squeezing his ribs. It felt as if someone—an angel, maybe—were flying above him, holding on, guiding him to earth.

When he was little, Ferguson's mind had been filled with stories about angels. He'd had vivid dreams of them, including one in which an angel grabbed him in his or maybe her arms and whisked him from danger.

The danger happened to be a particularly nasty Catholic nun—one of his teachers that half year—but that hadn't seemed to bother the angel.

The altimeter buzzed, telling him it was time to pull the rip cord. The harness yanked hard against his body as the chute deployed. Ferguson made sure it had deployed properly, then checked his position with the GPS device.

He was roughly two hundred meters north of the spot he'd set for his target, but he still had a long way to fall. Ferguson moved his right toggle downward, working against a slight breeze that wanted to push him east.

Finally he saw the dim outline of the clearing in front

of the perimeter fence off to his left. A sudden surge in the wind threatened to take him into the wilderness area; Ferguson dipped the wing of his chute and corkscrewed in the direction he wanted to land. The maneuver got him onto the right side of the fence but nearly collapsed his chute. He came down hard on the side of a hill about fifty yards behind the cameras. Collapsing onto his left knee, he slid for a few yards until he managed to twist downward and stop.

"Auspicious," he said aloud in a mocking tone. "That's what happens when you start thinking about angels."

Rankin landed nearly thirty yards away, a nice walking touchdown on level land. Both men quickly gathered their chutes, bundling them with the rest of their jump gear. They stowed them near some bushes at the base of the hill where Ferguson had landed, then went to take care of the video camera and sensors that covered the fence where they wanted to get out.

The camera could be pivoted by remote control to cover the fence area; it was also set to respond to a motion detector covering the area in front of it. Ferguson identified the wires from the motion detector, then, with a penknife, carefully stripped small bare spots through the insulation. He clamped alligator clips on them, testing the connection to a small black box and antenna. When a light on the box indicated current, he clipped the wire, eliminating the motion detector from the circuit. He took out what looked like a cell phone and began pressing the arrow keys; the camera responded as if it had detected a large animal in the brush.

With the camera pointed all the way to its stop, Ferguson unscrewed the rear housing. He'd just gotten the last screw off when it began moving; the security people were panning it by remote control.

Ferguson waited for the camera to finish moving, then gingerly lifted off the back. He identified the wires supplying power to the circuit board and clamped a fat clip over them. Then he plugged what looked like a thick cell-phone battery into the other end of the wire and tucked it onto the camera chassis. He picked up the ersatz cell phone and pressed the center key. The screen over the keypad turned white, then slowly began to fade to gray, indicating the operation had been a success.

"Fader works," he told Rankin, putting the housing back on the camera.

Ferguson used his short-range radio to call Guns, who was watching the plant's main entrance and the administration building from a rise about a hundred yards from the gate.

"Anything going on?" Ferguson asked, adjusting his night-vision goggles before setting out down the hill.

"*Aniyo,*" said Guns.

"Learning the lingo are we?"

"I got the MP3 player with me."

"Great. Just don't get so caught up in the pronunciation that you forget about us, right?"

"*Ne, dwaetseoyo,*" said Guns. "OK."

Ferguson and Rankin picked their way through trees and rocks for about an hour before coming to an old stone wall. The vegetation had been cleared on the other side of the wall, and within fifteen minutes they could see the buildings at the center of the complex.

They continued down a ravine that ran behind the low-level waste storage area. The radioactive dump had been sited inside the side of the hill. The entrance to the area looked like a mine shaft, albeit one large enough for a pair of trains to drive through. The actual disposal areas were shafts dug deep within the hillside. There were no fences blocking off the entrance, nor were there security cameras. The nearby ground was flat and open, though obscured from the rest of the site by a parking area for the train cars.

"First tab is over near those trains," said Ferguson, pointing. "We'll get it, then split up."

They hadn't taken more than a few steps before Guns warned them that the security people were starting a round in their pickup truck. Seconds later, Ferguson saw the vehicle's headlamps swinging in their direction.

"No place to hide around here," said Rankin.

"Into the mine shaft."

"There's radioactive waste in there," said Rankin.

"There's radioactive waste all over the place here, Skippy. Better to glow than get shot."

Actually, the waste was stored far below, in containers and compartments that prevented contamination. The entrance looked like a train tunnel or a very large mine shaft. The roof and walls were tiled with large cement blocks, reinforced at intervals by triangular-shaped steel pillars and crossbeams. The train tracks ran along the floor, bending to the right as the shaft turned and disappeared from sight.

Ferguson stopped at the first set of pillars, watching as a four-door pickup circled in front of the shaft opening, then darted away.

"Gone?" Rankin asked.

"Gone," said Ferguson, stepping out. "The radiation is all contained, Rankin. You don't have to worry about it."

"Yeah, all right."

"You remember that from the briefing, right?"

Rankin shrugged.

"You don't believe them?" Ferguson asked.

"Who the hell knows what to believe?"

They trotted across fifty yards of open ground to a pair of railroad flatcars and a small diesel shunting engine. They could see the truck in the distance as it returned to the administration building, the patrol over.

"You should have at least thirty minutes before the next security run," said Guns. The irregular intervals was intentional, designed to make it difficult for anyone who might try to time them. "Maybe as much as an hour."

"You get the three on that side," Ferguson told Rankin,

pointing to the left of the operations station. "One's in the rail there, another is over by that little power transformer set, and then there's the one in the siding of the building."

"I remember, Ferg. Jeez."

"You got one camera on the corner of that building there." He pointed to it. "Go."

Rankin nudged forward, moving in a half crawl to the shadows on the other side of the railroad track. He got down on his hands and knees and began groping for the tiny sensor.

Ferguson, meanwhile, trotted in the opposite direction, running through a dark shadow toward the fence guarding the recyclable reactor rods. It was the hardest tag to get, because it was within view of the recycling area's guard post. Ferguson reached the fence and threw himself on the ground. As he did, he saw the pant leg and boot of a man in the round glow of light ahead. Fearing he'd been seen, he reached for his pepper spray; there would be enough trouble if they were caught without killing the guards.

But the sentry continued without noticing him, walking across the macadam toward the administration building. Ferguson watched his boots disappear into the shadows, then snuck to the corner. Thera had stuck the sensor into the metal loop connecting the fence to the pillar; he retrieved it and retreated back toward the reception area for the other tags.

"Truck comin' down toward the plant," warned Guns. "Going to the front gate."

"What, are you kiddin'?" said Rankin. "It's way after closing time."

"No shit, man. Really."

"Where are you, Rankin?" said Ferguson.

"Other side of the reception building, near the little power cabinet."

"Truck is at the gate. Going in," said Guns.

"Rankin, stay where you are until the truck goes through."

Ferguson hunkered down as headlights swept in front

of him. The truck was a six-wheeler, a bit stubby looking, the type used by small firms in the States for local deliveries. It headed in the direction of the low-level waste disposal area, bumping over the tracks close to the railcars where he was supposed to meet Rankin.

"Guns, they question these guys at the front gate?"

"Just let them through, Ferg. The patrol should be starting in another five minutes or so. Any time after that, I mean. It's been twenty-five minutes."

Ferguson retrieved the second tag from the side of the reception building and then began looking for the last, which Thera had planted on top of a barrel opposite the corner of the building.

The problem was, he didn't see a barrel.

Thinking Thera had gotten the corner wrong when she drew her map, Ferguson got down on his hands and knees and crawled along the side of the building. He was about midway when he heard voices coming from the direction of the administration station. Cursing, he jumped up and got back to the reception building as the men crossed toward the recycling area.

"They're going for the truck," warned Guns.

Ferguson was now trapped. He couldn't stay where he was because he'd be easily visible once the truck started in his direction. Two of the other sides of the building were visible from the administration station itself; the front, with its large doors, was covered by cameras.

He considered running across the open lot to his left but decided that was too risky. Instead he backed against the building, hoping to hide in the shadows. The metal ribs extended out nearly a foot, but he didn't think they were quite big enough to hide him. As he examined them, he thought it might be possible to climb up between them, leaning against one rib with his feet and the other with his hands. He gave it a quick try, pulling upright a few feet off the ground.

The sound of the pickup approaching convinced him this was going to have to be the solution. Ferguson reached the metal overhang of the building and pulled himself on top as the patrol truck swung in his direction.

As soon as the truck passed, Ferguson took out his night-vision glasses and used them to scout the nearby yard. The barrel was about ten yards from the corner of the building; he'd gone by it earlier without realizing it was where Thera had put the bug. Obviously her map hadn't been drawn to scale.

Meanwhile, the truck that had come through the gate had disappeared into the entrance to the low-level waste storage area. Ferguson could see the top of the opening but not inside.

"Ferg, where are you?" asked Rankin over the radio.

"On top of the situation."

"Where the hell is that?"

"On the reception building. Where are you?"

"Over near the back of the administration building. I got one more to get."

"Hang tight. Guards are coming back."

The pickup swung around the reception building, slowed near the entrance to the recyclable waste area, and then returned to the administration building.

"Clear," said Ferguson. He was about to jump down when he saw the headlights from the truck that had come in earlier heading in his direction. "Hold it," he told Rankin, and he leaned down against the metal roof.

Blessed Peak was a state-run facility; the users weren't charged. Why would they need to bypass the standard procedures by bringing a single truck in late at night, skipping around the classifying and tracking station?

Ferguson reached into his pocket and grabbed three small wireless bugs, then crawled to the edge of the roof. When the truck passed the building, he tossed the bugs onto the top of the truck body. One bounced onto the ground, but the others stayed.

"Guns, see if you can follow that truck," Ferguson said. "I dumped a couple of bugs on top."

"On it, Ferg."

Though not as good as dedicated tracking devices, the bugs could be used as primitive range finders with roughly a three-mile range.

"Ferguson, where are you?" asked Rankin.

"About to break my legs getting off the reception building roof," said Ferguson, looking over the side and realizing there was no easy way down.

15

SOUTH CHUNGCHONG PROVINCE, SOUTH KOREA

Guns ran down the hill and jumped into the car. He fumbled with his backpack, finally locating the audio bug's receiving unit in a case at the very bottom. He had to squint to see the directional arrow in the screen.

Then they were gone. The bugs worked with line of sight radio waves, which would limit their range in this terrain.

At least he had the advantage of knowing which way the truck had come from. He eased down the dirt road toward the highway and waited for it to go by.

Five minutes passed before he realized his assumption was wrong; the truck had to have left by now and must be going the other way. Sure enough, he got the signal back as soon as he passed the waste facility.

It was weak; the truck was more than a mile beyond him, possibly close to the outside limits of the bug's range. He stepped on the gas.

"Going east," he told Ferguson. "He came from the west."

"Just follow him until he gets somewhere. Check in later. We'll meet you at the park."

Guns had to slow down to take a series of curves as the road descended, braking so sharply that the receiving unit fell off the car seat. He grabbed for it, then lost it again as the road jerked right in front of him. Cursing at himself, he waited until he came to a straightaway, then reached down and grabbed the unit, holding it in front of the Hyundai's dash.

They were straight ahead, about a half mile away.

Guns decided to trying ramping the volume on the unit, but the only thing he heard was a *whoosh*ing noise. Only one bug seemed to be working, even though Ferguson had told him he'd thrown more than one.

Five minutes later, Guns came to a north-south intersection. As he started across, he saw that the directional indicator had swung to the right. He veered across the shoulder and opposite lane of the deserted highway, scraping the muffler on the median curb. The car's exhaust rumbled a bit louder as he got into the right lane, but at least he was going in the right direction.

While the immediate area was deserted, the truck would soon reach a built-up area where there were lots of intersections and turnoffs. Guns decided to close the gap. Within a few minutes the meter showed he was steadily gaining on the truck, and he started looking ahead for taillights, expecting them to appear at any second. Every so often he glanced at the receiver; his target was dead ahead.

And then suddenly it wasn't.

The strength needle began backing off, and he lost the directional compass. Guns realized he'd somehow passed the truck.

He spun into a quick a U-turn. The strength gauge climbed again, showing the bug was dead ahead.

And then behind him.

He cursed, realizing the bug had fallen off the truck onto the road.

16

It took Ferguson and Rankin nearly three hours to hike out of the waste plant property and down through the nearby park. Guns was leaning against the car near the fence, waiting for them, his arms crossed and a scowl on his face. Ferguson laughed, then slapped him on the back and told him not to take it so hard.

"I'm sorry I messed up, Ferg."

"The bug fell off the truck. What are you going to do?"

"I shoulda been closer."

"Don't worry about it."

Rankin, tossing his gear in the trunk, couldn't help thinking that Ferguson would have ridden his butt if it had been him rather than Guns who'd lost the truck.

"I checked the area out. Couldn't find anything," said Guns as they got in the car. "I took a picture of the truck coming into the plant. Maybe we can use that."

"Maybe," said Ferguson.

"Probably getting around some no-dumping law," said Rankin.

Ferguson plopped into the front seat of the car. He'd hurt his right knee getting down off the roof, and he grimaced as he pulled it in.

"What'd ja do?" asked Guns.

"Roof was a little higher than I thought it was," Ferguson told him. "I tried sliding down the ribs, but it didn't work too well. Nothing a good belt of Irish whiskey wouldn't cure," he added.

Rankin snorted from the back.

"They have Irish whiskey in Korea?" asked Guns.

"Guns, they have Irish whiskey everywhere," said Ferguson. He dug into his pocket and took out the sensors, examining them. Only one had gone red, the one that had been on the barrel. It had been positioned near the tracks to the permanent low-level waste area, right next to the route the truck had taken.

"Gonna be a nice day for a change," said Rankin, looking out the window. The sun had just started to peek over the horizon.

Ferguson repacked the tags in an envelope, then sealed everything in a large carrying case. He snapped the lock closed, then reset the digital lock.

"Give this to Van and tell him to send it back ASAP," he told Rankin, handing it back to him. "I'll let Corrigan know it's coming."

"I thought we were all going to shadow Thera," said Guns.

"This is more interesting," said Ferguson. "Besides, Skippy likes to be alone with the Delta boys. They stay up late and talk all that blanket-hugger stuff while they roast MREs over the fire."

"You're a laugh a minute, Ferg," said Rankin. "You oughta go on Jay Leno."

"Keep working on it, Rankin. There's a comeback in there somewhere," said Ferguson.

17

CIA BUILDING 24-442, VIRGINIA

Corrine Alston got out of the elevator and walked down the narrow hallway to a stairwell guarded by two CIA security officers. The men stared straight ahead as she approached, doing their best to pretend that they didn't notice her. She descended one level—the stairwells and elevators were separated to prevent a smart bomb from flying all the way down—and walked through a well-lit hallway. The walls had recently been painted a soft blue on the advice of an industrial psychologist to add an air of calm, but it was a futile gesture. So much went on here that it was difficult for anyone to be calm.

Corrine put her thumb on a small panel next to the first doorway on the right. After a second's delay, the doors swung apart, and she entered a vestibule leading to a small, secure conference room. In contrast to the rest of the building, the room was bereft of high-tech gadgetry. There was a whiteboard at the front and an old-fashioned slide projector on the table. The table and chairs were at least thirty years old, having been salvaged from another building.

Daniel Slott, the CIA's deputy director of operations and the head of the agency's covert operations division, sat alone at the table, fiddling with a plastic Paper Mate mechanical pencil. He looked up when Corrine entered, nodded, then went back to staring at his pencil.

Corrine pulled out a seat opposite him and sat down. "So?"

Slott cleared his throat. "I thought I'd wait for the DCI."

DCI was Agency-talk for "director of Central Intelligence Agency"—the head of the CIA, Thomas Parnelles.

"When will he be here?"

"Hard to tell." Slott twisted the lead from the pencil. "He said he was on his way an hour ago."

When she had first become involved with Special Demands, Corrine had assumed that Parnelles and Slott—generally considered the number-two man at the CIA—were close allies, but over the course of several operations she had come to realize they weren't close at all.

Parnelles didn't consider that a problem. Slott, though, felt the director not only second-guessed him but also undercut his authority, giving many of his deputies too much leeway, in effect encouraging them to subvert the normal chain of command. Parnelles wanted results above all; Slott often found himself trying to rein in operations that were veering toward the sort of abuses that had laid the agency low in the past.

Not that Slott would discuss this with Corrine.

"Maybe you and I should get started," said Corrine. "And when he comes in—"

The door opened before she had a chance to finish the sentence. Parnelles stalked in, a frown on his face. Slott put the pencil down.

"Ms. Alston. Daniel." Parnelles pulled a chair out and sat. "What's going on?"

"The First Team found evidence of bomb material in South Korea," said Slott.

It took Corrine a second to process what he had said. "*South* Korea?"

"Yes, South Korea. At the Blessed Peak South Korean Nuclear Waste Disposal and Holding Station, thirty miles northwest of Daejeon. Thera brought tags in to get a baseline so the scientists could compare it to the North Korean waste site. All of the tags were somehow exposed. Ferguson thought it might be a mistake or a screwup in the instruments. The devices are new, and since the underlying nanotechnology—"

"We don't really need the details, Dan," said Parnelles.

"We stipulate that they made the right decision to double-check."

"They planted a full set again," said Slott. "One showed a serious exposure. It's on its way back to the States to be examined."

"Is it a bomb or bomb material?" asked Parnelles.

"We can't be sure," said Slott, going on to explain that the sensors were "tuned" to discover the main ingredient of a bomb and one common contaminant. The ratio indicated that weapons-grade plutonium was present, but they could not definitively say how it had been used.

Parnelles rolled his arms in front of his chest and leaned back in his chair. "Has the president been told?"

"No. I only just found out about this through Lauren. I haven't spoken to Ferguson myself." Slott glanced at his watch. "It's roughly six a.m. in Korea, and they'd been working on getting this all night. I figured I'd let him sleep."

"But you're sure of the results?" said Parnelles.

Slott bristled. "There's always a possibility that the sensors malfunctioned," he said. "But the technology people tell me it's unlikely. They've been tested, I'm sure you recall."

"I think we have to tell the president immediately," said Corrine.

"That goes without saying." Parnelles's voice boomed in the small, sealed room. "Are you sure, Daniel, that this isn't a mistake?"

"We have two scientists on their way out to a lab in Hawaii. We should know more definitely in eight or nine hours. But I don't think it's a mistake, not with two sets."

"It makes sense that they have a weapon," said Parnelles. "It makes a lot of sense."

"Whether it makes sense or not, it's going to be a problem," said Corrine.

Parnelles held out his hands. The skin around his eyes was thick and rugged, as textured as a rubber Halloween mask, but his hands were remarkably smooth and unblemished.

"This could kill the nonproliferation treaty and God knows what else," said Corrine.

"I think it's still a little premature to jump to the conclusion that they have weapons," said Slott. "It's possible this is just part of an exploratory program."

"You think they stole the material from the North Koreans?" asked Parnelles.

Slott hadn't considered that. "Maybe," he said.

"Why didn't we know about it?" asked Parnelles.

All Slott could do was shake his head.

"Nothing anywhere in any of the analyses hints at it?" asked Parnelles.

Slott shook his head again. While he couldn't be expected to know everything the CIA knew—no one did—Asia was an area of special interest. So was Korea, where he'd been station chief. There had been South Korean programs in the past but none aimed at plutonium-fueled weapons. At least as far as the Agency knew.

"Who's going to tell the president?" said Parnelles, looking over at Corrine.

Corrine interpreted it as a challenge. "I will."

"You'll want to tell him in person," suggested Parnelles, "and alone."

Corrine nodded. The president was in Maine this evening, staying at a private home; he'd be in New Hampshire tomorrow. She'd catch an early flight and meet him there.

"We should have the report from the scientists within a few hours," said Slott, screwing the lead all the way out his pencil. "I can get you a copy."

"All right. Start reviewing what we already know," Parnelles told Slott. "See what's there."

"Absolutely. But it's a sensitive time. Thera's on her way to Korea."

"It's always a sensitive time," said Parnelles, rising.

"Better talk to Ferguson and find out exactly what the hell he knows. The president is bound to ask some very uncomfortable questions."

Slott waited until the others had left the room before getting up from the table. The discovery of the plutonium had shaken him, not merely because it implied that the South Koreans were doing something he'd never believed they would but also because it implied that the CIA's operations in the country had failed miserably. No matter where the radioactive material had come from, the Agency surely should have known about it before now.

And for it to involve Korea, of all places, a country he knew intimately, having spent the better part of his career there . . .

Granted, he hadn't been back in a number of years. Still, he knew Ken Bo, the station chief in Seoul, reasonably well. Until now, Slott thought he was a very good officer.

Knew he was a good officer.

Careers were going to be ruined if the information panned out. Including his, maybe.

He should take steps . . .

All his life he'd derided officers who put their careers above the needs of the country and the Agency. He hated the cover-your-ass mentality. But as he walked down the hall toward the Special Needs communication center, he realized he was thinking along those very lines.

He wasn't going to do that. He was going to take it step by step, do what *should* be done, no matter the personal consequences.

Jack Corrigan was just coming on duty as mission coordinator and was being briefed by Lauren. They stopped talking as he walked across the "bridge," an open area of space between the communications consoles and the high-tech gear that lined the room.

"I'd like to talk to Ferguson as soon as possible," Slott told them.

"He's still sleeping I think," said Lauren. "His phone isn't on—"

"Why the hell isn't his phone on?"

Lauren glanced toward Corrigan. Ordinarily Slott was the personification of cool; he showed so little emotion at times, she was tempted to take his pulse.

"Ferg's afraid that the phone might, you know, that there would be a bad time or something," said Corrigan. "And I don't think he totally trusts the encryption either."

"That's ridiculous," said Slott. The encryption was an NSA standard, all but theoretically impossible to crack.

"He usually leaves it off unless something important's going on," said Lauren. "The transmissions can be detected and—"

"Something damn important is going on," said Slott. "Who's with him? Sergeant Young?"

"Um, Guns turns his phone off, too," said Lauren. "I'm sure Ferg tells him to."

Slott struggled to control his anger. It wasn't Lauren or Corrigan's fault that he couldn't talk to Ferguson—they couldn't control what the op did—and, to be honest, neither could he.

He liked Ferguson's results—who didn't?—but the op had always struck him as being arrogant, acting as if he didn't have to follow the rules everyone else did.

"I called the hotel desk," said Lauren. "He left orders not to be disturbed. Maybe—"

"I want to talk to him now," Slott told them. "Get somebody to get him. Have him call me."

"Colonel Van Buren's operation has his men tied up," said Corrigan.

"Tell Seoul to send someone down there," snapped Slott, referring to the CIA's South Korean office.

"How much should I tell them?" asked Lauren.

Slott hesitated. There were two separate problems he had to deal with: the plutonium itself and his people's failure to discover it. If he had Seoul work on problem number one, he might not be able to discover the seriousness of problem number two. What he needed for now was to keep the two problems separate if at all possible.

On the other hand, he needed to talk to Ferguson ASAP, not when Ferguson felt like checking in.

"Dan?" said Corrigan.

"Don't tell them anything. Ferguson is just an American who's supposed to call home."

Corrigan and Lauren glanced at each other.

"I'll come up with something," said Corrigan.

18

DAEJEON, SOUTH KOREA

The knock on the hotel-room door was not quite loud enough to wake the dead, but it was sufficient to jostle someone with a mild hangover. Ferguson lifted his head and grunted, "Yeah?"

"Robert Christian?"

It was the cover name Ferguson had used to check in. The voice speaking was English with an American accent.

"Yeah?"

"Your uncle wants to talk to you."

"What time is it?"

"Going on ten o'clock."

Ferguson groaned and slipped out of bed. "My uncle, huh?" At least his knee felt better. "Where's he live?"

"Washington."

He grabbed his Glock and a flash-bang grenade and walked to the door, flipping on the TV as he went. Ferguson had chosen the hotel because it had eyepieces in each room's door; Ferguson had replaced his with a wireless video camera whose wide-angle lens allowed it to view the entire hallway.

The image on the TV screen showed that there was a man and a woman outside, both dressed in suits, both Western, more than likely American. They didn't have guns showing, and they didn't have backup down the hallway, unless they were hiding in the stairway. No headsets, no radios.

The man leaned against the door, apparently in a misguided attempt to peer through the spyglass.

"My uncle hasn't lived in Washington in twenty years," said Ferguson. Silently, he slid back the dead bolt and unhooked the chain.

"We're from the embassy," said the man, still leaning against the door.

"Which embassy would that be?" asked Ferguson. As he did, he yanked the door open. The man fell inside, helped along by Ferguson, who grabbed his arm and threw him against the bureau. Ferguson kicked the door closed behind him, then knelt on the man's chest, his pistol pointed at his forehead.

"I'm hoping you're new," Ferguson told the CIA officer, who clearly was. "Like maybe you just got off the plane."

"I've been in Korea three months," managed the man.

"That's long enough to know better."

Ferguson quickly searched him; he wasn't carrying a weapon. His business cards indicated he was Sean Gillespie and a member of the U.S. Commerce Department's Asian Trade Council, the cover du jour obviously.

"What's going on in there?" yelled his teammate from the hall, pounding on the door.

"Let her in," Ferguson said, getting up. "Before I shoot her."

Gillespie opened the door, and his fellow CIA officer, a thin brunette with thick glasses, came inside, her face flushed. Like Gillespie, she looked about twenty-three going on twelve.

"What is this?" she sputtered, mesmerized by Ferguson's gun.

"Lock the door and lower your voice," Ferguson told her. "Then you have about ten seconds to tell me why you're here blowing my cover."

The brunette's cheeks went from red to white.

"Why are you here?" said Ferguson.

"You're supposed to come right away to the embassy and call home," said Gillespie. "We were told to bring you."

"Why?"

"They didn't say."

"You're not on official cover?" asked the brunette.

"Do these boxers look official?" said Ferguson.

Official cover" meant that the officers held positions with the government and had diplomatic passports. It also meant that just about anyone who counted knew they were CIA.

Someone traveling on unofficial cover, like Ferguson, had no visible connection with the Agency or the government. Other officers were supposed to be extremely careful when approaching them, since anyone watching might easily put two and two together and realize the other person was a spy.

Unsure whether the two nuggets had been followed, Ferguson told them to leave without him. They refused; they had their orders after all and insisted on accompanying him to Seoul. After considerable wrangling, he convinced them to meet him on the train to Seoul. Ferguson gave them a head start, then he called The Cube and asked what the hell was going on.

"There you are," said Corrigan.

"Two bozos from the embassy just woke me up. What's the story?"

"Oh. Slott needed to talk to you and—"

"So you got Seoul to blow my cover?"

"No."

"You need to talk to me?"

"Dan does. Listen—"

"I'll call back."

Ferguson hung up, looked at his watch. Guns wouldn't be up for several hours. He decided he'd let him sleep; they weren't supposed to meet until the afternoon anyway.

Ferguson turned off the phone, gathered his gear in an overnight bag, then left. Outside, he took a cab to a hotel near the science museum, checked in, then strolled downstairs to the coffee shop. When he was sure he wasn't being followed, he went out on the street and caught another cab at random, waving the first one off, and took it a few blocks to a park they'd scoped out the other day where he had a good view of the surrounding area.

He dialed into Slott's number but didn't get an answer, so he called back over to The Cube.

"Where have you been, Ferg?" asked Corrigan.

"Hello to you, too, Jack. Where's Slott?"

"Seoul called me—"

"Yeah?"

"They were supposed to meet you on the train, and you didn't show up. They thought you were dead."

"Tell them I jumped out the window."

"Hang on. Slott's standing right here."

"Ferg, what's going on?" said Slott when he came on the line.

"I was about to ask you the same question."

"You found bomb material."

"Lauren didn't tell you?"

"I want to hear it from you."

"The tags were hot. All of them the first day, one the second. We didn't find the material itself. I have an idea where it might be, though. I'll go back tonight."

"No. I don't want you going anywhere until you hear from me."

"Why the hell not?"

"I really don't feel like discussing this with you right now."

"Well maybe you better," said Ferguson.

"At the moment, I don't want to do anything that will jeopardize Thera."

"How is this going to affect her?"

"I understand you contacted her—"

"No, she contacted me. Look, Dan, if you want to second-guess me, fine, but I'm a little cold right now, so why don't we do it some other time?"

Ferguson glanced around, making sure no one was near.

"I'm not second-guessing you, Ferg," snapped Slott.

Ferguson, realizing he was feeling a little cranky himself, remembered he'd forgotten to take his morning dose of thyroid-replacement medicine. He reached into his pocket for the small pillbox he carried, and slipped out the three small pills.

Amazing how such a small amount of chemical could have so much control over a person.

Ferguson recounted what had happened, essentially repeating everything he had told Lauren before going to sleep a few hours earlier.

"The tag that went red the second night was the one next to the entrance to the low-level waste area," added Ferguson. "I want to get a look at it. I'll bring a gamma meter in, look around, take some soil samples, plant some more tags."

"Not yet."

"Not yet? How long do you want me to wait?"

"Until I decide what I want you to do."

Ferguson put his head back on the bench and looked at the thick layer of clouds overhead. He exhaled slowly.

As supervisors went, Slott was generally reasonable; Ferguson couldn't remember being second-guessed, let alone being jerked around like this.

"This is a bad decision, Dan," said Ferguson finally. "You're not thinking this through."

"Why is this a bad decision?" snapped Slott.

"Because they could move the material."

"I'm not debating this with you."

"Does Seoul know about all this?"

"Not yet."

"You telling them?"

"I haven't decided yet."

"I don't think we should get them involved. They sent a couple of rookie bozos down to Daejeon and blew my cover. I don't think they can be trusted."

"That's not really up to you, is it?" snapped Slott, instantly defensive.

"You sure they don't know about this already?"

"Good-bye, Ferg." Slott cut the line.

**P'YÖNGYANG AIRPORT,
NORTH KOREA**

A gust of wind rushed into the plane as the steward folded the 737's forward passenger door back. Thera, standing directly behind Dr. Norkelus, hunched her shoulders together under her parka to ward off the cold, watching as a boarding ladder was rolled across the concrete toward the airplane. The metal stairway, a throwback to the 1950s, groaned and shook ominously as Norkelus stepped onto it.

"Come along," Norkelus said to Thera under his breath. "Let's look professional."

Two men in heavy military overcoats stood at the bottom of the steps, their right hands welded beneath the visors of their caps in salute.

Norkelus, who did not speak Korean, addressed them in English. The men apparently didn't understand what he was saying, for they responded by gesturing in the direction of one of the two large buses that were parked nearby. A short woman in an oversized parka stepped from the bus and began walking slowly toward them, taking tiny steps, her head bowed as if she were a beaten dog.

By now a good portion of the inspection team had come out of the plane and formed a small knot behind Norkelus. Most stared at the nearby three-story terminal building, where a large photo of North Korea's supreme leader, Kim Jong-Il, returned their gaze.

P'yŏngyang Airport was the country's main international airport, but it typically saw no more than four flights in any given week. No other aircraft were parked on the expansive concrete pad in front of the terminal. A half-dozen old Russian airliners, turboprops mostly, and all showing signs of serious neglect, stood in a row by the taxiway closer to the runway, or the place might not have seemed like an airport at all.

"You will board bus, please," said the translator, looking at her shoes as she spoke.

"I am Dr. Norkelus," said the director. "Please tell our hosts we are happy to be here."

"You will please now board bus," said the woman.

Norkelus, slightly confused, began shepherding his people toward the bus. Two of the techies stayed behind to supervise the unloading of the equipment. This bothered the two military men, and it took quite a while for Norkelus to explain through the translator that the protocols called for the equipment to remain in the team's custody and care. The words *regulations* and *our orders* seemed to impress them finally, and they stopped complaining. But then came a fresh problem: Some of the gear was too bulky to fit in the bottom luggage compartments of the bus. A pair of military vehicles were finally called to transport the boxes.

During this entire time, the bulk of the inspection team remained on the bus. Thera, whom Norkelus wanted to "chronicle the events of the trip," was among the handful of exceptions. She stood a few feet from the inspection team leader, shivering in the cold. Finally, with the gear loaded and the military leaders satisfied, Norkelus boarded the bus, and the inspection team rolled out . . . to the terminal building, all of two hundred feet away.

The inspectors were led to a set of tables in one of the large downstairs rooms. Even though they were traveling under special UN-issued passports guaranteeing them diplomatic immunity, the North Koreans insisted on detailed checks of the baggage and personal items being brought into the country. Norkelus decided this wasn't worth a fight, and the team members queued up with their bags.

Thera took her red suitcase and rolled it behind Julie Svenson, listening as the scientist complained. Submitting to a search set the wrong tone, Julie said. It would make the Koreans think they were in charge.

"Wrong, wrong message," said the scientist as she hoisted her bag up and then banged it onto the table. "They'll think they can boss us around."

One of the engineers nearby had an American Tourister bag with its red, white, and blue logo on the ID tag. The North Koreans pointed at the logo and began questioning the man closely. In a country still officially at war with the U.S.—and with a museum dedicated to America's "war crimes"—even such a seemingly innocuous commercial symbol aroused suspicion. The fact that the engineer was from South Africa hardly seemed to matter.

Thera's stomach began churning as the customs official riffled through Julie's bag. She saw herself being hauled away, dragged out the large glass doors behind them, and shot on the stained cement.

"OK, Miss," said the young man, pushing Julie's bag to the side and turning to Thera. His light tan shirt had ballooned up from his waistline, and he was sweating, despite the fact that the terminal was rather cool. "We check. OK?"

Thera snapped open the suitcase. Four cartons of cigarettes sat at the side of the bag.

The man looked up at her expectantly. Thera, guessing he wanted one of the cartons, nodded. The customs official took one, slit open the end, and poured the boxes of cigarettes onto the table. He chose one pack and opened it, again emptying its contents. Then he selected a cigarette.

I should light it for him, Thera thought to herself, but before she could, he had pushed the cigarette back into the box and began to repack the carton.

He put the boxes back and went through the rest of the things. Thera reached into the pocket of her jacket and took out an unopened pack of cigarettes.

"You could have one," she said, holding it out to the man. "Sir?"

The custom official's face turned beet red. He shook his head quickly, then, without even looking in her pocketbook, shoved her suitcase to the side and waved the next person toward him.

"I'm sorry," whispered Thera.

"Go now," said the man, without looking in her direction.

20

DAEJEON, SOUTH KOREA

After talking to Slott, Ferguson spent a few hours lining up new backup hotel rooms and renting cars under a new set of pseudonyms, erasing any connection with the man the Seoul CIA officers had called on. If he'd been operating somewhere else—Cairo, for example—he might not have gone quite so far; it seemed unlikely that they had been followed. But he didn't know Korea, and the last thing he wanted was to be blindsided here because he wasn't careful enough.

Running a bit late, he found Guns in the National Science Museum, puzzling out a historical display of Korean weaponry. The captions were almost entirely in Korean, but the marine had a connoisseur's appreciation of the tools of the trade.

"Better than rifles, huh?" said Ferguson as Guns bent over an ancient sword.

"Not better exactly, but I wouldn't mind putting it to the test."

"Maybe later. You have lunch?"

"Like two hours ago at the hotel."

"Come on and have some again."

They found a small, inexpensive restaurant about a mile away, took off their shoes, and sat at a low table. A laminated menu hung on the wall next to them. All of the words were in Korean, punctuated by idealized pictures of the dishes that both men had learned from experience had little to do with what they'd actually end up being served. A gas burner sat in the middle of the table; they ordered steak and grilled the raw strips themselves when the dish was brought over.

Ferguson, who hadn't eaten in more than twenty-four hours, wolfed the food down as soon as the meat reached medium rare. He also devoured most of the kimchi and rice. Guns, still adjusting to the spicy food, looked on with a mixture of wonder and shock as the meal disappeared into his companion's mouth.

"So what's the next move?" he asked when Ferguson came up for air. "We go in and look for the material?"

Ferguson shook his head.

"OK," said the marine.

That was one thing about Guns, Ferg thought: He always went with the program. No muss, no fuss.

"So what do we do?"

"Talk to a man about a truck," Ferguson told him, counting out his money to pay the bill.

This is all you got?" said Corrigan after Ferguson uploaded the photos to him.

"What, the driver isn't smiling?"

"Jeez, Ferg, these are blurry as hell. I can't even read the logo on the grill."

"Get some truck expert to look at it. Once you get the make narrowed down, we can talk to the police, get a list of licenses."

"Even if we *could* talk to the police, which we can't," said Corrigan, "you know how many trucks there are in Korea?"

"Corrigan, stop whining and see what you can find out."

While they were waiting for Corrigan to come up with something, Ferguson and Guns drove back to the highway near the waste plant and found a spot to plant two video units, hoping they might spot the truck if it came back. The units were outfitted with miniature hard drives; time-lapse photography let them record for thirty-six hours before transmitting their images to The Cube and starting all over.

Ferguson guessed it would be a long shot that the truck would return. He also had no idea if it was important or not. But he couldn't stand just hanging around with nothing to do.

They were on their way back to Daejeon when Corrigan called Ferguson on the sat phone, greeting him with a question about what truck model was the most popular in Korea.

"Ford?" guessed Ferguson.

"Hyundai," said Corrigan. "This isn't that. You know what number two is?"

"Daewoo."

"Exactly. This isn't one of those either. It's pretty rare, *Namhan Hoesa Teureoka,* South Korean National Truck Company."

"Very creative. Who owns the truck?"

"I don't know. They were only made for about two years. This was about a decade back. See, there was this rich guy named Park tried to set up a company to compete with the Japanese and—"

"Whose truck is it, Jack?"

"I told you, Ferg. I don't know."

"Have you run the registrations?"

"I can't just call up the division of motor vehicles."

"Why the hell not?"

"For one thing, they'd get suspicious. Slott says we're not supposed to do anything that will tip anyone off, especially the government."

"Lie to the Koreans. Tell them it's a drug thing. Just get me a list."

Ferguson snapped off the phone.

"Problem?" asked Guns.

"Corrigan still thinks he's in the army."

Guns laughed.

They passed a Hyundai sedan whose side had been caved in from an accident.

"Hey, back up," Ferg told Guns.

"What?"

"I want to grab a picture of that banged-up car. Turn around."

Guns checked his mirror, then jammed the brakes and made a U-turn.

"What are we doing now?" he asked after Ferguson came back with two digital photos of the car.

"Looking for a police station. We just had an accident."

Ferguson reasoned that he was more likely to find a sympathetic policeman in a small town, and so he and Guns got off Route 19, wandering around the local roads. They finally found a likely looking place just outside of Baekbong, where buildings with curved-tile roofs clustered behind a row of two-story stores on the narrow main drag. After brushing up on his Korean with the help of his handheld translator and a phrase book, Ferguson left Guns up the block and went inside.

"I want to report an accident," he said in Korean, addressing the squat woman behind the desk at the police station. *"Sagoga nasseoyo."*

"Dachin saram isseoyo?" said the woman.

It took Ferguson a second to untangle the phrase, even though he was prepared for it.

"No, no one's hurt," he told her in English, "but my car was damaged."

"Da-majj-ed?"

Ferguson pulled out the camera with the picture of the damaged car. "It was a little road near Songnisan National Park, about a mile from the highway."

By now three other officers had appeared. One spoke excellent English and began acting as translator.

"I need to fill out this insurance paper," Ferguson told him, waving a form from the rental agency. "I need to find the truck."

"What was the registration?"

"I'm not sure, but I know the kind of truck: *Namhan Hoesa Teureoka.*"

"Namhan Hoesa?"

"Maybe I'm not saying it right. The words mean 'South Korean National Truck Company.'"

The officer gave him a strange look, wondering how he would know what the words meant if he could not pronounce them properly.

"I have never heard of the truck," said the policeman. "Are you sure it was not a Hyundai?"

"No, I'm positive. That's why I figured you could help me track it down. Probably it would have damage on it.

Couldn't we search on the computer?" Ferguson stepped around the desk, pointing to the workstation. "For trucks? It's an odd model—"

Going behind the desk meant passing over the invisible line separating police from civilians and was a major faux pas. The Koreans reacted quickly and fervently, shouting at Ferguson that he must get behind the desk. Ferguson raised his hands and backed away, trying to cajole them into giving him the information, but it didn't work, and in the end he retreated, probably fortunate that he wasn't arrested as a public nuisance.

"Didn't work?" asked Guns when he got back to the car.

"Fell flat on my face." Ferguson smiled. Then he reached into his pocket for his synthetic thyroid hormones, which he was due to take.

"Pep pills?"

"Oh yeah." Ferguson dumped two into his palm, then swallowed. They tasted bitter without water.

"Why do you have to take that stuff, Ferg?"

"I never told you, Guns?"

The marine shook his head.

"I don't have a thyroid," Ferguson told him.

"Wow. How'd that happen?"

"Birth defect. Let me see if Corrigan has anything new."

Corrigan—or rather the analysts working for him back at The Cube—had managed to come up with a list of the South Korean National Truck Company vehicles registered in South Chungchong Province. As rare as the trucks supposedly were, there were nearly three hundred.

"We're working on the rest of the country, but this is a start," said Corrigan.

"I thought you said this was a rare truck?"

"It is. You know how many trucks there are in Korea?"

"We have to narrow it down."

"There's about fifty that look like they might have

something to do with hospitals or different companies, that sort of thing," Corrigan added. "They deal with radioactive waste. Why don't you start with them?"

For once, Corrigan had a good idea. Ferguson hooked the sat phone to the team's laptop and downloaded the information from an encrypted Web site. Then they headed to the nearest hospital.

Parked near a small laundry building on the hospital grounds was a trio of trucks. One was a National.

"Wait for me a second," said Ferguson. He got out of the car and walked over, took a picture of the license plate, and then used a handheld gamma detector to scan for radiation. The needle didn't move off the baseline.

The gamma meter was designed specifically to find trace material. As powerful as it was, it couldn't definitively tell whether the truck had been used to transport material, since properly shielded plutonium could have been transported without leaving any trace material behind.

Ferguson, though, theorized that the shipment hadn't been well shielded at all, which would explain why all of the tags had turned positive the first time Thera visited the site. He also thought it possible that the plutonium had been moved after that first day, one possible explanation for the weaker hit on day two. And what better place to hide millions of dollars worth of plutonium than in a laundry truck?

None, but not in this truck. Ferguson opened the rear door and climbed into a compartment filled with stacks of linens bundled between brown paper. The needle still didn't move.

"Anything?" Guns asked when he got to the car.

"Nada."

"You think this is worth the effort, Ferg?" asked Guns. "I mean, all that's probably going on is that these guys are illegally dumping waste, you know?"

"Yeah." Ferg reached down for the bottled water. "Here's the thing, Guns. We want to get into the site, right?"

"Yeah."

"We can parachute in, or we can go over the fence. Either way is doable, right? Because me and Rankin just did it, and anything me and Rankin can do, you and I can do better, right?"

"I don't know about better, Ferg."

"But let's say there's something in there that's pretty heavy, and we want to take it out—"

"Oh."

Ferguson made his hand into a gun and fired at his companion.

"How'd you get to be so smart, Ferg?" asked Guns as they left the parking lot.

Ferguson laughed. "I'm not that smart."

"You are, Fergie."

"My dad taught me," said Ferguson, suddenly serious. "He was the smartest guy I know."

"He's a spook?"

"Was. He died about a year and a half ago." Ferguson smiled, realizing the unintended double entendre. "Yeah, he was definitely a spook. A good one. The best. So good he got screwed."

"How'd that happen?"

"Long story, Guns." Ferguson unfolded the map to find the next truck. "Basically he trusted somebody he shouldn't have."

"Double agent?"

"No. His boss."

Ferguson and Guns found the next hospital but couldn't locate the truck, nor did they find one at the next place they tried, a small machine shop. This area of the city—technically, it was one of the suburbs, though a visitor would find it difficult to find the border—was a curious mix of business and science, part Berkley and part Silicon Valley, with what looked like old-line factories thrown in every so often for variety.

Two trucks belonged to a company whose name indicated it was a medical testing lab. Confused by the Korean street signs, Ferguson and Guns had a hard time finding it, and when they finally did they were stopped by a security patrol outside the building. Ferguson grabbed the map, hopped out, and began pointing excitedly, saying in Russian that he was truly, truly lost. The officers did not speak Russian, but one of the men patiently began to explain in Korean and then halting English how to get back to the road.

After a few minutes of gestures and nodding, Ferguson thanked the man profusely and stuffed a business card into his hand. This was an honorable gesture in Korean culture that could not be ignored, and the security officer not only examined it carefully but reciprocated by giving him his own.

The card came in handy an hour and a half later, when they checked on a trio of trucks owned by Science Industries. Ferguson drove through the main entrance without spotting a guard, only to find a pair of security officers standing in front of a gate a short distance from an intersection a quarter mile from the entrance. Before Ferguson could decide whether they should go left or right, one of the officers approached the car with his hand out in the universal sign of "halt."

His other was on his holster.

Ferguson rolled out his Russian again, then went to pidgin Korean, saying he had lost his way. When that didn't work, he found the other guard's card and handed it to the man. Mollified, the security guard called over his partner for advice on how to best send the foreigners on their way.

Ferguson got out of the car to better understand the directions and to get a better look around. There was a loading dock at the side of one of the buildings about a half mile away, down the road that was outside the gate. Three trucks were parked in front of it.

The security officers agreed that his best bet was to go

back the way he had come, taking a right on the main road and then heading to the highway a short distance away. From there he would have an easy time finding downtown Daejeon, his supposed destination.

"This way?" said Ferguson, pointing in the direction of the warehouse.

"No, no, straight."

"Straight, then this way," said the other guard.

Ferguson thanked the men and got back into the car. He turned around and began heading down the road.

"Those the right kind of trucks?" he asked Guns.

"Hard to see from here, Ferg."

"Yeah, hang on."

Ferguson turned off the lights, then veered to the right down the narrow dirt road that ran inside the perimeter fence. After about fifty feet he spotted a fire lane that led down to the lot in front of the warehouse.

"Hop out and hold the meter by them," he told Guns, reaching up to kill the interior light.

As Guns got out, Ferg spotted headlights coming up the road in his direction.

He pulled forward into a three-point turn, ready to go.

"How much longer, Guns?" he called out the window.

"It's still, like, calibrating."

The headlights were growing larger very quickly.

"Never mind," Ferg yelled. "In the car. Let's go."

The security patrol was less than a hundred yards away by the time Guns jumped into the car. The man inside turned on the side spotlight and moved the car into the middle of the street, trying to block their way.

"That's the kind of crap that really annoys me," Ferguson said as Guns hopped in. He stomped on the gas, homing in on the spotlight.

"Aren't you going the way we came?"

"He'll just follow us and radio to his buddy to cut us off. This is faster."

"Jesus!" yelled Guns, covering his eyes with his arm.

The security officer, either taken by surprise or simply

stubborn, remained in the middle of the road. Ferguson kept the pedal floored and, at the last second, jerked the wheel to the right. The car flew over the curb, rising up on two wheels.

Ferguson had cut it too close; his left fender and door sideswiped the security vehicle with a loud screech. The rental rebounded across a cement sidewalk, flattened a sign, and then landed back on the access road.

Something was scraping under the car, but this wasn't a good place to stop and investigate; the security officer had jumped out of his battered vehicle and was firing at them.

A tracer round flew past Ferguson's window.

"They're not screwin' around," said Guns.

As Ferguson reached the main entry road, a burst of red illuminated the rear of the car. Thinking at first this was just the reflection of a police light, Ferguson ignored it.

"We're on fire," said Guns. "One of the tracers must have hit us."

"Shit. I hate that."

Ferguson slammed on the brakes and threw the car into a skid.

"Out!" he told Guns as the vehicle stopped perpendicular to the road, blocking it. He yanked off his seat belt, grabbed his backpack, and threw himself to the pavement as the gas tank exploded.

21

Rankin studied the satellite photo as the AH-6 Little Bird helicopter veered toward the North Korean shore. According to the GPS coordinates, the site where they had to plant the first cache "dump" was exactly three miles dead ahead, a few hundred yards off the coastal highway heading north.

While the highway was deserted at night—and indeed for much of the day—an unmanned Global Hawk reconnaissance drone was flying overhead just to make sure. The feed from the unmanned aerial vehicle was being monitored by Colonel Van Buren in Command Transport Three, a specially equipped C-17 flying a hundred and fifty miles to the south.

"Bird One, you're go for Cache One," said Van Buren.

"Bird One acknowledges," said the pilot.

Their job, though dangerous, was relatively straightforward. Bird One would land in a field near the highway, where Rankin and the two soldiers with him would hide two large packs with emergency rations, weapons, a special radio, and a pair of lightweight, collapsible bicycles. The gear would be used by Thera in an emergency or by team members sent to rescue her. There were three spots along the coast, stretching from this one, about thirty miles south of the waste plant Thera was inspecting, to a spot on dry land in the marshes five miles north of the muddy mouth of the Ch'ŏngch'ŏn or Chongchon River.

Rankin didn't see much point in leaving the gear. It wasn't a mistake, exactly, just a waste of time. A forward rescue force would be parked on an atoll about twenty miles offshore. This was about seventy miles from the plant where Thera would be inspecting. If anything went wrong, they'd scramble in, grab her, and get out. The caches were just CIA fussiness, "just-in case" BS that the Langley planners liked to dream up to pretend they had all the bases covered.

That was typical CIA, though. They went crazy planning certain elements of a mission, then ignored others.

Like the possibility that *South* Korea might have nuclear material, for example.

"Here we go," said the helicopter's pilot, dipping the aircraft downward.

The helicopter arced over the roadway, the pilot making sure everything was clear before settling down in the field nearby.

Rankin and the two men in the rear of the chopper hopped out as the Little Bird settled down. While the other soldiers hauled the gear to the brush, Rankin located the large rock near the road that was to serve as a signpost. When he found it, he took out a can of white, luminescent paint and put a big blot on the stone. Then he ran to a set of rocks near where the others were burying the gear and sprayed them.

By the time he finished, the others were already hopping into the Little Bird. Rankin kicked some of the dirt where his paint had gone awry, hiding it, then hustled back to the helicopter.

22

The heat from the explosion was so intense Ferguson rolled on the ground, thinking he was on fire. By the time he realized he wasn't, he could hear sirens.

"Guns?"

"Here, Ferg," yelled the marine from the other side of the car.

"We want the highway."

"Yeah, no shit."

Ferguson leapt to his feet and began running in the direction of the road, crossing toward the perimeter road and then climbing the fence; with his arm, he pinned down the barbed wire strands at the top, ripping his parka but getting over without tearing his body to shreds. As he hit the ground, he saw a car approaching from the direction of the highway. Ferguson ducked behind some trees. Once the car passed—it turned out to be just a car, not the police as he'd feared—he climbed one of the trees and looked back in the direction of the plant they'd just escaped from.

"What's goin' on?" asked Guns from below.

"They're putting out the fire," Ferg told him. He slid back down. "You got the gamma meter and the laptop?"

"Left it in the car, Ferg. I'm sorry. I got everything else."

Almost on cue, a fireball rose from the vehicle. The laptop had self-destructed.

"Sorry," said Guns.

"It's all right. Wouldn't have been a good idea to go back and get them anyway. Most of those guys were carrying submachine guns instead of fire extinguishers."

23

OFF THE COAST OF NORTH KOREA

Thirty minutes after leaving the emergency supplies, the pilot of Bird One homed in on a small blot of black in the center of his green night-vision goggles. The blot was an uninhabited atoll eight miles east of North Korea's Taehaw Island, itself a dozen miles off the mainland. During the early spring and summer, North Korea's small fishing fleet regularly plied these waters, but in late fall the fishing was terrible, and the potential for ferocious storms kept the area nearly empty.

"We're sixty seconds from go/no go," the pilot told Rankin.

Rankin switched his radio onto the command frequency, linking with Van Buren.

"Bird One ready," Rankin told Van Buren.

"You're good to go," said Van Buren. "Be advised there are two fishing vessels approximately three miles southeast of your target."

"What are they fishing for at one o'clock in the morning?"

"Thinking here is that they're smugglers, bringing goods back from China," said the colonel.

"Thirty seconds from go/no go," said the pilot.

"Roger. Team is committed," said Rankin. He switched into the shared frequency, talking to the other three helicopters that made up the emergency extraction force. They'd all rendezvoused en route after dropping off their caches. "We're committed. Two minutes to target."

An officer might have said something like, "Make it look good," but Rankin left it at that. The bullshit pep talks always bugged him when he'd been a member of Special Forces.

Technically, he still was a member of Special Forces, and, in point of fact, several of the men on the mission with him outranked him. But joining the First Team had put him into his own special category, not only in terms of rank—there was no question Rankin was in charge of the extraction team—but also in terms of the government bureaucracy. Officially, he was assigned as a special aide to someone at the Pentagon whom he'd never met. Unofficially, he worked for Ferguson and the CIA. They took their orders, to the extent Ferguson took orders, from Corrine Alston and maybe—Rankin wasn't entirely clear because he didn't get involved in that end of things— from the head of the CIA.

The First Team gig was the sweetest assignment Rankin had ever had, a grab bag of action that never got dull. Working with Ferguson was the only downside. The CIA officer was extremely clever and could handle SpecOps as well as the fooling-people spy stuff, but Rankin didn't appreciate his wisecracks and know-it-all attitude. Without the CIA agent around, though, things were good.

"Beach is clear, sir," said the pilot.

"Let's get in," said Rankin.

The helicopter zoomed over the rock-strewn beach and turned toward a small knot of trees. Rankin leapt out as it touched down, racing through the copse to make sure no one had managed to hide themselves here. The two Special Forces soldiers who'd been in the back of the chopper fanned out, making absolutely sure the spies in the sky hadn't missed anything.

The small island was barely two and a half acres, so it didn't take that long to search.

"Landing area is clear. Chopper Two, come on in," Rankin said over the radio when the reecee turned up nothing beyond a few pieces of driftwood. Then he went to help the pilot get the camo net on Bird One, just in case the smugglers decided to bury their loot here.

24

Corrine Alston tried to look nonchalant as she was ushered into the back of the elementary school auditorium by one of the president's traveling staffers. Three or four hundred kids sat at the edge of their seats, quizzing President Jonathon McCarthy about the presidency.

"What's the best thing?" asked a gap-toothed third-grader in the fifth row.

"The best thing about being president is that no one can give me time-outs," said McCarthy.

The kids thought that was pretty good and began to clap.

"Plus, I get to have ice cream at any time of day I want, and no one can tell me no."

The applause deepened.

"And, if I want to stay up past my bedtime, I just go right ahead."

There were loud cheers of approval. McCarthy segued into a story about a frog he had brought to school in his pocket when he was in second grade; the amphibian had gotten loose.

"Not that you should follow my example," added McCarthy at regular intervals, relating the havoc the creature caused as it worked its way through gym class and into the principal's office, where it cornered the principal for fifteen minutes before he rescued her.

"Now there's an important moral to the story," said the president, wrapping up, "which many people do not realize. And that is this . . ."

He paused for effect. The kids and their teachers were practically breathless, waiting for some pearl of unexpected wisdom.

"Never bring a frog to school," mimed Corrine, edging toward the door as the auditorium erupted with laughter.

Fred Greenberg, the president's chief of staff, was standing just inside, a cell phone pressed to his ear. One of the Secret Service people opened the door, and Corrine slipped into what turned out to be a cafeteria.

"He's running late," said Jess Northrup, McCarthy's schedule keeper. "You're going to have to talk to him in the car."

"Here we go," said someone else, and Corrine heard the auditorium erupt in one last thunderous round of applause. The small group of aides began filing toward the rear; McCarthy was suddenly alongside her, joking with one of the local congressmen about how he had to be careful not to give students too accurate a picture of his childhood, lest he be accused of leading them "down the crooked path."

"Hello, Counselor, glad you could make it all the way up heah from Washington," said McCarthy, tapping her arm. "You know Mark Caren, don't you?"

"Congressman."

"Josh Franklin is outside, and Senator Tewilliger," said McCarthy. "Come ride with us to the hospital."

Tewilliger? Corrine wanted to ask what he was doing here; New Hampshire was a good distance from Indiana.

Unless, of course, you were planning on running for the presidency in three years . . . against McCarthy.

Corrine put on her courtroom face as she walked to the limo and SUVs. Secret Service agents flanked the procession, aides scurried to the vehicles, and the national press corps sauntered toward their bus, trying to pretend they didn't like looking important in front of their local brethren.

Corrine couldn't talk in front of the others, so she simply followed along as they walked to the limo. Franklin and Tewilliger seemed to have just finished sharing a private joke and were smirking like schoolboys as they got in. Congressman Caren gave the president a pitch for more funding in a highway appropriations bill, mentioning that the road they were to take was one of those that would be improved.

"And there are plenty of potholes in it," said Caren. "I have to warn you."

The president winked at Corrine as he got into the limo.

Though in theory there were six passenger seats in the back, three facing front and three facing rear, the president generally sat without anyone next to him. Corrine found herself sandwiched between Tewilliger and Congressman Caren, her arms folded.

"Senator, I was surprised to see you in New Hampshire," said Corrine.

"My Senate subcommittee is holding a hearing on the coast guard," said Tewilliger smoothly. "This afternoon as a matter of fact. I made my plans before I knew the president was coming."

"The Senator joined me at the state party dinner last night," said McCarthy, grinning. "It was quite a night."

"They put on a good party," said Caren, oblivious to the president's irony.

Tewilliger, of course, had arranged to be in New Hampshire specifically to attend the dinner, where many of the state's top politicos could be glad-handed at the same time. It was hardly an accident that he'd shown up when the president did, nor was it likely that he had made his plans before the president. Everyone in the car knew it, though general political etiquette kept them from contradicting him.

"Are we making progress on Korea?" asked Tewilliger as the sedan began moving toward the president's next appointment.

"I think we are," said McCarthy.

"The Undersecretary seems to think North Korea is holding out," said Tewilliger, turning to Franklin, "if I'm reading him correctly."

"I just think it's a possibility, not necessarily a fact," said Franklin.

"What do you mean?" asked Caren.

"I think it's very possible that they have nukes we don't know about."

As a general rule, First Team missions were kept secret from the cabinet, and neither Franklin nor his boss had been informed of this one. The president gave nothing away now, his manner still pleasantly accommodating. Talking to children always charged him up; he had dozens of schoolboy stories and loved to tell each one. Chatting with the kids, even from an auditorium stage, made him feel as if he were breaking out of the bubble that surrounded the presidency.

"If the international organizations do their jobs, we won't have to trust North Korea," Caren said.

"Assuming the North Koreans cooperate," said Tewilliger.

"A difficult thing to assume," said Franklin.

Corrine had not realized that Franklin was so skeptical. Defense Secretary Larry Stich was a proponent of the agreement, partly because he believed the North Korean regime was on its last legs and the agreement would not only freeze developments but also avoid the possibility of the weapons disappearing if a successor took over. But Franklin clearly had a different opinion; he began speaking about increases in the size of the North Korean army recently, mentioning improvements in the forces around the capital and the pending purchase of new Russian equipment. Details rolled off his tongue. There was a program to replace the type 63 light tank and another to update the North Korean version of the Russian type 85 armored personnel carrier, equipping it with better armor and fire-and-forget missiles.

"I'm sorry. I didn't mean to monopolize the conversation," said Franklin, suddenly cutting himself off midsentence. He turned to Corrine. "Ms. Alston, what do you think about the Koreans? Can we trust them?"

"I don't really have much of an opinion on trust," she said. "And in any event, my opinion would be the same as my client's."

McCarthy started to laugh.

"What brings you to New Hampshire, Ms. Alston?" asked Congressman Caren.

"I have a few things to go over with the president," she said, "and since he couldn't come to me, I came to him."

Caren nodded. He suppressed a smile, as if he were afraid his oval egg of a face would crack.

"I haven't been to your state in a long time," added Corrine. "It's beautiful in the fall."

"You should have seen the trees a few weeks ago. It is pretty, though. But chilly, very chilly."

He could have been describing the temperature in the limo for the ten minutes it took to reach the hospital where the president was scheduled to meet with staff and patients before meeting with a doctor who had won a humanitarian prize for helping wounded children in Iraq. McCarthy picked up the phone just as the limo arrived; the others, sensing not only that the president wanted to be alone but that they would have a chance at giving exclusive interviews to the media, got out quickly.

"Just a second, Corrine," said McCarthy. He asked the person on the other end to connect him to Senator Freely, then looked at her. "Assistant Secretary Franklin is here to accept an award from his alma mater this evening. I thought it would be useful to have him nearby; hold your enemies closely, as the philosopher once said."

"Josh Franklin is an enemy?"

"Only of late and only with respect to Korea," said McCarthy. "A slight difference of opinion. We can tolerate that. Sometimes I even disagree with you."

Senator Freely picked up on the other end. McCarthy asked him how he was, how his family was, how his grandchildren were, how his constituents were.

"Now by and by, Lawrence, are you coming back to Washington for the treaty vote? It will help us get a great many other things done, both in that region and else-where. . . . Well I do appreciate that, I do. Yes, I share your concerns. They are serious concerns. Nonetheless . . ."

Corrine watched the president listen to the senator. Like all the great politicians, McCarthy had a remarkable ability to make the person he was speaking to believe that he or she was the only person in the world he wanted to be with at that moment.

"Senator Tewilliger and I have been discussing your very point this morning," the president told Freely. "Your very point. We both have concerns, but we feel they can be dealt with. Yes, Senator Tewilliger, though I can't pretend to say I know which way he'll vote. . . . Yes, he is a very *accomplished* senator in that regard."

McCarthy bantered for a few more minutes, then hung up the phone.

"Still on the fence. They're probing for weakness," McCarthy told her. "Freely was in favor of the treaty six months ago."

Corrine nodded.

"I would like to see what treaty they could obtain, that would not cost us any blood or gold, but they don't see the big picture," added McCarthy. "Now, to what do I owe this unexpected pleasure?"

"We've found nuclear material in South Korea. The same isotopes that we were looking for up North. Plutonium weapons-grade material."

The president stared at her for a few seconds, genuinely surprised.

"Do they have a bomb?" he asked finally.

"I don't know, Jonathon. It's a possibility. We're trying to track it all down."

McCarthy folded his arms and stared straight ahead. "Not the best timing, dear."

Corrine couldn't argue with that.

"Has the IAEA inspection team found it?" added the president.

"No. It was at the waste site, near or in an area where low-level waste is ordinarily stored. They didn't take samples from that area, and we don't believe that what they did take will detect it. But of course we won't know that until they get back and run their tests in a week and a half," said Corrine.

"Right before the Senate vote."

"Yes, sir."

"What do you think North Korea would do if they found out that their brothers on the other side of the border had their own nuclear weapon?"

"The State Department would be in a better position to answer that."

"Oh, I don't think we need the State Department to know that the hound dog will bark when the fox slithers into the barnyard. Do you, counselor?"

Corrine shook her head.

McCarthy frowned, then reached for the door to the limo.

"What do you want me to do, Mr. President?"

"I want you to find out what's going on, dear. If South Korea has a weapon, I want you to find it. I want you to be very quiet about it, but I want you to proceed very quickly. Very, very quickly," said McCarthy, getting out of the car.

ACT 2

Walls of iron
Rise to the sky.
Demons surround her
On the road to the Dead.

—from "The Seventh Princess,"
traditional Korean song for the dead

P'YŎNGAN-PUKO (NORTH P'YŎNPAN) PROVINCE, NORTH KOREA

After taking them on a brief bus tour of the capital—the giant statue of the Great Leader was a special highlight—the North Koreans escorted the inspection team some ninety miles northward, installing them in a school dormitory about three miles from the waste plant.

The accommodations were not exactly deluxe; even the senior scientists found themselves sharing rooms barely big enough for the bunk beds that dominated them. Their hosts did not intend this as a slight; the quarters were the best available in the area. The military leaders who had met them—General Namgung, the commander of the armed forces in the capital area, and General Woo-suk, an official with the strategic weapons division—hosted a lavish dinner that lasted well past midnight, as toast after toast was offered to the visitors and their mission.

The next morning, the inspection team was presented with an elaborate breakfast featuring a variety of foods from around the world. Besides fried eggs and Korean-style pancakes filled with fruits, vegetables, and even meat, there were Western-style dishes, including bacon, potatoes Dauphine, and cheese Danishes. For a country where perpetual famine was a fact of life, the spread was obscenely impressive.

The provincial governor and some of his deputies sat at the head table with Dr. Norkelus. Thera, sitting across the room with her roommate, Lada Rahn, watched for a while as he tried to make conversation with the help of the translator. It clearly wasn't getting far, but it was better than she was doing with Lada, who spoke English fluently with noticeable haughtiness; the syllables practically had ice dripping off them.

Thera's adventure with the cigarettes in South Korea had given her a new status as the team's bad girl, eliciting the interest of not only Evora but also many of the other male inspectors. This was charming in a junior-high-school kind of way: About midway through breakfast Evora came over to check on her coffee, asking if she needed a refill. She had no sooner given him the cup than another man, this one arguably the world expert in uranium isotopes, sprung up and galloped across the room, pointed at her plate of half-eaten toast, and asked if she would care for a fresh piece. She turned him down as politely as she could; as he left the table he shot Evora a glance several times more radioactive than anything they were likely to find today.

The attention continued as the team loaded up for the trip out to the site. Thera turned down several offers of rides and got into her usual truck with Julie Svenson, about midway in the pack.

"You're awful popular today," said Julie.

"They're all looking for free smokes," said Thera, buckling her seat belt.

Thera's light mood held all the way up the twisting, rutted road to the waste plant. Then at the gate panic grabbed her by the throat. Foreboding welled inside her. She couldn't shake the thoughts of what would happen if she were captured, as if the idea of being tortured was fluid choking her lungs.

She knew, absolutely *knew,* she would fail.

Four or five men with submachine guns watched the bus and trucks pull to a halt in the center of the compound.

They were going to shoot her.

Thera forced herself to her feet. She started to slip as she came down the steps. A man extended his arm outside the bus. She reached forward and grabbed it, holding tight, supporting herself, afraid that were she to let go she would melt into the ground.

"OK?" said the man. His English surprised her.

"I guess."

"Nervous because you are in North Korea?"

"No. Just need a cigarette." She looked up at him and smiled.

He smiled back. In his late forties or early fifties, he was about her height though considerably heavier. His temples had turned silver, and he had a perfect smile, his teeth radiant in his mouth.

"Cigarettes are bad for your health," he told her.

"Everyone needs some bad habits."

He smiled and wagged his finger at her, as if he were a kind uncle.

His finger brushed away enough of her fear to let her walk again. The paranoia retreated to her chest, hiding in some secret chamber of her heart as she joined the others for the introductory tour.

The layout of the plant was almost meter for meter the same as that of the site in South Chungchong Province, South Korea. There were fewer video cameras and slightly more soldiers outside the gate, along with a pair of very old tanks near the fence, but the buildings themselves were in precisely the same locations. The vegetation was browner, but the buildings were just as bright.

The North Korean officials were more long winded

than their counterparts in the South, perhaps because they felt it necessary to insert the praises of the Great Leader into every other sentence. Thera found herself struggling to stay awake as the tour of the administration station proceeded in slow motion.

The man who had helped her from the bus stepped forward to speak. She'd thought he was simply one of the army of assistants, but he turned out to be a scientist responsible for "supervising precautions against pollution of the workers," as the translator put it, reading from a prepared vitae. "Ch'o Tak has studied in Russia and France and is one of the world's top experts in waste handling. A very important scientist for the People, who takes his duty most seriously."

Dr. Ch'o kept his eyes fixed on the floor as she spoke, the tips of his ears turning bright red. When she finished, he raised his hand in a half wave.

"I have been blessed with good fortune," he said, speaking in Korean and then immediately translating his words to English. "Korea's Great Leader has directed us to answer any questions you have and to lay ourselves bare. I humbly pledge myself to cooperate fully. You may ask whatever you wish, and I shall answer."

Norkelus glanced toward the rest of the group. When he realized no one was going to ask a question, he put up his hand, rose, and asked whether it had been difficult to install necessary safeguards. It was an extremely obvious attempt to be polite, but Ch'o took the question very seriously, saying that there had been great concern about expenses "and other considerations" among officials at different levels, but the directives of the Great Leader himself had prevailed and focused the actions of all. Money had been found and state-of-the-art precautions installed.

Norkelus thanked him. Ch'o, relieved, gave way to another official.

"What a ham," whispered Julie as they passed out of the hall.

"He seemed sincere," said Thera.

"Right. And Kim Jong-Il deserves the Nobel Peace Prize."

2

CIA HEADQUARTERS, LANGLEY, VIRGINIA

A long sleepless night followed by a morning and afternoon filled with meetings had only increased Daniel Slott's anxiety over the South Korean plutonium. He did his best to control it, but it was a losing battle. By midday he was wound so tight that when his daughter called him from college to say hello he nearly hung up on her.

Corrine Alston had called from New Hampshire to tell him what the president had said. It wasn't exactly a surprise. Slott resented Corrine, but he thought it was probably better that she had told the president what was going on rather than Parnelles. This way, he figured, Parnelles looked as bad as he did.

It was more cover-your-ass thinking, and he hated it. He absolutely hated it.

When his four p.m. budget meeting finally dragged to a close, Slott headed toward his office, intending to call his daughter and apologize for being so abrupt.

"Daniel, there you are," said Parnelles, intercepting him just before he got there. "Come and let's have a quick chat."

Slott followed silently as the CIA director led him down the hall to his office. Unlike many of the more recent DCIs, Parnelles was a CIA insider, a man who'd worked in the field as a case officer and held a host of other Bureau jobs before being appointed to head the CIA. There had been a gap of roughly ten years—he'd left the Agency and worked as, among other things, a bank vice president before being appointed—but otherwise he'd spent his entire adult life with the CIA, a throwback really to the handful of old hands who'd learned the business from the ground up.

"Where are we with Korea?" asked Parnelles when Slott sat down.

"Still trying to get more information."

"What's Seoul's opinion?"

"I haven't consulted them."

Parnelles raised his left eyebrow slightly.

"I wanted to make sure we knew what we were dealing with," explained Slott. "That it wasn't a false alarm."

"Is it?"

"The scientists say no. The first batch of tags were brought very close to a source, though it's impossible to say where. The second set, which Ferguson recovered, had only one exposure. We've narrowed down the possible location, but we need more work."

"And you don't think Seoul can help?"

"I guess I'm wondering why they didn't know about it in the first place," said Slott. "Just as you are."

"Do you think they purposely withheld information?"

"I've thought about that. I have thought about that."

He had, for hours and hours.

"But I don't," Slott added. "I just can't see Ken Bo doing that. I can see . . ."

The word *incompetence* seemed too harsh, so he said nothing.

"We may to have involve them," said Parnelles, "if we're going to find out anything. This has to have been a far-reaching operation, and I don't know that we'll gain anything from delaying at this point."

"If the information comes out, it will jeopardize the

disarmament treaty," said Slott. "And if Seoul gets aggressive about pursuing it, sooner or later the ROK government will realize what we're doing. Once that happens, I doubt we can keep the information under wraps."

"That's not really an intelligence concern, is it?"

"I guess it's not," said Slott, "but I wouldn't want to do anything that would jeopardize the disarmament treaty."

"How would you?"

By having the information leak out, thought Slott. It was obvious. Any bad publicity now—and certainly a reaction by North Korea—would send the Senate running for cover.

"I'm having a little trouble reading you," said Slott. "I know you're against the treaty, but—"

"That has nothing to do with it," said Parnelles. "I'm not interested in politics. I'm interested in information. And our security."

"If Seoul pokes its nose around, and something comes out, it would have a very negative effect."

"Why should something come out?"

Slott couldn't decide whether Parnelles was being disingenuous.

"You don't trust your people in Korea?" Parnelles asked.

"I do trust them."

"Then tell them to be discreet, but let's find out what's going on."

"We're going to have to find out why they missed this," said Slott.

"Yes, but that's of secondary importance right now," said Parnelles. "Find out what it is they missed, first."

"I guess you're right," said Slott, guessing Parnelles had probably already decided to clean house there. "I'll get on it."

3

NORTH OF DAEJEON, SOUTH KOREA

Park Jin Tae ran his fingers over the fabric of the twelfth-century armor, admiring the fine craftsmanship of his ancestors. Park had made several billion dollars in his sixty-seven years; he had built more than a dozen companies from scratch and taken over so many others he'd lost track. He was among the most important businessmen in South Korea and, though he operated entirely behind the scenes, an important player in its politics as well. But nothing brought the South Korean businessman more pleasure than his collection of antiquities, and this suit of armor was the pinnacle.

The brigandine or fabric-covered armor had belonged to a high-ranking Korean official. The man's wealth was evident from the rich cloth of the exterior. The metal plates beneath the armor were roughly nine and a half centimeters thick, strong enough to withstand a great blow. Yet the suit was constructed to allow the warrior great freedom of movement, for a Korean warrior was expected to use his feet as well as his hands as weapons if need be.

He would use his very breath, Park thought. The men of ancient times were different, hardier and tougher. Just to wear the suit into battle took great strength.

What would such men say if they looked at Koreans now? They would scoff at their weakness.

Not every Korean was weak—Park knew many brave men, hundreds who would gladly sacrifice themselves for Korea—but the country as a whole had been seduced by Western materialsm. It had forgotten its birthright and its past, both ancient and recent.

How else could one explain the fact that the South Korean president had spent yesterday showing the Japanese emperor Korean factories? The *Japanese emperor,* son and grandson of a criminal, son and grandson of Korea's most hated and brutal master.

The South Korean government had suggested that some of Park's companies be included in the tour. He had declined, even though this was a breach of etiquette. Ordinarily, one had to be polite when dealing with visitors, but politeness would only go so far. It would not extend to Japanese criminals.

The enmity between Japan and Korea went back thousands of years, but Park's familial hatred of the Japanese took its severe shape in 1941. It was the year Park Jin Tae was born. It was also the year his mother was made a "comfort woman," a slave to the Japanese soldiers, an unwilling prostitute.

She had triumphed in the end, ending her life and that of one of her tormentors in a glorious fury of blood and revenge. But it was a bitter victory for her family, who were persecuted as a result. Her husband and brother were killed and their children sent to an orphanage where they were given Japanese names and taught to hate their country.

Park considered himself lucky. The war ended well before he attended school, and his personal memory of the outrages was, mercifully, dim. But his anger at the humiliation of his mother, the murder of his family, and the rape of his country burned ever stronger with each year he aged.

It burned so fiercely that if he spent too much time thinking about it, he would surely explode.

Park shook himself. There was considerable work to do. Thousands of employees worked for him—he was a man of great wealth and status, a respected man—and he could not afford to indulge himself in distractions. He left the display room and went to start the day.

DAEJEON, SOUTH KOREA

It took Ferguson and Guns several hours to walk back to
Guns's hotel from Science Industries. Ferguson sat down
on the couch; the next thing he knew it was several hours
later and Guns was shaking him awake.

"Corrigan needs to talk to you," Guns told him. "Sorry
to wake you up, Ferg."

"What time is it?"

"Oh eight hundred hours."

"In real time that's what, eight in the morning?"

"Something like that. It's six o'clock at night back
home. Eighteen hundred."

"What, you got two clocks to keep track?"

"Only my head."

Ferguson rolled out of bed, splashed some water on
his face, and went down to the hotel café to get some
coffee. All he could find was tea. He took two cups back
to the room, did a quick scan for bugs to make sure no
one had managed to sneak in while they were sleeping,
and called The Cube.

"Ferg, how are you?" asked Corrigan.

"Can't party like I used to," he told him. "You get that
information I told Lauren about? Science Industries?"

"Yeah. There's an encrypted PDF file waiting for you
to download. You can read it at the embassy."

"Why the embassy?"

"Slott will explain. Hold on."

"Great."

Slott came on the line after a short pause.

"Good morning, Ferg."

"What's this about the embassy?" said Ferguson.

"We want soil samples from the waste plant, and as much other information as we can come up with. Seoul's got to be involved."

"I can get the samples without them."

"There's no need to cut Seoul out," said Slott. "I want you to brief Ken Bo. He's the station chief."

"Me?"

"You have someone else in mind?"

Ferguson scratched the side of his head. Tea was fine as far as it went, but it wasn't a substitute for coffee.

"It'll take me a while to get up there."

"Listen, Ferg, this situation is volatile, seriously volatile."

"Yeah, I know the drill."

"Ferguson, for once, will you listen to what I say?" snapped Slott.

"I always listen to you, Dan," said Ferguson, who found Slott's uncharacteristic anger amusing. "The question is whether I pay any attention to it."

"If you need backup, ask for it, all right?"

"My middle name is Please," said Ferguson. He took a swig of the tea and practically spit it out. "Listen, I gotta go. I think somebody's trying to poison me."

5

The North Koreans set up a midday feast for the inspection team in the reception building, once again importing massive amounts of Korean and Western specialties. Large banquet tables were placed in the center of the building with chairs clustered nearby. The team members and the Koreans escorting them ate with their plates in their laps.

The lunch might have had the air of a picnic or perhaps a wedding, except that it was hard for the guests to ignore the fact that the space they were sitting in had been designed for vehicles carrying nuclear waste. Julie Svenson shook her head the whole time she was eating, gulping her food and then going to the far side of the building.

When Neto Evora saw that Thera was alone, he came over and sat down beside her, asking how she was enjoying North Korea.

"It looks like the perfect place for a nuclear waste dump, doesn't it?" said the scientist. "Deserted, cold, and desolate."

"Actually, the countryside is very beautiful," she said. "It looks almost like heaven."

"Heaven? I don't think so."

"I don't mean the government. Just the open fields."

"If you are like me, a city boy, then you want excitement."

"I guess I'm not like you," said Thera.

Evora smirked. "Maybe we'll chance a party this evening."

"Here?"

"You never know."

He got up. Thera watched him strut across the room,

very full of himself. There was a thin line between confidence and conceit. Evora was far over the line.

Why hadn't she realized that the other night?

Temporary insanity. And drinks.

She hadn't actually gone to bed with him, so she deserved *some* credit.

Some people could push the line between conceit and confidence. Ferguson, for example. Fergie could push it very far. He exuded confidence but not really conceit—not in her opinion at least—maybe because he could back it up.

Not that he was perfect. He could be casually cruel and impish, like the way he loved baiting Rankin, even though he trusted him with his life.

He was nice to her. But maybe that meant he didn't take her seriously.

Still hungry, Thera got up and went over to the food table.

"You should try the *bulgogi*," said Dr. Ch'o, the scientist who had helped her out of the SUV earlier. "It is beef, marinated and grilled."

"Thank you," said Thera, holding her plate out for him to dish the food.

"My pleasure," said the scientist, bowing his head slightly.

"You speak very good English," said Thera. "Better than mine."

"Oh, you are very good. What language do you speak as a native?"

"Greek." Thera rolled off a few sentences about how she lived near Athens, then returned to English. "But everyone speaks English these days."

"You have an American accent."

"Yes, I have worked there. For the UN. A very interesting place."

"Yes. I have never been myself. But I have been to Russia and Europe."

"Really?"

"Oh, yes. Some years ago. When I received my degree."

Another member of the inspection team asked Ch'o where he had been in Europe. Thera drifted away, then returned to her seat and finished eating. The beef was tasty, but a bit too spicy for her.

When she was done, she went outside to have a look around. Unwrapping her pack of cigarettes, she pounded the box end, then took one and put it into her mouth. She had just lit up when she saw Ch'o and another North Korean walking swiftly toward her, concerned looks on their faces.

Oh, crap, they don't allow smoking here either, Thera thought to herself. I'm going to be arrested.

SEOUL, SOUTH KOREA

Ken Bo glared at Ferguson as he walked into his office, both hands on his desktop as if he were bracing himself against a gale. Ferguson pointed at him, smirked and sat down.

"How are ya?" said Ferguson. Bo had kept him waiting more than fifteen minutes in his outer office. Ferguson wouldn't have minded so much if his assistant had had decent legs.

"Why did you pull a gun on one of my people the other day?" said Bo.

"I thought it was a cigarette lighter. He looked like he wanted a smoke."

"I've heard about you, Ferguson."

"Oh, good. You know why I'm here?"

"Slott told me."

"Can we talk here?"

Ferguson glanced around. Generally offices in embassies were not used for very sensitive conversations, even though there was only a remote chance that they would be bugged or overheard.

Bo looked down at his desk, glancing around it as if looking for the answer. Suddenly he jumped into motion, leading the way out of the room.

Halfway down the hall he stuck his head into a door and called in to his deputy chief.

"Chris, I want you to hear this."

"No," said Ferguson. "Only you."

"That's ridiculous."

"Take it up with the boss."

"Hey, no problem," said the deputy chief, backing away.

Bo shook his head and started walking again. Ferguson followed as the station chief went up two flights of stairs to a secure room within a room that had been built for sensitive discussions. There were no chairs or other furniture in the room—most likely to keep conversations short, Ferguson decided.

"What do you know?" asked Bo.

"Plutonium was detected at the Blessed Peak Nuclear Waste Processing Plant. An isotope that indicates there's bomb fuel present. It looks like the South Koreans are building a nuke."

"Impossible!"

"I wouldn't say impossible."

"Your data is wrong."

Ferguson laughed. "You don't even know what data I have."

"It's impossible. I'm sure it's wrong. Or can be explained."

"Yeah, probably you're right." Ferguson, realizing he was done, turned around.

"Where are you going?" Bo grabbed his arm.

"I have work to do."

Bo glared at him. Ferguson glared back.

It didn't take ESP to know what the station chief was thinking. A bomb project like this would have taken years to get to this point, and Bo had missed it. Good-bye job.

Ferguson hadn't really been sold on the idea of working with the locals to begin with, but even if he had, Bo's attitude warned him away. The station chief was looking at this as a threat to his job. He was going to be interested in covering his butt, not in finding out what was going on.

Not that he was surprised. Disappointed, maybe.

No, not even that. It was to be expected.

"Wait," said Bo as Ferguson once more started for the door. "We can work together."

"Don't think so."

"That's all the information you have?"

Ferguson stopped and turned back around. "I don't have much more, no. If you want the technical stuff, you'll have to get it from Slott. I really don't know it," Ferguson said. "Listen, I need to use the secure communications center. If you don't mind."

"Bob— Can I call you Bob?"

"I *really* don't know anything else. Honest."

They stared at each other. Ferguson was so much taller than Bo that he thought he might get a crick in his neck if Bo didn't blink soon.

"Well, keep us updated," said Bo finally, looking away.

Ferguson didn't feel like lying, so he simply shrugged as he left the room.

7

Thera braced herself as the North Koreans approached. There was no sense hiding the cigarette; both men had clearly seen her.

"You must be away from the building," said Ch'o. "I'm sorry, Miss."

"It's a nonsmoking area?"

Ch'o gave her a strange look. "No. The train car. We are demonstrating the train car. You are on the track."

He pointed behind her. Thera turned and saw that one of the remote-controller train cars was heading slowly in her direction from the temporary waste-storage area.

The other Korean began speaking in a very excited voice, telling her that she would be run over if she did not get away from the embedded tracks.

"The trains have sensors," said Ch'o, "but they do not always work. There have been close-call accidents. We do not trust them."

"I'm sorry," said Thera, stepping out of the way.

Ch'o and the other man stood by her side as the train car went slowly by. The rest of the inspection team had gathered inside the building and was watching the train as it made its way slowly toward the reception building's door.

"I didn't know there were accidents," said Thera when the train passed. "The South Koreans have the same system. They didn't mention accidents."

Ch'o translated what she said for his colleague. Thera picked up some of the reply but not all of it.

"Very possibly our cousins have not been one hundred

percent candid," said Ch'o. "Assuming that we have the same system."

"You do."

Ch'o glanced at her cigarette.

"You smoke?"

"Bad habit, I know," said Thera, dropping the butt on the ground. "Thank you for warning me."

She touched the scientist's arm. He turned light red.

"Very welcome, very welcome," he said, leading the other man away.

The rest of the afternoon passed slowly, the tour a slow-motion replay of the one they'd had in South Korea. Finally, the site director led them to the administration building for refreshments: seltzer water and kimchi-style hors d'oeuvres. Thera took a few sips of the seltzer, then went outside, ostensibly to grab a smoke but really to get another glimpse of the area and make sure she could plant the tags tomorrow.

It looked like it would be easy. There were no cameras covering the interior of the compound, and the guards stayed close to the buildings. Thera took a short walk, testing to see if she was being watched.

No.

Could she get the tags in exactly the same places she had in South Korea?

Probably. But was that important now? The baseline they'd been looking for was from a plant with no plutonium.

Thera swung around to head back toward the administration building. The door opened, and a number of team members came out, followed by three or four North Koreans, one of whom was Ch'o.

"Miss," said Ch'o. "Oh, Miss?"

"Me?"

"You must try these," said the scientist in English,

bowing his head slightly and holding a small package out toward her. It was wrapped in brown paper.

Thera took it. Two other Korean officials nodded behind Ch'o, motioning for her to open the package.

She pulled the rough string and opened the paper. There was a pack of cigarettes inside. It was only about half full; obviously Ch'o had improvised the present.

The package had Marlboro's color scheme, but the words were in Korean.

"Our own," said Ch'o. "Try."

"You like, yes," added one of the other men. "North Korean cigarettes number one."

Thera felt herself flushing. "I—"

"You mentioned to the guard at the door that you needed a cigarette," said Ch'o.

"Oh," said Thera. "It was just an expression."

By now other members of the team, including Dr. Norkelus, had come over to see what the fuss was about. More North Koreans joined them, and Thera found herself at the center of a small crowd. She held up the package; Norkelus rolled his eyes. Julie Svenson shook her head. Evora and some of the others laughed.

"I guess I should try one," said Thera.

She took two of the cigarettes from the pack, then held the cigarettes out to the Koreans. They all shook their heads furiously. Finally, Dr. Ch'o, his lips gritted together firmly, stepped up and took one.

"I will try just a puff with you, out of hospitality. We cannot let a guest be alone."

He turned and repeated what he had said in Korean, in effect scolding them for their bad manners. The others grinned sheepishly.

Thera took a drag and immediately began coughing. Horror flooded onto the faces of the Koreans nearby.

Then Ch'o laughed, and the others laughed, and Thera laughed as well.

"It's good but very strong," she said.

The translator, squeezing through the knot around her, explained in Korean. Everyone laughed again, nodding and saying in Korean that their cigarettes were good but took some getting used to.

"I'm afraid we should all get back to work," said Norkelus finally. "We should continue."

"Yes, we must continue and be perfect hosts," said Ch'o. He walked off very proud of himself, Thera thought.

She took a short draw on the cigarette as the others left. It tasted just as terrible as before, though this time she managed to keep herself from coughing.

Thera put her finger into the top of the package to pull the flap closed. When she did, she noticed there was writing on the margin of the paper. At first glance, it looked like a trademark notice, but of course that couldn't be right.

The letters were so small she had to hold the package right in front of her face.

She nearly dropped it as she read the words: *Help me.*

OFF THE COAST OF NORTH KOREA

Rankin took the binoculars from the lookout and panned them across the sea to the south. The small fishing vessel was just under a mile away. It had been sailing toward them for more than an hour, moving so slowly that it was hard to tell if it was being propelled by anything other than the current.

"I say we grab them if they get any closer," said Michael Barren. Barren was the assault team's first sergeant, the ranking noncommissioned officer on the atoll.

Grabbing the people in the boat was the safe thing to do, unless, of course, they botched it, or the people in the boat were expected somewhere else or managed to get a radio message off.

"No," said Rankin. "We wait. They'll pass by."

"What if they don't?" asked Barren.

The others moved a little closer, interested not only in finding out what they were going to do but also in seeing who was going to get his way.

"If they don't, we deal with that then," said Rankin, handing the binoculars back.

The boat kept coming. Fifteen minutes later, it was a hundred yards offshore. Rankin, Barren, and two other soldiers crouched behind a fallen tree trunk on the island's high point overlooking the beach. The helicopters were about a hundred yards behind them, down the hill. The rest of the assault team was spread out in hidden positions around the atoll.

"We gonna let them come ashore before we kill them?" asked Barren.

"We ain't gonna kill them," said Rankin.

"What?"

"We're going to stay down, hidden, unless it's absolutely necessary to grab them. Then we grab them. We don't kill them."

Barren thought this was the most ridiculous thing he'd ever heard.

"Can we talk, Sarge?" asked Barren.

"We are talking."

Barren glanced at the two other soldiers nearby. "We might want to make this private."

"Nothing I say is private."

"All right," said Barren. "Why won't we shoot them?"

"Because we don't have to."

"Jesus, Sarge. They're North Koreans. The enemy."

"Look, you can call me Stephen or Skip if you want," Rankin told him. "Not Sergeant."

"You're not a sergeant?"

Rankin ignored the challenging, almost mocking tone. "This is my call," he told Barren. "We leave these people be if we can. They come on the island, they see anything, we grab them. We don't kill them."

Frustrated, Barren turned away.

"Looks like they're landing," said the lookout.

Rankin moved to the end of the tree trunk, watching through his glasses as two men jumped from the front of the small vessel and pulled it onto the beach. A third man stayed with the boat.

If he gave the order to fire, they'd be dead inside of thirty seconds.

If he delayed, it was possible they might alert someone via radio.

But the best thing, the right thing, was to wait. It was much better for the mission that these people leave without seeing them. Kill them, and maybe someone would come looking for them.

Rankin knew in his gut he was doing the right thing, balancing the different chances in the mission's favor. But it wasn't like he could put it into a mathematical formula. The others would just have to trust him.

The Koreans took a large barrel from the boat. Rankin was baffled, until he realized they were making dinner.

He rolled back behind the log and told the others what was going on. Smoke was already starting to curl from the fire.

"What do we do?" Barren demanded.

"We hang loose and let them eat. If they get frisky and go exploring, then we grab them. Otherwise we wait and hide. It's already getting dark. It won't be hard."

Barren shook his head, but said nothing.

"Relax," said Rankin. "Food smells kind of rancid anyway."

Only later, when the North Koreans had pulled out without seeing anyone, did Rankin realize that what he'd said was exactly the sort of line Ferguson would use to put him off.

"Ferg's still a jerk," he mumbled to himself, going to get some meals-ready-to-eat for dinner.

SOUTH CHUNGCHONG PROVINCE, SOUTH KOREA

With the fader still in place on the security camera at Blessed Peak, Ferguson and Guns didn't have to make another night jump—which was fine with Guns, since he hated parachuting during the day, let alone at night. They hiked into the nature preserve around four in the afternoon, getting their bearings before the sun set. They hid and waited until dark, when they hiked up the trail near the mountain that backed into the waste site, then headed in the direction of the fence. Between the sliver of moon and the clear night sky, there was enough light to see without using their night-vision gear, though every so often Ferguson stopped and put his on while he scouted to make sure no one was lurking nearby.

It took roughly two hours for them to reach the clearing in front of the fence. Ferguson led Guns through the pine trees to a rock outcropping that stood almost directly across from the video camera.

"You got clips?" Ferguson asked.

Guns nodded. The clips were large clothespins that were used to hold down the barbed wire at the top of the fence. He also had a Teflon "towel" tied around his shoulder to throw on top of the wire and keep it from snagging them as they went over. Because of the camera angle, they could leave the gear in place until they came back.

Ferguson took the remote from his backpack and sent the signal to the camera to move to the right. It didn't budge.

Ferguson cursed and tried again. Still nothing.

"What's going on?" Guns asked.

"Not sure. Let's see if the fader's working."

The screen turned white, then grayed. Ferguson let it come back to full.

"I don't know why the camera's not moving," he told Guns, "but the fader is."

"You sure?"

"Only one way to find out."

"All right."

"If I yell retreat, retreat. OK?"

"Sure."

"Hey, I thought marines never retreated," said Ferguson, hitting the fader button and jumping to his feet.

Laughing, Guns scrambled to the fence, leaping about halfway up and climbing hand over hand to the top in about two seconds flat. He clamped down the wires, untied his towel, and twirled himself over and down to the ground.

Ferguson, several steps ahead, ran straight to the camera. Dropping down behind it, he saw the problem: One of his clips had fallen off the wire. He fixed it, made sure it worked, then went with Guns in the direction of the plant.

They had more than a mile and a half to go when Ferguson noticed a glow he hadn't seen the other night.

"What's up?" asked Guns.

"Looks like there's a used-car lot down there, doesn't it?"

Guns peered through the trees.

"What do you mean?"

"Place wasn't lit up like this the other night. There are spotlights down there."

"They going to see us coming?"

"I don't know."

Ferguson started walking again. About a half mile from the low-level waste area, he emerged from the ravine he and Rankin had used the other night, circling above and around the cavelike entrance. The rise in terrain gave them a better view of the area, though the brush and rocks were fairly low and they had to stay close to the ground to avoid casting shadows.

A dozen security guards stood near the reception building, warming themselves around large burn barrels. Another four or five stood around a barrel near the tracks, about a hundred yards from the low-level waste site but within full view of it. The train cars had been moved.

"This is new," Ferguson told Guns.

"You think they saw something with the video camera?"

"No. They'd've sent somebody up to fix it. Or shoot us."

"I mean when we went over."

Ferguson studied the compound. It was *possible* that there had been an alert, but surely the response would have been more emphatic. This looked more generic, like something you might do if you heard bank robbers were over at the saloon having a drink.

Or if word had leaked out of the Seoul office that something was up.

A pickup truck swung around the compound. It was the same truck that had been used for patrols the other night, only this time there were men in the back. The pickup stopped in front of the low-level waste area, and the men got out, took a look around, then hopped back in.

Ferguson and Guns lay on the cold ground for another hour and a half, timing the patrols. There were seven during that time, almost nonstop. The men varied their patrol route as well.

"Something tipped them off," Ferguson told Guns. "There's no way we're getting where we want to go without being seen."

"What do we do?"

"Follow me."

"We leaving?"

"Not yet."

Ferguson retreated about a hundred yards up the hill, then began circling toward the far side of the entrance to the underground waste depository. He had to move slowly, trying not to kick too much dirt or rocks downhill. And every time the pickup truck came in their direction, he and Guns had to flatten themselves to make absolutely sure they weren't seen.

Nearly two hours passed before they had reached the other side. Ferguson stripped off his pack and took out his small shovel and baggies.

"Chill for me here, Guns."

"Hey, don't get lost, man."

"You're getting a sense of humor. That's dangerous in a marine."

Ferguson got down on all fours and crawled out in the dirt toward the entrance to the low-level waste area. After roughly fifty yards, he reached the edge of a macadam parking area that sat off the loop road used by the pickup patrol. He was just about to get up and run across it when the security patrol swung in his direction.

Ferguson flattened his body in the dirt, nudging his face against the pebbles. His nose and mouth filled with the fine, claylike dust as he waited for the truck to pass.

Guns, standing in the shadows, watched helplessly as the truck veered in Ferguson's direction. He had a smoke grenade in his hand, but what good was that? He reached for his pistol, even though Ferguson had told him they weren't supposed to shoot anyone.

Ferguson heard the engine, then the staccato rhythm of the Koreans' voices. The wheels crunched the gravel, spraying it to the sides. The truck jerked to the left, then sped up. They'd just missed seeing him.

Ferguson waited a full minute, then scrambled across the lot and the road, throwing himself down in the dirt. Two shovelfuls later, he had the bag filled.

"I thought they were going to spot you," said Guns when he got back. "They were like, ten feet away."

"Eleven at least," Ferg told him. "Let's get the hell out of Dodge."

10

NORTH P'YÖNPAN PROVINCE, NORTH KOREA

Thera lay on her cot, staring at the bottom of the empty bunk above her. Lada Rahn snored a few feet away. The sound rattled all of the metal in the room, like a kind of counterpoint to the hum of the fluorescent light fixtures from the hall.

Thera had destroyed the message in the cigarette box, but the words had been seared into her brain.

Dr. Tak Ch'o wanted to defect.

Why had he picked her? Was it a trap? A trick?

Thera wasn't sure what to do. The scientist might be a big prize, but was he worth jeopardizing her mission for?

And even if he was, how would she go about arranging for his defection?

If there were answers, they weren't in the dark gray light around her. But Thera continued to stare, unable to sleep.

11

Ferguson picked his way slowly across the rocks, crossing the hill behind the entrance to the underground low-level waste area. The whole night had been pretty much a waste—the soil samples were the lowest priority on the wish list the specialists had given him—but he had to contain his bile until they were out.

Ferguson stopped as he came to a deep crevice. He didn't remember the fissure, which was about three feet wide and extended at least twenty. Unsure where he had gone off course, he stopped and took off his night-vision glasses to get his bearings.

"What's wrong, Ferg?" asked Guns, tagging along behind him.

"You remember this hole here?"

"No."

Ferguson reached into his pocket and took out his satellite photos. They'd gone farther up the hill on the way back than they had on the way in. It wasn't a big difference, but if they kept going they'd end up at a cliff.

"We need to angle down this way," he told Guns, pointing.

Within a few yards, the soil became extremely loose. Afraid that they were going to send enough down to alert the patrols, they backtracked again and looked for sturdier ground. They went over a steep stretch, finding handholds in the thin vegetation, finally arriving at a ledge about thirty feet from the ground.

Once again, Ferguson consulted the photos. They

hadn't made enough of a correction and were a good five hundred yards farther east of the spot where he thought they would come out. But that wasn't necessarily bad. The ledge was out of sight from the compound, and though the ledge was narrow—maybe eight inches—following it would save them considerable time. Ferguson eased out slowly, keeping himself flat against the wall. After what seemed like forever, he reached a large boulder. He hugged it, spun his legs around, and landed on the side of the hill.

"Downhill from here," he whispered to Guns, who was just starting across.

The marine grunted. He kept fighting the temptation to look down, narrowing his view to the rocks in front of his face. As far as he was concerned, the problem wasn't that the path was narrow; the problem was that there were no handholds. He had to keep his weight pitched in toward the wall, which was difficult not only because he was carrying a backpack but because the ledge was angled the other way. He found himself sliding across on his tiptoes the way he imagined a ballet dancer would move.

Guns's foot hit against the side of a rock he hadn't seen. Surprised, he jerked his weight forward, then twisted to see what he'd hit. The shift in momentum threw him off balance, and the next thing he knew he was falling straight down.

Ferguson, barely two yards away, dove forward to grab his companion.

He caught the top of his shirt. Instead of stopping Guns, Ferguson was yanked downward with him, somersaulting around before losing his grip. He slid a good twenty feet before managing to snare himself on a rock.

Guns stopped about eight feet below him. He'd smacked the side of his head on a stone and gotten a mouthful of dirt. Much worse, he'd banged and twisted his knee as he fell.

The pain held off for a second. Guns felt as if he'd

been plunged into a cold lake, totally numb. Then a hatchet seemed to chop the side of his kneecap. The pain reverberated up and down his leg, and he felt incredibly hot, sweat pouring from his forehead.

"Ferg."

"Hey, Guns, I'm here," said Ferguson. Gingerly, he made his way down to the marine, retrieving his night glasses as he went.

"Hurt my leg. I can't tell if it's my knee or what," said Guns. "The right one."

"No compound fracture," said Ferguson, gently running his fingers above and below it.

Guns sucked air and bit his lip to keep from screaming. "This hurts like a mo-fo."

"If we slide down a little way, we can get to the base of the ravine we used to come in. See it?"

"Can't. Can't see anything, Ferg."

Guns's glasses were attached to his face, held there by elastic at the back of his head; Ferguson wasn't sure whether they malfunctioned or if Guns was losing consciousness. He pushed the glasses down so they fell around Guns's neck, then wrapped his arm around his.

"All right, let's go down together," Ferg told him. "I know it's gonna hurt, but we gotta get out."

"It's all right."

Ferguson tucked his leg under Guns's to cushion it. "On our butts. Ready?"

"Go."

Guns ground his teeth together to keep from crying out. Ferguson kept his arm around his, but Guns's leg jerked to the side and smacked against some of the rocks as they went down.

"All right, let's get the hell out of here," said Ferguson, standing a little awkwardly. He checked their gear, making sure they hadn't lost anything.

"Leave me, Ferg," croaked Guns.

"Yeah, right. Like that might work." Ferguson laughed, barely able to keep his voice down. "Hang on, Gimpy."

He dipped down, maneuvering his shoulders to get leverage, then lifted Guns up and onto his back.

"You're going to have to go on a diet if you plan on doing this again," he grunted, starting back in the direction of the fence.

Guns insisted he could pull himself over the fence. Though doubtful, Ferguson preferred climbing to cutting a hole, and agreed they would try it. To his surprise, Guns was able to pull himself up hand over hand, all the way to the top.

"Nothin' compared to boot camp," grunted Guns.

Guns had trouble getting over the Teflon blanket covering the razor wire, scraping his good leg on the sharp knife point next to it. He straddled the fence top, hyperventilating.

"All right, that was the hard part," Ferguson told him.

"Yeah. Downhill from here."

With Ferguson's help, Guns managed to get reasonably close to the ground before letting go, hoping to land on his good foot. But he collapsed immediately, falling backward in a swell of pain.

"Wow," he said, looking up at the dark sky. "Imagine what being shot feels like."

"Piece of cake compared to this," said Ferguson, standing over him.

He meant it as a joke, but Guns took it seriously. "Gotta be ten times worse."

Ferguson got the blanket and the clips, then pulled Guns onto his back and began hiking toward the exit. It was slowgoing; by the time they made it outside and to the car a half mile away, dawn had broken.

"I'm sorry, Ferg," muttered Guns as they drove back to Daejeon. "I'm really sorry."

"Don't worry about it. Just rest for a while. We'll get you cleaned up, then take you to a doctor and get that knee fixed."

"I'm really sorry, man. I'm really, really sorry. I screwed up."

"You didn't screw up. Somebody must have tipped them off. And I have a pretty good idea who it was."

12

Thera took out the pack of cigarettes, pulled two out, then pointed one in the direction of the North Korean soldier. The man—he looked more like a teenager, with dark peach fuzz above his lip—blinked his eyes, then looked left and right before taking it. Thera smiled and gave him her matches; he lit up furtively, turning from the wind.

In the six or seven seconds it took him to get the cigarette lit, Thera slipped the last tab into the slot between the metal panels of the reception building.

She was done. It had been easier to plant the devices here than in South Korea.

Her relief lasted about as long as it took her to light her own cigarette; she saw Tak Ch'o approaching from across the complex. The scientist had a big smile on his face, nodding and laughing as he caught her glance.

The young soldier stiffened and started to move away. Ch'o told him something Thera couldn't understand. Though it was meant to put the young man at ease, the guard barely relaxed.

"You like our cigarettes then?" Ch'o told her in English. He immediately translated into Korean for the soldier.

"Oh, yes," said Thera. "Very good."

"And interesting?"

"Very interesting." Thera stared into his eyes. If there had been any doubt that Ch'o had given her the message, his gaze erased it.

"So, you are Greek?" he asked in English.

"Yes."

"From where?"

Thera described the town, adding that it was near Athens. Ch'o nodded, then turned to the soldier and told him what she had said. He clamped the young man on the shoulder and turned to her.

"My young friend comes from Hamhun, in the east," Ch'o told her. "His father is an important and brilliant general."

Before Thera could respond, the scientist continued, "It's good to see two young people getting along. Scientists are not blind to matters of the heart."

The soldier looked on quizzically, clearly not understanding what was going on.

"I— I'm probably too old for him," said Thera.

"Old? You are so beautiful I couldn't guess how old you are," said Ch'o.

He turned to the soldier and told him enough of what he had said that the young man turned beet red. This made the scientist laugh.

"Well, then, I will see you both at lunch," said Ch'o. He started away, then turned back quickly, pulling a cigarette pack from his jacket pocket. "I almost forgot . . . another present for you. I see you are low."

Thera took the package.

"Save some for your trip. You will want to share with friends, no doubt," said Ch'o. He laughed again, turned toward the soldier, then with a sideways glance as if he suspected someone were watching, took another pack from his pants pocket and pressed it into the young man's hand.

"*Haeng-uneul bireoyo,*" he told the soldier, glancing at Thera. "Good luck."

13

Guns had torn several ligaments in his knee, damaged his kneecap, and broken the top of his tibia. The knee was splinted so it couldn't be moved until some of the swelling went down and he arranged to see a specialist. He had a large cast and a pair of crutches that were awkward to use.

Ferguson decided—over Guns's protests that he was starting to feel much better—that Guns should go home immediately, taking the dirt back with him for analysis. Corrigan arranged a military flight and even got an army driver to pick him up at the clinic where he was examined.

"I don't want to leave, Ferg," said Guns. "You need backup."

"I got plenty of backup," Ferguson told him as they waited for the car.

"I feel like a quitter."

"What are you going to do, chop off your leg and march on?"

"If that's what it takes."

Ferguson laughed, but Guns was serious.

"Give it a rest, Guns," Ferguson told him. "That dirt has to go back anyway."

Guns shook his head, but there was nothing he could do. Ten minutes later, he grimaced as he pulled himself into the van that had come for him.

"Don't forget to take those painkillers," Ferguson told him as he closed the door.

"I will."

"Two every six hours."

"I only need one."

———

Two hours after packing Guns off, Ferguson walked into Ken Bo's office in Seoul.

"Why'd you tip off the waste site?" said Ferguson, pulling over a chair.

"Tip them off to what?"

"They were waiting last night when I went back. I couldn't do what I had to do."

"You went there?"

"Yeah, I went there."

"We—" Bo stopped midsentence, trying to collect his thoughts. He'd been ambushed and was talking from the hip, not a smart thing to do.

"You *what?*" demanded Ferguson.

"I thought you were going to work with us," said Bo angrily, turning to the attack. "You were going to keep us informed."

"What does that have to do with you telling the South Koreans what's going on?"

"We didn't tell them. They don't know anything."

"Then why were they waiting for us last night?"

"We needed a way to go in, a cover story. So we came up with one."

"Why?"

"What do you think, we're sitting on our hands?" Bo's eyes were pinpoints in the tunnel created by his furrowing brows. "Slott told us to get this figured out. We're pulling out all the stops."

"Slott told you what was going on because he didn't want you messing it up. This is my gig, not yours."

"Bullshit, Ferguson. Just because you're the golden-haired boy around headquarters doesn't mean you're the only one who's working around here."

"My hair's black."

Ferguson folded his arms. He told himself that as long as he remained in his seat, he could be calm. As long as he didn't mention Guns getting hurt, he could control himself.

"Start explaining," Ferguson said.

"I don't work for you."

"Be damn glad of that. Now what the hell did you do there?"

Reluctantly, but realizing there was no point in not telling him, Bo explained that they had invented a story about having intelligence claiming that the North Koreans would try and infiltrate the waste site "to cause problems." They had offered to conduct a security analysis to counter the threat.

"We needed a way to get in legitimately," said Bo, "without tipping them off."

"And what did you find?"

"We haven't found anything yet. We're going in next week."

"Next week? Next week?"

"I need time to get our specialists in place."

"You gave them a heads-up that something was going on, and then you gave them a week to get rid of whatever they've got there. Jesus F. Christ, Bo. How the hell stupid are you?"

Bo leapt to his feet. "Get out of my office, Ferguson. Out."

"No, I want a fuckin' answer. How the hell stupid are you?"

"We're watching the facility. Nothing goes in or out without us knowing about it."

"Oh, that'll work."

Ferguson got up from his seat. Bo leaned across his desk, his face red.

"You should have told us you were going in," said Bo. "You were going to work with us. You screwed up, not me."

"I screwed up?" Ferguson gave him a half laugh. "I screwed up? I screwed up. Yeah, that's it. I screwed up. Oh, boy, did I screw up."

"You think you're a one-man show, Ferguson. That's your problem. The Agency doesn't revolve around you."

"No shit."

Ferguson's father had taught him a great deal about life and the espionage business, but one of the most important rules the son had learned was one his dad failed to follow: Don't get screwed by your own people.

In the early nineties, Ferguson Senior had been sent to Moscow to retrieve a high-level Russian agent from the Kremlin. Unbeknownst to his father—but probably not to the CIA's deputy director of operations at the time, who felt they owed it to the man to try and get him out—the Russian agent had already been betrayed. Ferguson's father walked right into a trap.

The thing was, Ferguson Senior was too good an operative to be blindsided. He turned the tables on the KGB team that was watching him, shot them, and got the spy out anyway.

Except it wasn't the spy.

The KGB had replaced the agent before Ferguson Senior got there. Two people in Moscow supposedly knew the agent's real identity; Ferguson Senior went to both after the gunfight for help. For reasons that never became clear, neither one said anything to alert him. It wasn't until he got to Berlin that Ferguson Senior realized he still had a real problem on his hands. Once again, though, he managed to turn the tables on a KGB ambush.

That was his dad. Always pulling a rabbit out of his hat.

But the roof caved in anyway. Ferguson Senior was injured in the attack, and a bystander was killed. The German police got involved, and within a few days there was talk of a congressional investigation to "rein in the CIA cowboy."

Ferguson Senior was cut loose by the Agency. The only person who stood up for him was his old friend and fellow officer Thomas Parnelles, the General. But Parnelles, who'd essentially been exiled to a meaningless headquarters job for his own supposed indiscretions, had little influence within the Agency and none outside of it. Ferguson

Senior was forced to retire; he was told he was lucky he wasn't going to jail.

Maybe it was his family history, but Ferguson couldn't help but feel he'd fallen into a snake pit here in Korea. Even if he accepted Bo's story at face value, which meant that Bo was a dope, how could the South Koreans have produced plutonium without the local CIA people finding out about it?

In some ways, it was an unfair question. The CIA operation was designed to spy on North Korea, not the South. Besides, intelligence agencies were historically more notable for their failures than their successes. This wasn't quite on the scale of Pearl Harbor or 9/11.

Still, by definition it was an intelligence failure. And it seemed to Ferguson that something else was going on here that he didn't know about. Slott had never directly interfered in an operation before.

If he'd been in the Middle East or Russia, Ferguson would have felt much more sure of himself, but Korea was very foreign. He needed some sort of backup, a check on his superiors just in case they were gaming him.

The sole possibility that came to mind was Corrine Alston.

A measure of his desperation, that.

But he needed some sort of insurance, just in case.

In case what?

He stared out the window of the train, not wanting to answer his own question.

14

Thera was walking with Julie Svenson toward the lunch buffet in the reception building when Dr. Norkelus stormed up, an angry look on his face. She looked at him expectantly, trying to think what she would say if he asked about the package of cigarettes she'd just been given. She knew there'd be another message in them, though she hadn't had a chance to look for it.

She had the first pack, which was almost empty. She'd give that to him.

"I need a message sent to the secretary general's special committee," said Norkelus, practically shouting at her. "It's absurd."

"You want me to help prepare it?" said Thera, trying not to let her relief show.

"Yes." He took a voice recorder from his pocket. "The details are there. It must go out by one p.m., our time."

"One?"

"I know. It's ridiculous. Bureaucratic fools," replied Norkelus, turning on his heel and stomping off.

ALEXANDRIA, VIRGINIA

Corrine Alston was just about to curl up in bed with a good mystery when the phone rang. Thinking it was her mother, she picked up the phone on the night table in the bedroom.

"Hey, Wicked Stepmother, it's Prince Charming."

"Ferg?"

"I need you to get to a secure phone, but don't go to The Cube."

"Ferguson, what the hell are you doing?"

"Encrypted phone. Call me. You have my number."

"But—"

"No buts. You have five minutes."

The phone line went dead. Corrine scrambled to get her secure satellite phone. She punched the buttons, not entirely sure she remembered Ferg's number.

"Grimm Brothers. Fairy tales are our business."

"You're not very funny, Ferguson, especially at midnight."

"It's only two o'clock here," he said. "Must be the problem. Humor's jetlagged."

"What's going on?"

"I need you to do me a favor."

"What kind of favor?"

"Guns is on his way back home with a soil sample. He messed up his leg. Corrigan tell you that?"

"No."

"One of the reasons he messed up his leg is that the South Koreans tripled security at the waste site where we found the plutonium. You know about the plutonium, right?"

"Yes, of course. Why did they up the security?"

"Sixty-four-thousand-dollar question. The leading theory is that our CIA station chief here is a boob, but there are other suspicions."

"Like what?"

Ferguson ignored the question. "I have some things to check out, and I need, uh, I just need someone I can trust."

"You mean from the Team?"

"This isn't a team job I have in mind. I want them to do some translating maybe, and I may send them back with something for you."

"For me?"

"Maybe more soil samples . . . I don't know. I don't want to use Seoul."

"Why not, Ferg?"

Ferguson didn't answer.

"Ferg."

"Because, Wicked Stepmother, if they're merely incompetent, they'll screw it up. If they're more than merely incompetent, who knows what will happen?"

So why was he cutting out Corrigan, Corrine wondered. And why had Slott decided to get the Seoul office involved in a First Team mission without telling her?

"You still there, Stepmother?"

"I'm here, Ferg."

"Hey listen, one of these days you're going to have to trust me," he told her.

"I trust you."

"Then see if you can find this guy for me. He's retired. Used to work for the Bureau. Name is James Sonjae. Call him now and wake him up. Tell him to come to Seoul."

"Ferg, it's two o'clock in the morning."

"He doesn't sleep very well anyway."

"But—"

"Like I say. Trust me, OK? Gotta go do some barhopping now. I'll talk to you in a bit."

———

Two hours later, Corrine arrived at a diner about a mile and a half off the Beltway. James Sonjae sat in the far corner, slumped down in the booth, a coffee and half-eaten bagel sitting on the table in front of him. He kept his gaze toward the window as she approached; it was only when she leaned over to ask who he was that she realized he was able to watch everything from the reflections there.

"Mr. Sonjae?"

"Please have a seat, Ms. Alston."

"Corrine, please."

He turned from the window and straightened in the seat. "You're the president's counsel?"

"Yes, I am."

"You don't have bodyguards?"

The remark surprised her. "I don't need Secret Service protection."

"I see."

He picked up his coffee cup. He looked considerably older than his Bureau records indicated. His face was pockmarked and worn, his hair thin and gray. He was dressed in a light windbreaker, despite the night's chill. A short, compact man, his shoulders sloped, giving Corrine the impression of someone who had been worn down by his years in government service.

"Bob Ferguson asked me to contact you," Corrine told him.

"Ferg works for you?"

"In a way. He's in Korea."

"Korea?" Sonjae put down his coffee cup. "South Korea?"

"Yes. He needs . . . He needs a translator he can trust. And he asked for you. He needs someone right away. Very much right away. The sooner the better."

Sonjae leaned back in the seat. Corrine guessed that he was trying to think of a way to say no politely.

"His father saved my life," said the ex-FBI agent finally. "What does he need me to do?"

16

Thera rode back to the dormitory with two engineers who'd finished for the day and needed to record their findings. The two men headed off to have lunch; Thera jogged to her room to write up the report.

She took the cigarette pack out of her pocket and examined it while she waited for the laptop to boot up. She assumed the room was bugged, and thought it possible that there was some sort of camera monitoring what she did as well, even though she hadn't been able to spot one. So she tried to be as nonchalant as possible.

The package was wrapped in cellophane, unopened. She slit it open with her fingernail, pulling the top off and crumpling the wrapper in her hand. She slit the top open and folded back the paper, looking for a message.

There was nothing on the flap, no paper between the cigarettes, no writing on the interior, at least not that she could see.

Was yesterday's message an illusion?

Thera put the pack down and went to work.

I t was only as she started to type Norkelus's terse response to the committee that Thera remembered what Tak Ch'o had said: save some cigarettes.

Maybe the message was *in* the cigarettes.

Of course.

Thera out took the pack and tapped a cigarette free, playing with it as if to relieve tension or boredom. The cigarette quickly began to fray. She moved her hands back and forth, agitated, nervous. Absentmindedly she crushed the side of the cigarette and dropped it on the desk. Then, seeming to realize what she had done, she picked it up and flipped it toward the wastebasket.

It missed.

She pulled the paper apart as she dropped it into the can. Nothing.

Back at her desk, Thera started working on Norkelus's report, which said that the team had found nothing but was still "in preliminary stages." She transcribed everything he said; his accent made it difficult to understand some of the sentences, and she had to stop and rewind, stop and rewind, and even then ended up guessing at spots.

If there was a message inside one of the cigarettes, it would look slightly different than the others, wouldn't it?

Thera typed a few more words, then got up, and with exaggerated movements gathered her things so she could go outside for a smoke. Here she was definitely being observed, so she made a good show of things: opening the package from the bottom, taking out one cigarette, examining it, lighting it. A gust of wind came up; she scooped her hand over the end of the cigarette to shelter it, and dropped the pack. Most of the cigarettes scattered.

She dropped to her knees, picking up the cigarettes one by one.

The third was slightly fatter than the others. She slid it behind her ear and scooped the rest into the box.

Inside, she palmed it, rolled the tobacco out in her pocket, and finally unfolded the wrapper, revealing a message so tiny she had to squint to make out the letters.

Nov 8 124.30.39.52 MIDNIGHT

Thera's first thought was that the numbers referred to an Internet site where a message would appear tomorrow night. But as she went back to work on the report, she realized the numbers were actually longitude and latitude and referred to a spot roughly fifty miles south of the waste plant, whose own location she'd had to note for the records.

The team was leaving for Japan on the evening of November 8; they'd probably land by midnight.

Was it some sort of trap or trick?

Thera couldn't decide.

Best let The Cube figure that out.

The problem was how exactly to tell them. She could imbed a message in the report she was typing for Norkelus easily enough. But none of the prearranged message sequences came close to covering this situation.

Working Ch'o's name into the message was easy. Norkelus said they had been greeted warmly; Thera added a line quoting his brief speech the day they arrived.

She scanned down what she had, deleting some of Norkelus's extraneous comments. He'd included a to-do list that was basically the inspection team's agenda, ending with the flight at ten p.m. Nov. 8.

Thera added a line: Nov. 8 pckp 0000XXXX.

It looked as if it were something she'd stuck in, intending to finish or clear up later. She scrolled back, adding XXX's and zeroes to some of the earlier parts.

Norkelus had given some initial readings taken by air monitors. She could stick the numbers in there, claiming she'd misheard or mistyped something, but how would anyone know to look for them?

What if she put in a new line, mangled from Norkelus's notes?

She typed in the numbers, removing the periods. It looked more like an error than anything else.

Obvious enough?

Thera hit her spellchecker, which ran through the document quickly. She accidentally "corrected" one of the readings, replacing an abbreviation with the word *Pluto*. She left it, as if she hadn't realized her mistake.

The coordinates were just there, on their own line. It would take ESP to realize they were part of the message.

The whole message would take ESP to interpret.

Maybe she shouldn't send it at all. Maybe it was a trap.

A nuclear scientist who wanted to defect? Quite a prize.

Thera hesitated, her mouse over the Send button.

She had to make the coordinates obvious; otherwise there was no point to this at all. No point.

She scrolled to the findings list, looking at some of the samples. Particle quantities were noted.

Iron. The code for an emergency pickup was *Iron*; she was to insert the word or the chemical symbol, Fe, into a message to alert the Cube.

Thera typed FeBr into the list of first-day chemical samples—if anyone caught it, she would claim she couldn't decipher something from Norkelus's notes—then cut and pasted the coordinates in. Finally, she scrolled to the end of the message and put her initials in, making it clear she had prepared it.

Send, or not send?

Fear gripped her for a moment, fear, doubt and doom.

It filled her with anger. She zeroed the mouse on the SEND command and tapped furiously, practically breaking the plastic.

Gone, she told herself. Gone. And don't look back.

17

CIA BUILDING 24-442

"*Iron* is the code for pickup," said Corrigan, "and I double-checked just to be sure: There is no test for iron bromine, which is what FeBr would be, presumably."

Corrine glanced across the conference room table at Parnelles and Slott. Both wore grim expressions, clearly concerned about the message that had been imbedded in a routine UN report intercepted almost exactly three hours before. Corrigan had called them all immediately, waking Slott and Parnelles up. Corrine had only just returned from meeting with Ferguson's friend, so wired on coffee she wouldn't have been able to sleep anyway.

"There are other typos in the message," said Slott. "It may be nothing."

"I doubt she'd be sloppy with something like that," said Corrigan.

"November 8 at midnight, the team will be out of there by then," said Slott.

"Maybe it's tonight at midnight," suggested Corrigan. "See, it's out of sequence; maybe the wrong date was put there to throw anyone else off."

"She's not going to make a mistake like that," said Slott.

"Then why ask for a pickup after they leave?"

"Let's see where this is," said Parnelles, rising.

Corrigan had brought an extra-large map with him. The DCI unfolded it and peered down at the spot the mission coordinator had marked. A lock of jet black hair fell across his forehead. Parnelles's eyes had immense bags beneath them. The looks that appeared rugged by day seemed merely craggy at three in the morning.

"Fifty miles south of the site, along the coast, if you read the numbers as longitude and latitude, with minutes and decimals," said Slott softly. "Just due south of Kawaksan."

Parnelles grunted. "You have satellite maps of this?"

Slott slid over a folder.

"I think, uh, we ought to run the team in there," said Corrigan. His voice squeaked.

"How would Thera get there?" asked Corrine, looking at the map. "She wouldn't walk fifty miles."

"Yes," grunted Parnelles, continuing to stare at the map.

"Maybe she's planning on taking a vehicle from the site," said Corrigan. "I think we have to assume she's going to be there."

"Thank you, Jack," said Parnelles. He looked up at the mission coordinator. "I believe Corrine, Dan, and I can take it from here."

Corrigan didn't want to leave, but of course he had no choice. He felt as if he hadn't made a good enough case for a rescue mission; his gut told him Thera was in trouble, and he didn't want her abandoned.

"It just doesn't make any sense," said Slott after Corrigan left. "Why would she want a pickup after she's gone? And if the sequence is supposed to be a clue, if it's tonight, why did she give this location rather than O2, or one of the cache points? It doesn't make any sense."

O2 was a location a few miles outside the camp toward the coast.

"When you say midnight November 8, do you mean the midnight after the day of November 8?" asked Corrine. "Or the midnight that leads to the day of November 8? It might be interpreted either way."

"She'd mean midnight at the end of November 8," said Slott.

"Are you sure?"

"That's the way we do it."

"It would make more sense Corrine's way," said Parnelles. "She needs to be picked up before the UN team leaves, because she's worried about something that will happen to her when she tries to go."

"Midnight November 7—the way she should have written it—that would be tonight," said Slott.

"Then we better get there tonight," said Parnelles.

Slott was skeptical that the message was even a message; it seemed to him likely that Thera had accidentally typed the wrong letters for a legitimate testing compound. Analysts were always seeing things that weren't there, and Corrigan tended to be an overanxious den mother.

"Dan's point about how far it is from the base does make a lot of sense," said Corrine. "From this map, it looks like she would be driving right by one of the supply caches, not to mention O2."

"Maybe she saw something at O2 that made it inappropriate," suggested Parnelles. "Or maybe it's not her who's supposed to be picked up."

"What? A defector?" Slott picked up his plastic mechanical pencil and began tapping it furiously on the desk. "No. She'd never blow her cover like that."

"Maybe she didn't have to blow her cover," said Parnelles. "Can we get to this site without being detected?"

Slott glanced at the map. "I believe so. I'll have to check with Colonel Van Buren."

"Very good," said Parnelles, pushing back from the table.

"Which night should we go in?"

"Both, if necessary."

"Since we're all here," said Corrine, "there's something I wanted to mention. Sergeant Young broke his leg and is on his way back to Hawaii for treatment."

"I hadn't heard," said Parnelles.

"He fell off the side of a ravine," said Slott. "It didn't affect the mission."

"The circumstances seemed odd," said Corrine, looking at the deputy director.

"Guns and Ferguson went into the South Korean waste site," explained Slott. "Security had been increased, and they took a risk getting out. In any event, as they were leaving, the sergeant slipped down a ravine and got injured."

"Why had security been increased?" asked Parnelles.

Slott let the pencil slide down through his fingers to the table. He resented Corrine for bringing this up now; her only motive, it seemed, was to embarrass him.

"Seoul had a plan to get into the facility," Slott told Parnelles. "Unfortunately, they didn't coordinate properly with Ferguson. Actually, it's very possible Sergeant Young would have gotten hurt anyway. The site is very hilly."

"Why is Seoul involved?" said Corrine.

"Why wouldn't they be?" said Slott.

"This is a Special Demands mission."

"Special Demands doesn't have the resources for what we need to do. This is more a bread-and-butter assignment."

"You should have told me," said Corrine.

"Seoul is involved because I told Daniel to pull out all the stops," said Parnelles. "Blame me."

"Why didn't you tell me?"

"You don't run the CIA, do you?"

"Mr. Parnelles." Corrine gave him a don't-screw-with-me look.

"The president wants to know about the bomb material. We're pulling out all the stops," said Slott.

"Did Ferguson know?" Corrine asked.

"Apparently not. I sent him to talk to Ken Bo." Slott picked up his pencil again. "Obviously, they didn't play together very well."

"I'd appreciate being informed when something directly involves Special Demands," said Corrine. "I should have been told."

"You want me to tell you every little thing?"

"I don't think that's a little thing, but yes," she added. "Everything that has to do with Special Demands."

Slott turned to Parnelles.

"I don't think it's unreasonable that Ms. Alston be kept in the loop," said the director. "She is the president's representative."

Slott had intended to tell Corrine but got caught up in other matters and simply forgot. But her demand now—and, more important, Parnelles's backing it up—seemed like an unconscionable attack on his authority. In effect, they were saying he couldn't do anything without getting her approval. Or at least that was the way he interpreted it.

"I don't know that that's going to work," Slott said.

"Make it work, Dan," said Parnelles, getting up. "You better get moving; you have only a few hours to get this pickup arranged."

18

DAEJEON, SOUTH KOREA

According to Corrigan, Science Industries was owned by the same man—Park Jin Tae—who had owned the truck company, though for the moment Ferguson saw that only as a coincidence. What was more interesting was the fact that Park—in Korean, it was pronounced like "bark"—was an important behind-the-scenes political player, albeit a frustrated one. Several years before, he had donated a considerable amount of money to a now-banned political party named March 1 Movement. The left-leaning group had argued for peaceful reunification with North Korea. It had also called for a dramatic boost in military spending, a measure that to Ferguson seemed contradictory with the goal of peaceful reunification, but was somehow compatible in the tangled world of Korean politics—or at least the March 1 Movement members thought it was.

The CIA report forwarded to Ferguson stated that Park hated Japan, apparently because his family had been persecuted during the Japanese occupation. Supposedly he had retired from politics since the banning of the March 1 Movement, though in the last few years he had worked to strengthen ties with the North. Park was a part owner, with the North Korean government, in several factories in a special area near the capital. He also owned stock in a North Korean bank established by a Swede. The business arrangements were encouraged by the South Korean government and, while profitable, were not entirely about making money. Anyone who believed in reunification realized that the greatest barrier to it, besides the intransigence of dictator Kim Jong-Il, was the North's great poverty. Economic development in the North was absolutely essential if Korea was ever to be reunited.

"Now here's the interesting part," Corrigan told Ferguson. "Just before the political party was banned, some of the principals were being investigated for trying to buy weapons on the black market. Scuttlebutt was that it was just a trumped-up charge. But . . ."

"What sort of weapons?"

"Lots. Tanks. Artillery. Everything they could get."

"Were they planning a coup?" asked Ferguson. He was walking through Daejeon's shopping district. Even though the late afternoon air was cold, the streets were still crowded.

"Not clear. We have a news report here where one of the lawyers claimed that the weapons weren't going to be used in South Korea. They don't show up in any of the other reports, ours or the media's."

"Thanks."

"So, Ferg. What are you going to do with this?"

"Process it."

"Are you working with Seoul?"

"I'm in touch with them. Did you tell them about the trucks?"

"Well, no. Am I supposed to?"

"No," said Ferguson. "I'm handling that myself."

"Slott wants to make sure you're cooperating. He doesn't want a repeat of what happened to Guns."

"Neither do I."

Ferguson killed the communication, then turned down a side street, aiming for a motor scooter rental company he'd scouted a few days before.

Whether the trucks were a coincidence or not, Ferguson decided Science Industries was too interesting a place not to check out. His first thought was that he could scout the grounds from one of the hotel rooftops nearby, but it turned out that the one with the best view—

the Han—showed the entrance driveway and two nondescript two-story buildings, nothing more. In fact, it was
difficult to even get an idea of the size of the campus
from the hotels; the landscape included a large number of
evergreens on the hills and knolls that blocked the view.
Only by going to four different high-rises was Ferguson
able to determine there were six different buildings. The
one where the trucks had been parked looked like a warehouse or perhaps a garage. It was arranged in a way that
someone could make a drop-off or pickup without going
through the rest of the campus; in fact, an inner fence cut
off all but the rear of the building from the rest of the
complex.

Two other buildings were very small cement structures, possibly for storage or machinery. One was round,
the other square.

The last three were brown-brick structures with narrow, slitlike windows. The largest was three stories and
only about two hundred feet long; the others were smaller
two-story structures.

With a rough idea of the layout, Ferguson went to check
out the perimeter, examining what sort of security mea-
sures protected it. A double fence topped by barbed wire
protected the perimeter, limiting access to the single road
Ferguson and Guns had taken two nights before. Security
cameras were placed at irregular intervals, accompanied
by floodlights to illuminate the grounds at dark. The building doors were all equipped with electronic locks that
worked with card readers.

Ferguson found a spot on the road between the highway and the plant where he could watch for cars to come
out of the facility. He hoped to follow them to a bar or
restaurant, any place where he could get more information and maybe steal an ID card to get inside the buildings. But it was like playing the lottery—the first car he
followed went onto the highway toward Seoul, and the
second disappeared into a residential area west of the city.

The third was more promising—a Mercedes sedan

with a driver and a passenger in the back. Ferguson had a little difficulty keeping up on the highway, but after about ten miles, the car turned off onto a local road. They drove past a series of high-rises until evergreen-clad hills burst around them, as if Nature had pushed man back and retaken its land.

The grade became steeper and steeper. When the road leveled off, Ferguson could see Daejeon laid out in the distance to his right. The afternoon sun gave the city an ethereal glow. It was a phenomenal view, but not one shared with many others—the road abruptly narrowed and turned to packed dirt.

The Mercedes turned into a gated driveway a few hundred yards beyond the end of the macadam. Ferguson slowed down, watching from the corner of his eye as the gate opened and the sedan pulled through.

Just after the driveway, the road veered to the left. A group of very old structures hugged the shoulder; a dozen men were working on one, refurbishing it with hand tools. Ferguson pulled around in a U-turn.

"Nice work," Ferguson told the workers, getting off his bike. They either didn't hear him or didn't understand English, since no one paid any attention. This only encouraged him; he walked to the side of the building, staring up and nodding his head in admiration.

A man in a white shirt and tie came from around the side of the building and asked, in Korean, who he was. Ferguson stuck out his hand in greeting, then reached for the small phrase book, looking for the words for "very nice carpentry" while the man with the tie told him he should be on his way.

"They don't have a section on carpentry," said Ferguson cheerfully, closing the book. "But I hammer, saw." He mimed the work, as if he were a carpenter. The man with the tie seemed to think he was looking for a job.

"No, no. On vacation. Love old houses. And big houses. Great work. I'm a contractor myself. Back in the

States. Great work here. Fantastic. Make a lot of money doing this back home. You ever been?"

Ferguson's admiration for the craftsmanship was so effusive that the man in the tie began showing him around the exterior. Ferguson, who in his entire life had been no closer to woodworking tools than the parking lot of Home Depot, bent over an ancient wood plane, admiring it as if it were the Grail.

It wasn't the Grail, but it may have been older. The men were refurbishing the buildings with period tools to preserve the authenticity. Two of the older men began explaining their methods in great detail—and in Korean. Ferguson understood perhaps one word out of twenty, but he could be enthusiastic in any language. He spent more than a half hour admiring the project, and by the time he left he was sure he could show up in a day or so with a camera and have an enthusiastic audience.

He was also sure that the man who owned these houses and most of the surrounding mountain, including the property across the street, was Park Jin Tae: "a great and noble man, a leader of true Koreans and the heart of generosity and spirit," according to the man with the tie.

19

THE WHITE HOUSE, WASHINGTON, D.C.

One of the good things about being in the West Wing at a quarter to four in the morning was that no one was around to interrupt you.

One of the bad things was—it was a quarter to four in the morning.

Corrine waited as the coffee dripped through the cof-
feemaker, the aroma filling the small room. Her body
cried out for the caffeine, but she knew from experience
that the first quarter of the pot the machine made would
be cold and taste like metal shavings; for some reason the
pot had to be half full before the liquid was fit for human
consumption.

She leaned back against the cupboard, waiting. And
thinking of her conversation with Ferguson.

Clearly he didn't trust Seoul, and he didn't trust Slott.
Whatever his suspicions were, they must be pretty strong.
Ferguson didn't like her at all, though obviously he
trusted her to some degree.

Or he was using her.

Had she even done the right thing? Getting an outsider
involved, even one who'd worked for the government in
the past?

Slott's reluctance to tell her that he was involving
Seoul—even if Parnelles took the blame for the actual
decision—told her that something *was* going on. Maybe
it only amounted to Agency politics, but there was no way
for her to figure it out without considerably more information from the principals, Ferguson especially.

Had she done the right thing?

If Ferguson was up to something *illegal,* he surely
wouldn't have involved her.

On the other hand, was it really in the president's interest to be subverting the chain of command at the CIA?

Then again, some might say that her very presence on
Special Demands subverted it.

Slott would certainly say that.

The coffee machine gurgled at her. Corrine grabbed
the pot and poured herself a cup, then went down the hall
to get a jump on the day's work.

20

SOUTH CHUNGCHONG PROVINCE, SOUTH KOREA

By the time Ferguson got back to Science Industries, it was nearly six p.m. Even so, there were plenty of workers in the complex, and within a few minutes five cars came out in a bunch. He went with the two that turned off the first highway ramp, following as they went into the bar district. Seven young women got out of the cars, joking and laughing as they went down the stairs to a *hof,* a Korean bar that served food and drinks.

By the time he parked the scooter and got inside, the women had found a place at the far end of the bar. Ferguson made his way over to them nonchalantly, ordered a *maekju*—beer.

"*Saeng maekju?*" said the bartender, asking if he wanted a draft.

Ferguson gave her one of his best goofy smiles. "Hang on," he said, taking out his phrase book.

One of the women next to him glanced over.

"You speak English?" he said in a lost voice.

"English, a little," said the woman.

"Do I want *saeng maekju?*"

The woman giggled, and tapped her friend. Within a few minutes Ferguson was surrounded by young women who found the handsome but clueless foreigner quite amusing. They got him a Hite—a brand of bottled beer popular in Korea—and a plate of food whose identity he couldn't decipher.

Midway through the beer, Asian techno-pop began playing in the background. Ferguson proved deft on the nearby dance floor, dancing with three and four of the women at a time. When a slow song came on, he took the girl named Lin-So in his arms and held her close; she clung to him furiously, her head against his chest and shoulder.

She didn't want to let go when the music stopped, but the punchy, driving beat of the next song got her moving. Ferguson took her by the hand and twirled her backward and forward, around and around several times before segueing into a kind of jig and sharing himself with two of the other young women, who'd been shooting jealous glances in their direction for several minutes now.

When the song ended, he excused himself to find the restroom; he went down the hall and slipped outside, having obtained what he wanted: Bae Eun's identity card, with its magnetic key to open the doors at Science Industries.

Had Ferguson looked even the vaguest bit Korean, or if he had thought the plant routinely employed foreign workers, he would have used the ID card to go in the front gate; most guards rarely took a good look at credentials, especially when they were outside on a cold night. But the circumstances called for a slightly more creative approach: hopping the fence.

At half-past nine, a limo drove up the drive to the front gate. The driver told the guards that he had come to pick up Mr. Park. The men immediately ordered him out of the car. The driver objected, and within seconds one of the guards was holding him down on the pavement while the other was frantically calling for backup.

Ferguson, meanwhile, scaled the first perimeter fence, clamping down the barbed wire strands at the top with a pair of oversized clothespins. Though the spot he had chosen was only a few yards from the front gate, it wasn't covered by a video camera, not so much an oversight as a commonsense decision by a security designer who had only so many cameras to work with and saw no reason to cover an area under constant human surveillance.

Now inside the compound, Ferguson trotted up one of the interior roads, circling around to a set of lights that indicated where one of the surveillance cameras had been placed. He blinded the camera with a rather low-tech application, the wrapper of a local fast-food restaurant artfully tangled and stuck on with a gob of mayonnaise. This done, he sprinted past it, racing for a second camera, located at the base of a tree.

This camera covered one of the nearby buildings as well as the route he wanted to use to get out, and here he had to rely on something more dependable than tainted mayonnaise. He inserted a fader in the back housing, hit the button to dim the view and then ran in front of it toward the nearby building.

By now other guards had responded to help their brother at the front gate. Red and yellow lights were flashing, illuminating the grounds. Ferguson trotted to the largest building on the campus. He walked around the side farthest from the gate to the back, trying to see through the windows as he went. But the windows had been designed to prevent that, and all he could catch was a glimpse of his own reflection.

The door at the back didn't have a card reader or handle. It was also hooked to an alarm. Ferguson decided he'd leave the building for later, after he took some soil samples and checked out the trucks.

Getting across the compound without getting caught by the video cameras took a bit of work. It was relatively easy to see where the cameras were and what they covered—each used floodlights to illuminate its view. Ducking around them, though, was like running through a free-form maze. It took nearly two hours to get to the warehouse area where the trucks had been parked. Ferguson filled a dozen bags with soil on his way over.

The first thing he did was calibrate the gamma meter—

a replacement for the one Guns had lost—and hold it next to the building. The needle didn't budge.

Ferguson took two shovelfuls of dirt from the northwestern corner of the building, then climbed the eight-foot chain-link fence that separated all but the front of the building from the parking lot.

A camera sat under the front eave of the building, covering the lot. Unsure how far he could go before getting in its view, Ferguson considered climbing up and disabling it, but one look at the slick metal sides of the building made his knee ache. He decided he could reach the trucks without being seen if he stayed close to the wall. Ferguson slipped off his backpack and got down on his hands and knees to crawl.

He didn't pick up anything from the gamma meter at the first truck. Pausing near the tailgate, he slid a gamma detection tag into the chassis just beneath the truck bed. Then he rolled to the next truck, repeating the process. When he reached the third truck without getting any indication from the gamma meter, he pressed the button to initiate the self-calibration sequence again, wondering if it was malfunctioning.

As he did, he heard the rumble of a car approaching.

21

DUE SOUTH OF KAWKSAN, NORTH KOREA

Rankin leapt from the helicopter, rushing with the others as they ran into the open field overlooking the rocky shore. The team spread out: Half ran in the direction of a stone wall that stood near the road, the rest took positions along the cliffside. It was not quite pitch-black, but seeing more than ten feet was impossible without his night goggles.

The field was empty, as was the nearby road.

Rankin scanned the area, turning slowly to make sure he hadn't missed anything. Then he took out the handheld global positioner and walked to the exact coordinates Colonel Van Buren had given him.

Nada.

"We making a pickup, or what?" said Sergeant Barren, his voice more a demand than a question.

"We'll see what happens," spit back Rankin.

"Fuggit," muttered Barren, trotting off to check on the men near the road.

Rankin couldn't necessarily disagree with Barren's assessment. They were only a few miles from a North Korean army base. Sitting on the ground here for any particular length of time wasn't all that good an idea, especially since they had to do it again tomorrow night if no one showed up.

But that's what they were going to do.

Rankin went over toward the cliffside, checking on the men there. He squatted next to each one of the men, not saying anything—what was there to say?—just showing them he was there.

"Oh-twenty," said Barren finally, coming over and pointing to his watch. "What do you say?"

"Ten more minutes," said Rankin.

"You briefed fifteen, not thirty."

"I want to make sure."

"Right."

The ten minutes passed more slowly than the first twenty. The wind stiffened. It wasn't bitter cold—the temperature had climbed to the high thirties, a veritable heat spell—but it added to the discomfort nonetheless.

Finally, Rankin hopped over the wall and trotted to the middle of the road, taking one last look himself.

Nothing.

"Saddle up," he told the others. "Let's hit the road."

22

SOUTH CHUNGCHONG PROVINCE, SOUTH KOREA

The lights grew stronger. Ferguson tried to sink into the ground, hiding from them in the musky, oil-scented dampness.

This is what the grave will smell like, he thought.

The lights moved to his right, then came back. The car stopped and moved, stopped and moved; it was making a U-turn.

Finally the lights moved away for good. Ferguson planted a tag, then made his way back to his pack, retreating around the building to find a way inside.

The door in the rear of the building had a wired alarm, with the wires running along the top and the sensor near the upper-left-hand corner. Ferguson worked a long, flexible metal strip into the gap between the door and molding, pushing it until it struck the alarm connection plate on the jamb. He used the current meter to make sure he had a connection, then taped the metal in place.

The lock was a high-quality German-made model that used mushroom pins in its works, a difficult challenge to pick. Ferguson had to alter his usual technique, gently and loosely prodding the inner workings of the lock before getting it to give way.

The door opened into a vast empty space. The concrete floor was swept clean, the ribs of the building bare. Ferguson made sure there was no motion detector, then slipped inside. He checked for radiation contamination—none—and put tags near the overhead doors at the front of the building.

Ferguson circled back across the compound, aiming at

one of the two smaller buildings. Just as he approached the front door, he caught a glimmer of something on his right and jerked back.

It was a video camera.

He froze, silently cursing. Slowly he backed away, wondering how he had missed it.

It took him a few minutes to spot the light that was supposed to be illuminating the camera's area. It was out.

So had he been seen? Or was there simply not enough light?

Ferguson ran his fingers around his mouth, considering the situation. Given how the guards had responded the other night, if he had been seen, the entire security force would be racing here.

No sense wasting time then, he thought, stepping to the door.

Ferguson swiped the card in the reader and tugged on the latch. The door didn't open. He swiped the card again, but it remained locked. Leaving the card in the reader didn't work either.

Maybe the security people had a way of locking down the campus buildings and were on their way.

Ferguson jumped back into the shadows, fingering a tear gas grenade. But after ten minutes passed, he realized no one was coming. The problem had to be with the card. It must be programmed to allow its user access only to certain areas or at certain times.

"OK, Miss Secretary," he whispered to the card. "Let's try you at door number two."

Ferguson slinked through the shadows to the next building, the largest on the site. It had three stories and—most important for Ferguson—a card lock on the door at the rear that wasn't covered by a video camera, not even one with a broken light. He checked for alarms, then took out his pilfered identity card.

The door buzzed as soon as he put the card into the reader. Ferguson held his breath on the threshold, listening to make sure the place was empty.

Red exit lights and pairs of dull yellow bulbs posted along the ceiling lit the hallway. Each door was made of wood; placards with Korean characters hung next to each. Ferguson photographed the hall and the placards, then chose an office door about midway down the hall. It was locked, and not just with a run-of-the-mill, any-screwdriver-will-do lock, but a Desmo, an eight-pin isolated key tumbler that was almost impossible to pick.

Almost.

Ferguson had to dig deep into his lock-picking tools to take it on, fiddling with a custom-made tension wrench and wirelike spring. The lock gave almost no feedback before suddenly giving way. Ferguson was so surprised that he dropped the screwdriverlike tension wrench on the ground.

"Real quiet, dude," he whispered, scooping it up. He left the door slightly ajar and slipped inside.

He found himself in an office shared by three people; each had a small desk and his or her own computer. Stealing a hard drive would have been easy, but it would also be pretty obvious.

Pulling one of the computers out, he saw that they were networked, and that the LEDs were flashing. Unhooking it or even just leaving it and booting up might alert a remote system administrator, or at least leave a record of the intrusion.

Ferguson was debating whether the risk was worth it when he heard a sound from the hallway. By the time he got back to the door, footsteps were coming in his direction.

Easing the door back against the jamb, he kept his hand on the knob rather than risking the sound of a click as it snapped into place. Then he took a long, slow breath, pushing the air from his lungs as silently as possible.

Whoever was walking toward him was wearing plastic-soled shoes that squeaked loudly as he walked. Ferguson eased his right hand into his jacket and took out his pepper spray.

Keys jangled.

The steps were next to him.

Then they were past.

Ferguson heard the door to the next office open. The person who'd gone in began to whistle.

He glanced at his watch. It was already quarter to five. The operation had taken him considerably longer than he had thought it would. If he was going to get out to the fence before it got light, he had to leave now.

Ferguson looked back at the room. There were boxes of backup disks next to the PCs. Reasoning that they were less likely to be missed, he helped himself to a couple from each desk, choosing at random since he had no idea what the Korean characters meant.

Outside, light from the next office flooded the corridor. Ferguson got down on his hands and knees and crawled to the doorway, looking up from the bottom to see inside. A man sat with his back to him, facing a computer a short distance away.

Ferguson tiptoed past, stopped to make sure he hadn't been seen, then continued to the end of the hallway.

He was just about to put his hands on the door's crash bar when he heard the squeak of the man's shoes once again.

Ferguson threw himself into the open stairwell to his left. As soon as he did, he realized this was a mistake; a set of vending machines sat on the landing between the floors above. He scrambled down the nearby steps, ducking just out of sight before the man and his squeaking shoes trotted up the steps to the vending machines.

The doors below the stairwell had narrow glass slits on them. Curious about what might be on the bottom level of the building, Ferguson eased down and tried one.

It wasn't locked. He pulled open the door and entered a vast room of computers. Large mainframes and server units lined the walls and formed clusters around the pillars. Metal cabinets formed low-rising walls at different points in the space, which extended the entire width of the building.

The cabinets were locked, but it was a simple matter to pick them, and as soon as he was sure there weren't any monitoring devices or alarms, he slid his tools in and opened one up.

Large tape discs, the type used to store and back up massive amounts of data, sat in the cabinet. Most if not all had been there awhile—there was a layer of dust on the bottom row. Ferguson selected one, then closed up the case. He took some photos with his small camera, and went back the way he'd come.

23

NORTH P'YŎNPAN PROVINCE, NORTH KOREA

Thera rose before dawn, once more unable to sleep. Her roommate's snores rattled the room, but it was the adrenaline of the mission that was keeping her awake. She wondered about the scientist, and at the same time wanted to be gone, back to Japan and then home.

She'd be back in three months to pick up the tags, and have to go through all of this again. But it'd be much easier then.

Unless Ch'o deserted.

Had they gotten the message? There was no way of knowing.

There'd always be tension, anticipation, adrenaline. She could handle that. It was fear she had trouble with, unfocused fear. But who didn't?

Dressed and wrapped in her heavy coat, Thera slipped out into the hallway and walked down to the door. The night air was frigid and sky dark. Without even thinking, she took one of the cigarettes from her pocket and began to smoke.

God, I'm addicted, she thought, tossing it to the ground and stamping it out. She took one last look at the overcast sky, then went inside to get a head start on work.

24

CIA HEADQUARTERS, LANGLEY, VIRGINIA

Slott thumbed through the preliminary technical report on the soil that Ferguson and Guns had gathered at the South Korean waste site. The report contained several pages of graphs and esoteric formulas as well as a dozen written in almost impenetrable scientific prose, but the data could be summed up in one word: *inconclusive*.

No plutonium had been found, though the scientists weren't sure that was because there was none there or because the field equipment they'd taken to Hawaii simply wasn't strong enough to detect it. A further analysis of the soil would take place in two days at a special CIA lab in California. There, the dirt would be compressed in a chamber and pounded with a variety of radioactive waves in a process one scientist had compared to high-tech gold panning. If there were any stray plutonium-239 atoms—actually, there would have to be a few more than *one*, but Slott wasn't up on the specifics—the machine would find them.

There was one technical caveat. The analysis relied on the fact that anyone trying to hide plutonium would go only so far as necessary to prevent its detection by standard equipment. The nano technology the Agency was using was exponentially more powerful; still, in theory a scientist who was aware of the lower detection threshold might be able to counter it. But if that were the case, Slott reasoned, they wouldn't have found anything in the first place.

Directly below the report was a response from Ken Bo regarding the plutonium and its possible origin. Stripped of its many qualifications—and complaints about the "unusual" operation that had found it—was a theory that the material had come from the closed TRIGA Mark-III research reactor in Seoul. The reactor had been used in the 1980s and probably the 1990s to conduct experiments testing extraction techniques from depleted uranium. Other experiments, continuing until 2004, had produced other isotopes.

While not generally known, those experiments had been detected by the IAEA roughly five years *after* they'd been reported to the president and the Intelligence Committee by the CIA.

Bo's contention—he phrased it as a hypothesis—was that the plutonium that had just been discovered was merely waste material left from those activities.

The theory would make a certain sense to a layman; the readings had been found at a waste dump, after all. But Slott knew that wasn't what was really going on. First of all, the experiments had never been aimed at or succeeded in producing plutonium. TRIGA Mark–III had been shut down, and all the material, even potential waste products, accounted for. Slott knew this because it had all happened on his watch in South Korea.

But few other people, even within the CIA, did. Much of the data on the experiments was highly classified and had not been found or reported by the IAEA. Information about the program had not been included in any of the briefing papers on the new treaty, and it was obvious to him that neither Corrine nor Parnelles for that matter was aware of it.

Bo's theory could get Seoul—and, by extension, Slott—off the hook if they were criticized. By carefully controlling the release of information about the TRIGA experiments, Slott could easily make it seem as if the CIA knew about this material all along and had in fact told Congress and the president.

Bo would never put this in writing, of course. He was counting on Slott to understand and play along.

Slott got up from his desk and began pacing around his office. Five people had known the entire TRIGA story from the Agency's perspective. Slott was one; Bo was another. A third was now dead. That left the former head of the CIA, now dying of Alzheimer's disease, and an officer now working in a staff position in what amounted to semiretirement.

He didn't even have to manipulate the records. If anyone asked, he could say that plutonium had been mentioned but not put in the reports for some reason he no longer knew.

Had it been found?

No. Definitely it hadn't. Definitely not. They had access to the South Korean documents, and it wasn't there.

And they were *all* the documents.

He knew that, because he'd verified it with the Korean document tracking system. But who in Congress or the administrative branch would know that? Even Parnelles wouldn't know that.

They could find it out, if they knew the right person to ask, but it would be difficult.

Slott rubbed his eyes. He couldn't lie. And he wasn't going to play the CYA games. He wouldn't. He couldn't. That wasn't who he was.

Slott stopped in front of his desk, looking at the picture of his wife and kids. It was a year old, taken when they'd moved into their new house. His only boy—they had three older girls—had just lost his first tooth.

If he didn't play the games, he might very well lose his job. They'd lose their house, have to move. He'd end up selling cars or insurance somewhere out West where no one knew who he was.

Or he could just keep his mouth shut and see what happened. Protect Bo, even though this raised some serious questions about Bo's competency.

Everyone was entitled to one screwup, wasn't he? And it wasn't even clear this was a screwup.

Slott went back behind his desk. He still had his son's baby tooth in the top desk drawer, an accidental souvenir he'd retained after exchanging it for a gold dollar.

The tooth fairy—a little white lie.

Not even that. His son had brought up the tooth fairy and the promise of money. Slott hadn't said anything, one way or another.

Daddy didn't lie, David. He was just protecting the family.

Would that be better to tell his boy or his girls than: *Daddy's not the incompetent screwup the congressmen are claiming?*

Slott pushed the desk drawer closed. He told himself he needed more information before he could decide what to do.

It wasn't true, but it was the sort of lie he could live with.

25

DAEJEON, SOUTH KOREA

Ferguson stuck his head under the shower's stream, shaking as the ice-cold water sent shivers through his body. It was a poor substitute for sleep, as was the weak coffee he got in the lobby.

"Corrine wants you to talk to her," said Corrigan when he checked in.

"What, does she think I'm working for her now?"

"You are."

"You find anything else out about Science Industries?"

"Thomas Ciello got a list of some of the people who work there," said Corrigan. "One of them is pretty interesting."

"Who dat?"

"Guy named Kang Hwan. Wrote a paper on extracting nuclear material using some sort of laser technique. Real technical stuff."

"Jack, you think a shopping list is technical."

"Har-har. This is. I can upload a copy of it for you."

"In Korean?"

"You're a laugh a minute, Ferg. What if I busted your chops like this every time you called in?"

"You mean you don't do it on purpose?"

Ferguson laughed, picturing Corrigan fuming at the communications desk in The Cube.

"Post me a file of the open-source information on him that I can access from a café," Ferguson said.

"Anonymously?"

"No, Jack, I'm going to walk in and tell the people there I'm a spook. We lost the laptop, remember?"

"You can get the open-source stuff with a Google search. There's nothing there. I can't send the report that way."

"I don't want you to," said Ferguson.

"You can get it at the embassy."

"Don't send it to them."

"Jesus, Ferg. You sound more paranoid by the minute."

"Yeah, I'm channeling my Irish grandmother. Just do what I say."

"All right, but . . ."

After he'd finished with Corrigan, Ferguson called Corrine.

"It's the Black Prince," he told her cheerfully when she answered. "What's going on?"

"Your friend is arriving in Seoul at six p.m."

"Very nice. He may be returning home a little sooner than I expected with some things I want you to check out."

"What's going on, Ferg? Why are you bypassing the usual channels?"

"Insurance."

"Against what?"

"Against things disappearing. Memories going bad. Interpretations of facts that can't be trusted."

"Who don't you trust?"

Ferguson lay back on the bed in his room. He hadn't planned on getting into this discussion right now—and, hopefully, ever.

"Maybe I'm just being paranoid," he told her.

"You don't trust Slott?"

He didn't answer.

"You trust me?" said Corrine finally.

"I pretty much can't stand you, Corrine. But I think you have a different agenda than those people do."

"You saved my life," she said.

Ferguson had to think for a moment before remembering. It had been in a nightclub in Syria. Or was that Lebanon?

"Yeah, well, that was a job thing," he told her. "Anyway, don't get your underwear all twisted up. I don't know that anything's going on. I just want to make sure I'm not screwed by it if it is."

"Well—"

"A deep subject. Now how about that flight number?"

Ferguson spent a few hours looking for more of the National Truck Company vehicles. None of the ones he checked out seemed like very good candidates for the truck he'd seen at the waste site. Four of the seven had open beds in the back. One was painted a garish pink that he thought would have glowed in the dark. The other two were in various states of disrepair and looked as if they hadn't been moved in months or maybe even years.

Checking on the trucks was the sort of necessary but tedious detail work that Ferguson had little patience for.

The more he did it, the more he was convinced that Science Industries was the best lead he was going to get for the time being, and that he ought to concentrate there until something told him he was wrong.

In the early afternoon he took the train to Seoul but got off a stop before the city, showing up at a hotel that advertised it had a "business center" with high-speed computer access. Ferguson inserted what looked like a small memory key into the hotel computer's USB slot and trolled for information on Kang Hwan, the scientist Corrigan had mentioned. The key contained a series of programs that enabled anonymous surfing and allowed him to erase any trace of the Web pages and files he looked at.

The Google search brought up several hundred references, but most were about a half-dozen papers the scientist had written. The English synopsis of two of the papers said they were on the possibility of using lasers to speed up the separation of radioactive isotopes, especially in uranium.

Almost as interesting was a fact Corrigan had neglected to mention: The scientist, fifty-three, had died two months earlier. None of the obituaries in the translated Korean newspapers gave the cause of death, but a small item in the Asian edition of the *Wall Street Journal* said it was suicide.

26

NORTH P'YÖNPAN PROVINCE, NORTH KOREA

Tak Ch'o took one last look around the small apartment where he had lived for the past year. It was not a look of nostalgia; he was glad to be gone. He just wanted to make sure that he wasn't leaving anything that would show where he had gone.

The bed was unmade; the medicine he had obtained for his supposed stomach ailment lay open on the table. It would look as if he had just stepped out when he left.

Ch'o had no way of knowing if the Greek girl on the inspection team had found either of the messages in the cigarette box, let alone if she had passed them along or been able to arrange for help. It didn't really matter; he knew that his time at the plant was over. He'd only been kept on because the governor did not want to cause any problems before the inspection team came.

Tomorrow, Tak Ch'o would be fired. If he was extremely lucky, he would be stripped of his job and made a nonperson, allowed to scrounge his way back to his ancestors' village on the eastern side of the country.

If he was not extremely lucky—and Ch'o had never been a man who believed much in luck—he would be put in prison for the rest of his life.

Not because he had committed a crime or even because he had failed to do his job well. On the contrary, he was being persecuted because he had dared to tell the ministry that several trucks had been turned away from the gate because they did not come with the proper paperwork.

Ch'o hadn't even mentioned that the men in the trucks had thrown their barrels into a field along the highway. He had not said that the waste was from P'yŏngyang's hospitals. He had not made a guess about the threat it might pose to the villagers who farmed the field and drew their drinking water from shallow wells nearby; in truth that was difficult to assess precisely, and Ch'o would not make an estimate without a great deal of study. The fact that the number of birth defects in the region, long used for haphazard dumping, was significantly higher than elsewhere in the country, was alarming, but not necessarily relevant to this particular case, from a scientist's point of view.

Even so, Ch'o knew that simply writing the report would have severe consequences. It implicitly alleged all of these things, and implied that powerful men were not doing their jobs.

But reporting it was his duty. And so he did.

For a while, he naively believed that it would not have dire consequences.

No, he'd always known. What he hadn't known was that he would be willing to leave Korea behind. Not to preserve his life, but to help his countrymen. The IAEA people would help him get the word out, and there would be a crackdown.

The officials, of course, would deny it. But then, quietly, the material would be picked up and dumped, the countryside scoured for similar transgressions. Party members would be reminded that they must follow the proper procedures—procedures Ch'o had helped write— or face dire consequences.

That was the best he could hope for.

Assured that everything was ready, Ch'o closed the door on his apartment and went outside, walking swiftly down the street to the shed where he had left the bicycle two days before. The bike lay against the brown grass where he had left it, wet now from the day's intermittent rain. Ch'o picked it up, tried in vain to dry the seat with the sleeve of his coat, then gave up and got on. He had a long way to pedal—more than seventy kilometers—and five hours to do it.

No matter. If he missed the rendezvous—if, as he feared, no one showed up—he would continue on. He would pedal south all the way to the border area, then find someone to help him across. Others had done it.

The wind blew a fresh spray of rain in his face. Even Nature was against him, he thought, as he started to pedal.

27

James Sonjae stepped through the Customs area, joining a surge of people flooding into the reception terminal at Incheon International Airport. He looked around at the waiting limo drivers, unsure whether Ferguson would send someone for him or meet him himself. When he didn't find his name on a placard, he began walking around the hall, scanning slowly and expecting at any moment to spot Ferguson's grin and raised eyebrows.

He didn't, though.

For nearly half an hour he walked from one end of the terminal to the other, unsure exactly where to wait. He felt off balance, his equilibrium disturbed by the cacophony of sounds around him. The chatter sounded both familiar and strange at the same time.

Though born in America, Sonjae had been taught Korean as a child and had used it a great deal at home and with close relatives. Over the past two decades, he'd practiced it less and less; with the exception of some old people he looked in on for his church every few weeks, he rarely used it these days. The Incheon terminal overloaded his ears, overwhelming him with a strange sense of déjà vu and eliciting all sorts of memories and associations— grandparents visiting when he was a child, distant relatives tearfully saying good-bye at Dulles. He struggled to keep his mind focused on the present, looking for Ferguson.

Sonjae tried to have Ferguson paged, but found it impossible to correctly decipher the operator's instructions. Finally he gave up and found a place to sit where he could gather his wits and decide what to do next.

Thirty seconds after he plopped down, Bob Ferguson hopped over the row of seats and sat down beside him.

"Had a good tour of the airport?"

"Ferg."

"Were you making sure you weren't followed?" Ferguson asked. "Because you know, you walked back and forth about twenty million times."

"A dozen. I wasn't followed," said Sonjae defensively.

"You're right. At least I think you are," said Ferguson. He pointed to the small carry-on bag perched on Sonjae's knees. "That all you got?"

"I didn't know what to pack."

"Don't worry. It's all you need." Ferguson grabbed the handle of the bag. "Come on. I have a limo waiting for us outside."

Ferguson led him out to the drop-off area, where the driver he'd hired was arguing vehemently with someone. The man raised his hand to pop the trunk with his key fob, not even bothering to interrupt the argument.

"What are they saying?" Ferguson said as they climbed into the car.

"Damned if I know."

Ferguson laughed. "Some translator you are."

Sonjae flushed. "I, uh . . . I'm out of practice."

Ferguson looked at his friend's face, tired and worn. Just as well that he'd decided to send him back tomorrow.

"You all right?" Ferguson asked.

"I'm OK. What are we doing?"

"Depends on whether you're going to fall asleep on me or not."

"I'm awake."

"Good. Then let's go barhopping."

28

"Iron Bird One, this is Van. Rankin, you hear me?"

"Iron Bird One. Rankin."

"Cinderella has gone over the line."

"Roger that," said Rankin. The message meant that the plane with Thera on it had crossed out of North Korean air space. She was safe. "We are zero-five from Potato Field."

"Be advised there is a flight of MiGs coming from the south on a routine patrol. Stand by for exact position and vectors."

Rankin turned to the pilot and tapped his headset, making sure he'd heard.

The helicopter bucked as they passed over the coastline. They hit a squall of rain head-on. Water shot against the bubble canopy as if bucket after bucket were being thrown against them.

"Rain's bitchin'," said the pilot, struggling to hold the small chopper on course. "Sixty seconds."

Rankin tensed. The rain made their infrared sensors almost useless. If anyone had seen or heard them the night before, a good hunk of the North Korean army might be waiting for them.

Buffeted by yet another gust, the helicopter tipped hard to the right. The pilot overcorrected, pitching the craft so low the skid bumped against the ground. The next thing Rankin knew they were down, stopped, in one piece and without crashing.

He jumped into the downpour, running toward the wall near the road as he had the day before.

"See anything?" he barked into the squad radio as he reached the stones.

A chorus of no's jammed the circuit.

Sergeant Barren cursed somewhere behind him.

Rankin leapt over the wall, landing in a ditch at the side of the road. He sunk in water up to his thigh. Climbing out, he pulled his binoculars from his tac vest and looked down the road. The glasses fogged; even when he cleared them, all he could see was rain and blackness.

It was two minutes to midnight.

29

ON THE ROAD SOUTH OF KAWKSAN, NORTH KOREA

Tak Ch'o hunkered against the handlebars, fighting to stay upright as the wind pushed against him. He'd stopped looking at his watch more than an hour ago when it became obvious that he wouldn't make it to the field by midnight. Now he simply pedaled, determined to get there as soon as he could, determined that he would at least accomplish the first stage of his journey. If he made it to the field at all, Ch'o thought, he would make it to South Korea and freedom as well.

Headlights appeared behind him. Taken off guard, Ch'o felt his entire body freeze. He tumbled into the road, a truck looming down on him.

Everything blurred together——the rain, the bicycle, his fear.

The truck veered to the right, crashing over the bicycle but missing Ch'o. As the vehicle disappeared into the raging night, a scream erupted from the scientist's belly, a curse that had been years in coming. He raged against the rain and fate, then, the yell still emptying his lungs, hurled himself forward.

30

DUE SOUTH OF KAWKSAN, NORTH KOREA

"Car or a truck," said Rankin, spotting the headlights as they came up over the hill. "This may be it. Hang tight."

He hopped back over the wall to wait. The vehicle came forward at a steady pace, no more than twenty-five miles an hour.

It was a truck, an army vehicle.

So there was a defector, Rankin thought. Hopefully he was important enough to justify the risk they'd taken.

Rankin started to get up but then stopped, realizing the vehicle wasn't slowing down.

"Shit," someone said as it drove past.

"What the hell we do now, Stephen?" said Sergeant Barren. He might just as well have spit the words from his mouth.

Rankin checked his watch. It was oh-thirty, a half hour past midnight.

"All right. Load 'em up," he said. He leaned over the wall, gazing up and down the road. The whole mission was a washout, in every sense of the word.

Had Thera screwed up? Had the people in Washington? Had something happened to the defector?

Most likely, no one would ever know. No one would

care, probably, unless something else screwed up—if the choppers couldn't make it back because of the weather.

A good possibility, Rankin thought, giving one last glance toward the road. The he turned and ran for the Little Bird.

Inside, he pulled off his sodden campaign hat and looked at the pilot.

"Ready, Skip?"

"Let 'er rock."

The rotor blades began churning above his head. The other helicopter took off first, twisting backward toward the ship they were supposed to rendezvous with to the south.

Rankin held on as the Little Bird bucked forward, stuttering in the wind. The wall loomed in front of them, suddenly taller than it was in real life, a trick of the shadows dancing in the rain. As Rankin stared at it, something seemed to shoot across their path.

"Flip the searchlight on," Rankin told the pilot.

"Searchlight?"

"I think there was something back by the wall, near the road."

Silently, the pilot complied, circling back.

There was nothing by the wall. Rankin had seen an optical illusion, a shadow thrown by the helicopter, but further down the road, a tiny figure appeared, waving its hands.

"There," he told the pilot, pointing. "There. Let's get him."

ACT 3

The wide, dark road leads to hell,
The narrow to Buddha's Heaven.

—from "The Seventh Princess,"
traditional Korean song for the dead

1

"I gotta be me . . . I just gotta be me," bellowed Ferguson, smiling at Sonjae as the karaoke music track pounded out the Frank Sinatra track sans vocal. It was almost four a.m.; they'd been at this for hours, and it was time to call it a night.

Past time: Sonjae's eyelids looked like disheveled bedcovers sagging toward the floor.

Ferg reached over and killed the machine midsong.

"Ready for some rest?"

"Sounds good," mumbled the former FBI agent. "Real good."

Ferguson gave him a thumbs-up. Despite hitting nearly every bar and karaoke joint within five miles of Science Industries, they hadn't come across the secretary he'd stolen the ID tag from the night before. Nor had he seen any Science Industries employees, or at least none who had admitted to Sonjae that they worked there.

A disappointment.

One of the managers came over as they were getting ready to leave and began peppering Sonjae with questions.

"He's asking if everything was OK," Sonjae told Ferguson. His Korean had started to improve, though he was a long way from being comfortable with it.

"Perfect." Ferguson handed over his credit card. "Except, Sinatra was off-key."

"I don't think I can translate that exactly," said Sonjae.

"The hotel's a couple of blocks away," Ferguson told him. "You'll be snoozing in a few minutes."

"Great." Sonjae shook his head, trying to clear it. "What do you have in mind for tomorrow?"

"We need to make a few phone calls, visit an apartment building, and look for nosey neighbors. Then I have you booked on an eleven a.m. flight to the States."

"I'm going home?" Sonjae asked as they walked up to the limo. The driver was sleeping in his seat.

"I need you to deliver a few things for me."

"Like what?"

"Dirt, mostly."

THE HART SENATE OFFICE BUILDING, WASHINGTON, D.C.

"The president may already have the votes he needs," Hannigan told Senator Tewilliger and Josh Franklin, the assistant secretary of defense. "My count shows the treaty will pass by two votes."

The senator nodded. There was one thing you needed to be able to do in Washington to succeed—count—and Hannigan was a genius at counting.

"Even if we lose this one vote—admittedly it's a big vote and I'm not ready to give up on it yet," the senator told the assistant secretary of defense, "but even if we lose it, we're not going to give up. Korea is the fulcrum of

Asia, and it will be for the next ten years. We can't lower our guard against North Korea."

"I absolutely agree," said Franklin. "I was afraid you wouldn't. I got the impression in New Hampshire that the president was convincing you to change your mind."

"The president can be very persuasive," said Tewilliger, "but he hasn't persuaded me on this."

"You haven't made a statement against yet."

Tewilliger glanced across his office at Hannigan.

"Going public in a speech might actually do more harm than good," said Hannigan. "Right now, McCarthy isn't exactly sure what he's up against. He's courting the senator, spending time with him rather than with other people who might actually be persuaded."

Franklin nodded.

"Right before the vote, that's the time to declare your intentions," said Hannigan, turning to the senator. They'd actually discussed this several times, but the aide made it seem as if this was a new idea. "When you can have some impact."

And when the media might actually be paying attention. A speech, a press conference, an appearance on the *News Hour* and one of the Sunday talk shows—that would all come. But only if he waited until the exact moment when the rest of the world caught up with the issue.

"Do you think the North Korean regime is as weak as people are claiming it is?" Tewilliger asked Franklin, changing the subject.

"I wouldn't trust that," said Franklin. "That sort of intelligence seems to go in cycles. Besides, if they are weak, that's an argument for taking a stronger stand."

"Invasion?" asked Hannigan.

"If it comes to that."

"Let's hope it doesn't," said Tewilliger. "I think we can be firm without necessarily going to war."

"Hopefully," said Franklin.

"So let's not give up," said the senator, getting up from his desk.

"No, of course not." Franklin got the hint and glanced at his watch. "I better get going. I still have a few more stops to make on the Hill."

"Keep in touch, Josh," said Tewilliger, showing him to the door.

"What do you think?" he asked Hannigan after closing the door.

"I think he wants to be defense secretary in a Tewilliger cabinet."

"Probably." The senator chuckled. "You don't think he's a McCarthy plant, do you?"

"Nah."

"He was with him in New Hampshire. They seem reasonably close."

"Franklin goes back to the last administration. I think he's being honest."

"Mmmm."

In Tewilliger's opinion, McCarthy was easily devious enough to send one of his people out to stalk for opinions, pretending to be opposed to the treaty to find out what he was really thinking. Probably Franklin was truly against the treaty, Tewilliger decided . . . but only probably.

"You know, if the treaty were to be defeated, I doubt anyone would get a better one," said Hannigan, getting up to go back to his own work.

"Probably not," conceded the senator. "Fortunately, that's not really our problem."

"Not yet."

"The future will take care of itself," said Tewilliger. "Don't be so pessimistic."

"I'm not," said Hannigan, closing the door.

3

ABOARD THE USS *PELELIU,* IN THE YELLOW SEA

The USN LHA-5 *Peleliu* was an assault ship, a veritable floating city that could deliver an entire marine expeditionary unit ashore in a matter of hours. Looking like an old-style aircraft carrier, it had enough hovercraft, airplanes, and helicopters to re-create a good portion of the Korean War's famous landing at Inchon, a bold stroke by 261 ships that broke the back of North Korea's army in 1951.

To Rankin, though, the USS *Peleliu* was a claustrophobic tin can that smelled like a floating gym locker. The navy people had strange names for things, and funny places to eat. The idea of being surrounded by water was not very comforting. And it was tough to sleep with the weird noises that echoed through the ship: bells, intercom whistles, and metallic groans that half-convinced him the whole damn thing was being ripped in two.

The Little Birds had come here after refueling aboard a frigate about a hundred miles off the Korean Coast. A CIA debriefer was due out any minute to meet Rankin and their "guest," who'd said very little before going to sleep earlier that morning.

"Helo's landing now, sir," said the ensign assigned to liaison with Rankin. "If you follow me, you can meet your party on deck. You'll want to watch those knee knockers."

Knee knockers. What the hell were they?

Rankin followed the woman out to the flight deck, lifting

his feet carefully over the metal thresholds—knee knockers—that came up from the deck to make the doors watertight.

A cold wind punched him in the face as he stepped outside. He turned to the side and was almost knocked down as a pair of marines passed quickly inside. The ensign grabbed hold of him and, smiling, pointed him in the direction of the helicopter as it landed.

The chopper was a bright blue Sikorsky, civilian, leased especially for the purpose of bringing the interrogators to the ship. The pilot was a CIA contract employee who had retired from the navy and was used to shipboard landings; he'd put down marine MH-53s on this very same deck. The helo swooped in, hovered for half a second then settled gently on its wheels.

The rear door opened, and two men in light jackets hopped out, holding their heads down as they ran out from under the still-rotating blades.

The helicopter lifted off before they reached Rankin.

"You Colonel Rankin?" said the first man.

Rankin, who was wearing civilian clothes, snorted, but decided not to correct him. "Yeah, I'm Rankin."

"You got a prisoner?"

"He's not a prisoner; he's a defector."

"Yeah, that's what I meant. I'm Gabe Jiménez. This is John Rhee. He's a Korean language specialist."

"OK."

"Can we get goin'? I'm freezin' my nuts off here," said Jiménez.

"Yeah, let's go," Rankin said, turning to the ensign to show them the way.

The touch seemed to come from the other side of the world. It pulled Tak Ch'o from a deep sleep, almost as if he had been ripped from the womb. He woke startled, unsure where he was.

"Sir, there are some people who would like to see you,"

said the young man standing over him. "I brought some tea. I can get you some breakfast."

Ch'o stared at the sailor.

What had happened to the IAEA people? Why was he on a military ship?

"I have some fresh clothes, sir," said the man. He pointed to a set of Western-style khaki pants and shirt on the desk. "If they're not your size we'll get you some. Some slippers and socks as well."

Ch'o nodded slowly.

"Are you all right, sir?" asked the sailor. "Sir?"

"Yes." Ch'o's voice sounded thin and weak, even to him.

"I'll just be outside when you're ready."

The sailor, who knew nothing about the Korean scientist except that he was to be treated with the greatest respect, smiled and went out to wait for him in the narrow hall outside the cabin.

Ch'o put his hands on the clothes. As he did, a heavy sense of doom gripped him.

What had he expected? He thought the girl would be there, the other scientists he had met. Not soldiers.

He'd seen the world; he knew America wasn't in charge of everything. They didn't run the IAEA or the UN.

But here they were.

What should he do? All his life, Ch'o had heard that the Americans were evil incarnate, the enemy not just of his country but of the entire world. And now they had him.

They'd been kind last night. But of course they would be—it was a trick.

The enormity of what he had done paralyzed Ch'o. He'd always been a logical man, but now his emotions overwhelmed him. He thought of his ancestors' graves, never to be tended again.

Their spirits will turn their backs on me, he thought. I've shamed them and cut myself off from my family.

He sat back on the bed, unable to move. After a few minutes, the sailor outside cleared his throat.

"Sir?"

Ch'o stared at the wall in front of him. Perhaps if he stared long enough, he would slip into a hole where nothing he did mattered anymore.

Rankin found Ch'o sitting motionless on his cot, exactly as the sailor had described.

"Sir? Mr. Ch'o? It's Stephen Rankin. I'm the guy that picked you up last night."

Ch'o didn't respond. He barely heard the words.

"These are some friends of mine. They can help you," said Rankin, gesturing over his shoulder. "All right?"

It was like talking to a wall.

John Rhee, the Korean language specialist, took a try, telling the man that he was among friends and would feel better after he had something to eat. His valuable information would not be wasted, added Rhee; he would be rewarded by the U.S. government.

Ch'o winced.

"We're friends," said Rhee. "We can help you."

Ch'o shook his head. That was the most Rhee got out of him.

"Did you have a doctor look at him?" asked Rhee outside the cabin.

"Last night," Rankin told him. "He was tired and cold, but he said he'd be fine."

"You better have him take another look. Guy's catatonic."

"Yeah," said Rankin.

"We can break down his resistance," said Jiménez. "Soften him up and—"

"You aren't breaking anything down," Rankin snapped. "This guy is a defector, not a prisoner. Something's wrong with him. He's sick or he's in shock or something."

"Relax, Colonel. All I mean is, we'll get him to talk to us. I've dealt with this before."

"Leave him alone until I tell you different," said Rankin, going to find the doctor.

4

THE WHITE HOUSE, WASHINGTON, D.C.

"The defector's name is Tak Ch'o," Corrigan told Corrine and Slott over the scrambled conference line. "Scientist in the nuclear weapons program for at least twenty-five years. Expert on handling by-products and, when he was younger, was probably involved in extracting weapons-grade plutonium."

"What do you mean, 'probably'?" asked Corrine.

"There are some significant gaps in our knowledge of the North Korean weapons program," said Slott. "Someone like Ch'o, who wasn't in that first top tier a few decades ago, we're just not going to have a lot of information about what he did then. Not readily."

"We're still digging in," added Corrigan. "This is just a preliminary report on him from Thomas Ciello, our analyst guy."

"What's Ch'o done lately?" Slott asked.

"He seems to have been doing a lot of things with waste and by-products. His name pops up in a couple of places where there's concern about radiation leaks," said Corrigan. "We have intercepts going back to the 1990s."

"Do they have anything to do with a bomb project?" asked Corrine. She reached for the yogurt container at the far end of her desk, her belated lunch.

"Doesn't look like it," said Corrigan.

"We'll know more when we debrief him," said Slott. "Even if he's no longer involved in the weapons program, what he knows of what happened in it would be invaluable. And of course he can tell us what's going on at the P'yŏngan Province site."

"Is this going to affect Thera?" Corrine asked.

"As a precaution, we should remove her from the program," said Slott. "But this was worth it," he added. "Ch'o is potentially an important prize. We'll recruit someone else to check the tags now that they're planted."

"The North Koreans haven't reacted yet," added Corrigan. "The NSA is monitoring it. Ch'o hasn't said anything yet. He seems a bit overwhelmed by the ordeal."

"How so?" asked Corrine.

Slott explained that it was not unusual for defectors to have second thoughts or even suddenly freeze once they escaped; as many as twenty-five percent suffered post-traumatic stress.

"We have a psychologist en route," said Slott. "We'll let him unwind on the ship awhile, then fly him to the States. It may be a few days."

"Is our Seoul office involved?"

"No," said Corrigan. "I'm keeping the First Team operation departmentalized."

"I think that's a good idea." Corrine wasn't sure what to say about Ferguson and his suspicions. She'd have to at some point, but at the moment she wasn't sure exactly what to say. She changed the subject. "Do we have any more information on the South Korean plutonium?"

"Nothing new," said Corrigan.

"OK, then," she took a quick spoonful of yogurt. Her computer's automated scheduler beeped at her; she was due at a meeting in five minutes. "Anything else?"

"No," said Slott, signing off.

S lott ignored the blinking yellow light indicating he had another call as he hung up from the conference call. Corrine Alston's remark about his decision not to tell Seoul had seemed offhand at the time, but now as he thought about it, he wondered at her tone.

Would she have suggested that Seoul be kept out?

Never mind that he had already made the decision, or that he had his own doubts about Ken Bo. To have Corrine telling him what to do in an area that did not involve Special Demands—that was just too far. Too, too far.

Bo's BS theory was beside the point.

Or a separate point, anyway.

Was she telling him what to do? Or was he just being overly prickly?

The latter. *But . . .*

But . . .

Should he tell her what Bo was up to?

It wasn't her business, was it? Not yet, anyway. Bo had only said that to him.

He'd make it clear what was going on when it was relevant. When he was sure. Or rather, when there was more information about the plutonium.

In the meantime . . .

He reached for the blinking button.

5

DAEJEON, SOUTH KOREA

Ferguson and Sonjae stepped out of the elevator into a brightly colored hallway on the thirty-seventh floor of the high-rise apartment building. Sonjae paused for a moment, gathering himself.

"Nah, just jump right in," said Ferguson, leaning in front of him and knocking on the door.

A middle-aged woman pulled open the door, a perplexed look on her face.

"Excuse us for bothering you this early, ma'am," said Sonjae in Korean. "We were looking for Professor Kang Hwan."

"Hwan?"

"A friend of ours," said Ferguson in English.

"There's no Kang Hwan here," said the woman. "We live here."

"What is it?" asked a man in a business suit, coming around the corner behind the woman. "What is going on?"

While Sonjae struggled to explain that he was looking for Hwan, Ferguson strolled across the hall to the next door. He knocked twice, then stood waiting with a big smile on his face.

A twenty-something woman answered.

"I was trying to find a friend of mine, Dr. Kang Hwan," said Ferguson in English.

"Hwan?"

"Yes. Do you know him? I'm from the States."

Her face began to cloud.

"Problem with my English?" asked Ferguson.

"He . . . He's dead."

Ferguson feigned surprise. The woman, whose English was fairly good, said he had passed away a few months before.

"How did he die? When?" said Ferguson.

The woman shook her head.

"He was young."

The woman started to close her door. "How did he die?" said Ferguson, putting his hand out to keep the door from closing.

By now, Sonjae had extracted himself from the couple who'd taken Hwan's apartment and come over.

"Is there anything you can tell us about our friend?" he asked in Korean.

The young woman shook her head and pushed against the door. Ferguson let it close.

"Suicide is a great embarrassment in Korea," said Sonjae.

"It's not big in the U.S., either," said Ferguson, going to the next door.

There was no answer; after four or five knocks, they moved to the last one on the floor.

Four knocks later, Ferguson and Sonjae were just about to give up when the door creaked open. A lady about the age of Sonjae's aunt peeked through the crack and asked what they wanted.

"Hello," said Sonjae. "We were looking for information about our friend, Kang Hwan, who used to live here."

The old woman frowned at him, starting to close the door.

"It's an important matter," said Sonjae. "This man is from the United States. He wants to make sure that Dr. Kang Hwan's memory is honored properly. Because of the circumstance of his death."

"What about it?" said the old woman.

"It was . . . The circumstances were not the best."

"Suspicious," said the woman.

"Yes," said Sonjae. "Could we talk about it?"

"I was going out."

"It won't take long," said Sonjae.

"We'll buy her some breakfast," said Ferguson, who was following maybe a tenth of the conversation.

Sonjae translated the offer.

"Just come in," said the woman instead.

Kang Hwan had kept to himself mostly, working late and rising early. His neighbor had spoken to him on average once a week, but most of these conversations were about simple things.

"He had great respect for his parents," said the woman. "They were both dead, but he brought them up in conversation often."

"Was he sick?"

The woman shrugged. His suicide had baffled her as well.

"Who claimed the body?" asked Sonjae.

"People from work." She shook her head. "Terrible."

———

O ne thing that seemed odd about it," Sonjae told Ferguson as they descended in the elevator. "He really loved his parents."

"That's odd?"

"He was an only child, right?"

"Right."

"Who will honor their memory if he dies? No one to make offerings—"

"You're assuming he's religious."

"Maybe. But your ancestors . . ." Sonjae explained how there would be a shrine in the home where offerings were made to make sure the deceased passed to heaven.

"If he killed himself, there would be no one to perform those duties," said Sonjae.

"Yeah, but he's a scientist. He probably doesn't believe in that," said Ferguson.

"I don't know. It's a very powerful pull."

"Not against depression."

"You're assuming he's depressed. His neighbor was surprised. He was relatively young, in good health. He had no reason to commit suicide."

"Maybe." Ferguson could think of plenty of reasons. And as far as being in good health, someone who spoke to him once a week wouldn't know.

Someone who spoke to him many times a week might not know either.

"The only circumstance I can think of that would make it all right," said Sonjae, "would be if he wanted to avoid bringing shame to his ancestors, but there was no note."

"She said that?"

"Yes."

"That seems odd."

"Who would he leave it to?" said Sonjae.

"People at work."

"Maybe he wasn't that close to them. Besides, what's he going to say?"

"Good-bye?"

The doors opened. Ferguson thought about who he would say good-bye to.

Maybe Sonjae was right. What would be the point?

"Breakfast?" Ferguson asked as they walked toward the car.

"Coffee, and lots of it."

"Let's see what we can find."

Fortified by several cups of strong coffee, Ferguson and Sonjae drove to the train station and took a train to Seoul and then the airport. Once the ticket was squared away, they found a phone booth near the entrance to the departure gates.

"She's a secretary," said Ferguson, handing Sonjae the number of the woman whose card he had stolen.

"She'll know I'm not a native Korean speaker."

"Yeah, be straight with her. Tell her you're an American colleague trying to figure out what happened to him. Then we can go from there."

That wasn't exactly being straight with her, Sonjae thought as he began punching the numbers written on the small card.

"Annyeonghaseyo," he said to the operator at Science Industries when she picked up the line. "Good morning. Can I have Bae Eun please?"

The line buzzed and clicked as he was put through. Sonjae's brain was still having trouble translating the words.

"Who is this?" demanded an angry male voice.

Taken off guard, Sonjae gave the name he'd made up and repeated that he was looking for Bae Eun.

"Why are you calling Miss Bae?" said the man, not mollified in the least.

Sonjae wanted to say it was a personal matter, but the words wouldn't come. He stuttered, then started to apologize, hoping the words would somehow work themselves into his mouth. *"Sagwa deuryyeoyo . . .* I really apologize . . . I—"

"Where are you calling from?" demanded the man.

Sonjae hung up the phone.

"What's up?" asked Ferguson.

Sonjae explained what had happened.

Ferguson glanced at the card where he had written the phone number. "Try changing the last two digits. See if we can get another extension and have them transfer us."

Sonjae got a message that he had dialed a nonworking number. Then he tried an old Bureau trick, dialing in and asking for Mr. Kim, essentially asking for Mr. Smith.

"One minute," said the operator.

Sonjae found himself talking to a jocular young man who laughed when he heard that there had been a mistake and that Sonjae really wanted Miss Bae Eun.

"Everyone wants Eun," said the man. "She's very pretty."

"I think so, too," said Sonjae.

"Are you her boyfriend?"

"A relative," he said quickly. "But how do I get her?"

"Wait, I'll connect you."

"What is the extension in case I lose you?"

The man laughed as if this were the funniest joke he'd heard all week. "I won't lose you. But it is . . . Let me see . . . secretary section two, four-four-seven-eight. Wait. I will forward the call."

A second later, Sonjae found himself talking to the same gruff man he'd been speaking to earlier.

"You had better turn yourself in and cooperate," he told Sonjae.

Sonjae glanced up at Ferguson. "Same guy," he said, holding his hand over the phone. "Wants me to turn myself in."

"Why?" prompted Ferguson.

Sonjae put the phone back to his ear. "Turn myself in, why?"

"Where are you?" said the man, softening his tone ever so slightly.

"I'm in Daejeon," Sonjae lied. "What sort of trouble is she in?"

"You're lying to me!" The man exploded. Obviously he had a caller-ID device or some other way of seeing the phone number Sonjae was calling from.

Caught in a stupid lie. He should have said Seoul from the start.

"What trouble is Eun in?" said Sonjae. "I am her . . . a cousin."

"Where are you?"

Sonjae hung up.

"Call the first guy back and tell him that you missed your cousin," said Ferguson. "See if you can get the extension of someone who knows her."

"Not Kang Hwan?"

"If you ask for the scientist, they'll automatically be suspicious. It's more natural to be looking for her."

Sonjae nodded. This sort of thing used to be second nature to him. Was it the jet lag, his language difficulties, or was he just getting old?

"It's me again," he told Mr. Kim a few minutes later. He claimed that there had been no answer at Bae Eun's extension. This was a real problem, Sonjae said, because his cousin was supposed to pick him up at the airport; he was just in from America.

"America. Oh, you live in L.A.?"

"No."

"New York?"

"Yes, New York," said Sonjae.

Kim gave him some instructions on how to deal with taxi drivers and how to get a train to Daejeon, then put him through to a woman whose office was next to Bae Eun's so Sonjae could leave a message.

"I'm looking for Bae Eun," said Sonjae, his Korean growing smoother as his cover story became more polished. "I'm her cousin from America and—"

The woman who'd answered the phone burst into tears.

Sonjae asked her what was wrong. The woman told him she couldn't talk.

"But my cousin—"

"They're watching," said the woman, and then she hung up.

Ferguson had already guessed what had happened: The security people had realized that her card had been used to gain access to the building. The card readers hadn't seemed that sophisticated, but it wouldn't take all that much to simply record reads.

He didn't explain to Sonjae. Instead, he had him make one more call to Science Industries.

"Ask for Mr. Park's office. See what happens. If you get a secretary, ask when he's usually there. Then let's get out of here. They probably have someone on their way here right now."

THE WHITE HOUSE, WASHINGTON, D.C.

Corrine's secretary, Teri Gatins, segregated her phone messages into three main piles: important, really important, and obscenely important. Messages in those categories were placed on the top of her computer monitor, an old-style CRT.

Messages in two other categories were placed on the ledge between the monitor and the keyboard: personal, and no idea.

Josh Franklin fell into the latter category, primarily because he wouldn't tell Teri what he was calling about, a fact the secretary noted on the pink slip with several exclamation marks.

Remembering their conversation about Korea, Corrine pushed the message to the head of the line and called Franklin back.

"This is Josh."

"This is Corrine Alston, Mr. Franklin. What can I do for you?"

"For starters, call me Josh," he said. "Mr. Franklin's my dad. I was wondering . . ."

He paused. Corrine stopped sorting through the messages, waiting for Franklin to continue.

"Maybe we could have dinner," he said finally.

"Dinner?"

"Just, uh . . . I wanted to hear your thoughts on Korea. The treaty—legally enforcing it, which I thought might be a problem. Just informal thoughts."

"I really don't have any thoughts," said Corrine.

"Oh," he said.

He sounded so dejected Corrine felt sorry for him. Then she remembered him sitting near her in the president's limo: handsome, earnest, a nice smell.

And nearly fifteen years her senior.

But that wasn't a big difference by Washington standards. Not in the right context.

"I'm not doing anything for dinner tonight," she told him. "If that's really what you're asking."

"Yeah. That'd be great." He sounded like a teenager, surprised and happy.

"Let's pick a place to meet."

Franklin suggested a Tex-Mex place not far from the Pentagon. He was waiting when Corrine got there, sipping a Beefeater martini. Corrine ordered a glass of the house chardonnay.

"You're really going to want a beer with dinner," said Franklin. His tie was still knotted at the collar of his gray suit. "Goes better with the food."

"I don't know about that," said Corrine.

"This place isn't too informal for you, is it?"

"No, it's fine," said Corrine. She glanced around at the soft-hued walls and granite tabletops.

"In D.C., I never know whether someone might be a foodie or not," said Franklin. "Where I grew up, food was just food; this would pass for fancy."

"Where did you grow up?"

"Idaho," said Franklin.

"And you like Tex-Mex?"

"I love the spices."

They traded innocuous small talk for a few more minutes, both sipping from their drinks. Franklin's nervousness, not far from the surface, added to his charm. It made him seem more real.

He told Corrine that he'd come from a small town in Idaho, was an only child, still had a house there he never went to. His parents owned a ranch. Small by local standards, it sounded immense to Corrine.

Along the way he mentioned that he'd been divorced, no kids. Didn't work out.

He quickly moved on to other topics.

When he spoke about hunting and hiking his voice hit a different pitch; he was more relaxed, not shy and anxious anymore. Corrine liked that.

Their dinners came. Corrine had ordered a fish dish in a lime sauce; it was a little overcooked.

"See I told you not to order that," Franklin said as she inspected it.

"Did you?" She was annoyed by his tone, but hid it.

"This steak is great. Want a taste?"

"No, thanks."

"So, Korea," said Franklin.

"I really don't have much of an opinion on Korea."

"Well, it's a very important place these days. As Senator Tewilliger was saying, it'll be the fulcrum of Asia for the next decade."

"Isn't that an overstatement?"

Corrine nibbled at her fish as Franklin held forth on why it wasn't. The tone he'd used when suggesting she'd ordered the wrong entree was back. He was earnest, but he was strident as well.

Not for me, she thought to herself, with the sort of sharp finality a judge's gavel might signal dismissing a case.

"Do you think the treaty will pass?" he asked finally.

"I really couldn't say. I don't watch Congress really."

"Not even on this?"

"Well, if the president asks me to do something, then I do."

"I got the impression the other day that you were really involved."

"Not really."

"You disagree with me, but you don't want to say that," said Franklin. "About the treaty . . . You think it's a good idea."

"I don't have a position on the treaty one way or another."

"Hmmph," said Franklin, not believing her. "I guess I just don't trust North Korea."

"I don't know that I do, either."

"Hmmph," he said again.

The waiter arrived to ask if they wanted anything for dessert.

"Try the flan," suggested Franklin.

"I think I'll have some of the cheesecake."

"Flan's better."

"Just cheesecake, thanks," said Corrine, handing the menu back to the waiter.

ABOARD THE USS *PELELIU,* IN THE YELLOW SEA

"You appear in good health, Mr. Ch'o," said the doctor. "Your blood pressure is a little high."

Ch'o wanted to tell him that he was in perfect health, but his tongue wouldn't move.

The doctor packed up his stethoscope and blood-pressure cup.

"I can give you a pill for anxiety," said the doctor. "It might make you feel more at ease. I think you're just— It was probably quite an ordeal coming here. You're still not over it."

Ch'o couldn't bring himself to say anything. He simply couldn't talk. He remained motionless on the bed.

"Do you want the pill? It's very safe."

With the greatest effort, Ch'o shook his head.

"No?" said the doctor.

No, thought Ch'o, shaking his head again. No devil poison. You'll have to kill me yourself.

The doctor found Rankin and the CIA people standing like bookends, arms folded and backs against the bulkhead a short distance from the cabin.

"It looks a lot like post-traumatic stress, something along those lines," said the doctor. "What happened to him?"

"I'm not sure," said Rankin. "He wanted to be rescued from North Korea."

"This happens," said Jiménez. "Let me try talking to him."

"No," said Rankin, putting out his hand to bar the way.

"What do you mean, no?"

"I don't want to spook him worse than he's spooked now."

"He can't get much worse."

"Pushing him around's not going to help us."

"I'm only going to ask him some questions. Relax."

"We have to go slow. I've seen people like this. It doesn't do any good to push them."

"You've been in combat, Colonel?" said Jiménez.

"Yeah, I've been in combat," Rankin told him. "And I'm not a colonel."

Jiménez scowled but said nothing.

"I agree with you," the doctor told Rankin. "I'd go very, very easy on him. I offered him a pill for anxiety, but he shook his head."

"Give it to me and I'll give it to him," said Jiménez.

"Absolutely not," said the doctor.

"We can go easy on him," said Rankin. "There's no rush."

"How do you know there's no rush?" said Jiménez. "If we don't talk to him, we don't know anything."

8

ALEXANDRIA, VIRGINIA

Corrine was just turning her car out of the parking lot when her cell phone rang.

"Sergeant Rankin wants to talk to you on a secure line," Corrigan told her. "He says it's pretty urgent. I can hook up a sat phone call."

Corrine had the phone in her pocketbook. She'd have to find a spot to pull over, a place where she could think.

"Can it wait a few minutes?" she asked.

"Not a problem."

"Can you call me in fifteen minutes at my office?"

"Perfect."

Exactly fifteen minutes later, out of breath, Corrine rushed into her office at the White House. Corrigan had set up the connection to the *Peleliu* and put her through as soon as she called.

"Sergeant Rankin?"

"Ma'am, sorry to bother you."

"It's not a bother, Stephen. What can I do?"

"Ch'o—the scientist we picked up—he's bugged out. Spooked. Like from shock, either from what he's seen or what he's gone through or just being here. I don't think the CIA debriefer really understands the situation," said Rankin.

"I heard that there's a psychologist on his way," said Corrine.

"Yeah. The shrink. But I had another idea," said Rankin. "It might be faster. Because, you know, we don't know if there's a time limit or something."

"What's that?"

"If we could get someone he already trusts."

"Who?"

"Thera."

"Did you talk to Slott about it?"

"Am I supposed to? Ferguson usually—"

"I'll take care of it," she said. "Don't worry."

9

INCHEON AIRPORT, SOUTH KOREA

Ferguson sat in the lounge area across from the phone Sonjae had used for a half hour, hoping someone might show up looking for them. But either he had missed them while he was getting Sonjae to the gate and aboard the plane, or they hadn't sent anyone.

Assuming it was the latter, the people Sonjae had called at Science Industries probably weren't connected with the government. The South Korean security forces were nothing if not efficient; they would have had the phone staked out by now.

Ferguson got up from his chair and stretched his arms, looking around nonchalantly, checking for a tail. No one seemed to be watching him, but he took a wide turn around the terminal anyway, moving back and forth, thoroughly checking his back.

Outside, he took a taxi to the city. As they were nearing downtown, he asked the driver in halting Korean if he could be dropped off at a park.

The driver obliged by leaving him at Tapgol Park, a tourist landmark. Ferguson got out and wandered near a tour guide, who was explaining the significance of the bronze relief on the outer wall.

"The historical protest movement known as March 1 began on these streets," said the guide, immediately catching Ferguson's attention. "The Korean people protested the Japanese occupation. Though Korean protest was nonviolent, the Japanese reaction was not. By early spring 1919, seven thousand five hundred Koreans were killed. At least fifty thousand were arrested. A great tragedy for my country."

Enlightened as to the significance of the name of Park's political party, Ferguson edged away from the tourists. He found a spot where he couldn't be overheard, took out his sat phone and called Corrine. By now it was after lunchtime here and close to midnight back in D.C.

She picked up her office phone on the first ring.

"Hey, Wicked Stepmother. Can you talk?"

"I'm in my office."

"That's a yes?"

"Yes."

"You sure you're a government employee? It's gotta be going on midnight, right?"

"Ferguson, what's going on?"

"I need you to meet a flight at Dulles tomorrow around five p.m. You'll see someone you know who'll have something for you."

"Someone I know?"

"Vaguely. Make sure you get to the airport on time."

"What's he bringing back?"

"You'll see when he gets there."

"What do you want me to do with it?"

"I'll talk to you tomorrow."

"Ferg, why don't you trust Slott?"

"Who says I don't?"

"*Ferg—*"

He killed the transmission.

10

After Korea, Japan was a vacation. Thera felt as if an immense block of concrete had been chiseled off her shoulders. She stayed next to Julie Svenson during the orientation tour of the waste treatment plant, joking about which of the dour-faced executives would ask them out at the reception planned that evening. They decided the most likely was a fish-faced man in his late forties who spoke of "mechanical containment systems" in the tones of a Baptist preacher.

Neto Evora, the Portuguese scientist who'd been flirting with her on and off since South Korea, jokingly berated her for avoiding him as the morning tour ended.

"We will have a proper party after the reception tonight," he told her. "We will celebrate our escape from the dour dominion known as the People's Democratic Republic."

He sounded so portentous that both women laughed. Evora told them that a number of nightclubs had already been scouted out; festivities would continue "till dawn or collapse."

"Collapse comes first," Julie said.

"With luck," said the scientist.

"He's cute," said Julie after he had left them. "Handsome. And he likes you."

"You think?"

Julie rolled her eyes. "If you play it right, he would be in the palm of your hand."

"Not my type."

"Does that matter?"

"Definitely."

They were on their way to lunch when Dr. Norkelus called Thera's name so sharply a shudder ran through her body. The grim look on his face seemed to foretell a serious scolding, and she braced herself for a tirade about misspellings in one of her reports, or perhaps a more serious warning about making fun of their hosts.

"Thera, please," he said, abruptly turning and walking from the caravan of trucks.

Norkelus reminded her of her parochial school principal, a Greek Orthodox priest who had run the elementary with an iron fist. Even now, two decades later, she remembered trembling as she walked down the hall to tell him her teacher had banished her from class for "being a Miss Chatty-Chat-Chat."

She couldn't remember the punishment. Probably sitting in his office the rest of the day. It seemed so trivial now, and yet so deadly then.

Paralyzing. Like the fear she'd felt in Korea as the mission got underway.

Fear was what your mind made of it; it wasn't necessarily proportional to the danger you were in.

"I'm very sorry. I'm very, very sorry," said Norkelus, turning around a few feet from the nearby building.

"Sorry?"

"Your mother . . . There's been a terrible accident just outside of Athens. She doesn't have long to live. The Red Cross has arranged an aircraft. One of the drivers will take you to the jet."

11

"Annyeonghaseyo," said Ferguson, bowing forward slightly at the waist. "Good afternoon. I am Ivan Manski, from the Russian State Federal Industries. I have an appointment to meet with the managing director."

It was a long run of Korean, and even though Ferguson had practiced it for nearly a half hour, his pronunciation was so spotty that the man at the reception desk blinked at him, unable to comprehend.

Ferguson reached into his pocket and took out a card. "Ivan Manski. Russian is my native language, but I can speak English. Perhaps is better than my Korean, no?"

The man took the business card and examined it. No matter how much attention he gave it, however, it was unlikely to mean much to him; the characters were all Cyrillic Russian.

"My office managed the appointment with your director, Mr. Ajaeng," said Ferguson.

The receptionist turned to his computer and keyed through several screens.

"Perhaps a mistake," the man told Ferguson in English. "Dr. Ajaeng does not have you scheduled."

Ferguson held out his hands, muttered a Russian curse, then told the man that the meeting had been set up more than two months before by the Russian trade ministry.

"Perhaps I should speak with Mr. Park," added Ferguson. "I think perhaps this would be better. We spoke informally when he was in Japan a few weeks ago. I was to say hello when I came."

The Korean flinched. "I'm not sure Mr. Park is in."

Ferguson knew that he was, since he'd seen the Mercedes arrive, but he didn't argue.

"Should I call embassy? I should call embassy," said Ferguson.

Confronted with the possibility that he might be insulting an important visitor who knew his multibillionaire boss, the man at the desk assured Ferguson that there was no problem and that someone would take him to see the managing director shortly.

After a brief phone conversation with the director's secretary—who knew nothing of the Russian either—the receptionist showed Ferguson to a seat nearby and went to fetch him a cup of tea. Within ten minutes, another young man came and escorted him down the hall. Taking the same set of stairs Ferguson had ducked into a few nights before, they went up the stairs to the third floor.

Ferguson knew it was possible the secretary's office was along here somewhere. If she saw him . . . Well, then she saw him. He'd play it by ear, depending on her reaction.

Ferguson was led to an office so small that his knees bumped against the front of the desk when he sat. He couldn't move the chair back any farther because it was already against the wall.

The male secretary began to quiz him about the appointment. Ferguson rolled out his Korean before switching to English, throwing in a little Russian for flavor. The man disappeared with his business card; ten minutes later he ushered Ferguson toward the managing director's office.

Dr. Ajaeng met him at the door, holding out his hand and greeting him as if he had been expecting him all along. The two men exchanged business cards, reading intently and then nodding deeply, as if the small white cards contained words from Confucius.

Dr. Ajaeng directed Ferguson to sit with him in the sitting area in front of his desk.

Though he was managing director of the company, Ajaeng's office was barely larger than the secretary's room. His desk was a simple wooden table whose polished surface gleamed from the overhead fluorescent light. There were a few small woodblock prints on the wall and a bookcase lined with pictures at the side of the room. The chairs were anything but plush.

Ferguson unzipped his small briefcase and took out his brochures, fanning them across the director's desk as if he were a real salesman on the make.

Printed on thick, glossy paper in bright colors, the catalogs showed a variety of instruments for measuring different processes and machine tolerances. As Dr. Ajaeng leafed through them respectfully, Ferguson took out another sheet, this one on plain paper, showing diagrams of canisters used for containing hazardous waste. The information on both handouts was in Russian and Korean.

"We do many things along these lines," he told Ajaeng, giving him the handout. "Custom work we can do. The price very cheap."

Ferguson leaned down to put his case on the floor. As he rose, he slipped two bugs under his chair.

"This is very nice material," said Ajaeng. "But we produce no waste."

"Oh," said Ferguson. Then he proceeded to ignore the statement. "Our shielding for gamma-ray applications is very diverse. We can handle any item, in any situation whatever."

"Our work has to do with industrial applications of gamma particles, but we do not generate them ourselves," said Dr. Ajaeng. "We are consultants."

"*Dah*, consultant," said Ferguson. He smiled. "We have products for alpha decay as well. With uranium—"

Ajaeng tensed. "What do you mean?"

"My English not good on tech-nik. Uranium and plutonium containment, processing as necessary."

Ajaeng stared at him. Ferguson knew that he had hit on something, but what exactly he wasn't sure.

"We have experts, if necessary, for hire," he said. "We have access to very big possibilities. Very big."

"Ah." The managing director rose. "I have another appointment now."

"Very sorry. *Annyeonghi jumuseyo*," he said.

"Yes, good-bye," said the director. Relieved to be so easily rid of his visitor, he had a look of a man who'd just had five hundred pounds lifted from his back.

"Perhaps I should say hello to Mr. Park before I leave," said Ferguson. "I would not insult him."

The managing director's expression changed once more.

"We have many mutual friends in Russia," continued Ferguson. "In the ministry and then of course Dechlov, with whom I believe he had done business."

The name clearly meant nothing to the managing director, but he nodded anyway.

"Just mention that I'm a friend," Ferguson added. "Take my card. And Dechlov. You know him?"

"Oh, yes."

"An interesting man, don't you think? Dechlov?"

"Dechlov. Very interesting."

Ferguson knew he'd been successful when he was followed out of the lot. He drove directly to the hotel where he'd rented a room as Manski, went upstairs and pretended to make some phone calls.

The great thing about posing as a Russian was that people naturally assumed the worst about you. So even if you came into a place as a seemingly legitimate businessman—as he did when he approached the managing director of Science Industries—they were utterly unsurprised when the conversation turned to less legitimate business.

Dropping the name of the most notorious Russian black-market arms dealer in Asia of the past decade didn't hurt either. Ajaeng didn't know it, but if Park had truly been interested in the weapons March 1 had tried to obtain, he or his people surely would.

Dechlov had been one of the most successful black-market arms dealers in Asia and the Middle East until just two years before, when an operation run by Ferguson rolled him up.

Literally.

The Russian mobsters who thought he had double-crossed them decapitated his body and rolled the torso in an Iranian rug. A few weeks later it turned up in Tehran. It wasn't entirely clear what had happened to his head; Ferguson's bet was that it had been served to pigs at a dacha on the Black Sea.

Dechlov's demise had never been reported or acknowledged by Western or Russian security forces, and he was well known in all the wrong circles throughout Asia and the Middle East.

Sure enough, within two hours of Ferguson's arrival at the hotel, the front desk phoned to say that a man wanted to meet with him.

The man was dressed in a tan suit and stood iron-spine straight in the middle of the lobby when Ferguson emerged from the elevator. Ferguson greeted him as Ivan Manski; the man bowed very formally and presented a business card. Ferguson took it with both hands, spewing in Russian that he was very pleased to meet Mr. Li. To his surprise, Li responded in very good Russian that the pleasure was his.

Li told him that they had many mutual acquaintances, though he mentioned none of them by name. Ferguson was very happy to hear this, and suggested that they discuss these friendships in the hotel bar nearby.

For the next forty minutes, Li quizzed Ferguson on his bona fides, dropping a variety of names, including several that Ferguson had never heard of and guessed were phony, though he answered diplomatically that the earth was a big place and it was impossible to know everyone worth knowing on it. The men Li mentioned ranged from the Russian defense minister, whom Ferguson had actually met in his cover identity, to a shady Chinese soldier of fortune whom he knew only by reputation, a fact he admitted.

At last satisfied, Li told him that he had come because his employer was interested in meeting him.

"And your employer would be who?" Ferguson asked.

"Park Jin Tae, of course."

"Of course," said Ferguson, lifting his glass.

ABOARD THE USS *PELELIU*, IN THE YELLOW SEA

Thera hopped out of the helicopter and trotted head down toward the assault ship's island, following the lead of a sailor who'd come to escort her. The man clamped his hand onto her forearm and wouldn't let go until they were at the side of the ship. Annoyed, she flicked her arm and finally got rid of his hand just as Rankin appeared from the nearby door.

"Hey," said Rankin.

"Hey, yourself. What's up?"

"We have a situation with your guy. Come on downstairs."

Thera followed through a maze of hallways. Rankin, abrupt and taciturn as always, didn't bother to introduce the two men escorting them.

It seemed funny to Thera that Rankin and Ferguson worked together. They were almost exact opposites: Ferg always talking everyone up, BSing with them, and busting; Rankin typically as talkative as stone. It wasn't surprising that they didn't get along, but what amazed Thera was that Ferguson, who could have anyone on the team he wanted, chose someone whom he didn't like.

Did that mean Ferguson always tried to choose the best, or that he just liked conflict?

Rankin turned the corner and entered a small compartment that would have made a good broom closet on land. The two sailors stayed behind as Thera entered.

"They tell you what the deal was?" Rankin asked.

Thera shook her head. "They didn't tell me anything except that you needed me here. My mother supposedly died in Greece. I've been traveling ever since."

"We picked the scientist up the night you took off from Korea. He was soaked, cold, but OK. Told me his name, that he was involved in nuke research, like that. Now he won't talk. His brain's frozen or something."

"What do you want me to do?"

Thera's question took Rankin by surprise. "You know him, right?" he told her. "Maybe he'll talk to you."

"He thinks I'm a secretary. He gave me cigarettes."

"Yeah, OK. Go with it."

"I'll try talking to him, but if there's something wrong with him, I don't know that I can help."

Rankin couldn't understand why Thera didn't understand what she had to do. It seemed pretty straightforward to him.

"Physically he's fine," he repeated. "It's gotta be some sort of stress thing. Take a shot."

C h'o lay on his back, his mind completely blank. He neither thought nor felt anything, floating in a gray swirl beyond emotion or intellect.

Gradually, he became aware of a buzz at the side of the room, a swirling noise that he couldn't comprehend. He turned his head slowly. A face appeared from a white cloud, a face he knew was familiar, though he couldn't precisely place it.

The face spoke.

"Dr. Ch'o. Are you OK?"

The voice was foreign and yet familiar. Ch'o struggled but could not recognize it.

"Dr. Ch'o, are you OK?" repeated the voice, a woman's voice, a gentle, friendly voice.

It spoke English. Did he know English?

"I wanted to thank you for the cigarettes," said Thera.

She got down on her knees and took hold of the scientist's hand, as if she were a supplicant.

"I can help you if you need help," she told him. "These people are good. They've sent for a doctor to help you."

Ch'o pursed his lips. The voice was extremely familiar, yet he couldn't quite make the connection. He closed his eyes.

Thera stayed on her knees for nearly ten minutes. Ch'o seemed to be sleeping, though she couldn't be sure. Finally she decided it would be best to let him rest.

"I'll be back," she said, rising.

Rankin met her outside.

"Well?"

Thera shrugged. "Got any cigarettes?"

"Cigarettes?"

"Yeah."

"You smoke?"

"It was part of the cover. He gave me a pack. Maybe it'll make a connection."

"Let's see if we can find some."

13

The sedan—a Mercedes, though not the same one that Park used—arrived at the hotel for Ferguson at precisely eight-thirty. The driver spoke no Russian and didn't appear to know English. After making sure that "Mr. Manski" was in the vehicle, he took his seat behind the steering wheel and silently began to drive through the city.

Ferguson had pretended to be an arms dealer so often—sometimes Russian, sometimes as a former member of the IRA—that the role was part of his personality, no more foreign than the doting nephew he might become when visiting one of his great aunts. He could do it in his sleep, or at least in bed, and in fact had.

The problem with this, though, was that often his thoughts tended to wander, his mind drifting from the very real dangers of his covert job to other things, some trivial, others not. Looking out the window at the well-lit city, he saw a massive crane in a cramped, tiny alley and wondered how it had been positioned there. He also thought of the cancer count and the fact that his body was gradually turning against him.

How would he go out? Die of thirst in a hospital bed? Plug himself with a Glock or a PK pistol when the end was in sight?

Maybe that had been Kang Hwan's problem; maybe he'd chosen to hang himself rather than drain away. Working around radioactive materials could cause any number of cancers, including thyroid cancer.

The doctors talked in percentages, possibilities, never in absolutes. Ninety percent chance of survival.

Which was great, unless you were in the ten percent that didn't make it.

Fifty-fifty chance of one-year survival.

Twenty-two percent possibility of breathing the fresh air of Maine two Christmases from now.

Was it twenty-two or eighteen? Thirteen?

Was the air fresh in Maine anymore?

The car whisked up the driveway of the Daejeon Science & Arts University, where Park was due to attend a gala reception announcing the construction of a new physics laboratory. Work had already begun on the building: Dump trucks and bulldozers and cranes were lined up in the lot. Ferguson looked at them, then saw the sign announcing the project. The main words were in Korean and English: "Home of a new nuclear research reactor."

Had the reactor been built already, the dots would have connected perfectly.

"Whoa," said Ferguson, spotting a pair of trucks in the parking lot. They were the same type he'd seen at the waste-processing area and at Science Industries.

Ferguson leaned forward and tapped on the driver's shoulder.

"That lot," he said in English. "Can you go there?"

The man gave him an odd look.

"*Jeogi,*" he told him, pointing. "There."

The man replied in Korean that the reception was in the main administrative building, dead ahead.

Ferguson waved his hand and settled back, telling him to never mind.

Mr. Li was waiting at the door with two large bodyguard types behind him. Their black suits blended into the night.

"I am very glad you made it," said Li in Russian as Ferguson climbed the concrete steps.

"I wouldn't miss it."

"I have to ask—"

"Yes, of course," said Ferguson. He reached beneath

his jacket and pulled out the two Glocks he was carrying—what was a Russian arms dealer without weapons?

Li turned to one of the bodyguards, who took the weapons.

Ferguson saw a gun detector in the foyer. "You want this, too," he told Li, reaching down and taking the last Glock from the holster near his ankle.

"More?" asked Li, looking at the other leg.

"I dress very light in Korea. A very civilized country."

"Thank you very much," said Mr. Li, handing over the gun to one of the guards.

"My pleasure."

Inside, they took an elevator to the top floor. The reception was already in full swing. Guests, the majority of whom were male and over the age of sixty, milled around a large ballroom, replete with crystal chandeliers and a floor so polished Ferguson could see his reflection.

"Dance a big major here?" Ferguson asked Li as they made their way toward the bar area.

"The room is often used for receptions."

"I can see why."

"Mr. Park paid for its construction."

"Generous man."

"The most generous in Korea."

A guest took hold of Li and Ferguson drifted off, nodding politely but not speaking as he strolled across the room. As he reached the table with the food he heard two men talking about Park in what seemed to be negative tones, using phrases that meant "aggressive" and "too fond of the North." He smiled at them; their conversation immediately ended.

"Ivan Manski," he said, sticking out his hand.

The men looked at each other, then introduced themselves. A polite exchange of business cards followed.

"So you know Mr. Park?" said Ferguson in English.

The men claimed not to understand. Ferguson

switched back to Korean, telling them that he was Russian and that his company sold many important scientific instruments. Both men smiled but said nothing.

"So you are Russian?" said another man by his side. He was a thin rail with glasses, so short Ferguson had to practically bend over to see his face.

"*Dah.* Yes. Russian."

"You're not a spy, are you? KGB?"

Ferguson laughed. "KGB no more."

"FSB, sorry. I was joking," said the man. "I teach the history of the Cold War. From the viewpoint of its technology. Professor Wan."

"Ivan Manski."

"I have a very good collection of Soviet and American bugging devices," said Wan.

"Really?"

"Very good. And encryption devices."

"Oh really?"

"I have a Fialka machine."

"What's that?"

The professor explained that the Fialka was a cipher machine based partly on the Germans' World War II–era Enigma device. It was quite a find if you were interested in how secret messages were sent during the early days of the Cold War.

Ferguson was spared a detailed dissertation on how the machine worked when the room erupted in applause. All eyes turned toward a man dressed in a tuxedo who was walking to the center of the room. He had a microphone in his hand.

"Thank you, honored guests," he said in Korean. "I have the privilege to introduce our dean of science and physics, who wishes to say a few words in tribute to your generosity."

Polite applause followed. The dean recited a number of statistics about the new science facility that was being constructed, then began praising the Korean educational system, which the year before had turned out more engineers and scientists per capita than any country in the world. The university was proud to be part of this "Korean Revolution," which was bringing the country to the forefront of scientific achievement.

"When the science reactor is built, Korean science will advance ten thousand years," said the dean. Impressed by the overstatement, the crowd once more applauded. "Until now we have had to make due with the government-sponsored reactors for our studies. This has been most generous. But the future will be grander."

Ferguson followed the two men he'd tried to make conversation with as they slipped toward the table with the food. Halfway there, he spotted a familiar face: the female CIA officer who'd rousted him from bed several days before.

She stared directly at him, mouth open.

Li stood to her right. He saw the expression on her face and glanced across at Ferguson.

Ferguson smiled and walked directly to her.

"*Здравствуйте*," said Ferguson. "Hello. And how is the U.S. trade council today?"

The CIA officer's mouth dropped even wider.

"Can I buy you a drinkski?" Ferguson asked, switching to Russian-accented English.

She shook her head.

"Very good whiskey. But the vodka, eh."

Another head shake.

"My loss," he said, turning to continue toward the bar.

Li pounced before he got there. "You know her?"

"I know all pretty women. Personal motto."

"She told you she is with the American trade council?"

"One never questions beauty." Ferguson shrugged. He could tell that Li knew she was CIA; it was a good bet that half the room suspected it, assuming they cared. "You have a diverse guest list."

"Many people come, whether invited or not."

"I have the same problem when I throw a party," said Ferguson, ordering a fresh drink from the bartender.

"Drink later," said Li.

He took Ferguson's elbow and steered him toward a small conference room at the right. They walked through it, then down the hall to one of the administration offices.

Park was already waiting. A silver-haired man in his early sixties, he had the quiet air of an ancient village elder. Short and squat, with a buzz cut that flattered his face's rounded features, he looked like a retired wrestler sitting on the long couch.

Mr. Li introduced him, using Korean and then switching to English. Park could not speak Russian.

"A great honor to meet you," said Ferguson in English. "I've heard very much about you."

The corner of Park's mouth turned up in a faint smile, but he said nothing. Ferguson remained silent as well, the two men staring at each other for a few seconds, their smiles gradually increasing.

"He is a sagacious one," Park told one of the men behind the couch in Korean. "Useful in his profession."

Park rose. "Take a walk with me," he told Ferguson in English. "Come."

Ferguson fell in alongside him as Park slipped out of the office and walked down the hall. His aides and Mr. Li trailed along at a respectful distance until Park reached a set of double doors. Then two of the assistants sprang forward and held open the doors.

Ferguson and Park walked through a small vestibule, and then out onto an open terrace. The city spread out before them, a million lights glittering in the night.

"Progress," said Park in English.

"Yes," said Ferguson.

"Three decades ago, this was a poor place. Then, men with vision for Korea stepped up. The nation began to move ahead."

"Looks like it," said Ferguson.

"What is it you want, Mr. Manski?" said Park, still gazing at the lights.

"To be rich."

Once more, a smile grew in the corner of Park's mouth.

"That is a dangerous desire," said the billionaire.

"Life is dangerous."

"The Russian embassy claims not to have heard of you."

"I hope they would say that." Ferguson scanned the well-lit horizon, wondering how much of what he saw Park owned. "I was told that if I made myself available, there might perhaps be a market for certain items difficult to find elsewhere."

"Is that so?"

"Dah."

"And who told you this?"

"Some information, it is in the air."

"Korea has its own industry. We can make whatever we need."

"Truly. And Koreans are very discreet. But Russians can be even more discreet, for some matters require discretion as well as expertise. That is what I deal in: discretion."

Park turned around and went back through the doors. Ferguson started to follow, but found his way barred by two of the men in the black suits. He was just debating whether to push through them when Mr. Li appeared. Though Li said nothing, the two men separated.

"Mr. Park is planning a journey the day after tomorrow," said Mr. Li in Russian. "Perhaps you would like to join him. He finds it considerably easier to talk to people while he is traveling. He's very busy otherwise."

"How long?"

"A few days."

"I might be able to arrange that."

"Very good."

"If he tells me what sort of items he would be interested in, I can be better prepared—"

"That would be for Mr. Park to say, not for me."

"Very good." Ferguson, getting cold, rubbed his shoulders. "Where are we going?"

"Don't you follow the news?"

"No."

"Mr. Park is leading a group of businessmen to North Korea, to encourage cultural and business exchanges. His friends meet informally with ministers and others, at receptions, hunting, dinner . . . You might find some business yourself."

"That territory is already taken," said Ferguson.

Mr. Li nodded. "There will be diversions. It is a pleasant time in a secluded lodge outside the capital. You will have an opportunity to talk to Mr. Park then. Of course, if you wish not to come . . ."

"No, no," said Ferguson. "I wouldn't miss it for the world."

14

ABOARD THE USS *PELELIU*, IN THE YELLOW SEA

"Dr. Ch'o, are you awake?"

Thera squatted next to the prone scientist, who didn't appear to have moved on his cot since she had last seen him. His dinner sat nearby, untouched.

"You were so kind to give me cigarettes. Are you sure you don't smoke?"

She took the pack out and held it where he could see it. Then, carefully, she unwrapped the top and tapped out a single cigarette. Smoking was forbidden inside the ship, but Thera lit up anyway, thinking it might break the spell. She felt bad for the scientist, worried about him, as if he were an old friend.

"Remember?" she asked as she took the first draw.

The sulfur smell of the match and the whiff of tobacco

pushed at Ch'o's consciousness. A flood of thoughts came to him, ideas that were in numbers as well as sights and emotions: the half-life of isotopes, his father's slow death from radiation sickness, his mother's cancer, his own attempt to save others from their fate.

The girl. It was the girl he had passed the message to. She had come—they had captured her, too.

"You," said Ch'o.

Thera reached to help the scientist as he pushed to get up.

"You," he said again.

"It's me, Dr. Ch'o. They told me you were sick."

Ch'o shook his head.

"Are you in trouble?" he asked her. "You must be in trouble. The Americans . . . We've been captured."

"It's OK," she said, clasping his hand. "The Americans are helping us."

"The Americans do not control the IAEA."

"No. They don't. They're here to help you. You needed help."

Thera steered him to the chair. When he sat, she pulled over the other chair and sat in front of him.

"The Americans can help," said Thera. "They want to know what's going on. I know you've heard many bad things about them, but you have been outside Korea. You know they are not all evil. Not all of them."

That much was true, Ch'o thought.

"They're working with the IAEA. They can get your message out. And you don't have to stay with the Americans; you can go where you want. You were in Europe when you were younger."

"People are being poisoned," said Ch'o.

"And you can stop that."

Someone pounded at the side of the cabin.

Not now, thought Thera, but the young ensign who'd been assigned to liaison with the First Team people came in anyway.

"Ma'am, the psychologist is in-bound. . . . Uh, you can't smoke in here," he said. "I'm sorry, ma'am."

Thera shot the private a look of death. She was about to tell him what he could do—a direction that would have been physically impossible—but then remembered that she was supposed to stay in character for Ch'o.

"I'm sorry," Thera said meekly, stabbing out the cigarette.

A wave of indignation rose up in Ch'o. "Get out," he told the man at the door. "Out!"

The ensign ducked away. Ch'o pushed his legs over the edge of the bed and put his arm around the young woman.

"Don't worry," he told her. "We'll be all right."

I told him I have my own cabin and would see him in the morning," Thera told Rankin two hours later.

"He totally snapped out of it?"

"Whatever shock he was in, he's out of that. But he's still wary. Very, very wary." Thera explained that Ch'o seemed to think that he was protecting her in some way. He was confused by the fact that he had been picked up by the U.S. and not the IAEA.

"The North Koreans think we're pretty close to devils," Thera told Rankin. "They have museums devoted to our criminal acts, so he doesn't understand how the U.S. could be helping."

"You helped him."

"He thinks I'm Greek, remember?"

"Yeah."

"He wants to talk," she told Rankin. "He has information that will save a lot of people. Thousands."

"A bomb would kill millions."

"This isn't about a bomb. He's concerned about waste. That's what he wants to talk about—pollution. Radiation poisoning."

"A dirty bomb?"

"Pollution. He was going to be put into prison and maybe shot because he tried to alert the authorities. It's North Korea he's worried about."

"That's what we rescued him for?" said Rankin. "We went through all this trouble because he was worried about *pollution?*"

"Sometimes you can be a real jerk, Stephen," said Thera, storming away.

15

DAEJEON, SOUTH KOREA

Jogging was as popular in Korea as it was in the U.S., and an early morning jogger, even a Caucasian one, rarely attracted attention on a college campus. Ferguson waved to the security men at the gate as he came up the university drive; the one paying attention shook his head at him, mouthing words in Korean to the effect of "you're a crazy nut job."

Crazy nut jobs could go just about anywhere, and ten minutes later Ferguson entered the parking lot where he'd seen the two trucks the night before. He took a lap around the perimeter, made sure he wasn't being watched, then stopped to tie his shoe near the first truck.

When he got up, he slipped one of the gamma-ray counter tabs into the back, wedging it into the space near the door. Then he took pictures of the license plates with the small camera he had in his fanny pack; it was easier than trying to remember the numbers.

Ferguson stretched out a cramp, sticking another tab in the second truck. Then he resumed his exercise, taking a lap near the building where the test reactor was being constructed.

Under normal circumstances, such reactors could not produce weapons-grade plutonium, nor could the government research reactor the school was currently using. But that assumed that no one wanted them to.

Large boards of plywood and a chain-link fence ringed the construction area. Curious, Ferguson squeezed beneath the metal chain holding the gate closed. Once inside, he saw that work hadn't progressed very far at all; at the moment the building consisted of a concrete slab and massive steel pillars, with cladding only on the corner facing the building where the reception had been held the night before. He took some pictures anyway.

Sightseeing done, Ferguson stopped at a PC bang, a public-access computer café not far from the campus. It was early, but already most of the fifty seats were filled. He slid his security dongle into the USB port and pulled up the browser. Then he typed the secretary's name into a general search engine and was rewarded with six million matches. Nine-tenths of the results, to judge by the first two pages, were of pornographic sites.

Not of her.

"Whoa," said the teenager sitting next to him, glancing over. "How'd you get past their filter?"

"Just lucky, I guess," Ferguson told him. "I'm looking for a girl's address, but I don't do Korean very well. Think you can help me?"

"You American?"

"Russian."

Ferguson put his hand out. The kid shook it, then wrinkled his nose.

"Yeah, I gotta take a shower. This is the name."

Ferguson took out the card with the secretary's name, then got out of the way so the kid could sit down. Barely containing his drool, the teen called up a phone directory and then typed the name into the search box.

"What is her husband's name?" asked the kid.

"Not married."

"No phone with this name."

"Maybe she lives with her parents."

"Many, many Kims," he told Ferguson.

"Give it a try."

The teenager typed the surname into the computer. Sure enough, there were over a hundred pages of results.

"OK for now," said Ferguson. He reached over and slid the dongle out of the slot.

"Mister?"

"Be my guest," said Ferguson. When he left the store, the kid was still bent over the computer keyboard, trying to figure out what combination of keys Ferguson had used to conjure porn past the browser filter.

16

DULLES INTERNATIONAL AIRPORT

Corrine saw James Sonjae as soon as he cleared Customs. He looked tired, even more tired, in fact, than he had when she'd met him in the middle of the night.

"Need a ride?" she asked.

"Oh, thank God. I thought I was never going to get out of there. The line was endless."

"Did you have trouble?"

"Not really. The line was a bit long, but it moved pretty quickly."

"My car's this way."

It had gotten dark and cold since Corrine had arrived at the airport. Her thin sweater did little against the wind.

"It's all in the bag," Sonjae told her as they drove. "Computer disks, a big tape, and dirt."

Corrine said nothing, deciding it would be best if she acted like she knew what the items were.

"How's Ferg doing, anyway?" Sonjae asked.

"You would probably know better than me," she said. "You just saw him."

"No, I mean, with the cancer."

What cancer? thought Corrine. But she kept her lawyer's face on.

"I think he's doing pretty well," she said.

"I hope so. He looked a little run down. Probably the jet lag and everything."

"Probably."

"Shame," said Sonjae. "I've known Fergie since he was a little kid, off and on. His dad and I go back. Long story."

Corrine nodded. "So you knew him before the cancer?"

"Oh yeah. I only found out about that because I was visiting his father a few years back, before he died. Ferg's kind of quiet about that. Always kept things to himself. Probably the way he was raised, I guess."

Sonjae fell silent. Corrine tried to think of something to say to prompt him to continue. His exit was coming up.

"Hungry?" she asked as she took the turn onto the ramp.

"I could use some food, yeah."

"Come on. I'll buy you dinner."

17

DAEJEON, SOUTH KOREA

When Ferguson returned to his hotel, he discovered that during his absence the room had been bugged—a very promising sign. He put the bug to good use, pretending to use his sat phone to call a contact in Russian Georgia and telling him that things were going nicely. Then he removed the bug. While it would have better to leave it in place, he wasn't an expert on them and would need to give it to someone who was to have it identified.

With the room now clean, he called Corrigan to check in and to tell Slott he was going to North Korea.

"Ferg, where the hell have you been?"

"Good morning to you, too, Jack."

"What are you doing over there?"

"Sightseeing."

"Slott is pissed. He wants to talk to you right away. And I mean *right* away."

"Here I am. Listen, before you get him on the line, I'm going to be out of touch for a couple of days. I'm going north of the border on a business trip."

"What?"

"Mr. Park is getting up a junket. I'm going as Manski, the notorious Russian arms dealer."

"Why are you going to North Korea?"

"Park wants to talk about something, but I get the feeling that he doesn't think it's safe in the South. I don't know exactly what he's up to."

"Ferg. You can't go north."

"I am Russian citizen. I go anywhere."

Corrigan slapped him on Hold. Slott, breathing hard and talking a mile a minute, came on a few seconds later.

"What the hell are you doing?" Slott asked. "Are you out of your mind? Have you lost your senses?"

"Following a couple of leads. I don't think so. And no. In that order."

"You outed a fellow officer. I can't believe you did that, Ferg. That's way over the line."

"When?"

"You blew someone's cover last night in Daejeon."

"Jeez, I almost forgot about that."

"*Ferguson.*"

"Look, I didn't blow her cover. I didn't say anything about her, except that she worked for the trade commission, which *is* her cover, right?"

"Why were you even near her?"

"I was undercover, she was staring at me, her jaw scraping the carpet; I had to do something. I left things vague." Ferguson, annoyed, sat down in the chair and put his feet up on the bed. "It was a reception that Park went to. Park's the guy who owns Science Industries."

"What the hell is Science Industries?" said Slott.

"Science Industries has a guy on its staff who's an expert in extracting bomb material. Or was an expert—he killed himself a couple of months back. It was a suicide. Suspicious."

"And what else?"

"You know Park Jin Tae?" Ferguson asked.

"Park Jin Tae? I know of him."

"What do you know?"

"Billionaire. Extreme nationalist." Slott calmed down as he spoke. "He was connected with March 1, a political movement. They may have been thinking about rioting. It was hard to know where the South Korean's charges ended and the truth began. In any event, he bought his way out of trouble."

"Well, he owns Science Industries. He wants to talk to a notorious Russian arms dealer up in the People's Democratic Hell Hole tomorrow."

"What arms dealer?"

"Me."

"You?"

"I figured it was the easiest way to talk to him."

Slott exhaled so loudly Ferguson had to move the phone away from his ear.

"Sometimes you go too far, Ferg."

"I don't think so, Dan."

"North Korea's pretty risky."

"Park goes there a couple of times a year. Something's gotta be up, right? Arms dealer comes to him, says I can get you whatever you want? And Park says, hey, take a trip to the outlaw paradise of the world."

"All right. I'll tell Seoul. We'll set up—"

"I wish you wouldn't tell them."

"Why not?"

"I don't trust them. I barely trust you."

Actually, he wasn't sure that he *did* trust Slott, but saying that wouldn't be particularly helpful.

Slott didn't answer.

"You still there, Dan?"

"Just because you're Parnelles's fair-haired boy, don't think you can get away with everything," said Slott.

Ferguson laughed. "My hair's black, Dan."

"Bo's thinking about bringing formal charges against you for outing his agent."

"That'll be fun."

He'd hedge his bets. Have Corrine take the dirt to the DOE, the disks to the NSA. He'd tell her where he was going, and why.

Not that that would save his sorry butt if Slott really was out to screw him. But at least he wouldn't get away with it.

"You still there, Bob?"

The truth was, though, Ferguson wanted to trust Slott. Bo seemed like a boob, but Slott had a good track record, a history. And he'd helped Ferguson do his job, which was pretty much the best thing you could say about any manager.

Not trusting him meant not trusting the Agency—and, ultimately, not trusting his country.

Was that how they got his dad? Was it your sense of loyalty to your nation that screwed you in the end?

"I'm still here," Ferguson told him.

"I won't tell Seoul. But take care of yourself. You don't have any backup."

"Always," said Ferguson, hanging up.

18

Corrine was in her car when the secure satellite phone rang.

"Corrine here."

"Wicked Stepmother, we really have to stop meeting this way."

"Ferg."

"Did you get the bag?"

"Yes."

"All right. Everything in that bag comes from a place called Science Industries in Daejeon."

"What do you want me to do with it?"

"That's the ten-million-dollar question. I don't trust Seoul, so I didn't want them getting their paws on it."

"Do you trust Slott?"

"Yeah."

Corrine heard a note of hesitation in his voice.

"I think I do," Ferguson added, "but that's not good enough. He's going to hate me, he may even fire me, but I want you to have them all independently tested. Take the computer things to Robert Ferro at the NSA. You know him?"

"Deputy director."

"Yeah. You can drop my name if you have to to get it done quick."

"I don't think that will be necessary." As the president's counsel, Corrine had more than enough political muscle of her own.

"Dirt goes to DOE. Tell them to test for plutonium."

"I'll do it first thing in the morning."

"Do it tonight," Ferguson told her. "It may take days to get the results. Tell Slott what's going on once you have a good idea what's on the computer disks or the tape, or once it's gone far enough that you're reasonably sure no one's going to lie to you."

"Why don't you trust Slott?"

"I told you, I think I do. But he was in Korea for a long time. And these guys over here work for him. See, if there is plutonium there, the fact that they didn't find it and we did is pretty embarrassing. So they have an incentive to keep it quiet."

"You're talking about treason, Bob."

"Maybe just incompetence," said Ferguson.

"How mad is Slott going to be that you went behind his back?"

"Real mad," said Ferguson. "Real, real mad. But maybe I'll get lucky, and he'll never talk to me again. Look, I'd love to stay and chat, but I have to get going."

Corrine wanted to ask about Ferguson's cancer, but it was too late; he hung up before she could find the words to bring it up.

19

ABOARD THE USS *PELELIU*, IN THE YELLOW SEA

The ship's captain gave them the officer's wardroom for the initial "debriefing." A civilian psychologist who'd worked for both the CIA and the Defense Department was scheduled to arrive on the ship in a few hours, but Rankin saw no reason to wait, and the CIA interrogator was chomping at the bit. The interrogator suggested that Thera meet Ch'o and bring him to the wardroom for breakfast; once they were settled, the others could join and take it from there. Thera agreed, intending to leave as soon as the others came in, but from the moment she saw Ch'o dressed in the borrowed khakis and waiting for her she knew she wouldn't leave unless he asked.

"Good morning," he told her, rising and bowing his head stiffly.

"Dr. Ch'o." She bowed her head as well. "Are you feeling well?"

"I am feeling . . . prepared."

"Prepared?"

Ch'o didn't explain. He had decided that he must do his duty, and his duty as a Korean was to protect the people who would be poisoned by the improperly handled waste. He trusted the girl, and so he must believe that the Americans, whatever else was true about them, would give the information to the IAEA and the UN.

His own fate was immaterial. He was just an ant. He would move forward calmly, doing his duty.

"They have breakfast for us in the officers' galley," Thera told him. "Would you like to come?"

"I'm not very hungry."

"You have to eat," said Thera. "You look very pale. It's more comfortable than your cabin."

"I'll have some tea."

Ch'o had been aboard several ships during his career, but this was his first time aboard a fighting vessel of any type. The ship seemed several times more crowded than civilian boats. A brusque energy emanated from the young people; there were women as well as men in uniform, which surprised him. Ch'o recognized the energy as a kind of shared purposefulness, a common motivation that reminded him of his own youth and of Korea as it should be: everyone moving in the same direction.

Why the government had deviated from such a path, he did not know. It saddened him, and when he arrived finally at the wardroom he felt as if a cloud of doom had fallen around him.

"You can tell the seaman what you want," Thera said to Ch'o. "He'll get it."

"Tea?"

"Tea, yes sir," said the waiter, whose pronounced southern accent was difficult for the scientist to understand. "The cook made some mighty fine biscuits this morning. Y'all might try some of them."

"Biscuits are a kind of bread," explained Thera.

Ch'o shook his head. He only wanted tea.

"I'll try some," said Thera. "And coffee."

"Yes, ma'am. Best coffee in the fleet, I promise."

Neither Thera nor Ch'o spoke until the man returned. Ch'o found the tea very weak, but this did not surprise him; only Koreans made very good tea.

"Some of the people who helped you escape want to talk to you," said Thera. "You may have information that could help save lives."

"I do," said Ch'o. "I have much information."

"Will you speak to them?"

"Yes."

"They should be here shortly."

Ch'o spent two hours simply talking about his background, telling the CIA debriefer and the others where he had gone to school, what he had studied, the ministries he had served. Thera and Rankin listened, and occasionally the translator explained particular words and phrases, but for the most part, only Jiménez and Ch'o spoke.

Both grew slightly impatient as the conversation continued. Ch'o wanted to talk about the toxic wastes; Jiménez wanted to find out just how valuable the scientist really might be. Neither man, though, felt he could change the course of the interview, and so they plodded on, concentrating on Ch'o's schooling and research interests until a chief petty officer came in and said it was almost time for lunch.

"Let's all freshen up and get something to eat," suggested Thera. "And then find a more comfortable place to talk."

"What is 'freshen up'?" asked Ch'o.

"Take a break," she told him.

"Yes, very good."

"We could all have lunch together," suggested Jiménez.

"I think the doctor needs a break," said Thera. "Let's get some air and move around a bit."

"Yeah, that's a good idea," said Rankin.

Jiménez didn't agree, but arguing in front of the subject was an even worse idea, so he got up without saying anything else.

A half hour later, the psychologist and translator met Ch'o at his cabin, and they went for a walk on the flight deck. Thera, Rankin, and Jiménez met in Rankin's cabin to discuss what to do next.

"Definitely an important scientist," said Jiménez. "But how important? We're going to have to bring in experts to talk to him, people who can understand the technical stuff and know the history of the bomb program. I don't have the background to question him; he lost me on his dissertation."

"Yeah," said Rankin.

"How long are we staying on this ship? I'd like to get someplace more comfortable, flexible."

Rankin shrugged. Corrigan had told him they were "on hold" until the bosses figured it out.

"Where does he go after this?" Thera asked.

"Back to the States," said Jiménez. "First to a military base where we can keep him secure, then maybe set him up in an apartment when he's feeling comfortable. Your people should be working on the logistics right now."

Jiménez took a gulp of his coffee. "Next thing we do this afternoon, we find out if he has family in North Korea. Who they are, where, etc."

"Why?" said Rankin. "We're not going to be able to protect them if he does."

Jiménez grinned. "He doesn't know that."

"He's not stupid," said Thera.

"I didn't say he was. It's leverage."

"You can't lie to him like that."

Jiménez rolled his eyes.

"You have to ask him about the pollution," said Thera. "He's worried about people dying."

"We'll get to that," said Jiménez.

"When?"

"This is a long process. I have to build up a rapport. You know? I've done this before."

"I'm just telling you what he's concerned about."

"Don't tell me my job, all right?" said Jiménez. "Just because you shook your bootie at him doesn't mean you're his friend, right?"

Without thinking, Thera delivered a perfect roundhouse to Jiménez's jaw. It caught him completely by surprise; he flew into the nearby bulkhead and tumbled to the deck.

Rankin sprung over and grabbed her, dragging her outside. Thera, slightly stunned by the intensity of her own anger, didn't resist.

"All right, settle down," Rankin told her. "Settle down."

"I don't have to take that."

"Yeah." Rankin didn't like Jiménez either. "But easy. All right?"

Jiménez, blood dripping from the side of his mouth, came to the door of the cabin.

"What the fuck was that for?"

"For being an asshole," Thera told him.

"Well you turned him. That's all I meant."

"I didn't *turn* him. I didn't do anything. He came to me. He picked me at random."

"You were out of line," Rankin told Jiménez.

"Look, either you let me do my job, or get somebody else."

"You can do your job. Just don't be a jerk about it." Rankin looked at Thera, who looked like she was about to unload another haymaker. "Let's get some air up top."

Regret mixed with anger as Thera walked down the corridor. They took a turn and found themselves on the hangar deck. Mechanics were looking over a Harrier Jumpjet a few yards away.

"I'm sorry I hit him," said Thera.

"He deserved to be hit."

Thera felt her arms shaking. She was still wound up from the mission, too wound up.

"Let's go up and have a cigarette," suggested Rankin. "If I can remember how the hell to get up there."

"It's back through here," she told him, leading the way.

How had she become so attached to Ch'o, worried about him? She shouldn't be. He was just . . . Well, he was just a defector with information that might be useful.

When you were on a mission, you had to remember things were black and white, good and evil. She was on the good guys' side. He was on the evil side. Even if he was useful, at the end of the day, he was still on the wrong team.

Except she didn't feel that way. She could see the other North Koreans like that, the ones who would have arrested her or shot her or whatever. The guard who'd smoked with her, the officious jerk in South Korea—they were all on the other team; she didn't feel any sympathy for them. But the scientist was different.

Why? Because he'd been nice to her?

Because he was concerned about innocent people being harmed.

"Look, maybe we should let Jiménez do his thing by himself," said Rankin as they reached the fresh air. "We were just sitting there anyway. Like bumps on a log. We listen to what the shrink says, and if he thinks Ch'o's cool, then we let Jiménez take it."

"You're right," said Thera abruptly. "I'd like to get the hell out of here anyway."

20

"So, who do you think would use a bug like that?" Ferguson asked the professor.

Wan scowled and turned it over.

"Very new. Two years old, design," said the spy buff. "Not government, though."

"Not American or not Korean?"

"Neither. Wait."

Wan went to the side of his office and hit his computer mouse. His machine woke up, the screen flashing with a screensaver showing an old substitution code wheel. In less than a minute, he brought up a Web site that featured the bug in question.

"Government would want to spend ten times as much," laughed Wan, pointing at the price: five dollars.

"Would the bug be ten times as good?"

Wan smiled.

Ferguson packed up his sat phone and electronic gear and left them in a small locker in a Seoul self-storage facility. From now until he returned, he would be only Ivan Manski.

Not having his bug detector when he got back to his hotel wasn't a real problem; it was easier to assume he was being bugged and act accordingly. But he was curious, and so he set about looking through the hotel room. It was a game in a way, seeing if he could figure things out the old-fashioned way, like a *real* spy would have done it.

Like his dad would have done it.

The bug that he'd removed from the TV set hadn't been replaced. But there was a new one in the clock radio.

A bit of an insult, really; the radio was probably the most obvious place to look, after the television and phone.

And the lamp, where Ferguson found another.

A third had been placed at the bottom of the small stuffed chair and two more in the bathroom, including one wired into the light fixture ($13.99 on the professor's Web site).

Ferguson gathered them all together, put them on the tile floor, then stomped them under his heel with a loud yell.

Laughing, he went downstairs to the bar, where, still in character, he ordered a vodka before going out for dinner.

There were two new bugs in the room when he came back.

"Points for persistence," he said in Russian before flushing them down the toilet.

21

ABOARD THE USS _PELELIU_, IN THE YELLOW SEA

"Maybe we stop now," said Tak Ch'o. He'd been talking for so long that his jaw hurt. "We stop."

"Yeah, that's fine," said Jiménez. "As good a place as any." Jiménez glanced at the translator. "Start back in tomorrow morning?"

"I want to know," said Ch'o, "is the girl OK?"

"Yeah, I told you, she's fine," said Jiménez.

Reflexively, Ch'o started to nod, accepting what Jiménez said. He had heard such excuses many times in his days in North Korea, and always, he had nodded.

Because he was afraid. Fear was the central fact of his life.

No more. That was why he froze when he woke up here. The fear had been removed, and he was incapable of everything, even breathing, without it. But somehow, when he'd seen that the girl might be in danger, he had been reborn.

That was who he wanted to be, who he was now: a man who could help others by acting, not by being afraid and paralyzed.

"The girl," said Ch'o firmly. "I will see her now."

"You sure?"

"Yes. I want to talk to her alone. And tomorrow, tomorrow we will speak of more important things."

"Well, now, listen, Doc, we have plenty of things to talk about," said Jiménez.

"We will talk about what I want to talk about tomorrow," insisted Ch'o.

"All right," said Jiménez, still clearly reluctant. "Sure. Whatever you want."

"Let the girl come to the cabin."

"She's got to decide that for herself, but I'll tell her."

Thera spent the afternoon hanging around her cabin, reading a mystery the last occupant had left behind. Attempting to keep contact with the ship's crew and marines to a minimum—and still in a dark mood because of her confrontation with Jiménez—she had a sailor bring her dinner. She flipped on the closed-circuit entertainment channel while she ate and began watching a sentimental tear-jerker about a kid looking for his father in the Alaskan wilderness. She guessed the ending five minutes into the picture—the boy's real father had disguised himself as the guide for the journey—but still felt her eyes welling up at the very end when the guide, fatally wounded on the trek, revealed himself after saving the boy's life.

Movie over, Thera fiddled halfheartedly with a computer game that was connected to the television set. Finally she flipped on the TV and began watching the Alaskan wilderness movie a second time.

Father and son were just about to be attacked by a Kodiak bear when Rankin knocked at the side of her door.

"Come on in," she said.

Rankin did so. Jiménez followed.

"Busy?" asked Rankin.

"Bored."

Thera flipped off the TV. She glared at Jiménez, daring him to apologize. He didn't.

"I was wondering," said Jiménez, "if maybe you'd come see Dr. Ch'o."

"Why?"

"He's worried something happened to you."

"Oh?"

"Yeah. The shrink says he's fine, a little, you know, culture shock. And maybe he's protective of you or something along those lines."

"Maybe he likes people who aren't jerks."

"Look, you're the one who hit me," said Jiménez. "My jaw still hurts."

"You're lucky I hit you there," said Thera. "Would it kill you to say you're sorry?"

"Would it kill you?" answered Jiménez.

"If I did anything to apologize for, I would."

They glared at each other, neither willing to give up any ground.

"Why don't you go talk to the scientist?" Rankin told her. "Just show him you're OK."

"I have no problem with that," said Thera, getting up.

"Hey," said Jiménez, following her out of the stateroom. "Yeah?"

"Look, I'm not a total jerk, all right?"

"You have a way to go to prove that."

"I jumped to the wrong conclusion. You're pretty, and that's the way it works with a lot of guys I deal with. I just jumped to the wrong conclusion. OK?"

"I'll let you know what happens," she said, turning toward Ch'o's cabin. Never before had being called pretty sounded like such an insult.

brought this to many people's attention. Personally, I took it to General Namgung. Personally. I had worked with him on many special projects, most recently four or five months ago, engineering special shielding for air transport of waste. He understood the hazards, but would he act? He did not act. This is a great shame to our country. Many people will die."

Ch'o stopped and looked up at Thera.

"You understand what I am saying?" he asked.

"Of course. But you should tell Jiménez this."

"I will. But you . . . you understand, don't you?"

Thera nodded.

"Maybe you could write this down," suggested Ch'o. "To keep a record."

"I can get Jiménez."

The scientist shook his head. "I'd rather talk to you now."

"All right. Let me get a pad and a recorder. Is that OK?"

"That would be very good."

Four years of college, and I'm back to being a secretary, she thought, leaving the cabin.

DAEJEON, SOUTH KOREA

Mr. Li had described the trip to North Korea as if it were a junket, but he hadn't done it justice.

Ferguson went down to the lobby a few minutes before noon, just in time to see a white passenger van pull up to the curb. A young woman dressed in a short, skin-tight yellow skirt hopped from the back and strode toward him, asking in English if he was the Russian businessman Ivan Manski.

"At your service," said Ferguson.

"Your bag, I take."

"Is fine," said Ferguson, laying on his heaviest Russian accent. "We go now?"

"We go, yes." She led him to the minibus, then stowed his bag in the back.

"Mr. Manski, we are pleased to have you," she said in a way that suggested any number of double entendres. "We can get you something, yes?"

"I'm fine."

"Vodka?"

"A little vodka maybe," said Ferguson.

She slipped back to a refrigerator chest at the rear of the van and took out a bottle of Zyr, an expensive vodka made in Russia, though the company was actually owned by an American.

"Straight," Ferguson told her. "Just ice."

"Ice? You are not a purist?"

"It's still early," said Ferguson, taking the glass and admiring the scenery.

A few minutes later they entered a residential area of

single-family homes and pulled into a private driveway. A short man in a gray suit was waiting. He left his bag for the young woman and climbed into the van. Ferguson introduced himself as Manski, giving him a card and examining the newcomer's. The man was an electronics salesman interested in opening his own factory up north in one of the special zones set aside for foreign endeavors near the capital. When the door closed and the van was underway, he told the woman that it was too early to drink, but since the other guest had already started, he would have a Scotch to keep him company.

The ritual was repeated four more times as the van made the rounds picking up its passengers. Everyone had a drink. And caviar. And a number of other treats Ferguson couldn't identify by sight or taste.

When all of the passengers had been picked up, the driver got on the highway toward Seoul. About five miles south of the capital, they were met by a pair of police cars. Lights flashing, the police escorted them to Gimpo, the airport to the west of Seoul generally used by domestic flights. There a private 727, already half-filled with other guests of Park, waited to take them north.

Ferguson circulated as much as he could among the other passengers. All were male, and all had relatively important positions in their respective companies, though none were as wealthy as Park.

Nor did any seem likely buyers for the goods an arms dealer specialized in. Ferguson chatted up the virtues of his supposed company's instruments just long enough to bore each listener, establishing his credentials before changing the subject to the trip or to the problems of doing business in the North or to Park himself.

The billionaire wasn't traveling with the rest of the party. He had already boarded a two-engined jet aircraft similar to a 737. Built by the Korea Commercial Aircraft Development Company as a demonstrator a few years before, the plane had the latest technology, from superefficient engines to a glass cockpit. It rivaled anything made in America or Europe, but because the company had no track record—and because it was primarily a Korean effort—other Asian countries did not place any orders, and the firm switched its efforts to spare parts.

Park, of course, had been the major investor.

"The Americans were the ones most interested in the aircraft," explained Ha Song, who sat next to Ferguson on the 727. Mr. Ha worked for an investment group with interests in cable television but had represented some aeronautics firms around the time of the project. "This was genuinely a surprise, since usually they look down on us as little brothers."

"A very *Americanski* attitude," said Ferg.

"Your government would have done very well to have formed a partnership."

"Undoubtedly," said Ferguson. "But I don't represent the government."

"Many good engineers in Russia."

"The best," said Ferguson. "Except for Korea."

Mr. Ha's face shaded slightly. Without prompting, he began telling him the story of his ancestors, ethnic Chinese who had been in Korea for several hundred years.

"Before the Japanese came to our country, my family had many, many shops," said Ha.

"Did they take them away?"

"Not at first, but, during the bad time, what we know as World War II, that was very trouble-matic."

"I'll bet."

"Many Korean peoples, same story," said Ha. "Japanese very evil."

"Good in business."

Ha made a face. "Their money not worth it. Very evil."

"It's too bad," said Ferguson.

"Russia have war with Japan, too: 1904." Ha was referring to the Russo-Japanese War of 1904–05, which was fought partly over Korea as well as Manchuria.

"*Dah*," said Ferguson. "And we get butts kicked."

Ha took a moment to translate the slang, then they both started to laugh.

A line of North Korean officials met them inside the terminal at P'yŏngyang. Ferguson bumped along with the others, nodding and smiling, nodding again. There was no passport check. If the bags were inspected, it was done by whoever had retrieved them; they were collected and sent on to their destination without being reunited with their owners.

As Ferguson was about three-fourths of the way through the receiving line, a short man approached him and asked in Russian if he was Mr. Manski.

"*Dah*," said Ferguson. "I am Manski."

"I am Mr. Chonjin," said the man. "I will interpret for you."

Chonjin's accent was so unusual that it took Ferguson a few seconds to untangle what he said.

"Your accent . . . Where do you come from?" Ferguson asked.

Chonjin said that, while he was Korean, he had spent much of his life in Vladivostok, a city on the coast of the Sea of Japan where he had been a member of the North Korean Trade Group. Ferguson assumed this meant that he had been a spy there, for surely he was a spy now, assigned to stay close to one of the more dubious members of Mr. Park's party.

He had the face of a pug—a pushed-in nose, large drooping eyes, a sad-sack mouth—but he was amiable enough, smiling and laughing as they worked their way through the rest of the officials gathered in the hall.

"All hope to do business very soon," said Chonjin as they reached the end. "We are the new China. Better."

"Of course," said Ferguson.

"You would like to open a factory here?"

"I keep an open mind."

The visitors were herded upstairs for a brief welcoming speech by an official Chonjin said was the local mayor. When the talk was over—"Better Than China" seemed to be the theme of the day—they were treated to a reception table at the far end of the large room. A half hour later, the entourage was escorted outside to waiting buses. A school band, heavy on the tubas but otherwise remarkably tuneful, serenaded them as they walked the few feet to the vehicles.

Another band, this time more balanced instrumentally and composed of older musicians, greeted them when they arrived at what Ferguson's shadow called a guesthouse about thirty minutes away. Obscenely lavish by North Korean standards, it reminded Ferguson of a European-style hunting lodge, the sort of place the kaiser would have brought guests to before World War I. The wall at the front was made of large wooden timbers, like a massive log cabin. The sides, however, were smooth stucco. Here and there the shadows of the large stones peeked through thin layers of cement, as if they were fighting their way out from behind the protective covering.

Park was waiting for them inside, standing on a balcony overlooking a large great room just beyond the entrance foyer. There were scores of North Korean officials there as well, along with young waitresses who fanned out with bottles of champagne.

"My friends, I welcome you here on what I hope will be a prosperous and exciting visit," said Park, raising his glass.

A long round of toasts followed. Park slipped out about midway through, leaving the others to mingle, drink champagne, and ogle the young women.

By the time the group began retiring to their rooms to get ready for dinner, Ferguson had introduced himself to nearly everyone and run out of business cards. Chonjin volunteered to get some made for him.

"That would be great," Ferguson told him.

The interpreter bowed his head. "Anything for a guest. I will see you at dinner."

"Can't wait."

23

General Namgung leaned forward and told the driver to stop. Instantly, the man obeyed, pulling to the side of the road.

Namgung ignored the questioning look from his aide, who was sitting next to him in the rear of the Russian-made sedan. He needed a moment to think. The enormity of what he was about to embark upon had settled on him, filling him with a dreadful sensation of foreboding. He knew from experience that he must take a few moments to let the sensation pass. Otherwise, he would not be able to make clear decisions. And the future depended very much on clear decisions.

At the age of fifty-three, Namgung was one of the top commanding generals in North Korea, in charge of the divisions around the capital and several in the northwestern provinces, including those on the Chinese border. Family connections had helped him launch his career, but in the thirty-plus years since he became a lieutenant he had worked extremely hard, outhustling and outlasting many rivals. He knew the supreme leader, Kim Jong-Il, extremely well and visited him often—or had, until Kim's recent sickness.

The dictator's health was a closely guarded state secret—even those of importance, like Namgung, didn't know exactly how bad off he was. But the general could guess that the supreme leader had perhaps six months to live.

After that, chaos supreme.

Unless Namgung acted.

There were many benefits to Namgung's plans, for him

personally as well as for the poverty-wracked People's Republic, but avoiding chaos was Namgung's primary objective. Chaos was an intense, immobilizing enemy, far worse than an opponent armed merely with guns and bombs. Chaos was to be defeated at all costs. It was a general's duty, a Korean's duty, to ward it off.

The general exhaled slowly. His moment of anxiety had passed.

"Mr. Park is waiting," the general said, leaning forward to his driver. "Proceed."

24

THE JOHN F. KENNEDY CENTER FOR THE PERFORMING ARTS, WASHINGTON, D.C.

Corrine glanced to her left as she walked up the steps and was surprised to see CIA director Thomas Parnelles right beside her.

"Mr. Parnelles, how are you?" she said.

"Corrine, well hello." Parnelles gave her a broad smile and gently prodded his wife. "Dianne, this is Corrine Alston, the president's counsel. Ms. Alston is probably the most powerful woman in Washington."

"Your husband is quite a charmer," Corrine told Diane.

"A scoundrel, you mean," said Dianne Parnelles, laughing.

"Are you here on a date?" Parnelles asked.

"Actually, with my secretary, Teri Gatins," confessed Corrine. "She got tickets from her son. I'm supposed to meet her in the lobby."

"Enjoy the show," said Parnelles, starting away.

"Tom, I wonder if I could ask you something."

"Classified?" He smiled, as if it were a joke.

"No. Not exactly."

"Well, surely then," said Parnelles. He told his wife he would meet her inside.

"I have a . . . theoretical question concerning a government employee. It just came up," said Corrine. "I wonder if I could bounce a situation off you."

"Theoretically."

"If someone were . . . If they had a life-threatening disease, would you think . . . If you were their supervisor, how would you handle it?" Corrine danced around the wording, trying to come up with a way to say what she knew about Ferguson without actually identifying him.

"Life-threatening disease? I'd be sympathetic to the person, certainly. I'd make sure that they were getting the sort of care that they needed, that sort of thing."

"Would you think it would affect their job performance?"

"I don't see how it couldn't. Assuming they'd be able to work in the first place."

"Assume that they could."

"I guess it would be a difficult situation. I think you would have to keep them on, though. By law, if nothing else," said Parnelles. "Don't you?"

"The Americans with Disabilities Act doesn't apply to the executive branch," said Corrine.

"I see. Well, in our agency, the decision would be rather easy if the person were on the operations side: A disease like that would eliminate them from active duty."

"Oh?"

"Yes, of course. The officer's judgment is the heart of the matter. You see, someone might be reckless if they knew or suspected they'd die anyway. That's not what we want."

"The decision would be that cut and dried?"

"We wouldn't kick them out the door, of course. We'd find something *suitable*." Parnelles drew out the last word, pronouncing it with special relish.

"Suitable?"

"There are things we could find, whether in the analytic areas or administrative. Perhaps you can do that as well. Lesser jobs," he added. "Are we speaking of someone I know?"

Corrine hesitated. If she told Parnelles about Ferguson's cancer—and clearly she should—she would be in effect asking to have him removed from the First Team. That would be a much harder blow to him than the cancer, surely.

But wasn't that her responsibility?

Parnelles must know. He knew Ferguson far better than she did.

That didn't guarantee that he knew, though. Sonjae had learned only by accident.

"It's just a hypothetical," said Corrine. "That's all."

"Let me know if it blossoms into a full-blown theorem," said Parnelles, tapping her forearm as he walked away.

The performance at the Kennedy Center seemed to go on and on and on, so Gordon Tewilliger was not surprised when he looked at his watch and saw that it was well after midnight. He considered skipping the reception but reminded himself that there would be plenty of potential contributors there, men and women who in the future might remember his handshake and agree to write a check in a time of need.

What a difference a decade makes, he thought to himself as he headed for the party. When he was younger, he'd have wanted to go simply to mingle with the pretty women. Divorced now longer than he'd been married, Tewilliger considered himself past that stage of life where sex had any importance.

Though occasionally he could have his head turned, as the woman in the short red dress who greeted him near the door proved.

"Oh, Senator, how good of you to come," she said.

Tewilliger struggled to remember if he'd met her before. He thought she might be with the National Endowment for the Arts, but had the sense to realize the connection his mind was making might be less than subliminal.

"I wouldn't miss it," Tewilliger told her, "but I can only say hello."

"Oh, look, there's Congressman Anderson," said the woman, taking off in the direction of the California representative. Tewilliger went in the other direction; Anderson was a member of the other party.

The senator spotted Thomas Parnelles, the CIA director, and his wife chatting with some military people. But before he could make it over to the old coot and ask how the Agency was shaping up, Parnelles and his wife had disappeared. Tewilliger sampled some of the hors d'ouerves as a consolation prize, then joined the fawning crowd around the actors he'd just seen perform. That was a mistake—he liked people who were fawning only when he was the one being fawned over. But he couldn't escape before the theater's PR director arrived, and he had to endure introductions to all of the "artists," as she called them.

They turned out to be much more polite than he'd thought, thanking him enthusiastically for his support of the arts. Tewilliger graciously accepted, even though his support had amounted to a single vote in favor of the endowment's budget in committee, a horse trade that meant nothing, as the matter was defeated.

Tewilliger moved on to the heart of the party, a knot of corporate types and their wives standing near the table with the champagne. Some of the people from GM and Ford were there; with practiced efficiency the senator managed to greet them all. After ten minutes of circulating among the heavy spenders, Tewilliger concluded that his flag had flown long enough and headed toward the door.

He'd nearly reached it when someone tugged his arm. He was surprised to find Harry Mangjeol, his Korean-

American constituent, who'd arranged for him to use a private company jet to get up to New Hampshire a few days before.

"Harry," said Tewilliger, instantly back in hail-fellow-well-met mode. "What are you doing in Washington?"

"Important business with GM," said Mangjeol, glancing toward the executives. "Wine and dine tonight."

"Do you need introductions?" A favor would be just the thing.

"No, no. We had dinner together. Lewis suggested I come to the theater."

"Did you like the show?"

Mangjeol nodded his head so enthusiastically Tewilliger thought of asking him to explain it to him.

"If I had known you were coming, Senator, I would have looked for you earlier," said Mangjeol.

"Yes. It is a late night, though," said the senator, plotting his exit.

"I have spoken to a great many of my friends in Korea these past days. They say, watch out for our brothers to the North. Something is brewing."

"Really? Who says that?"

"Many people."

"Many?"

"Prominent business people."

"I see." Tewilliger heard these sorts of rumors from constituents all the time. The worst were the ones from people who were sure they had stumbled onto a plot that would make 9/11 look like a Sunday school picnic. He was always tempted to put them onto a novelist he knew but didn't particularly like.

"I have associates close to Pak Lee, O Kok, Park Jin Tae," continued Mangjeol. "They all are worried."

"Very nice," said Tewilliger. The names meant nothing to him, though he could tell Mangjeol wanted him to be impressed. "I'll have to keep this in mind. Thank you. Pass along anything else you hear."

"I will," said Mangjeol. He'd had the impression that

the senator was blowing him off, but Tewilliger's forth-right tone brushed the thought from his mind.

"I'm afraid I have to leave now. Early session in the morning."

"Good seeing you, Senator. Very good seeing you."

"I'm sure," said Tewilliger, making his escape.

25

NORTH OF SUNG HO, NORTH KOREA

Ferguson's room in the lodge was bugged and not very creatively: A relatively large microphone was wired right into the light socket and "hidden" in the shade. Professor Wan would have been appalled.

Changing for dinner, Ferguson serenaded the North Korean secret service with a medley of Russian drinking songs. He carried the overinebriated Russian act into dinner. To have acted sober would have been out of place; nearly all of his fellow travelers were legitimately snockered.

Hostesses led each man to a seat at one of two long tables in the cramped dining room. Ferguson's shadow, Chonjin—hopelessly sober—was on his left. Mr. Ha, the Korean who had told Ferguson about Park's airplane in-vestment, was on his right.

Park sat at the head table with General Namgung, a North Korean general so important that he was intro-duced by name only.

"General Namgung is in charge of the guards here?" Ferguson asked his minder in Russian.

"General Namgung is one of the most important people in Korea," responded Chonjin.

"Do you know him?"

The question surprised Chonjin. "Of course not. He's too . . . He's too important. Much of the army, the air force—they answer to him. He would not know me."

"Maybe he can act on a contract for me," suggested Ferguson.

Chonjin shook his head. "You have a lot to learn about doing business in Korea."

"Teach me."

"The first step, have good time, mingle. On the next visit, then you bring up the subject."

"I don't talk business until the next visit?"

"You mention it on the next visit. Not talk. Talk—negotiate, a sale—that happens in the future."

"How far in the future?"

"Hard to say. Some day, perhaps."

Park stayed at the head table for only a few minutes before disappearing. Namgung stayed through the meal and led several toasts. Then he went off with some of the other North Korean officials.

The other guests were led back to the great hall for a reception that consisted of several rounds of drinks followed by several more rounds of drinks, topped off by many more drinks. The businessmen poured glass after glass for their companions, drinking and passing them on.

The Korean style of drinking, with companions essentially supervising one another into a stupor, made it hard to stay sober, and Ferguson finally retreated to a chair and pretended to nod off. When Chonjin woke him and suggested that he go to bed, he protested, but within a few minutes he had nodded off again, this time on a fellow guest. When a North Korean official sat down next to him, Ferguson flopped in his direction, his chin landing on the man's shoulder.

"Mr. Manski?"

"Oh, yeah." Ferguson roused himself. "Bedtime, I think."

"Yes."

Chonjin helped him up to his room. Ferguson's energy grew with each step.

"Open the window," he proclaimed as he entered the room. "Air, we need good cold air! All windows!" He flopped facedown on the bed, mumbling a Russian drinking song.

Chonjin and the attendant opened the windows, threw a blanket on him, and retreated.

Ferguson had no intention of spending the rest of the night sleeping, let alone singing. He'd staged his little act so he could go exploring, but to do that he needed to come up with a proper finale.

Ferguson started another drinking song, this one an obscure lament about the darkness of crows' feathers. As he sang, he studied the lamp where the bug was, considering how to best muffle it. Raising his voice ever higher and further off-key, he stumbled around, went to the bathroom, fell, got up, and finally knocked over the lamp.

The shade flew to the middle of the floor. Cursing, Ferguson stumbled around some more, left arm flailing while his right separated the bug from the shade. He left it on the floor near his bed and continued to sing, repeating the song over and over again, hoping to lull anyone unlucky enough to be listening into an autistic state.

Climbing into bed, Ferguson's lyrics gave way to snores. These slowly decreased in volume, until after a few minutes he began breathing normally. He wadded the blanket on top of the bug, grabbed his shoes, and tiptoed to the window.

Ferguson was on the third floor, facing the back of the compound. The window formed a small dormer similar to those in the Cape Cods he knew from Maine. Getting out as quietly as possible and climbing up onto the roof was more an exercise in nostalgia than a physical challenge.

The problem was to get down without being seen or breaking a leg. The front side of the lodge would have been easy to climb because of the logs, but the two guards at the front of the building meant this was out of the question. Besides being too smooth to offer any obvious handgrips, the opposite side featured the great room's large window as well as windows looking out from the kitchen and staff room. Likewise, the southern side, where Ferguson's room was, had far too many windows with light shining through them.

The north side had no windows above the first floor, but the only thing to climb on as he went down was the gutter at the corner. Ferguson had had bad experiences with gutters in the past, but it seemed his only option.

He worked his way down the peak and tested the metal by putting his right leg on it. The gutter groaned but didn't collapse.

Ferguson swung around, hung off the top, and then began pushing down the corner, using the downspout the way he would use a rope to climb down a mountain. By the time he reached the top of the second floor, the leader had pulled out several inches. Then, when he was just above the first floor he heard a loud and ominous creak from above.

There was no other option but to let go.

26

NORTH OF SUNG HO, NORTH KOREA

"The aircraft is the most advanced available," General Namgung told Park. "It can elude anything the South Koreans have. Or the Japanese, for that matter."

"What about the Americans?" asked Li.

"The Americans, too," said Namgung. He turned to his aide, Captain Ganji, who nodded quickly. "It does this partly by flying very low. And, of course, our spies have provided the radar profiles. We know just where the aircraft must go to avoid detection."

Park studied the general. He was a good man, a warrior of solid intention and dependability. Like many North Koreans, he had many relatives in the South, and believed as Park believed, that the country must be reunited.

But he had a warrior's hubris, a tendency to be overly optimistic. The MiG aircraft was formidable, but it was not invincible. They could not assume that it would triumph.

Park rose from his seat and walked to the french doors at the back of the cottage room. He studied his reflection in the glass, surprised to see that he looked much older than he felt. Then he pushed the glass door open, breathing the crisp air as he gazed at the waterfall to the left of the patio.

There was just enough moonlight to dapple the surface of the water with rippling white light. The sight was auspicious.

Before the division, this land had belonged to Park's grandparents. Among their businesses was a pottery factory, one of the finest on the continent, with more than a hundred skilled craftsmen. The main lodge up the hill had been built with its profits as a retreat for the family. The cabin where he and Namgung were meeting had been used as servants' quarters.

Much had changed in seventy years. The servants' quarters would be considered a palace by all but the most high-ranking North Korean party member. Even Namgung admired it.

Partition was difficult for most Korean families, and compared to many, the Park family had managed very well. They had held on to a great deal of their wealth, partly because so much of it had been concentrated in the South. Park hated the Communist principles that the Russians had imposed on the first Korean leader, Kim Il Sung; they were nothing short of theft, even though Kim at times mixed in true Korean ideas to make them seem more logical.

The dictator's attitude toward the people was, in many ways, more understandable. Park did not condone the police state, but it was natural that a strong leader would have to take a strong hand. History made this evident and not merely in Korea.

The dictator was irrelevant. As General Namgung himself had said a few minutes before, the government would soon collapse. The time was ripe to bring the Koreas together.

Park closed the door and turned back to his guests.

"I have studied the MiG," said Park. "You're surprised, General. You shouldn't be. My companies were involved in projects to build other aircraft. It is a very admirable aircraft, but it will be vulnerable. All aircraft are."

"On the ground, certainly," said the general. He was not one to retreat. "Once in the air it can avoid radars by flying low. By the time it is perceived as a threat, it will have reached its launch point. The enemy has no defenses in that sector."

Park looked at Li.

"We have a plan to make sure that it is not attacked," said Li. "It involves a certain amount of risk, but no more than if it were to proceed as you propose."

27

NORTH OF SUNG HO, NORTH KOREA

It seemed to take an inordinate amount of time for Ferguson to hit the ground.

When he finally did, time seemed to make up for the deficit. He flew backward so quickly he knocked his head with a fierce, welt-raising rap.

Ferguson lay on his back a moment, collecting his wits. Surprisingly, the gutter was still in one piece and attached to the building.

No way it would hold him on the way back. But that was a problem for later.

Scrambling to his feet, Ferguson trotted toward the nearby barn. A group of bored soldiers stood talking in the front, near where the buses had been parked. Ferguson circled around and found a window at the back. All he could see inside were a few Jeeplike trucks, parked up toward the doors; about three-fourths of the large interior looked empty.

A road ran on the other side of the barn. Curious, Ferguson paralleled it for about fifty yards downhill and then around a curve. Another pair of bored soldiers stood in the middle of the path at the end of the bend.

Ferguson doglegged past them, picking up the road as it made another S down the hill. A squat building sat at the edge of a clearing, overlooking a rushing stream and a waterfall so loud Ferguson could hear it over his breathing. Two large sedans were parked in front of the building. A pair of men in large greatcoats stood near the cars. Ferguson couldn't tell in the dim light if they were soldiers—they didn't have rifles—but they stood as still as statues near the second car, as if they expected someone to arrive and inspect them at any moment.

He slipped farther into the woods, approaching the back of the building by walking along the creek. A large terrace opened out from a pair of glass doors; he could see a fire in a massive fireplace at one side of the room.

Ferguson crawled up along the side of the terrace, hugging the wall. There was no cover, but the only light came from inside and most of the patio was in shadow. The inside light and glass would make it difficult to see outside.

Two men in uniform were sitting in chairs facing roughly in his direction. One, he thought, was General Namgung, though he couldn't get a good enough glimpse to be sure.

Ferguson saw the silver back of a head in the chair closest to the doors; he guessed this was Park. Between the glass and the nearby waterfall, he couldn't hear a word.

Li appeared behind the men in uniform, looking straight at him. Ferguson stepped back and flattened himself against the wall.

A moment later, the door opened.

Li stepped out, less than eight feet away.

Ferguson froze, trying to think of an excuse to be here that wouldn't sound ridiculous.

Someone else came from the house. Ferguson saw his back as the two walked away.

"A good night for a walk, Captain Ganji," said Li in Korean.

"It's gotten warmer."

Ganji handed two large envelopes to Li as they walked in the opposite direction. Ferguson eased toward the corner of the terrace, hoping to get down and hide before they turned around. He was about a yard from it when he saw them shake hands and start back in his direction.

He pushed back against the side of the building, hidden by a shadow if anything at all. His mind blanked. He had no excuse, nothing.

He waited to be discovered, holding his breath. But the shadow was darker than he thought, and the two men were so intent on getting out of the cold that they didn't even glance in his direction.

Escaping such a close call gave Ferguson an adrenaline rush, but he couldn't put the energy to much use; the general and his aide left within a few minutes. Park and Li left the room as well but stayed upstairs in the cottage, their presence announced by a series of lights on the second floor. A pair of younger men, guards, came down into the room near the terrace and warmed their hands by the fire.

Deciding he'd seen all he was going to see, Ferguson

made his way back to the guesthouse. Along the way he stopped at the barn. Sneaking in through the window, he scouted the large room but found nothing more interesting than a stash of heavyweight gear oil in the corner and a burned-out clutch plate that looked to date from the 1950s.

Climbing the gutter back to his room seemed dubious, so Ferguson slipped around to the front. The guards had disappeared, and the open door beckoned. He went up the steps and walked in, but before he could go up the stairs Ha spotted him and called out his name. He was standing near the great room, talking with a friend.

Ferguson went over, mentioning how warm the night was.

"Warm for now, yes," said Ha, several notches beyond ripped.

"Drink?" asked his friend, who wasn't far behind.

"Sure," said Ferguson, thinking he might ask a few questions about Namgung.

They walked inside, Ferguson helping steady Ha as he made for the bar.

"Mr. Manski. Having a good time?"

"Mr. Li," said Ferguson in English. He swept around, pretending to be drunk. "Drink?"

"No, thank you," said Li. "We must rest now for the morning. The hunting starts at eight."

"Eight."

"Where is your escort?"

"Escort. Don't know," said Ferguson. "A short drink."

"No, thank you," said Li firmly, taking hold of the bottle. The other men had already retreated.

"I will have a chance to talk to Mr. Park soon?" said Ferguson.

"Very soon," agreed Li.

"He's an important man."

"Yes."

"Does he know many army officers in the People's Democratic Republic?"

Li stiffened. "He knows many people."

"General Namgung was very impressive. Important."

"Namgung," said Li, correcting his pronunciation. "Mr. Park does not know him well."

"Yes," said Ferguson. He told Li in Russian that it was important to know many military people, because their discipline rubbed off on you, and they were very good drinkers.

Li accompanied him to the stairs. As they started up, Ferguson remembered he had left the door to his room locked.

Ordinarily, this wouldn't be a problem—a quick twist with his pick and tension spring, and he could easily get in. But he didn't have his tools with him.

Improvise.

"Maybe another drink," he said to Li.

"No, no. Come now, Mr. Manski. To bed."

One of the young women who'd been serving the guests was coming down the steps. Ferguson saw that her hair was pinned at the back, clipped by a pair of simple bobby pins. He lurched toward her, knocking her down. As she shrieked, he grabbed one of the pins from her hair.

"Sagwa deuryeoyo," he said drunkenly. "I'm sorry, I'm sorry."

Li shook his head but smiled, then wagged his finger as the girl escaped. "Naughty, naughty," he told Ferguson.

"To bed," said Ferguson, hoping Li would leave him. He didn't, though, following Ferguson as he walked up the steps.

Ferguson worked the bobby pin between his fingers as he walked down the hall. As good as he was with locks, it was tough to cover a pick. Under the best circumstances it took a few seconds to get the tools oriented properly. A simple lock could be fairly resistant to an improvised tool. Even Ferguson, who'd used bobby pins as a kid to raid the liquor cabinet, couldn't guarantee results.

Li stayed right behind him the whole way to his room.

Ferguson stopped, put his hand out on the door, then turned and stuck his face in his companion's.

"I thank you for this great opportunity," he told Li. "Thank you very much. Thank you."

"Yes," said Li, backing away from Ferguson's spit.

As he got out his handkerchief, Ferguson ducked down to the lock, working the pin into it. He grabbed at the handle as if drunk, then managed to get the tumbler to turn just enough to force the door.

He glanced over his shoulder.

Li had already disappeared down the hall.

Pushed it a little too far tonight, Ferguson thought to himself after he relocked the door and tiptoed to bed. But better that than not far enough.

28

If he was going to do the right thing, then he was better off doing it without hesitation. The sooner he clued Corrine Alston—and, in effect, the president—into what Ken Bo was doing, the sooner he would end the temptation to do the wrong thing.

Because really, the temptation was overwhelming.

Slott picked up his phone and dialed her office.

"I want to give you a heads-up about something," he told her when she picked up her phone. "Can you come to my office?"

"When?"

"As soon as possible. Now would be good."

"Is it about Korea?" she asked.

"I'd rather explain in person."

"I'll be there in about an hour."

Corrine told her secretary to rearrange her schedule, then began closing down the documents she'd been reviewing. She was about to pick up her pocketbook when the phone buzzed.

"Mr. Ferro from the NSA," announced Teri.

Corrine grabbed the line.

"The tape unit you gave me last night is very interesting," said Ferro. "The system this came from, that it's part of, uses a Cray X1E as the main computing unit. It's a very powerful supercomputer. Where exactly did it come from?"

"You can't tell from the data there?"

"Not without more study. It's a backup of a large number of data sets, and it's going to take a while to unravel."

"I see."

"There are several simulations that seem to deal with some sort of complicated chemical extraction. It seems to involve plutonium," added Ferro. "We have to have an expert look at it."

"I see."

"Should we proceed?"

"Yes," said Corrine. "What about the small disks?"

"Some correspondence in Korean regarding the purchase of office supplies. Looks like it's all from a place called Science Industries. We haven't translated it all yet."

"You can move ahead with both."

"All right." Ferro paused. "Have you spoken to the CIA about this?"

"I'm on my way there now," said Corrine.

The South Koreans tried to make their own weapons-grade uranium in the nineteen eighties and nineties," said Slott. The words practically gushed from his mouth, and it was a relief to get them out. "The program was exposed in 2004. Ken Bo is claiming this is part of it."

He pushed the paper across his desk to Corrine. There were only three lines on it, a brief secure e-mail that mentioned two code-word CIA projects and "Korean efforts believed related to M."

"M is a reference to that project. You see, if he contends that this was part of that program, he and his people will be off the hook," said Slott. "It's a CYA memo. Cover—"

"I know what CYA stands for," said Corrine. "Is his claim right?"

Slott shook his head.

"How do you know?"

"I know. For starters, the material was different. This was plutonium. The waste was accounted for. Blessed Peak wasn't built until three years ago. So they would have had to hide the waste all this time, then move it here. Unlikely."

"But the site was used as a waste site before they built the new plant."

"For cesium, nothing else. I know because I ordered it checked, and the man who checked it didn't make a mistake."

"Are you sure?"

"It was Ken Bo."

Corrine leaned back in the seat.

"Does this mean he's not really looking for the plutonium?"

"No. He's getting himself in a position to limit damage in the future. He is pursuing it. How hard I don't know." Slott rocked back and forth in his seat. "He is working on it. He has a plan to get people into the waste site and take measurements. And one of his officers has been nosing around where Ferguson was, though rather ineptly. And, frankly, it seems to have been accidental, part of standard contact gathering. Though it's difficult to tell from here."

Corrine put the paper down on the desk.

"I have to tell you, Dan, face-saving games . . . They're

not very important to me. I don't care whether someone was at fault or not. I want to get results. The president, I'm sure, would feel the same way."

"I realize that," said Slott. "Though that's not the way Washington works."

"Did Bo screw up?"

"We should have known about this." Slott picked up his pencil, twisting the lead out slowly as he continued. "It's our job. Something like this is very important—critical. So by definition, *we* screwed up. And, by definition, when we screw up, it's my fault."

"You're being awful hard on yourself."

"It comes with the job."

"I don't see Director Parnelles taking responsibility. If the buck is going to stop anywhere, it has to stop at his desk, not yours."

Well, he thought, that's something at least. Not the reason I told her, but something.

"Thank you for saying that," he told her.

"I mean it."

Slott smiled faintly. He'd thought his conscience would feel better when he finished, but it didn't. Now that he'd told her what he thought Bo was up to, he only felt more depressed about it.

Then again, it really wasn't her problem, was it? It was his.

On the one hand, he didn't want her interfering; on the other, he had given her ammunition.

But it was the right thing to do, he decided: cut off the games.

"I'm sorry if I wasted your time," he told her.

"It wasn't a waste," Corrine told him, slipping the paper back. "I didn't mean to imply it was."

Slott started to get up, but Corrine didn't.

"There's something I have to tell you involving the First Team," she said. "Bob Ferguson went into a place called Science Industries and gathered some material there. He sent it back. It's very interesting. There may be information on extracting plutonium. I don't have all the details yet."

"Corrigan didn't mention that when he briefed me this morning."

"I know." Corrine had debated how to present the issue all the way to Slott's office. She decided that the best way, for the good of the team, was to blame herself: protecting the client, an old lawyer's trick. "I had Ferg use a back channel to get the data here because I wasn't sure how much to trust Seoul, based on your comments the other day."

Slott folded his arms and sank back into his chair as she continued. It's me they don't trust, he realized, and it wasn't just Corrine. Ferguson was in the middle of it. And probably Parnelles, whom Ferguson was close to.

Because he'd worked in Seoul, and Ferguson figured he was covering up for the people there.

Damned if you do; damned if you don't.

"The NSA has the tape and the disks," said Corrine. "The Department of Energy has the soil samples and is scheduling the tests now. I'll refer them to you."

She got up to leave.

"Yeah," said Slott, not bothering to get up. "Thanks."

29

NORTH OF SUNG HO, NORTH KOREA

Korean breakfasts were traditionally skimpy, and when the party was roused at seven-thirty the morning following the reception, all that was available was a large metal pot of weak tea. Ferguson downed two cups, and was on his third when his "translator" Chonjin appeared.

Ferguson's pretend hangover amused Chonjin greatly, and the North Korean quickly suggested a cure: an ill-smelling concoction mixed with goat's milk from the kitchen.

Ferguson wouldn't have trusted the remedy even if he'd had a *real* hangover. But with Chonjin watching, he decided he had to take at least a sip. His stomach revolted; he ran to the nearby washroom as Chonjin nearly doubled over laughing.

Another man came in as Ferguson wiped his face at the sink. He was a North Korean soldier in full uniform.

"Captain Ganji," said Ferguson. "*Annyeonghaseyo.*"

The man, a corporal, looked at him and shook his head, explaining in Korean that he was not a captain and certainly not Ganji. Ferguson apologized, then switched to Russian, saying that he admired Ganji, a very shrewd thinker and a good drinker.

The soldier shook his head, and told him in Korean that he didn't understand.

"English?" tried Ferguson.

That didn't work either. The man rattled off something far too rapidly for Ferguson to understand.

"*Mworago hasyeosseoyo?*" said Ferguson. "I'm sorry, I missed what you were saying."

"He was explaining that the captain is an aide to General Namgung," said Chonjin, coming inside the room. "He spends all of his time at the capital, at headquarters."

"Oh, very good," said Ferguson in Russian. He laughed. "And did I meet the captain last night?"

"He wasn't here." Chonjin turned to the other Korean and began quizzing him. "He says you thought he was Captain Ganji," Chonjin told Ferguson when he was finished.

"Oh. I was actually trying to say good morning."

"*Annyeonghaseyo.*"

"*Annyeonghaseyo,*" repeated Ferguson. "Doesn't sound like Captain Ganji or General Nagtum to me."

"Namgung," said Chonjin curtly. There was no longer

any trace of amusement in his voice. "He is a very important man."

"I'm sorry," said Ferguson. He turned to the other man, who had a very worried expression on his face. "I am very sorry."

"Joesonghaeyo," prompted Chonjin.

"Joesonghaeyo," said Ferguson.

"You speak English very well for a Russian," said Chonjin as the other man slipped past them.

"Thank you."

"You know more Korean than you let on."

"I keep trying."

Chonjin told him in Korean that he was the bastard son of a three-legged pig.

Ferguson got the bastard but missed the rest.

"You may be right," said Ferguson in Russian. "My mother was rather loose."

"Come," said Chonjin, switching to English. "Let's go hunting, if your head has cleared."

"Dah," said Ferguson, staying in Russian. "My head feels much better."

"Wait," said Chonjin as they got to the door. He reached into his jacket, and for a moment Ferguson thought he was going to pull out a gun. Instead he presented him with a small package. "Your business cards," he said in English.

"Спасибо," said Ferguson. "Thank you."

Pickup trucks with benches mounted on the sides of the beds were lined up at the front of the lodge. When all the guests had boarded, the trucks set off, following the dirt road and passing the house where Park had met with General Namgung. They continued along the stream for about a half mile before coming to the edge of an overgrown field. Two other trucks were there already, waiting. These had shotguns for the men to use.

"What are we hunting?" Ferguson asked his escort in Russian.

"Grouse," said Chonjin in English.

"I didn't know there were grouse in Korea," said Ferguson, sticking to Russian.

Chonjin shrugged, and led him toward the truck with the shotguns. Ferguson examined one. It was a Chinese pump design similar to a Winchester Model 12, with an inlaid pearl pattern in the highly polished stock.

"They loaded?" Ferguson asked.

"They will hand out ammunition when we reach the starting line for the hunt," said Chonjin.

Ferguson checked the magazine anyway. As he did, he saw Li approaching out of the corner of his eye.

"Mr. Manski," said Li, nodding to Chonjin. "Perhaps you would like to hunt with Mr. Park."

"Love to."

"Come with me then."

Chonjin took a step to follow but stopped when Li shook his head.

"You have recovered from last night?" said Li, leading him around the trucks and back up the road.

"Yes," said Ferguson.

"Remarkable."

"No more remarkable than anyone else."

"Tell me, Mr. Manski, how did you come to be locked out of your room?"

"I was locked out of my room? *правда*? I guess I don't remember much of anything."

"Where did you get a key?"

"Couldn't tell you."

Li made a kind of humphing sound, but said nothing else, continuing in the direction of the house. As they rounded the first curve, a military-style jeep drove down the road. Ferguson stepped to the side, making room for it to pass.

The jeep stopped in front of them. Park sat in the front, next to a driver.

Li took Ferguson's shotgun, then gestured for him to get in the back of the vehicle.

"Mr. Manski, again we talk," said Park. He used English and stared out the front of the jeep, not looking at Ferguson. Li remained on the road.

"Happy to have the opportunity."

"Why would you come to me? What could you possibly have that might be of use to me?"

"That's for you to decide."

"Yes. I am a businessman, Mr. Manski, not a general or a politician. Not a terrorist."

"Of course not."

"But you deal with terrorists."

"I deal with businessmen," Ferguson replied. "And I am discreet."

"Some of your customers are not. You have a reputation."

"I can get things done when they need to be done. I can make arrangements that a man like yourself . . . You could certainly do what you want, but others might question it. It might look embarrassing."

Ferguson expected that Park would stop the conversation soon, handing him back to Li to do the dirty work.

That was really all he needed. He'd spend the rest of the day hunting, drinking. Get back, make his report.

Probably be told to come home. Play it by ear then.

"I have a vision for Korea," Park said. "We will be reunited. We will resume our historic place in the world."

Park twisted back to look at him.

"Do you know any Korean history, Mr. Manski?"

"Not much," said Ferguson. "I know the Japanese raped your country."

"That doesn't begin to describe what they did." Anger flashed in Park's eyes, but he quickly controlled himself. "The history I refer to goes much deeper. Koreans ruled Asia. A small nation ruled the larger ones."

The Chinese had actually done most of the ruling in Asia, but Ferguson didn't think it politic to interrupt.

"Korean intelligence, work ethic, tradition . . . We are

a great people," continued Park. "Your country, Russia, it is large, too varied, and corrupt. There are many thieves in Russia."

"I have to agree."

"America . . . earnest but a mongrel nation."

"At best."

"Mongrels and thieves have no place in Korea."

"Of course not," said Ferguson.

Park smiled, then turned back to the front. "Mr. Li will speak with you now."

"Pleasure doing business with you, Mr. Park," said Ferguson, leaning to get out. "Pleasure."

The jeep jerked into motion before Ferguson was completely out. He had to do a little twist to regain his balance. When he did, he looked up and saw that Li was holding a pistol on him.

"Problem?" said Ferguson.

"There is no place for mongrels or thieves in Korea, Mr. Manski." An SUV drove up. Li nodded toward the truck as it stopped behind him. "You will get in."

"I don't think so."

"For myself, I don't care; killing you here would be very easy. But Mr. Park fears that our hosts would not like to offend your government and desire a little time to contemplate the arrangements. So I advise you to get in, before I decide that their feelings are not worthy of consideration."

ACT 4

Are you human, or a ghost?

—from "The Seventh Princess,"
traditional Korean song for the dead

1

Corporal Wanju stared at the figure, disbelieving as it seemed to rise directly from the ground. He was manning a guard post about seventy yards south of the Demilitarized Zone separating the two Koreas.

How had he appeared there? A tunnel?

The man ran toward the roll of barbed wire to the corporal's left.

"An enemy!" hissed the private who shared the corporal's observation post. "Corporal, look."

Corporal Wanju had served in the army for more than three years, and had been stationed at this post for more than five months. He had seen North Korean soldiers before, but always at a distance, through binoculars.

What was the man doing? Attacking? He didn't seem to have a rifle.

Spies attempted to infiltrate South Korea all the time, but never here. Besides, it was the middle of the day; only a fool would attempt to sneak across the border when he could be so easily seen.

"Corporal, we must shoot him! He is attacking!"

"Wait," said Corporal Wanju.

As he did, one of the machine gunners at the observation post fifty yards to the west began firing.

The figure seemed to pause in midstride, turning slightly as if to begin a dance.

And then his head exploded as if it were a blood-filled gourd.

Corporal Wanju turned aside and threw up.

2

OUTSIDE CHUNGSAN, NORTH KOREA

Sitting alone in the back of the SUV, Ferguson watched the countryside pass by. He determined that they were going northwest, but since he had only a general idea of North Korean geography, he had no idea where he was being taken.

There were two men in the truck with him, both in the front seat. While it was tempting to throttle one of the men and try and take his weapon, Ferguson realized that would be foolish; there was another vehicle behind him, and even if he managed to overcome the driver and his companion he'd almost certainly be outgunned.

The fact that he hadn't been bound or blindfolded seemed significant. The North Koreans were dressed in plain work clothes, not military fatigues. They might be with the internal security force, but if that were the case, why hadn't the pug-faced interpreter Chonjin come with them? He didn't even seem to know what was going on.

Possibly this was simply Park's way of testing him, though Ferguson couldn't quite see the logic of that.

Had Park or Li realized he'd seen them meeting with the North Korean general?

Maybe, but if so it would have been much easier to dispose of him in the way Li hinted they could.

For the moment, he decided, he'd stay in character, angling to be released to the Russian embassy. That might involve other problems, but he'd worry about them when the time came. His cover was solid; he knew from experience it would check out, even in Moscow.

The SUV pulled down a dirt road lined with spools of barbed wire. It bumped through some ruts, then pulled up in front of a gate. The driver rolled down his window, and a man in uniform approached. After a few words, the guard looked into the back, glared at Ferguson, then waved them through.

The SUV drove past a pair of antiaircraft guns at least twice as old as the soldiers standing in front of the sandbags nearby. The truck rounded a curve, passed a small wooden building, and then stopped in the middle of a large parade ground in front of a large, dilapidated stone building.

The door opened, and a soldier ordered Ferguson out. As he stepped out, the man pulled him by the shirt and pushed him forward.

"*СТОЙ!*" said Ferguson. "Stop it!"

The man continued to prod him toward the entrance. Ferguson dug in his heels and put out his hands, shrugging the man off. Then he began walking on his own power.

"Inside," said his escort roughly in Korean. "Go."

Ferguson entered a small room dominated by a fat coal stove. Red embers glowed behind its cast-iron gate.

A short, balding man in an officer's uniform asked him his name in Korean.

"Ivan Manski," Ferguson said. "*Hanggungungmai mot hamnida.* I don't speak Korean."

"That is of no concern to me," said the man.

"I want to speak to the Russian embassy," said Ferguson, first in Korean, and then in Russian.

"You will speak when spoken to," said the man. He told the man who had pushed Ferguson inside to take him to a cell.

"I want to speak to the Russian ambassador," said Ferguson. He reached for his passport, but before he could he was grabbed from behind and thrown against the wall. Two men held him there while he was searched; they found the passport and the business cards, along with the commercial sat phone Ferguson had purchased in Daejeon, his wallet, and thyroid pills. Ferguson was then pushed into another room and ordered to strip.

He began to undress slowly. This annoyed the man behind him, who pulled down the back of his shirt.

No self-respecting Russian, let alone an arms dealer with a background as unsavory as Ferguson's, would stand for that. Ferguson spun and planted a fist in the man's jaw so hard that the North Korean flew back against the wall, stunned. Instantly, the others were on top of him, pounding him with their fists. Ferguson fought back hard, drawing blood and breaking at least one nose, before finally the officer from the other room arrived, yelling that they were fools and to let the Russian pig alone.

Lying on the ground, Ferguson worked his tongue around his mouth, making sure he hadn't lost a tooth. He rolled onto his knees and felt his face. His nose was bleeding, and he could feel the welts starting to swell around his eyes. His kidneys were sore.

"Much worse will happen if you do not cooperate," said the man, standing over Ferguson. He pointed to a pair of blue prison pajamas. "Get up and get dressed in those clothes."

Ferguson didn't understand all the words, but the meaning was clear enough.

"I need my medicine," he said in Russian, standing.

The officer didn't understand.

"Pills." Ferguson had learned the phrase in Korean but couldn't get it out. *"Jigeum yageul meok,"* he stuttered finally. "I need my medicine."

The officer waved at him to go and take off the rest of his clothes.

"Meokgo isseoyo. Jigeum yageul meokgo isseoyo," repeated Ferguson.

They were the right words, though his pronunciation was halting. His head was still scrambled from the pounding he'd taken.

The officer said something to one of the men, who disappeared into the other room. Then he told Ferguson to get changed.

Not seeing another option, he did so.

3

P'YŎNGYANG AIRPORT, NORTH KOREA

Park Jin Tae stepped from the sedan and walked briskly to the ladder in front of his plane. His visit had been an enormous success, but he had much to do at home. He'd waited until evening to leave only because the vice chairman of the Communist Party had invited him to lunch, and it would not have been politick to refuse, much as he hated the ignorant water buffalo.

His assistant, Mr. Li, met him at the top of the steps, just inside the aircraft. He bowed in respect, then told Park that the defector had been shot at the crossing.

"Dead?" said Park.

"Very. There have been no news reports yet, however."

Park slipped into the leather seat at the center of the cabin. A steward stood near the polished mahogany bar, waiting for him to nod; when Park did so, the man brought him a shallow cup and a bottle of *makgeolli*, a humble milky white liquor that never failed to ease his cares.

Li, as was his custom, declined the invitation to share the drink.

"Did they find the papers?" asked Park as the steward retreated.

"I have not heard. Should I inquire?"

"Not yet. Wait and see what develops in the morning, and what we learn from our usual sources. This must unfold without our hand being seen."

4

OUTSIDE CHUNGSAN, NORTH KOREA

Without his thyroid pills, most of Ferguson's vital organs would start to slow down. His body would have trouble maintaining its proper temperature; he'd feel cold even in a room of seventy degrees. His muscles would ache, a by-product of their difficulty removing built-up waste material. His energy would ebb, a pale of lethargy descending over him. Within two or three days he would begin to slide toward clinical depression and acute anxiety, his brain having trouble keeping its serotonin levels stable.

At some point Ferguson's tissues would begin to swell, and he would develop fluid around his heart and lungs. Along the way his brain would turn to mush, and he'd become psychotic, assuming he was still alive.

But skipping the *first* dose of T4 pills he took every evening had a paradoxical effect: It made him hyperactive. His heart rate bounded upward, and his mind raced as if maybe he'd drunk one too many pots of coffee.

Unable to sleep, Ferguson spent the night pacing the

small cell, one of a dozen in the dank basement block. He was the only one here. Every so often, he stopped moving, straining to hear sounds from outside or above him, but all he heard was silence.

He strode back and forth in the small cell: three and a half strides this way, three and a half that, four to the front, four to the back. He did it for hours, trying to puzzle out the situation and decide what to do.

Rather than getting tired, his energy seemed to grow with each step. So when his interrogator came for him around four a.m., Ferguson was not only wide awake but also fully alert, the opposite of what the North Korean expected.

The man stood outside the bars and introduced himself in Korean, asking if Ferguson spoke the language. Ferguson told him in Russian that he did not.

Chinese?

No.

"I can speak German or English if you want," said Ferguson, switching between the two languages. "My French might work."

"We can speak English," said the man. "What is your name?"

"Ivan Manski."

"What do you do?"

"I sell scientific instruments for the Redstreak Company of Moscow."

"That is what you do?"

"Yes."

"You should not lie to me," said the man gently. He had a round, sad face with owl eyes that blinked, as if he were missing his glasses. He wore a long gray tunic and pants, civilian clothes.

"I'm not lying," Ferguson said.

"I have been told that you are an arms dealer."

"Arms? I don't understand."

Owl Eyes blinked. "You sell weapons to outlaws."

"Never."

The North Korean reached into his pocket and took out Ferguson's bottle of pills. "This medicine is important to you?"

"Sure."

"If you are truthful, you can have it."

Ferguson shrugged.

Owl Eyes pocketed the pills and walked away.

5

ALEXANDRIA, VIRGINIA

Daniel Slott and his wife had slept together for more than thirty years. In all that time, Slott hadn't lost his affection for the touch of his wife's body at night. The weight of her leg against his reassured him somehow, even when he was dreaming.

He felt the weight as he woke, then he heard the chirp of his beeper nearby. It had been buzzing for a few seconds.

The code on it told him to call one of the overnight people at headquarters. He palmed it and got out of bed, gingerly sliding his leg out from under his wife's. He grabbed his robe but not his slippers, gliding quietly down the steps to the first floor and then to the basement, where he had a small office.

"This is Slott," he said, dialing into headquarters on a secure phone.

"Boss, Ken Bo has something urgent to tell you in Seoul."

"What's going on?"

"I don't know."

"Hook me up."

Slott sat back in the old leather chair, a relic from his

wife's brother, waiting while the deskman arranged for him to talk to Bo. The paneled wall in front of him was lined with photos of old haunts and career stops, most of them in Asia.

There was a particularly amusing picture of him bowing to the statue of the Great Leader in P'yŏngyang on an official visit. He'd taken a lot of ribbing about that when he got back to D.C. Some of his colleagues laughingly suggested he might be changing sides, and the DDO at the time claimed he wanted Slott to bow to him in the same manner.

"Dan, I'm sorry to wake you up," said Bo when he came on the line.

"Go ahead."

"The Republic of Korean government yesterday afternoon recovered documents from a DPRK soldier indicating that the forces are to be mobilized within the next few days. The mobilization plan is one that we identified about a year ago as Wild Cosmos, Invasion Plan Two."

"Wild Cosmos? They're invading?"

"They're mobilizing. Supposedly."

"Was this a plant by ROK ahead of the elections?" ROK was the Republic of Korea, South Korea; DPRK was the Democratic People's Republic of Korea, the North.

"We're not sure," said Bo. "The circumstances are a little . . . vague. It looks to us like the guy was trying to defect, and the ROK soldiers screwed up. We're still pulling information out. They haven't shared it with the news media, and the ambassador wasn't told. In light of everything else," added Bo, "I thought you'd want to know personally."

In other words: I know you think I'm a screwup; here's some evidence I'm not.

"All right. Stay on top of it. Obviously."

"Will do."

An hour later, Slott arrived at Langley and began reviewing the situation with headquarters' Korean experts, most of whom had been sleeping barely an hour and a half before. They went over the latest satellite and electronic intelligence. There was no indication—yet, anyway—that a mobilization was imminent.

Judging from their actions, the South Korean government didn't seem to know what to make of the documents. They'd put a unit near Seoul on alert, yet hadn't notified any of the units guarding the DMZ. And the incident that had led to the discovery of the orders still hadn't been reported in the media.

When it came to human intelligence north of the border, the U.S. generally relied on South Korean intelligence, which had a good though not stellar network of agents there. Slott had never trusted the South Korean intelligence agency, known as the National Security Council. During his days in Korea, he'd found his counterparts consumed by agendas that had nothing to do with the North. Even a simple assessment of the fighting strength of an army division could become a massive political football, with the data skewed ridiculously according to whatever ox was being gored.

In this crisis—or noncrisis, if that's what it turned out to be—the Agency would have to rely primarily on information from the Koreans.

Except that he had his own officer somewhere north of the border. Ferguson's observations might be useful, especially since he was with Park, who had access to the highest reaches of the dictatorship.

Assuming Slott could contact him. Alone in his office, he picked up his secure phone and called over to The Cube.

"Corrigan."

"This is Slott. Is Ferg still north?"

"Uh, yes, sir."

"When's he due to check in?"

"Um, he's not due exactly. He thought regular check-ins would be too dangerous up there. He's not supposed to call in until he gets back and gets settled."

"Where is he exactly?"

"I'm not positive. He's north of the capital somewhere."

"Track him on his sat phone."

"No can do. He left the Agency phone in Daejeon and bought a local unit. He wanted to make sure he was clean."

Ferguson's precautions were entirely reasonable. That far under cover, in an extremely hostile environment, the slightest slip or unexpected coincidence meant death.

But they were certainly inconvenient, thought Slott.

"You want me to try calling his phone?" asked Corrigan. "I do have the number."

Slott weighed the danger of an unexpected phone call against the information they might get.

If he'd done that a few days ago, before sending the Seoul people down to get Ferg, would the op still trust him?

But it wasn't his fault the Seoul people had been so inept or that Ferguson had overreacted to the situation.

Let it go. It's past now.

But he couldn't let it go, not completely.

"Should I call?" repeated Corrigan.

"No," said Slott. "When is he due back?"

"Sometime soon. The 727 that brought them is still in P'yŏngyang. It hadn't been refueled the last time the satellite passed overhead. The billionaire's plane came back this evening. He generally leaves the night before his guests do. But the schedule isn't always predictable. Could be a few hours, could be a day or two."

"Let's get someone to wait for him at the airport. Tell him to call in as soon as he gets back. And I mean the second he gets there. Tell him to go right over to the embassy and get on the line back here."

"Uh, boss?"

"Yeah?"

"Last time, uh, we used the Seoul office, it didn't go too well. Ferguson—"

"Well, that's too bad. I need to talk to him."

"How about Thera? She's just killing time offshore with the scientist. We could fly her in, have her wait."

Slott thought about it. "All right," he said finally. "I'll call her."

"What's going on?"

Slott explained, briefly.

"Should I tell Ms. Alston?" asked Corrigan.

Slott felt instant heartburn.

"I'll tell her myself when she gets in. Get Thera for me."

ABOARD THE USS *PELELIU*, IN THE YELLOW SEA

Thera typed the notes on what Ch'o had said during their morning session for the CIA debriefer. She'd come to a working relationship with Jiménez, each taking turns listening to him talk.

The scientist was truly concerned about the effects of radiation poisoning on sites throughout North Korea and had provided her with a long list of sites that he said were poisoning people. Ch'o also told her, almost as an aside, that there were no other weapons aside from those that had been announced. Two of the weapons had been assembled without the proper amount of weapons-grade material, a fact supposedly kept from the dictator. It was a critical piece of information, since it could be verified during the inspection process and then used to test Ch'o's real knowledge of the program.

"Hey," said Rankin, popping his head into her cabin. "You busy?"

"No."

"Slott wants to talk to you. Up in the communications shack or whatever the hell name these navy people use for como."

Thera followed Rankin up to the communications department, where she picked up a secure phone and found Corrigan on the line.

"Stand by," said the mission coordinator.

"Thera, this is Dan Slott. How are you?"

"Fine, Dan. What's up?"

"I'd like you to go over to Gimpo Airport in Seoul and wait for Bob Ferguson. We need him to call us right away, as soon he's back from North Korea."

"He's in North Korea?"

Slott explained that Ferguson had gone north with Park, trying to talk to the billionaire because of the possible link to the plutonium.

"This isn't about that, though," he added, explaining the situation.

"I realize this is a messenger's job," he added. "But it's important, and for reasons I don't want to go into, you're the best person available."

"Not a problem. I'll leave as soon as I can say good-bye."

"I'm sorry?"

"Nothing. I can go as soon as you want."

"Good. Corrigan will give you the details."

7

Ferguson found himself running across the desert, going up a dead ringer for a hill he'd ridden over near the Syrian border with Iraq a few months before. Thera was there, running a few yards in front of him. Every so often she would turn around and glance over her shoulder. She had a terrified look on her face.

She wasn't scared of him, but just what she was frightened of he couldn't tell.

Metal clanged.

Ferguson fell out of the dream and onto the cot in the North Korean prison.

He looked up. A guard was walking away.

The man had slid a plate through a metal hole at the front of the cell. A half cup of cold rice sat in a mound near the middle.

Ferguson got up and carried the plate back to his cot. His hyper phase was over. He felt as if he'd been up all night and gotten only an hour or so of sleep, which was pretty much the case.

Picking up a few grains with his fingers, Ferguson forced himself to chew as slowly as possible. He was halfway through the dish when footsteps approached down the hall. He steadied his gaze on his food, concentrating on each grain of rice.

"Are you ready?"

Ferguson raised his head slowly. Owl Eyes blinked at him from behind the bars.

"Have you called the embassy?" asked Ferguson.

"Why would I call the embassy?"

Ferguson took another bite of the food. He heard a

clicking noise and looked up. Owl Eyes was shaking his pill bottle.

Ferguson went back to eating. When he looked up again, the interrogator was gone.

8

THE WHITE HOUSE, WASHINGTON, D.C.

Corrine sat down at her computer, checking her e-mail before leaving for an early-morning meeting at the Justice Department. The first note was from Slott, who'd posted it nearly two hours ago. It read simply:

Call me. First thing. Secure line.

She picked up the phone and dialed. As it connected, she braced herself, expecting he was still mad about her going around him.

Or actually Ferguson going around him, though she'd taken the blame.

"Slott."

"It's Corrine Alston, Dan. What's up?"

"The South Koreans picked some interesting documents off a North Korean soldier who may have been trying to defect. They seem to indicate that a mobilization order has been issued, getting the country ready to invade the South."

Slott continued, explaining that, if legitimate, the order would be hand-delivered to units throughout the country. They would begin mobilizing within a few days.

"The order would seem to set the stage for an attack," added Slott. "So far, nothing has happened."

"All right."

"I'm going to ask Ferguson to report on anything he might have heard when he comes back. I've asked Thera to meet him in Seoul to make sure he calls in. Being Ferguson, that's not always something you can count on. I thought you'd want to know."

"I do. Thank you," said Corrine.

"There's no new information on the computer disk. They're still working on it. I checked this morning."

The words sounded almost like they were a challenge, or maybe a question: Is there something else I should know?

"I see," said Corrine. "If I hear anything myself, I'll let you know."

It was a lame reply. She thought maybe she should apologize or at least get him to admit he was mad, but he hung up before she could think of a way to say any of that.

GIMPO AIRPORT, SEOUL, SOUTH KOREA

Thera got to Gimpo about seven a.m., driving over after landing at Osan Air Base, a U.S. Air Force facility not far from Seoul. She'd had her hair cut before leaving the *Peleliu* and picked up a pair of glasses to help change her appearance.

Once Korea's largest airport, Gimpo had been overshadowed in recent years by the larger Incheon Airport, but it was still a busy place, with over a hundred passenger flights every day. Park's 727 had been directed to use a special gate in the domestic terminal; a Customs officer had already been sent to meet them. A guard stood outside the waiting area, but Thera could see in easily enough by standing in the hallway. She leaned against a large round column, sipping a coffee as if she were waiting for a friend.

The first clump of men off the plane looked seriously hung over, shielding their eyes from the overhead fluorescents. The second and then a third group of men came in, looking even worse. The men were all in their forties and fifties, all Korean.

It was just like Ferguson to keep her waiting, she thought. At any second, she expected him to come sauntering out of the boarding tunnel, a big, what-me-worry grin on his face.

But he didn't.

As Park's guests were led through a nearby door to their vans waiting below, Thera slipped into the jetway, walking toward the cabin of the 727.

"Nuguseyo?" said a startled steward, turning around as she entered the plane. "Who are you?"

"Hello?" said Thera in Korean. She glanced down the wide aisle of the jet. "No one aboard?"

"What are you doing?" asked one of the pilots, appearing from the nearby cockpit.

"Just looking for a passenger."

"They're gone. All gone."

Thera craned her neck, making sure. The pilot started to grab her wrist. Thera jerked her hand up and grabbed his instead, pressing it hard enough to make him wince.

"Not a good idea," she told him in English before letting go.

10

Oh, they were dead, they were dead, they were all dead, bodies leaping out of windows and doors at him, faces contorted, leering, falling with blood and bruises and obscene grins.

I'm not going to die damn it, Ferguson told himself. Not today today today, and who cares about tomorrow?

A snatch of a song came into his head, then a memory of a mission, a flash-bang grenade going off almost in his ear.

He had to push on anyway.

Ferguson got up from the cot, shaking off the nightmare. He began pacing the cell.

He was hungry and cold and his legs hurt like hell, but the thing he couldn't stand was his brain bouncing back and forth, gyrating with thoughts.

He couldn't turn it off.

They hadn't tortured him yet. They must believe that he was *someone.*

Or else they were saving all their fun for later.

The dank air pushed against his lungs. His body ached where he'd been pummeled. His knee felt as if it had snapped. But the worst thing was that he couldn't think.

"I need to focus on something," he said as he paced.

Belatedly, he remembered that his cell was probably bugged.

Better not to show them any sign of weakness.

Ferguson sat back on the cot, willing himself back into control.

He tried thinking of fun times with his dad, but that

was no good; within seconds images of missions just came flooding in, the association too strong.

He pictured Maine, thinking of what it would look like now, an early snow on the ground.

Thanksgiving dinner.

That was a safe image, except it made him hungry.

Better to starve than go insane, he thought, picturing himself eating a large bowl of sausage stuffing.

11

DAEJEON, SOUTH KOREA

Thera took the train to Daejeon. When she got there, she checked the hotel where Ferguson had been staying as Ivan Manski. His room was empty, and he wasn't in the restaurant or one of the nearby shops.

Needing a place to stay herself, she took a room two floors above where he'd been staying. Then she called The Cube.

"Ferguson didn't make the flight," she told Lauren Di-Capri. "He's not in Daejeon, either. Has he checked in?"

"No."

"He didn't show at the embassy or anything like that, did he?"

"That would probably be the last place he'd go, knowing Ferg."

"Check, would you?"

"Of course. Thera, are you sure he wasn't on that plane?"

Thera laid her head back on the overstuffed chair. What the hell had happened to him?

"Thera?"

"No, he wasn't on the flight. I thought maybe I missed him." She knew she hadn't; it was a wish, not a thought. "Try his sat phone, all right?"

"Now?"

"Yes, now. I'll wait."

"It's off-line," said Lauren a minute later.

"I was afraid of that," said Thera softly. She pressed the button to disconnect the call.

12

NORTH OF P'YŎNGYANG, NORTH KOREA

General Namgung stood at attention as the tanks passed out of the camp, returning the stiff salutes of the crews. Dust and exhaust swirled around him, but he didn't flinch. His father had taught him long ago that a leader inspired with poise as well as words, and the old man would be proud of his bearing now.

What he would think of his plan to oust Kim Jong-Il was another matter entirely.

The senior Namgung had been a close comrade of Kim Jong-Il's father, Kim Il-Sung, the father of modern Korea. Kim Il-Sung was a true liberator, a gifted ruler who had saved his people. Kim Jong-Il was a poor shadow of his father, a debauched tyrant who had contracted venereal disease as a youth and was now slowly dying of kidney disease brought on by alcohol abuse.

His son, Kim Jong-chol, promised to be even worse.

Not that he would have the chance to rule.

Namgung dropped his arm as the last tank rolled out of the camp. An American spy satellite should be almost directly overhead, recording the movement. By now, alarms were going off in Seoul, where Park would have delivered the bogus plan by Kim Jong-Il to mobilize and attack. Over the next few days, a variety of North Korean army, navy, and air force units would mobilize.

Then, the unthinkable would happen, and everything would fall into place.

Namgung glanced upward as he got into his car. He smiled at the thought that some intelligence expert back in Washington might get a glimpse of his face.

Let the smug Americans try and guess what was really going on.

13

DAEJEON, SOUTH KOREA

The black leather miniskirt was a little stiff, but there was no doubt it was effective; the security officer at the gate of Science Industries had trouble getting his eyes back in their sockets before waving Thera and her driver into the complex. The male receptionist was more influenced by cleavage; he stared at her chest as he dialed the managing director to tell him his appointment had arrived.

"But you do not seem to have an appointment," he told Thera.

"I would think he'd talk to me, wouldn't you? It has to do with a mutual business acquaintance, a Mr. Manski. The Russian. Would you remember him yourself?"

Thera leaned over the desk. The receptionist, in his early twenties, looked as if he was about to have a coronary.

"No. I wouldn't remember anything," said the man. He got back on the phone and persuaded the managing director's secretary that the boss would definitely want to meet the visitor.

A few minutes later, Thera was escorted into the director's office. She was playing the role of a jilted business partner, out to find Ferguson because he owed her money. In theory, she was Irish, the redheaded daughter of a one-time IRA member who'd done some business with Ferguson in the past, Deidre Clancy. There was a *real* Deidre Clancy, but she was presently serving time in an Angola prison after being caught short of bribe money on a deal Ferguson had arranged for her.

Thera told herself to tone down her performance, afraid she was going too far over the top. But it was like trying to stop yourself from skiing downhill in the middle of the slope.

And besides, wasn't that one of Ferguson's rules? When in doubt, push it as far as it will go?

The managing director's secretary said that Dr. Ajaeng was very busy and might not be able to see her before lunch.

"Then perhaps he and I should have lunch," suggested Thera. She took a seat opposite the secretary, adjusting her skirt.

The managing director's schedule cleared up within minutes. The secretary personally escorted her, stroking the back of Thera's fake fur coat.

"How can we help you?" said the managing director.

"I am looking for a friend. Or, rather, a business acquaintance. A special business acquaintance."

As Thera sat in the seat near his desk, she pulled out a pack of cigarettes and offered it to the managing director. He shook his head. There had been signs downstairs saying that smoking was not allowed in the building, but the director didn't object as she lit up.

This was a trick she had learned from Ferguson. Breaking rules always had an effect on a subject. Sometimes it annoyed them and made them want to get rid of you. Other times it created an unspoken intimacy, making them a partner in crime. Either way, it gave you something to use.

The effect on Dr. Ajaeng was somewhere between the two.

"I don't know what friend we might share," he said, shifting uncomfortably in his chair.

"Ivan Manski. Call it a business associate, for I'm not feeling very friendly toward him today. He was here some days ago trying to sell . . . ," Thera paused. "Scientific instruments."

"Manski. No I don't recall him."

His expression indicated otherwise.

"Mr. Manski and I, we have an interesting arrangement. He happens to owe me a spot of money," said Thera.

She stopped right there. That was enough.

"I'm afraid I don't know anything about that," said the managing director.

"Of course not." Thera smiled, then rose to go. "Is Mr. Park in?"

"Mr. Park?"

"I believe our friend went to North Korea with him. Perhaps he might know where he has gone to."

"Mr. Park never comes here."

"I thought he had an office. My mistake." Thera started for the door, then abruptly turned back, catching Dr. Ajaeng staring at her. "I'm at this hotel. Ask for me. Deidre. They'll know."

Too much, too much, too much, Thera told herself as she left. Even so, she made a point of saying good-bye to both the secretary and the receptionist, and waved at the guard as her driver took her out of the complex.

Are they working?"

"Loud and clear," Lauren DiCapri told Thera. "What are you wearing, anyway?"

"Well, now, do you think I'd be telling you that?"

Lauren laughed. "They want to jump your bones."

"I'll bet."

"You dyed your hair orange?"

"Kind of an orange red. Goes with the new haircut."

"It must be a stunner."

"Thank you."

"The managing director called someone named Li and told him about you. Li seems to be an assistant to Park; I have Ciello checking it out."

"Have they called the hotel?"

"No. There's been no attempt to check out your room, either."

During her visit to Science Industries, Thera had left bugs under each chair she had sat in. The units transmitted what they heard to a booster station—it looked like an old-fashioned transistor radio—outside the grounds. The booster uplinked to a satellite, which in turn relayed to The Cube. The tiny bugs would work for roughly four hours.

Thera told Lauren she was going to change, then run some errands. "Let me know if anything comes up."

"What kind of errands?"

"I want to check out the trucks at the university where Ferguson planted the gamma tabs."

"Be careful, Thera. Really careful."

"That would take all of the fun out of it."

Thera had dismissed her driver after the visit to Science Industries, so she had to navigate the clogged and confusing local roads herself in a rented Daewoo. The traffic wasn't that bad, she decided after a few minutes, as long as you followed the golden rule of international driving: Once moving, don't stop for anything.

Thera spotted both trucks near a loading dock at the university. She pulled in next to them, ignoring the sign that indicated she wasn't allowed to park there.

Thera had no idea where Ferguson would have put the gamma tags, and it took quite a while before she finally discovered one in the space near the door of the first truck. Thera rolled up the door and dug it out with her fingernails; it had not been exposed to any radiation.

She was just opening the back of the second truck when a gruff voice asked her in Korean what the hell she thought she was doing.

Two men in overalls with university emblems stared at her from the asphalt.

"What are you doing in the truck?"

"Are these your trucks?" she answered, using English. "The trucks. Oh, do you understand English?"

Her brain spun for a second, trying to translate. The Korean word for truck, *teureok*, was easy, but she had to gather it into a sentence to show, no, to *ask*, about possession. By the time she did, the shorter of the two men had told her, in English, that these were the school's trucks, and by the way, Miss, you're not allowed to park here.

"I need to have some things moved," Thera told him, jumping on the pretense as it flew into her head. "And I was wondering if these were big enough."

"These are school's trucks, Miss. Teachers can't use them."

"Well, yes, of course." Thera pushed open the door. The tab was on the right side, in the crack at the bottom.

Was the top red?

No.

"Can they be hired?" said Thera.

"What do you mean?"

Thera climbed up into the back. "I have to move some furniture. I've been staying in the city, but I'm going to have to fly back to Ireland and I need to ship things. I don't know what to do."

The taller man told her in Korean that she was crazy and that she must come out of the vehicle instantly.

"I'm not crazy," she said. "But I have only a few days."

"You can rent a truck," said the shorter man. "There are many places."

"I was told there weren't. If you want to ship in an airplane, you have to make special arrangements."

"Well, that is not always true. They have containers for shipments. We brought one to the airport just the other day."

He raised his hand to help her down. Thera pretended not to see it, squatting down.

"Yesterday?"

"Two, three days ago."

The day Ferguson had gone to the airport?

"Which day?" asked Thera.

The man shrugged. "Three days."

"So you can carry heavy things," she said quickly.

"Of course."

"Really heavy?"

"The container was very heavy," said the man. "So heavy we almost were in trouble."

Keep the conversation moving, Ferguson had told her. Don't give them time to realize how truly odd your questions are.

Did he say that, or did she imagine he said that?

"I do have a lot of things that need to be moved," Thera told him.

"Don't say anything to her," said the other man, again in Korean. "She's a lunatic."

"But pretty," said the other man.

"You have air in your head," his companion told him. "You're thinking with your privates."

The other man walked toward the other truck. Thera sat on the edge of the truck, swinging her blue-jean–clad legs.

"Maybe you could rent a truck for me?" she asked. "I love Korea, but sometimes it can be difficult to understand what needs to be done."

The man seemed willing to help, though he wanted a lot more than just a few thousand *won* out of it. Thera quizzed him on where he had been under the guise of asking about his truck-driving abilities. Again he mentioned the delivery to the Gimpo airport, where he and his friend had taken a relatively small but very heavy cargo container. He was an extremely careful driver, he said, and had even taken his vehicle to explosive plants.

"To carry explosives?" Thera asked.

"No."

"Just went there?"

"I go where I'm told."

Special licenses were needed to transport explosives, and it was not clear whether he was avoiding the question to make himself seem more competent or to stay out of trouble.

His companion blared the horn in the other truck.

"You must move your car. The police will have it towed," said the man.

"You're very sweet," Thera said, touching his shoulder. "Give me your phone number so I can call you."

OUTSIDE CHUNGSAN, NORTH KOREA

Shapes and faces and stabs of knives in his head.

No, I want to think of something pleasant, Ferguson told himself. No more missions.

Swallow the radioactive pill and let it kill the poison.

"Far away for death," Ferguson whispered. "Just far away."

He forced his brain to roam into the past . . . to prep school.

Not always pleasant. The Jesuits were a tough crew, toughening up the boys they taught.

Literature? When was it: the American school in Alexandria, the Jesuit school, the Korean school?

He'd never been to a Korean school.

What if they grabbed him now, stuck him in ice-cold water, threatened to freeze him to death if he didn't talk.

It was freezing here already. Couldn't get much colder.

"Hence! Home, you idle creatures, get you home."

The beginning of *Julius Caesar*. Brother Mark used to say it to end class.

Now that had been a good year. They'd even done that play. He'd been Anthony.

Antony.

Marcus Antonius.

Anthony.

"Friends, Romans, countrymen, lend me your ears; I come to bury Ferguson, not praise him. The evil that men do lives after them. The good is oft interred with their bones."

No good I've done.

"Jesus, it's cold," said Ferguson, rolling up from the cot and walking to generate some heat.

" 'Oh judgment, though art fled to brutish beasts,' " said Ferguson, the words from Antony's famous speech springing back from some recess of his brain. " 'Men have lost their reason!' "

Good God almighty, it was cold.

15

DAEJEON, SOUTH KOREA

"They went to the airport probably the day Ferguson left," Thera told Corrigan when she checked in with him after returning from the university. "They delivered some sort of cargo container. It sounded to me like it was the first time they ever did something like that. It was unusual—they were bragging about it—and it was very heavy."

"A shipping container?" asked Corrigan.

"One of the drivers said it was very heavy, heavy enough that he was worried about having the right license. They're fined personally if the police stop them and their trucks are overweight."

"What kind of cargo container?"

"One that goes on an airplane."

"You're talking about a unit-load device?" asked Corrigan.

"Like a baggage thing?"

"OK. That's what it's called: a unit-load device." Corrigan typed search terms into one of his computers to get background information. "How could something like that be so heavy he was worried about weight restrictions?"

"You tell me."

Her room phone began to ring.

"Hang on just a second, Corrigan."

Thera went to the bed table and picked up the phone. It was the downstairs desk, telling her that someone was asking for her.

"Tell him I'll be down in fifteen minutes," Thera told the clerk. "I'm just taking a shower. No. Better make it thirty."

Thera put the phone down and immediately took out her gun.

"What's up?" asked Corrigan.

"I'm betting it's someone from Science Industries. Maybe for Park. Hold on."

She turned the water on in the bath and stepped back into the room, waiting, half-expecting whoever had come to the desk to try sneaking in while she was vulnerable. But no one came.

"I'm going down," she told Corrigan finally.

"If I don't hear from you in ten minutes, I'm calling out the dogs."

"I'll need more time than that," said Thera.

"Don't take too long. Everybody's jumpy. Slott wants to send over some of Van's SpecOps people to shadow you."

"The last thing I need right now is an audience," said Thera. She stuck her head in the shower, then wrapped her hair in a towel. "I'll call back."

Mr. Li spotted Thera as soon as the elevator doors opened. He rose from the sofa where he had been waiting patiently and walked toward her, admiring her swift stride as much as the trim body that produced it.

"You are Miss Deidre?" he said.

"Just Deidre," Thera said, holding out her hand.

Li didn't know whether to shake it or kiss it. Instead, he bowed.

"Who are you?" she asked.

"Mr. Li. Very nice to meet you."

"And I you. To what do I owe the pleasure?"

"You were making inquiries about Mr. Park?"

"He and I have a friend in common." Thera noticed that Li was uneasy about standing in front of the elevators and talking; she decided to keep him there as long as possible.

"Mr. Park has many friends and acquaintances."

"This one owes me a great deal of cash." Too harsh, Thera realized; she tried to backtrack. "On the other hand, Mr. Manski has many positive traits."

"Mr. Manski. Ah, yes, he accompanied us to North Korea."

"I see. Why, exactly?"

The question took Li by surprise. "The other half of our country is an interesting place. There is a great deal of history. In the future—not very long from now, I hope—we will be reunited."

"Mr. Manski has very little use for history."

"Perhaps it was for the hunting, then."

"What was he shooting? People?"

"Birds," answered Li, stone-faced.

"I guess. But he didn't return with you?"

"He told us he was making other arrangements. He said he had business with some northerners."

"That's unusual. Mr. Manski doesn't ordinarily work in the People's Republic."

Li shrugged.

"Perhaps Mr. Park can tell me more," she told him. "When can I meet him?"

"I don't know that Mr. Park will be available."

Thera reached up behind her head to the towel, unwrapping it and drying her hair. The gesture was not overtly sexual, and yet Li stood transfixed, watching as if she were unwrapping a great jewel.

"I don't know what I should do," Thera said as her hair fell loose. "Would you advise contacting the police? Mr. Manski does owe me a spot of money. A rather large spot."

"How much?" said Li.

"Oh, dollars and cents aren't the issue," said Thera, realizing that Li thought she was shaking him down. "I just want to find him. I hope Mr. Park can help."

"Mr. Park is a very busy man."

Thera smiled. "Give him my regards, please." She turned and walked back to the elevator.

Li hesitated, then followed. "What exactly are you going to do?" he asked as she waited for the elevator.

"Find Mr. Manski and settle up."

The elevator doors opened. For a flicker of a second, Thera thought that Li would take out a gun and try to force her to come with him. But he remained motionless, watching as she got into the elevator and pushed the button to go upstairs.

"Thank you," she told him as the doors closed.

He frowned, then curtly lowered his head.

16

ABOARD THE USS *PELELIU,* IN THE YELLOW SEA

Rankin folded his arms as the ship's executive officer explained to Colonel Van Buren the difficulties involved in sailing closer to North Korean territory. First of all, they had orders to maintain their position two hundred miles off the coast of *South* Korea. And second of all, anything they did would attract the attention of the North Korean Navy—not only against their orders, but a detriment to any mission Van Buren hoped to launch.

"Maybe you oughta let the colonel worry about that," said Rankin, unable to stand the BS any longer. "He's done this before, you know?"

The ship's exec and intelligence officer looked at him like he was a cockroach that had just run across the galley deck.

"We need to be within a hundred miles of the target area," said Van Buren, his voice smooth but firm. "So we need to be further north."

"You know, Colonel, it would be helpful if you could tell us precisely *where* the target area is," said the ship's captain, who had said nothing until now. "It's difficult to plan for something when we don't know where it's going to take place."

"I don't know myself," said Van Buren. "We're working on it."

"Generally, we like to know where the hell we're going before we get there," said the exec sarcastically.

"By then it'll be too damn late," said Rankin.

"We have only the most general idea," said Van Buren smoothly. "We're positioning for a rescue mission. If we knew where we had to go, I assure you we'd be underway already."

"You don't even know if there's going to be a mission," said the intelligence officer.

He sounded like he was making an accusation rather than stating a fact.

"That's right," said Van Buren calmly. "Exactly."

"Colonel, even if I wanted to accommodate you," said the captain, "my orders are pretty specific."

"I'll take care of your orders. Let's have another look at that map."

"You'll take care of our orders?" snapped the exec.

Rankin had listened to all he could stand and walked out of the meeting. No one tried to stop him, not even Van Buren.

When they found out that Ferguson was missing, Rankin had suggested they launch a search-and-rescue mission immediately. There were two problems with that: First of all, they weren't exactly sure where Ferguson had gone after landing at the capital, and, second, Slott said there was too much else going on in Korea to risk an incursion, certainly not without hard evidence of where Ferguson might be.

Even if they had evidence, though, at the moment they were too far away to get him. The Little Birds' range was at best three hundred miles on a combat mission. If word came right now that Ferguson was standing on the double-loop roller coaster at *Mangyongdea Fun Fair* near the North Korean capital, it would take the *Peleliu* several hours to get into position to pick him up.

Van Buren at least understood the problem, and had come to the ship personally to get the idiot commanders here to cooperate. Van was an exception to the rule that officers were jerks—the exception that proved the rule. The colonel thought and acted like a noncom, but had the eagle on his collar to back up what he said.

"Giving up making nice to the navy?" said Jiménez when Rankin walked into the officers' wardroom to see if he could get some coffee. Jiménez was sitting with the translator at a table, going over their strategy for the next interview session.

"The navy's fine. It's officers I can't stand," Rankin told him. "Where's Ch'o?"

"Taking a nap."

"Tell you anything important?"

"Mostly he wants to know where Thera is and whether she's really OK." Jiménez smiled. "He has good taste in women."

"I guess."

"You don't think she's cute?"

"She'd bust you in the mouth again for saying that."

Jiménez flushed.

"Don't worry, I won't tell anybody," said Rankin. "Besides, she's beaten the crap out of a lot tougher guys than you."

17

DAEJEON, SOUTH KOREA

Thera had only just returned to her room from the elevator when the room phone rang. It was Mr. Li, calling on his cell phone.

"Mr. Park would like to invite you to dinner," he told her. "This evening. A car will pick you up at eight p.m."

"That would be very convenient," she said.

Thera glanced at the clock. It was nearly five; she had less then three hours to find a dress suitable for an arms dealer's first date with a billionaire.

18

Hugh Conners picked up the pint of Guinness Stout and held it in front of Ferguson.

"Look at it, Ferg. Aye that's a beer," said Conners, his Irish accent far thicker in death and dream than it had been in real life. "You'll be wantin' to drink up now, lad, if you know what's good for ya."

"Hey, Dad," said Ferguson, using the dead sergeant's nickname. "How's heaven?"

"Ah, it's a grand place, Fergie, simply grand. A parade every afternoon, and the taps never run dry. Drink up now."

"Can't."

"Ah, you have to. We have a place saved for you. We've been waitin' a whole long time fer ya, a whole long time."

"Gotta go."

"Stay awhile and have a song."

"I'm sorry I couldn't save you," said Ferguson.

Suddenly overcome with grief, he began to cry.

"Ah, now, there's a good lad. No savin' to be done," said Conners gently. "Yeh did yer best."

"You shouldn't have died. It should've been me."

"A song to brighten your mood." The sergeant, killed during a First Team mission a year before, began singing "Finnegan's Wake."

"Gotta go," said Ferguson, and the next moment he was awake, back in North Korea, heart pounding and head spinning.

He hadn't had his drugs now in what?

Twenty-four hours?

Forty-eight?

Longer. And he hadn't eaten and was run down to start with.

If his hands were this cold, it had to be three days at least, and it felt like twice that, maybe because he hadn't eaten and had had almost nothing to drink.

Plus, it was cold, cold and damp. So maybe it wasn't the lack of drugs but just something stupid like lack of sleep and isolation.

Stupid things he could beat. Those things he could beat. He couldn't get by the lack of the hormones, but thirst and fatigue he could beat. He'd been cold before and hungry plenty of times.

So, really, Ferguson told himself, things weren't that bad. Because he'd only been off the drugs two or three days, maybe just one now that he really thought about it, now that he decided it was one day, twenty-four hours, and probably, certainly, not even that.

What was that? Nothing. Nothing at all.

He could last for a long time. He'd gone two weeks without them during the worst of the treatments . . . two whole weeks.

A *hell* of a two weeks. But he'd made it.

So this was nothing. He could do this on his head. He could last months if necessary.

And when the time came, when he couldn't do it, he'd make the bastards shoot him.

"Ivan, are you ready for your medicine?"

Ferguson looked up from his cot.

"I don't need it," he told Owl Eyes.

"You look tired."

"I've been sleeping like a baby."

The North Korean took the bottle from his pocket and popped off the cap with his thumb. The white disk rolled across the floor.

The two men locked glares. Owl Eyes raised his hand, then slowly upended the bottle. The pills, large T3s, small T4s, tumbled out to the ground.

The North Korean put the toe of his right foot over the

ones closest to Ferguson's cell. Well in reach if he dove for them, Ferguson thought.

He wasn't going to; that was what Owl Eyes wanted.

Diving was the same as giving in. Diving was surrender. And he would never ever fucking surrender.

Slowly, the North Korean put his foot down and crushed the pills as if he were putting out a cigarette. He dragged his foot back across the floor, pulling the powder back out of reach.

Owl Eyes systematically crushed the remainder, one by one. When he was done, he motioned to someone down the hall, and had him bring a mop and bucket.

"When you are ready," Owl Eyes told Ferguson as the floor was mopped, "perhaps we will be able to find replacements."

"Have you spoken to the embassy yet?" said Ferguson, staring at Owl Eyes.

"I have no need to speak to your embassy." He started to walk away.

"Then do me a favor and call General Namgung. Tell him the Russian who was outside during his meeting at the lodge hopes to be of use."

Owl Eyes continued to walk down the hall.

"If the general isn't around, have him send Captain Ganji," Ferguson said, his voice just under a shout. "Mention the meeting. It was at the lodge. I was there. Tell him."

19

Corrine had arranged her schedule today so she could start by going to the dentist. Not among the most pleasant ways of beginning a day, though it had one benefit: She could stay in bed until seven, since her dentist's office didn't open until eight. So when the phone rang at six, her response was to curse and roll over in bed, trying to ignore it.

Then she realized it was her secure satellite phone that was ringing. She grabbed for it, hoping it was The Cube telling her that Ferguson had just shown up in some bar in South Korea.

But it wasn't The Cube.

"Stand by for the president," said the operator.

"Well, dear, I hope I did not get you out of bed too early," said McCarthy a moment later.

"No, sir."

"Good. We are on our way to Green Bay this morning to see some dear friends and even more fervent enemies, so I wanted to make sure I caught you early. You have been following the information the CIA has developed out of Korea, I would imagine."

"Yes, sir, of course."

"Good. What do you make of that bucket of string beans?"

"Twisted and gnarled," she said. "As your grandmother would say."

"She put it that way many times," said the president. There was a faint hint of nostalgia in his voice, as if he were picturing her in his mind. The tone always accompanied that expression, which he used at least twice a week. Corrine had never been able to determine if it was genuine or just part of his shtick. Perhaps it was both.

"I wonder if you would mind doing me a favor today?" McCarthy added.

"Sir?"

"I wonder if you would sit in on a briefing that is being arranged for the Security Council this morning. I believe the time is eleven. You may have to check on that."

"That's not in my job description, Mr. President."

"Well, now, are we going to have the job description conversation again, Miss Alston?"

She could practically see his smile.

"It would be unusual for me to attend," she said.

"Well now, tongues may wag. That is very true," said McCarthy before turning serious. "I want you there to consider the implications of our treaty with the North. Officially."

"Yes, sir."

"Unofficially, of course, the information may be useful to you in your dealings with our First Team. And as always I would *appreciate* your perspective. Now, dear, this all may well prove to be a wild rumor," continued the president. "The timing of it seems very suspicious to me. Consider: the North has been making *conciliatory* gestures over the past year. The dictator is rumored to be ill. All of this is not a context for planning an invasion. Assuming they are sane, which some might argue is a poor assumption."

"I'd agree with that."

"Well, now, of course we must take it very seriously. Very, very seriously, dear. And one of the things that taking it seriously entails . . ."

The president paused. That *was* part of his shtick, to make sure the listener didn't miss what followed.

". . . would be *not* doing anything that would entice action by the North Koreans."

"Understood, Mr. President. The portion of, uh, the matter in North Korea that might have caused concern has concluded. The results so far appear negative."

"Very good timing, Miss Alston. And on our other matter, regarding the Republic of Korea?"

"We're still working on it. Nothing new."

"Very well. Do your best."

Corrine put down the phone and got out of bed to start the coffee.

Oh, well, she thought to herself as she headed to the kitchen, at least I don't have to go to the dentist.

20

DAEJEON, SOUTH KOREA

Thera had never been much of a clotheshorse, but even she had to admit that the clingy black and silver satin dress reflected in the elevator's mirror looked stunning on her. She tossed her red hair back and set herself as the elevator reached the lobby, ready for dinner, and whatever else followed.

Park's Mercedes waited at the curb outside the hotel. Thera slid in, sinking into the leather-covered seat. A passerby gave her a jealous glance as the chauffer closed the door, no doubt believing that the Westerner was living a fairy tale.

Which was true enough, in a way.

Roughly forty-five minutes later, the sedan pulled through a set of gates on the side of a mountain road north of the city and drove up a long, serpentine driveway. The concrete gave way to hand-laid pavers within a few yards of the road. The car's headlights caught elaborate castings inset among the bricks: Dragons, gods, ancient Korean warriors lay at her feet as the Mercedes drove up the hill toward the mansion.

The house seemed like a gathering of squat, chiseled stones and clay-clad roofs, as if an old village had been compressed into a single building. The scale was deceiving; only as she reached the door did Thera realize that the single-level building was as tall as a typical three-story house.

A butler in formal attire met her at the door. The entry alcove was slightly lower than the rest of the floor, a reminder to guests that they should leave their shoes. A pair of slippers sat on a cushion nearby.

"Ms. Deidre, Mr. Park is waiting inside," said the butler as Thera slipped off her shoes.

"Thank you," said Thera.

"You understand, please, that it would be rude to search a guest."

Thera smiled. Her dress was not so slinky that it couldn't conceal two holsters, one on each thigh.

"A host should not stare," Thera told the butler.

It took a second for him to get the hint and turn around. Thera hiked her skirt and removed the weapons, deciding that she would leave both out here. This proved a good call—as she passed through the nearby doorway she noticed a series of LED lights embedded in the molding; the polished wood hid a metal detector.

Park's servant led her down the hall to a room that looked as if it belonged in a museum. Ancient pottery, small statues, and antique armor and weapons were displayed on boxlike pedestals in the low-lit, moisture-controlled hall. The walls were adorned with paintings and scrolls, all very old.

Park wasn't here; clearly she was expected to spend a few minutes admiring his taste in antiquities, adding to the suspense of his grand entrance. Thera folded her arms and turned toward a grill she suspected of harboring a video cam, staring at it with her most cynical expression.

"Miss Deidre, good evening."

"Mr. Park," said Thera, turning as the white-haired gentleman appeared from the side of the room. He was in his midsixties, not much taller than she was, on the stocky side though not fat.

"I am so very glad you could make it," said Park. He reached for her hands, grasping them with surprising strength. He kissed them as if she were a medieval princess. "Mr. Li told me that you were ravishing, but he did not do you justice."

"You are very kind, Mr. Park. You have a wonderful collection," she added, sweeping her hand around the room. "All Korean?"

"Most but not all. I have some Chinese and even Japanese items. Either for context or because they interest me." Though accented, his English sounded as if he had lived in America for many years.

Park showed her around the room, talking about the antiquities and where they had been found. Thera let him lead her through, inserting the proper *oo*s and *ah*s. Just as they were running out of display cases, the butler appeared in the doorway.

"Would you like to eat Western-style or Korean?" asked Park.

"Korean, of course," said Thera.

Park told the butler in Korean that they would use the traditional dining room. He then led Thera through a door at the side of the room into a large dining room. Scrolls with Korean characters and ink-brush paintings lined the stucco walls. A low table surrounded by mats sat in the middle of the room. Two of his servants stood next to it.

Thera lowered herself to the table, curling her legs under her on the cushions. A stream of food began to appear: small dishes of different kimchi, then a local fish dish, then another, then a grilled duck. Thera worried that she would split the dress when she got up.

Park did not speak during dinner. Thera remained silent as well.

When they were finished, he led her down the hallway to another room, this one a cross between a study and an artist's gallery. Park showed her a *minhwa*, a traditional Korean painting, in this case a landscape that he had been working on. The rustic style was deliberately primitive, meant to evoke a simpler people living in a simpler time.

"You have many talents," she told him.

He acknowledged the compliment by lowering his head.

"I would not have accused you of liking simple things," added Thera. Deciding the time had come to push Park, she ran her fingers down his arm.

"The advantage to the style is that one's lack of artistic skills are assumed," said Park, ignoring the stroke of her hand.

"Your desk does not look very rustic."

Thera let go and walked over to the desk, a modern glass and metal table. A computer and a phone sat to one side. A few mementos—a small car, a model airplane, a misshapen glass marble—sat at the front. Otherwise the surface was clear.

"Does your company make these planes?" Thera asked, pointing at the model.

"No," said Park, amused. "Those are Russian planes, the latest MiG fighter. A handsome design, don't you think?"

"Very. Are you buying these?"

"I don't have a need for such a toy."

"I meant for your business."

"My venture in aircraft a few years ago ended poorly. One of my firms makes aircraft parts. We may try and make some parts for the Russians. Their designs are good, but the executions are not as dependable as Korean craftsmanship."

"It depends on the item," said Thera, a salesman sticking up for her wares.

"A Korean-built fighter would be very potent," added Park. His voice was almost wistful. "Perhaps some day."

"I would think it would be an excellent aircraft, especially if you were involved." Thera put her finger on the tip of the plane, bobbing it on its stand. "I wonder, Mr. Park, what do you think happened to my friend Ivan Manski?"

"I wouldn't know."

"He was with you in North Korea, wasn't he?"

"He was with my party. I don't believe we had a chance to say more than a few words."

"And where was that?"

"A lodge near the capital where I often go. Very nice hunting. Once, it belonged to my family."

"He didn't return with the others."

Park gave her an indulgent smile, then walked to a large lacquered chest at the side of the room. "Would you join me in a drink, Miss Deidre?"

"Surely."

"In the past, Korean farmers brewed this," said Park, handing Thera a small bowllike cup. He filled it nearly to the brim with *makgeolli*. Park looked at the bowl of milky white liquor as if it were a sacramental offering, bowing slightly and waiting as Thera drank.

The liquor was extremely strong, but the taste very smooth, much smoother than what Thera had sampled as she familiarized herself with Korean customs prior to the mission.

She finished, then handed the cup to Park, filling it for him.

"My friend is still in North Korea?"

"I'm afraid I don't know. You really should find a higher class of acquaintance, Miss Deidre."

"I already have."

He answered her smile with one of his own.

"But Mr. Manski and I have certain entanglements," added Thera. "And I wish to get them unwound."

"I don't believe he will be a problem for you."

"Where exactly did you last see him? Was it in the capital? Or did everyone stay at the lodge?"

"You sound as if you are a police detective," said Park.

"Just someone anxious to recover what is mine. And to prevent further complications in a . . . difficult area."

Park put down the cup. He walked to one of the unfinished canvases, contemplating it. Thera watched him, not sure what he was going to do or say. Finally, she walked over and looked at the painting.

Park took her hand.

For an instant, she thought he was going to make a pass at her, but the pressure he applied to her wrist dispelled that notion. Intense pain shot up her arm to her spine.

"My assistant Mr. Li would be happy to indemnify any loss you suffered from your disagreement with your friend," Park told her. "Beyond that, it would be most wise to change your associations permanently."

"Mr. Park, I believe you are threatening me." Thera struggled to keep her voice level.

"Not a threat. I would not like to see a pretty woman such as yourself harmed."

Thera jerked her arm upward and then down, breaking the hold, though not easily. As she did, two men in black silk suits appeared in the wide doorway facing the desk.

"Miss Deidre is leaving," Park told them, turning away. "Please show her to the car."

THE WHITE HOUSE, WASHINGTON, D.C.

Corrine was on her way downstairs to the National Security meeting when she heard Josh Franklin's rich baritone echoing in the hallway.

"This is exactly what I warned about," said the assistant secretary of defense, standing outside the conference room. "They're going to attack. We should authorize a preemptive strike. That would be my recommendation."

The small group of aides clustered around Franklin murmured their approval. Corrine said nothing, hoping to pass by and get into the room unnoticed. But Franklin saw her out of the corner of his eye.

"Corrine, how are you?" he asked.

"Very well, Josh. Yourself?"

She wondered if he would mention the cell-phone call she'd "forgotten" to answer after their nondate date and was relieved when he didn't.

It figured though, didn't it? One of the few men who actually followed up on a promise to call, and he turned out to be a frog rather than a prince.

"Are you attending the NSC briefing?" Franklin asked.

"The president asked me to be here," she told him, "simply to monitor possible developments vis à vis the treaty."

She struggled to get the words out, then wished she'd said something, anything, more graceful. She sounded like a tongue-twisted freshman law student presenting a case citation for the first time.

"Still pushing the treaty, huh? It's dead now," declared Franklin. "No one will vote for it. Which is just as well."

"I'm just monitoring, not advocating."

"Josh is right." Christine Tuttle, the deputy national security advisor for Asia, separated herself from the rest of the group. "We have to be aggressive; we have no choice."

Tuttle turned toward Franklin. Corrine saw something in her expression as their eyes met.

Oh, thought Corrine. *Oh.*

"Didn't you write a briefing paper favoring the treaty?" Corrine asked.

"I changed my mind recently," said Tuttle, just a hint of her annoyance showing through. "Partly because of Josh's arguments, I must say."

"He can be very persuasive," Corrine said, walking toward the room, "but that doesn't mean he's right."

In the president's absence, the session was chaired by
Vice President Edward Wyatt. Wyatt was from the
Midwest, and differed from McCarthy in almost every
way, from appearance to temperament. Baby-faced and
chubby, Wyatt's main asset to the administration was the
fact that he had been governor of Illinois—a post he'd actually inherited when the elected governor died. He con-
tinually deferred to National Security Advisor Stephanie
Manzi, who introduced the briefers and labored to keep
the discussions on point.

The CIA handled the first part of the session. Parnelles
had Korean expert Verigo Johnson present satellite photos showing the troop movements in North Korea and
their possible implications. Though large and potent, the
North Korean Army was rather ponderous; a full-scale
mobilization would take several more days, even weeks.
Still, there were enough artillery units in place near the
border that a devastating attack could be launched at almost any time, with very little warning.

There was one positive note: The nuclear weapons the
North had declared were all present at their missile
launching station, and no move had been made to prepare
them for launch.

"That would require their being reassembled," added
Johnson. "Which would take several days. We'll have
plenty of notice. We can have them targeted and destroyed at the first sign of preparation."

"We are also monitoring other sites where missiles
might have been hidden," added Parnelles. "As of yet,
we've seen nothing to cause alarm. But we're watching."

"Any reaction from the Chinese?" asked Wyatt.

"So far, they don't seem to have picked up on anything," said Parnelles. "The Russians will have seen what
we saw via satellite, but there's been no action out of
Moscow. Neither the Australians nor the Brits have made

any comment, though I would assume they will take notice shortly."

The CIA director said there was a fifty-fifty chance of an attack, which, in his opinion, would be launched because Kim Jong-Il was angry over South Korea's refusal to provide more aid for heating oil.

"We can expect some sort of ultimatum along those lines when the forces are in place," said Parnelles.

"There's been no hint about the seriousness of the oil dispute in North Korean propaganda," said the national security advisor.

"That's not Kim's style," said Parnelles. "He waits until he has everyone's attention before making his demands."

Secretary of Defense Larry Stich had his own analysts provide a briefing on what was going on. It paralleled that delivered by the CIA. Their interpretation, however, differed. The military people were not convinced that this was in fact a prelude to an attack. Stich explained that the North Korean units had been used in the past as pawns in internal power struggles.

"I suggest we put our troops on their highest alert, but reserve further action," said Stich. "And I would suggest we refrain from anything that could be misinterpreted as a prelude to an invasion. Our bombers are on alert in Okinawa already; we can obliterate the North within a few hours. But long-term, that will create an entire range of problems."

"Amen to that," said Secretary of State Jackson Steele.

Josh Franklin fidgeted in his seat, and continued to do so as the chairman of the joint chiefs of staff concurred with Stich's recommendation.

"Josh, did you have a point?" asked Manzi.

Franklin glanced at his boss before speaking. Until the last two or three months, the two men had gotten along very well. Things would probably be different from now on.

So be it.

"Whatever the situation is north of the border," said Franklin, "whatever their motivation, this gives us an opportunity to deal with North Korea once and for all. If we act quickly, we'll never have to worry about them again. Strike their nuclear capability, wipe out their artillery at the border, just take them completely down."

"If we were successful," said the secretary of state. He ran his ebony fingers through the thick curls of his white hair. "A *big* if."

The assistant secretary of defense continued, laying out the case for a preemptive strike in a calm tone, though the action he proposed was anything but. Corrine glanced at Tuttle, wondering if she would come to Franklin's defense as the others began poking holes in his argument.

She didn't. Her boss told the group that he agreed with the secretary of defense, and Tuttle sank lower in her seat.

"Are we agreed then?" said Manzi, as the conversation became repetitive. "We go to alert but hold off on aggressive action?"

She looked around the room. "Then that's the recommendation I'll take to the president."

Belatedly, she glanced at the vice president, who nodded.

Corrine took her time packing her things as the meeting broke up. She fell in alongside Parnelles as he walked out of the room.

"Mr. Director," she said.

"Ms. Alston, how are you?"

"Fine."

"I'm glad you're taking an interest in foreign affairs."

"The president asked me to sit in. In case there was anything of interest regarding the treaty."

"Yes. He mentioned he would do that. Was there?"

"Not directly. Though if news of this comes out, it won't help."

"No. But I would suggest it's a matter of when, not if."

Corrine nodded. It wasn't simply that many people

knew about it; now that a decision had been reached on what to do, there was bound to be dissension.

"Any word on Ferg?" she asked.

"I'm afraid not. We think we know now where they stayed during the visit. Park uses a hunting lodge northwest of the city. But the satellite photos show nothing unusual there."

"Van suggested a mission to North Korea," said Corrine. "Can we go there?"

"Out of the question."

"Is it?"

Parnelles stopped, glancing around to make sure they were alone in the hall. His eyeballs seemed to bulge slightly as they moved, before returning to their sockets as he fixed his gaze on her.

"The great problem here, Corrine, is that Mr. Ferguson is entirely expendable. We can't decide what to do based on the small possibility that we might get him back."

"I understand that. But—"

"There are no buts," said Parnelles. "His father was my closest friend. I've known Bobby since he was born. Don't you think I want to save him? Duty comes first. The fires of war, Corrine, they always burn what we love."

He turned and walked away, a much older man than the one who'd come to the meeting.

22

DAEJEON, SOUTH KOREA

Thera scanned the room for bugs as soon as she got back to the hotel. Still wearing her slinky dress, she collapsed in the chair and called The Cube to report in.

"Are you OK?" were the first words out of Corrigan's mouth.

"Of course I'm OK."

"It's past one o'clock there."

"Well, I didn't get lucky, if that's what you're trying to ask."

"Jeez, Thera."

"Park tried to buy me off. He claimed Ferg had business with people in the North, but then he tried to buy me off. And intimidate me."

Thera described the dinner and Park's house, recalling the conversation almost word for word.

"I want to talk to other people who were on the trip, and I want to bug his house. The security there didn't look all that difficult to get around."

"I have to clear that first."

"Why?"

"I just do. Anything that's going on in Korea, I have to clear."

"They stayed in some sort of lodge near the capital and hunted. Park's family owned it. Can you find it?"

"We already did. Ciello made the connection a few hours ago."

"Well, let's go search it."

"We can't, at least not until we get evidence that he's there."

"Screw waiting. Where else could he be?" said Thera. "We should kidnap the son of a bitch Park and find out what the hell happened."

"You can't do that, Thera," said Corrigan. "Jesus. Don't do that."

"We should."

"Listen. You're supposed to concentrate on the plutonium now. Slott says—"

"Whose side are you on, Corrigan?" she said angrily. "Ferg is part of the team. I can't just leave him."

"We're not leaving him."

"Whose side are you on?"

"We're all on the same side."

"Then act like it. If we don't do something, he'll be dead."

Thera ended the call, fearing Corrigan might say the obvious: There was a very good chance Ferguson was already dead.

OUTSIDE CHUNGSAN, NORTH KOREA

Ferguson lay face up on the cot, staring at the ceiling, trying to remember the Chaucer he had learned with the Jesuits in prep school.

> Whan that Aprille with his schowres swoote
> The drought of Marche hath perceed to the roote,
> And bathud every veyne in swich licour,
> Of which vertue engendred is the flour;—
> What Zephyrus eek with his swete breeth

What did Zephyrus *eek*?

Eek, eek, eek. Something, something, ". . . the tendre croppes."

Ferguson pictured his teacher, Father Daedelus, saying the words.

Father Daedelus was the only fat Jesuit Ferguson could ever recall meeting. Jesuits as a rule were tall and thin, and most often gray, at least at the temples.

Ferguson went back to the beginning of the poem. Chaucer was harder than Shakespeare because Middle English was almost a different language, so this must have been tenth grade when he learned it.

Tenth or twelfth or college?

Where did you go to college, lad? Do you recall?

Tenth.

Princeton. With summers off to get shot at.

Taking the training and then the mission to Moscow, pressed into service, and almost getting his balls cut off—literally—by the Red Giant.

Now that was a close escape. Seeing the girl cut up before his eyes . . .

Jesus.

So this is what you do for a living, Dad?

Yet he came back, kept coming back.

The knife against his thigh.

Really he *is* going to do it.

Jesus H. Christ.

Ferguson forced himself to concentrate on Chaucer, vanquishing the other jagged tatters of memory from his mind.

About midway through the third line of the poem, he heard someone walking down the hallway for him. He remained staring at the ceiling, reciting the poem in his mind as the door was opened.

Expecting Owl Eyes, Ferguson was surprised when he tilted his head and saw two guards in the cell. They ordered him to rise.

Make a break for it? Make them kill him now?

Ferguson hesitated, then gave in, rising slowly and letting himself be prodded, gently, into the corridor.

The guards led him down the hall to a lavatory and shower. There was no soap and the water was close to freezing, but he stayed under the water for several minutes. The chill gave him a rush, pushed him forward.

Onward, Christian soldier!

A towel waited on the rack. There were also fresh prison pajamas and wooden clogs. The two guards who'd come in with him gazed discreetly to the side as he dried and dressed.

Ferguson felt a chill on his damp hair as he followed his minders out of the shower room and back into the hall. They stopped in front of a rusted steel door that was opened to reveal a set of rickety wooden steps upward.

As Ferguson reached the top of the steps, a flood of sunlight blinded him. It was daytime; he'd thought it was night.

He rubbed his eyes open and saw that he was rising in the middle of a very large room, bounded on both sides by floor-to-ceiling windows. A pair of long tables were set up in the middle of the floor to his right; a man in a uniform sat at the table to the right.

Captain Ganji.

Ferguson's jailers remained behind him as he sat across from the captain.

"Do you speak Korean?" asked Ganji.

Ferguson shook his head.

"I do not speak Russian," said Ganji, still using Korean.

"Français? Deutsch?" said Ferguson, asking if he spoke French or German. He could tell from Ganji's expression that he did not.

"We can use English, if you know this," said the captain.

"English will do," said Ferguson. The room was cold and seemed to steal his voice. He wasn't sure if the room was really cold, or if it was a symptom of the lack of thyroid hormones.

He glanced back at the guards. "You should send them away."

"They do not English speak."

Ferguson shook his head slightly. "You shouldn't take chances."

Ganji stared at him. His English was not very good: He had trouble with word order, which had a significance in the language that it didn't have in Korean. But the Russian's warning was clear enough. He looked over at the men and signaled with his hand that they should leave him. They were reluctant; the prisoner was taller than Ganji, and, while depleted by his captivity, still looked considerably stronger. But Ganji was not intimidated.

"Who are you?" the Korean captain asked Ferguson when the men retreated down the steps.

"Ivan Manski. I was to help Mr. Park on some small items, but there was a disagreement, apparently, with some of my superiors." Ferguson paused between his words, as if picking them out carefully. "A business disagreement they neglected to inform me of. Nothing personal. Or political."

"How does this concern me?"

"It doesn't," said Ferguson. His voice was hoarse and cracking. He needed a drink of water, but there was none on the table, and he didn't want to risk being interrupted by asking for it. "I was at the guesthouse when General Namgung met with Mr. Park. I felt that the general should understand that I was there and that I would not want to be responsible for what happened, for what I might say if I were tortured."

"You will not be tortured."

Ferguson didn't answer, staring instead at the captain.

"You were not at the meeting," Ganji said finally.

"The house was down a twisting road a half mile from the lodge and the old barn," said Ferguson. "There were two men out front, guards. Others were inside, though not in the room with you. You met in the large room on the first floor at the back. When you were almost through, you went out with Mr. Li and gave him envelopes. I assume he gave you money."

Ganji felt his face flush. The Russian had been there, surely. But why had Park brought him, only to then discard him?

"If you're thinking of having me shot," added Ferguson, "that is a solution. But you should know that the people I work for, the people who know where I was, they will not be happy. They had me tape the meeting as a precaution, and they have the tape."

Ferguson spoke in a monotone, his voice no more than a rusty croak in a dry throat.

"They hold no enmity toward the general," he added. "They can be incredibly helpful to you if things go as planned. Or, they could be very angry."

Ganji leaned back in his seat. Park's aide, Li, had claimed the man was a Russian arms dealer, but the way he held himself, the calm manner in which he spoke—clearly he must work for the Foreign Intelligence Service, the *Sluzhba Vneshney Razvedki* or SVR.

Namgung did not like the Russians, but angering them was not wise.

"How much do you know?" Ganji asked, trying to decide what to do.

"I'm just a foot soldier," said Ferguson, staring in Ganji's face, soaking in his fear. The man had been chosen for his intelligence, not his courage—a good thing for Ferguson.

"I know nothing," Ferguson told him. "I don't even know my own name."

Ganji rose without saying another word.

Ferguson raised his eyes toward the window. He thought it must be morning, perhaps as late as noon, and even though the sun was still out, he noticed that it had just begun to snow.

24

ARLINGTON, VIRGINIA

When he had no evening engagements, Senator Tewilliger liked to end his day by riding his exercise bike, taking a shower, and then relaxing with a Southern Comfort Manhattan. Or two.

His staff was not supposed to call him after ten p.m.,

which gave him a solid half hour to ride, and thirty minutes for a shower and a nice drink before catching the network news and nodding off.

So why was the phone ringing at 10:32, just as he got off his bike?

The answering machine picked up. He heard a male voice he didn't recognize at first tell him something was up with Korea.

Tewilliger realized it was Josh Franklin. He grabbed the phone just before Franklin hung up.

"You're working very late, Undersecretary," said Tewilliger.

"I apologize for calling you at this hour," said Franklin. "But I wanted to make sure you'd heard: The North Korean Army is mobilizing."

"What?"

"We had a National Security session on it. It's still pretty tightly wrapped, but I would imagine word will start to leak out tomorrow or the next day, if not from us then from the Australians or the Brits, whom we've been updating. I would have called sooner, but I didn't get the chance."

Of course not, thought Tewilliger; Franklin wanted to use a phone whose calls weren't logged.

"What's going on?"

"I really shouldn't go into detail, Senator."

"Josh. Come on now."

Franklin told him what he knew, including the administration's planned response, which he characterized somewhat harshly as sitting around until the peninsula caught fire.

"There have been troop movements and mobilizations in the past," said Tewilliger. "What makes you think these are different?"

"The timing is suspicious," said Franklin. "I would bet that they used the treaty as a way of lulling us into complacency."

"Maybe." Tewilliger had already begun to discount the information, at least as a harbinger of any sort of attack by the North. Still, it would help torpedo the treaty. "I appreciate the heads-up, Josh. I'll remember it."

"Thank you, Senator."

Tewilliger went across the room to his desk and began flipping through his Rolodex. It was never too late to call a sympathetic reporter, especially with information like this.

OUTSIDE CHUNGSAN, NORTH KOREA

Ferguson was well into the "Knight's Tale" in Chaucer's poem when he was interrupted by two guards who told him in Korean it was time for him to get up from his cot. He had no idea how much time had passed since he'd met Ganji. He'd eaten once, a few fingers' worth of rice. That had been hours and hours ago.

The guards put iron manacles on his hands and legs, then brought him to the front hall, where he had first entered the prison. A car waited outside. It was dusk.

Ferguson's clogs crunched through a small crust of snow as he was led into the sedan. Two large, uniformed men slid in on either side of him. The doors closed, and the car sped down the rutted dirt road.

Within a few minutes Ferguson had lost track of the direction. He reverted to Chaucer, going back to the Prologue where the knight was introduced:

> A Knight ther was, and that a worthy man,
> That from the tyme that he ferst began
> To ryden out, he lovede chyvalrye,

Trouthe and honour, fredom and curtesie,
Ful worthi was he in his lordes werre

The poem sprung up from his unconscious, unraveling from the depths of his memory. His old teacher stood before him, regaling the class. "Great literature, boys. Great lit-er-a-ture."

Ferguson and his friends would roll their eyes and in the hallway mimic the portly priest's pronunciation, "lit-er-a-ture." But he was a good man, a good teacher who'd tried to share some of his experience. Left his mark on the world, however humble.

What mark had Ferguson left?

Well, there were the missions. Saving lives.

Dust scattered on a car window.

"Truth and honor, freedom and courtesy, full worthy was the knight."

Full worthy, are you.

Lit-er-a-ture boys. Lit-er-a-ture and death, the only real things in life.

After two or three or four hours of driving, the car pulled up in front of a small hut.

"I overplayed my hand," Ferguson mumbled to himself as the car stopped.

Namgung had decided he was too much of a liability and would simply kill him here, out in the woods, where no trace would be found.

"Good, then. Better this way than other ways."

He'd pushed the damn thing to its limit. Better to die like that than like a slug attached to the hospital's death support, everything but your soul pumped out of you.

The North Koreans got out of the car. Ferguson leaned toward the door, debating whether it would be better to make a break for it and be shot or simply to let them do it at their own choosing.

No, he had a better idea, a much better idea. He'd use

the chain holding his hands together, take someone down with him.

"Out of the car," said one of the guards.

Which would it be? Who would get close enough to die with him?

All three kept their distance as he got out. The wooden clogs hurt his feet; he stumbled, almost lost his balance, but the men didn't help him.

"Inside," said one, pointing at the dark hut.

Ferguson decided he would wait to be pushed. Then he would twist around into the next nearest man, throw his chain around his neck, throttle him.

"Please," said the North Korean. "The hut will be warm. There are clothes inside. Go ahead."

The man's voice was soft and pleading. He turned and walked to the door, pulling it open.

OK, thought Ferguson. You're it.

He made his way around the front of the car, trying to catch up to the man. But the chains on his legs and his awkward clogs made it hard to walk fast.

The North Korean stepped aside. Ferguson gathered his energy, ready to spring.

The man smiled.

For some reason, Ferguson found that amazingly funny, hilariously funny: an executioner who would smile at his victim.

The man took a step backward, then another. He was gone, out of reach.

Ferguson tensed, waiting for him to pull a gun from his pocket. He'd lost his chance and now would have to die alone.

All right, then.

"Go ahead," said the man.

No gun.

Ferguson glanced over his shoulder. The others were back near the car. If they had weapons, they weren't showing them.

Ferguson stepped into the cottage, spinning to the side to wait for his assassin, but the only thing the man did was push the door closed.

Ferguson stood in the middle of the darkened room, waiting. Gradually, he realized there was no one else inside.

Maybe they were planning on blowing up the house.

He closed his eyes and waited.

After ten minutes passed, Ferguson realized nothing was going to happen. He made his way around the small room, banging into all four walls before determining that there was no furniture here, nothing, in fact, except plain wooden planks and a dirt floor. When he had covered every inch, he dropped down to the ground, took a deep breath, then lay flat to sleep.

26

THE WHITE HOUSE, WASHINGTON, D.C.

News of the North Korean troop movements had finally reached the media, and the White House congressional people found themselves talking nonstop to congressmen worried about the treaty. Already there were rumors that the vote would be put off for at least a month.

Just before noon, the Department of Energy called to tell Corrine that the soil tests from Science Industries had been finished ahead of schedule; they were negative. She immediately called Slott and told him.

"*Hmphh,*" he said. Then he fell silent.

"Dan? What's going on with Ferguson?"

"Still no word."

"I can talk to the president about a reconnaissance mission, if you think it's a good idea."

"It'd be suicidal under the circumstances. It's too close to the capital."

"I see."

"We had a Global Hawk fly down the coast," added Slott, referring to an unmanned spy plane. "It was tracked briefly but got away. Even that was a risk I probably shouldn't have taken."

"Did it see anything?"

"Nothing out of place. It looks abandoned."

The spy flight was little more than a gesture, but it was something at least.

"I'll keep you informed," said Slott, abruptly hanging up the phone.

27

DAEJEON, SOUTH KOREA

Thera spent the day doing a lot of nothing, installing GPS trackers in the trucks at the university, poking around Park's planes and his hangar at Gitmo, even checking on a few more trucks. It was all a waste of time. She was supposed to concentrate on finding the plutonium, not Ferguson.

On their first mission together, an attaché case of jewels had gone missing. She'd become the obvious suspect. Ferguson stood by her—and checked her out at the same time, believing she was a thief and yet not wanting to believe it either.

She'd been *so* mad at him, so damn mad.

She wanted to take it all back.

God, he couldn't be dead.

Fergie, you handsome son of a bitch. Come back and laugh at me, would you?

She got back to her hotel around eleven and checked in with The Cube. Lauren was on duty, shuffling time slots with Corrigan.

"What's going on?" Thera asked.

"Nothing new."

"Listen, I want to talk to the people who went north with Ferguson. They have to know something."

"Slott wants you to work on the plutonium angle, Thera. He needs to know what's going on with that."

"We need to find Ferguson."

"We're working on it."

"How? Analyzing intercepts? Looking at satellite data?"

"Well, yeah. Things like that."

"That's a waste." Anger swelled inside her. "Let me talk to Slott. Better yet, give me Corrine."

"I don't know if I can."

"You can get her."

"I'll call back."

Thera turned on the television, checking the local news. So far, there was no word of the troop movements across the border.

A half hour later, Corrine called on the sat phone.

"You needed to talk to me?" Her voice sounded distant and hollow, more machinelike than human.

"I wanted to know what we're doing to find Ferg."

"We're working on it."

"I want to interview the people he went north with. They may have information."

"Have you talked to Dan?"

"No. You're the one who's really in charge, right?"

"Dan handles the specifics of the mission," said Corrine coldly. "You have to do what he says."

"We have to find Ferg."

"I realize the situation is difficult, Thera. It's hard for everyone. We all have to do our jobs."

"Yeah."

"It's not easy for me, either."

It's a hell of a lot easier for you, Thera thought, but she didn't say anything.

"Do you need anything else?" Corrine asked.

"I'm fine." She turned off the phone.

ON THE KOREAN COAST, WEST OF SUKCH'ÖN

Ferguson woke to the sound of waves crashing against rocks. At first he thought it was a dream—his mind had tangled through several while he slept—but then he realized his body ached too much for him to still be asleep.

Light streamed through a thin curtain next to the door of the hut. Ferguson got up slowly and went to the window. He saw the back of a soldier ten yards away. Beyond him, the horizon was blue-green: the sea.

A tray of food sat on the floor a short distance away. Ferguson got down on his hands and knees and looked at it. There was rice, some sort of fish stew, and chopsticks. A bottle of water sat at the side.

A short distance away sat two buckets, one with cold water, presumably so he could wash, the other empty, for waste.

Ferguson opened the bottle and gulped the water, so thirsty there was no way to pace himself. He jammed the rice into his mouth with his fingers, barely chewing before swallowing. But as hungry as he was, the fish stew smelled too awful to eat. He left it and began exploring his prison.

Flimsy wooden boards nailed to cross members made up the walls. They were arranged in two separate courses, the top row slightly misaligned with the bottom. The tongue-and-groove joints were mostly snug, but here and there daylight was visible where the edges had eroded away. They were flimsy, no more than a quarter-inch thick.

Someone knocked on the door. Ferguson reminded himself that he was Russian and started to say "come in."

His mouth wouldn't cooperate; somehow the word *annyeonghaseyeo*—Korean for "hello"—came out instead.

The door opened, and a thin man entered. He was a soldier with the insignia of a lieutenant, though he seemed far too young to be one.

"You speak Korean," said the man.

"Jogeumbakke moteyo," said Ferguson, admitting that he spoke a bit.

"A little. I see, yes. I was told you can speak English?"

"Yes."

"You did not eat the stew," said the lieutenant.

"I need a fork."

"Fork? Not chopsticks?"

Ferguson could use chopsticks, but a fork would be more useful. He shook his head.

"I will bring you one. And more water. Would you like to read?"

"Sure."

The man turned to leave. "Where am I?" asked Ferguson.

"Do you know Korea?"

"Not very well," admitted Ferguson.

"We are on the Bay of Korea. The west coast. A beautiful place."

"Near the capital?"

"Farther north. South of Unjon. Do you know that city?"

"Chongchon River?" said Ferguson.

Amused by the mispronunciation, the lieutenant corrected him and then told Ferguson that he was correct. Three rivers including the Chongchon came together near Unjon and flowed to the sea. They were a few miles south of that point.

"Do you know where you are now?" asked the North Korean.

"No," confessed Ferguson. "Sorry."

But he did know, roughly at least. One of the three emergency caches that were to have been planted for a rescue mission North was located five miles north of the Chongchon along the coastal road. If Ferguson could reach it, he would be rescued.

Just ten miles, at the most, away.

Easy to do.

Easy, easy, easy to do.

Not with the leg chains and clogs.

The clogs were all right—his feet were so swollen he'd never get them off anyway—but the chains had to go. He'd have to swim to get across the river and hike through marshes.

Never. He'd never make it. Not like this, depleted, cold, half dead. His body felt as if it had been pushed into a crevice, squeezed there for days, pounded on.

Ferguson huddled against the wall, shivering beneath the blanket. The lieutenant returned about an hour later, a bag strapped over his shoulder.

"A fork," said the North Korean proudly, holding it up. "Difficult to obtain. You must hold on to it."

"Thank you."

The lieutenant put down his bag.

"Books." He pulled one out. "Finding things in translation, it is not very easy in our country. No Russian. These are Korean, children's tales. Perhaps you can work on your language."

"Yes."

The man looked at him. "You should take a walk after eating," he said.

"There's an idea," said Ferguson, some of his usual sarcasm slipping into his voice.

"Do you need anything?" asked the lieutenant.

The key for the chains, a plane south—those would be nice.

"I'm cold," Ferguson said. "Very cold."

The lieutenant said something in Korean that Ferguson didn't understand, then said good-bye and left.

When he was gone, Ferguson forced himself to eat the stew. Then he examined the fork. It was made of thin metal, and the prongs were easily bent—just the thing to slip into the lock at his feet. But the prongs were too big to fit the manacles on his hands.

The door opened. Ferguson slipped the fork into his pants and looked up as one of the guards came in, holding a thick winter coat.

There was no way he could put it on properly because his hands were chained, and the guard wouldn't remove them. Instead, he helped Ferguson drape the parka over himself and buttoned the top button, making it into a cape. It wasn't exactly airtight, but it was far better than nothing.

"Fresh air?" asked the man in Korean.

Ferguson followed the soldier outside. The muscles in his face seemed to snap as the wind hit them. The air smelled of salt and raw sewage.

Ferguson rolled his head back and forth, vainly trying to stop the muscle spasms in his neck and shoulders. He walked a little way, getting his bearings, taking stock of what was around him.

A path nearby ran along the sea, paralleling the rocks and shoreline. The road zigzagged away to his right.

His escape route.

There weren't many paved roads in this part of Korea, and this one must eventually go to the coastal highway, a two-lane hardtop road used mostly by trucks and official vehicles. Like all roads in the North, it wasn't very heavily traveled; if he could get there, Ferguson could follow it to the river, then find a place to get across.

He was guarded by two soldiers. Both had AK-47s. They kept their distance as he sat down on the rocks.

He could get out of here. He could do it. He *would* do it.

Two guards—that was child's play.

Not now.

Wait until dark. Use the fork. Undo the lock on his feet, pry off a board, slip away.

They wouldn't realize until dawn that he was gone. By then he'd be at the cache.

Or home. Probably home. Definitely home.

Wherever that might be. As long as it wasn't here, anywhere would do.

He felt so tired and cold and dead.

Back inside the hut, Ferguson examined the boards and found two he thought he could push out. He used the fork to help ease them apart, moving slowly so he didn't make too much noise. When the boards were loose enough, he went down and sat near the window, pretending to read one of the books while he bent the tines of the fork to use as a pick.

The lock was ancient and simple, but it still took over an hour for him to open. Finally it sprang free with a click so loud he was sure someone outside would hear.

Ferguson grabbed one of the books and held it over his lap. When he was sure no one was coming, he fiddled with the other chain and undid the lock, leaving the clamps over his ankles so it appeared he was still confined. He pulled the blanket over his legs.

Dark. When would it be dark?

Hours.

All he had to do now was wait. Ferguson picked up the children's book again. He hadn't learned enough written Korean to read more than a few characters, all used on common road signs. His brain was too flaccid at this point to recall even those. But he leafed through the pages anyway, and gradually realized he'd seen the woodblock prints that illustrated the work before.

The story was a version of "The Seventh Princess." They'd read it in Romanized Korean text during his language class. In the ancient Korean song, a girl—the seventh princess—journeyed to the land of the dead to save her parents and bring salvation to the Korean people.

What was the Korean? He tried retrieving the words from the corner of his brain where they'd fled.

The figures blurred in front of Ferguson's eyes. The book dropped form his hand, and he fell back against the wall of the hut, fast asleep.

29

CIA HEADQUARTERS, LANGLEY, VIRGINIA

"If it's not a mobilization for an attack, it's a damn good approximation," said Ken Bo as the secure conference call wound down. "ROK Army intelligence now thinks it's for real."

"Not much of an endorsement," said Verigo Johnson, the Agency's chief Korean expert.

Slott cut the conversation off before it degenerated. The evidence remained contradictory. Key elements of the North Korean army were moving toward the border, and the navy was on high alert. But the transmissions from army and air force units in the eastern parts of the country intercepted by the National Security Agency were entirely routine. Johnson interpreted this to mean that they were seeing the early stages of a coup, a significant change in what he had told the National Security Council only a few hours before.

Parnelles wasn't convinced, holding on to the blackmail theory. Slott was trying to stay neutral: No matter what was going on, the situation was extremely dangerous.

"Ken, I need to have a word with you now that we're done," said Slott as the others signed off. He glanced across the secure communications center at the specialist handling the call, waiting for the signal that he and Bo were the only ones on the line.

"What's up?" asked Bo.

"I'm looking for an update on the South Korean plutonium."

"Two of our people are going into Blessed Peak today," Bo told him. "I'll send a report as soon as I hear from them."

"Good."

"Listen, Dan. How much priority do you want us to give this thing? It's obviously nothing."

"Why are you dismissing it?"

"You saw my note, right?"

Bo was referring to the theory that the material was the remains of the earlier South Korean project.

"I saw it," said Slott.

Bo was silent.

"All right," the station chief said finally. "Ferguson is still working on this?"

"Ferguson went across the border a few days ago and hasn't been heard from since," said Slott, deciding there was no sense keeping it from him any longer.

"You're kidding. He went north?"

"He traveled with Park Jin Tae."

"About the plutonium? Jesus. He's off on this one,

Dan. I know he has a great reputation, but, honestly, he doesn't know garbage about Korea."

"Maybe not," said Slott.

"You want us to put feelers out?"

"No." Putting feelers out—asking about Ferguson, even in his covered identity—might inadvertently tip off the North Koreans to his true identity. That would be tantamount to signing a death warrant. A crooked Russian arms dealer was far safer in North Korea than a CIA officer.

"Do you want to give me some information about his cover? Maybe we'll hear something unusual."

"Let's leave it the way it is for now, Ken. Update me on the waste site as soon as you can."

30

FIRST AIR COMBAT COMMAND, KAECH'N, NORTH KOREA

"The plane is prepared," General Kang told Namgung. "You have only to choose between the two pilots."

Namgung nodded. He had known the head of the First Air Combat Command since he was six years old; he trusted Kang with his life.

Literally, now, since word from Kang could ruin the plan and brand him as a traitor.

"How will you choose?" asked General Kang.

Namgung had pondered the question for the past several days. Both pilots were highly qualified; both were committed to striking a blow against their ancient enemy. They were so evenly matched that he could have them simply draw straws and be pleased with the result.

But it was his job as commander to decide.

"I will make a decision right before takeoff," he said. "I will be there personally. One shall go."

"And the other?"

"He, too, will do his duty."

"Very good," said Kang. "As it should be."

Namgung held out his arms, and the two old friends embraced.

"We will succeed," said Namgung. "I have no doubt."

31

NEAR DAEJEON, SOUTH KOREA

The Cube had used a Korean speaker to call hospitals in the area along the DMZ, inquiring about Caucasian patients who had been admitted unconscious. They found one in a small facility northeast of Seoul, and sent Thera to check it out.

She hadn't realized exactly how much she was hoping she'd find him until she broke into tears when she saw that the patient, who was hooked into life support in the critical center, wasn't him.

CIA officers weren't supposed to cry—women CIA officers especially. If a woman wasn't ten times as tough as a man, she was labeled a liability.

Thera couldn't help herself, though. She was still sobbing when she boarded the train back to Daejeon.

Thera's sat phone rang when she was about ten minutes from the Daejeon station.

"Yes?"

"Can you talk?" asked Corrigan.

"A little." The two rows around her were empty.

"We have something new for you to check out. It's a real long shot but that's all we've been playing."

"What?"

"We were checking a list of vehicles that used the Korean waste site where your tabs found the plutonium. There's a truck used by a medical facility that happens to be owned by Park. It's down in Jiro, which is a couple of hours from where you are."

"What's that got to do with Ferg?"

"You're not looking for Ferg, remember? You're looking for the plutonium. That's our priority."

"I just came back from the hospital looking for him." Thera realized she'd spoken far too loudly. "I have to go."

"Thera."

"I'll call back," she said, hanging up.

32

ON THE KOREAN COAST, WEST OF SUKCH'ÖN

The pungent smell of the awful fish stew woke Ferguson. The room was dark; he was lying on his side near the wall, the parka still wrapped around him, his book on the floor where he had dropped it when he fell asleep.

Fear shot through him. Had he slept through the night?

He leapt to his feet, chains clanking dully on the dirt, and went to the window. A few faint lines of purple curled around the shadowy outline of the horizon. The sun had only just set.

Ferguson crawled to the food. He wolfed it down, then

drank half the bottle of water. He'd save the rest for his journey.

Finished eating, he went back to the window, looking to see if he could spot his guards. One stood about ten yards in front of the door, near the road. He couldn't find the other man.

If the guard was behind the house, he'd see Ferguson when he came out, but taking that chance was the only way to escape.

Ferguson, his hands still chained, pushed the boards to get them out of the way. The first came off easily, but the next stuck. Frustrated, he lost control for a moment, launching his fist toward the wall. He pulled it back at the last moment and collapsed on the floor, wrestling with his anger.

This is because I don't have the right hormones.

Do it step by step.

Don't go weird.

Step by step.

He retrieved the fork and pried at the pair of nails holding the bottom of the board. The wood came loose but then stuck somewhere toward the top. Ferguson pushed, gently at first, then more forcefully. Suddenly whatever was holding it gave way, and the board slipped from his grasp, clanking onto the ground outside.

Ferguson froze.

Don't stop now. Go!!!

He squeezed through feet first, rolling onto the ground. He sprung up, chain between his hands, a weapon, ready to confront the guards.

No one was there. The sound had been too faint to be heard over the lapping waves.

Ferguson propped the board back against the house, then crept to the corner of the building. The two soldiers were together now, standing next to the road a few yards from the front of the cottage.

He gave them a wide berth, circling out about a hundred yards before crossing the road and then going over to the path. His feet had swollen so much that the clogs were now tight. This was an advantage, really; it meant he could trot without worrying about losing them.

The parka flew behind him. He felt like a kid on Halloween, pretending to be a super hero.

"Trick or treat, Kim Jong-Il," he whispered to the moon over his shoulder as he ran north. "Trick or fuckin' treat."

It seemed to take the entire night to get to the mouth of the river. Ferguson jogged as much as he could, bouncing along to keep warm, never stopping. The highway was deserted, but he was too fearful to walk along it for very long. Instead he kept within ten or twenty yards, using paths and fields and occasionally hard-packed roads that led to the sea. Twice he had to backtrack to skirt small villages that lay near the water, then walk along the shoulder of the highway until he was safely past.

Eventually Ferguson found that the land on both sides of the road was too marshy to walk on, and he had no choice but to walk along the main road. He kept looking over his shoulder, prepared to jump into the nearby ditch or a clump of reeds if a vehicle appeared.

After what seemed like hours—the moon had arced high across the sky—Ferguson gave in to fatigue and stopped for a rest. He decided he had gone much farther than a few miles; the Korean who had told him the river was nearby had been lying to throw him off.

Maybe he could steal a boat from the next village he came to, take it north across the mouth of the river, find the cache from the water.

Or go south. It was farther, but he wouldn't have to wait to be rescued. He wouldn't have to depend on anyone but himself.

The waters were patrolled, but smugglers made it past all the time; surely he could.

Ferguson got up and started walking again. He began

humming "Finnegan's Wake" to himself, then whispering the lines from Chaucer, whipping up his strength. There was no wind to speak of, and while the prison pants he wore were thin, the parka was relatively warm, even as a cape.

I'm so cold I don't even know I'm cold anymore, he realized. Then he pushed the thought away.

It was just a matter of time before he found a boat. Maybe the river really was close. He'd steal a boat and paddle across the muddy mouth of the sea, skirting the shallow mud flats.

Make land, keep going, keep going, always keep going.

Keep going.

Keep . . .

The horizon brightened as Ferguson pushed on. He walked and ran along the road, moving as quickly as he could. His side ached, and his legs stiffened. He didn't want to stop, fearing that if he did, he wouldn't be able to get back up. But finally he had no choice. He felt his balance slipping. He steadied himself, then took a few steps off the road, slipped down the embankment and let his legs slowly collapse beneath him. He slid onto the ground.

Lying in the damp coldness, he thought how ironic it would be to die here, but then realized that irony and death didn't really go together; irony was something for the living. Death was just death, and this was as good a place to die as any.

He thought of Chaucer, then of his father, wishing he could have seen the old man one more time before he'd died, have a drink maybe, a lot of drinks, talk to him in ways they hadn't talked since he was small, about things they'd never had the strength to mention.

Have that chance in heaven. Maybe. If it worked that way. If he got there.

In the distance, a seabird called. His body suddenly felt warmer.

The bird called again.

Dawn, thought Ferguson.

He pushed upright. In the gray twilight, a flock of shadows crossed overhead, descending to his right. As they passed just out of sight, he heard the sound of pebbles being thrown into the water.

Rocks maybe.

Or the birds, landing in a sheltered arm of water.

Ferguson stared in the direction the birds had taken for several minutes, before realizing he had come to the river.

33

DAEJEON, SOUTH KOREA

Thera spent a restless night at the hotel after talking to Corrigan, then set out just before dawn for Chain, a town southeast of Taegu. She'd been using the rental for a while now; she decided she would change cars in Taegu, just in case someone had developed an interest.

Someone like Park, though he showed no sign of it. Her room hadn't been bugged, and she wasn't being followed.

She wished she were. Then at least she would feel as if she were on the right track.

Park *had* to know something about Ferguson; he simply had to.

As she saw the sign for the highway, Thera had an urge to take the ramp north and head up to Park's estate. She could see herself grabbing the old bastard and holding a gun to his mouth. She'd make him tell her where Ferguson was, or she'd shoot him.

She'd shoot him anyway.

Gritting her teeth, Thera bypassed the ramp, heading south toward Chain like she was supposed to.

DAEJEON, SOUTH KOREA

One more thing remained to be done—the way had to be cleared for the jet.

Leaking the information to South Korean intelligence was easy; Mr. Li would accomplish it through his usual intermediaries. To get to the Americans, however, required subtlety.

Park glanced at his watch. It was five a.m.—three p.m. in the States. He turned on his computer, waiting while it booted up.

He would supply the final touch himself over lunch with the Republic's president. It was a pleasure he could not deny himself.

The screen flashed. Park sat and began to type.

NEAR THE MOUTH OF THE CHONGCHON RIVER,
NORTH KOREA

The boat was longer than a three-man canoe but just as narrow. Flat-bottomed, it was propelled by a long pole-like paddle worked from the side. Similar vessels had been made according to the local design for two or three hundred years at least. It was a serviceable craft, more than capable of doing what Ferguson needed.

The wood creaked as he put one leg over the gunwale, pushing off into the soft mud with the other. The boat rocked beneath his weight, its sides giving slightly as he leaned the rest of his body inside and rolled into it. He turned onto his stomach, then knelt upright, half-expecting to feel his leg going through the wood. But the hull held.

The boat shifted back and forth abruptly as Ferguson took up the oar and tried to figure out how to work it. The water was very shallow, making it easier to push than to paddle, and after a few strokes he got a rhythm going.

He'd found the boat near a cluster of houses overlooking an arm of water that was separated from the rest of the bay by a swampy peninsula. To get into the main part of the channel where he could get across, Ferguson had to turn in front of the settlement, rowing directly past the houses.

It was still before dawn, but already smoke rose from several chimneys. There were other boats, bigger, tied to a dock closer to the houses. If someone saw him they would have an easy time coming after him; he was moving at a snail's pace.

He couldn't blame them if they came after him. The boat he had stolen undoubtedly represented a good portion of the community's wealth.

Ferguson thought of the girl he'd stolen the ID from at Science Industries: fired probably, though now he wouldn't put anything beyond Park.

He'd done things like that a million times. He never thought about the consequences.

He couldn't. Once he started to, he couldn't do his job. The girl, the villagers—they had to remain in the background, part of the scenery. If he stopped to think about them, if he focused on the pawns instead of the players, he was done.

Push, he told himself. Push and don't think. Go. Go! *Go!*

No one would think about him as anything but another piece of cannon fodder, ultimately expendable. It was the way it had to be.

The chain that connected his arms clanged against his chest as Ferguson started the turn. He leaned forward, pushing through the muck that lay barely a foot below the boat's shallow hull.

A gust of wind hit him in the side as he cleared the marshy finger of land. He turned into the teeth of it, poling so hard against the mud that he nearly lost the paddle.

Go, he told himself. Go.

Ten strokes later, the river deepened, and Ferguson once more struggled to figure out how to paddle properly. He barely made headway at first. He finally tried standing up, and after nearly losing his balance two or three times, started stroking steadily across the gaping mouth of water.

The rays of the sun lit the squat white faces of the houses on the opposite shore as he passed the halfway mark. Ferguson tacked to his left, in the direction of the sea, hoping that by staying far enough away from land he would seem just another villager. In truth he had no idea what a villager would look like; the real keys to his survival were the shadows on the water around him and the indifference of people trained by the dictatorship to keep their eyes focused firmly on the ground.

When he neared the other side, Ferguson saw that the land wasn't really land at all but muddy swamp and wild vegetation. He continued to paddle westward. Perhaps an hour passed before he saw ground solid enough to walk on. As he approached the embankment, he spotted a vehicle moving just beyond the reeds. He ducked down, waiting until it had passed, then landed and abandoned the boat.

A one-lane dirt-packed road ran through the swamp

about twenty yards from where he had beached. Ferguson
followed the road for roughly a mile before it curved
northward. Twice he ducked off the road when he heard
bicycles approaching. The marsh on both sides made for
plenty of cover.

Shortly after it turned northward, the road joined a
paved highway. Ferguson guessed it was the coastal highway. He was no more than five miles, and probably closer
to three, from the emergency cache.

He told himself he had less than half that: one mile, a
fifteen-minute stroll, an easy jaunt.

It wasn't a very effective lie, and as the sun climbed
higher he felt bad about it. As a CIA officer he lied all the
time but never to himself. He'd required brutal honesty
his whole career; he was the one person he could count
on for an honest assessment.

Honesty became even more important when the cancer was diagnosed. No one—not the doctors, not the lab
people, not anybody—told him the whole truth. They
thought they did, maybe they even tried, but they couldn't
really face it. In the end they slanted things to make
themselves feel better.

Not that honesty changed the thing that counted. The
cells mutating out of control cared not a whit for truth.

What had Chaucer said about the knight?

Forget the knight, forget Chaucer, just walk. Just go. *Go!*

Think of it as two miles, Ferguson told himself, pushing his stiff legs faster. Two miles. A cakewalk.

Ferguson had no idea how far it really was. He started
looking for the signs way too early and then when
he was near, almost missed it.

The blotch of white was on a rock about five feet from
the road. It looked so random that even when he stood
over it he couldn't be absolutely sure.

Because he wanted it, desperately wanted it, to be the
sign.

He stood over the rock, found the direction due west, then counted off ten yards, or what he thought was ten yards.

Another splotch.

I'm here, he thought. Here.

He'd planned to circle and scout the area but that was nothing more than wishful thinking. He began looking for the hidden packs. Before he'd taken more than two steps he tripped over something. He got his hands out to protect himself, but he was too weak and they collapsed. The chain cracked his ribs.

Wincing, he saw the packs lying beneath the nearby brush.

I'm here. I am Goddamn here.

Ferguson crawled to them on all fours. He grabbed at the nearest one, pulling it open. He took out a small Russian PSM pistol, then took out one of the bottles of water. He drank so fast his stomach cramped, and he had to lay down on his back for a good half hour, watching the white puffy clouds passing in the bright blue sky until the pain eased.

"Long way to go," he told himself as he got back up. "Long, long way to go."

ACT 5

The dead shed their covers
  And the gate of Knife Hell opens.

—from "The Seventh Princess,"
traditional Korean song for the dead

1

"Jesus, Ferguson."

"No, it's just me, Corrigan. Jesus is holding off until the Second Coming."

"Ferg, where *are* you?"

Ferguson's laugh turned into a cough. "North Korea. Where the hell do you think?"

"Ferg—"

"Puzzle it out, Corrigan. Check the line. The sat phone. I'm at Cache Point Zed."

Each satellite radio phone included in the cache gear was hard-wired to a specific frequency; these phones also included GPS gear that showed their location at The Cube.

"That's not what I meant," said Corrigan. "I *meant* are you OK?"

"I'm better than OK," said Ferguson, eying the small tool kit to see what he could use for a lock pick. "But I need a ride."

"Oh, jeez."

"Not the response I want to hear, Corrigan. You're supposed to tell me the bus will be here in a half hour."

"I have to get a hold of Slott."

"Well, let's move."

"Hang tight, Ferg. We're with you."

Yeah, right beside me, thought Ferguson.

He put the radio down and took the smallest screwdriver from the pack, but the blade and shaft were too large to fit in the lock. A small metal clip held two of the MRE packages together. He bent it straight, then broke it in two. But the wire was a little too rounded and not quite springy enough, or maybe he was just so tired that he couldn't get it to work.

The lock itself was extremely simple, little more than a kid's toy, which added to Ferguson's frustration. After trying to work the clip in for a half hour, he gave up and tried something new: chiseling the metal off with the help of a rock and the large screwdriver in the kit.

He'd just broken the link on his left hand when the phone buzzed, indicating an incoming transmission.

"Ferg?"

"Hey, Evil Stepmother. How are ya?"

"Corrigan arranged a conference call. I'm on with Mr. Slott and Parnelles."

"Guys."

"You sound terrible," said Slott.

"Good to talk to you, too, Dan."

"We're going to get you out of there, Ferg," said Slott. "We will."

"Yeah, Great place to visit but . . . shit."

Ferguson stopped midsentence. He could hear the sound of a truck, several trucks, coming toward him. "I'll get back to you."

"Ferg—"

"I'm OK."

He snapped the phone off and ran toward a clump of bushes to his right, stumbling over the rocks before reaching the thick cover. The first truck that passed was a military transport, similar to an American deuce-and-a-half. A stream of similar vehicles, some open in the back, some with canvas tops, followed. All were jammed with troops. Ferguson counted thirty-six.

He waited a few minutes after the trucks had passed, then called back.

"Robert, are you OK?" asked Parnelles.

"Yeah, General, I'm fine. Cold, though. And hoarse." He grabbed the broken chain in his hand and threaded his arms into the jacket, zipping it tight.

"Ferg, North Korea is going crazy," said Slott. "They're mobilizing. It looks like a coup, or maybe even an attack on the South."

"I just counted thirty-six trucks heading south. Troop trucks. Mostly full," said Ferguson. "So what would you figure that: thirty-six times twenty, thirty? About a thousand guys?"

"The point is," said Slott, "we want to know if you can wait until tonight for a pickup."

"Actually, Robert, waiting is imperative," said Parnelles.

"Sure," said Ferguson. "Not a problem. I'll work on my tan in the meantime. Maybe go a few rounds of golf later."

"We have a team off the coast, but it will take a while for them to get into position. The North Korean navy is on patrol all up and down the coastline, and army units are moving up to the border and down to the capital," said Slott. "Waiting for nightfall will be much safer."

Ferguson hunched over the packs and the bicycles. There was a pair of simple pants and a long shirt. Once he got the other chain off, he could pull them over the pajamas.

He wasn't going to fool anyone into thinking he was local, but the pants had to be warmer than the prison clothes.

"Ferg," said Corrine, "are you really OK?"

"Hell, yeah. All right, here's what I got." He told them that Park had probably had him arrested because it looked like he knew something was up.

"Why didn't he just kill you?" Slott asked.

"Because I'm a nice guy, Dan. He thought I was Russian. They couldn't decide whether I was working for the Kremlin or the mafyia. The North Koreans didn't want to piss off one of their major creditors, so they put me on ice."

Ferguson took a breath. He could feel the mucus in his chest, as if he had bronchitis.

He might actually *have* bronchitis, now that he thought about it.

"Park met with a Korean general named Namgung. There's something up between them. Something big enough that Namgung had me taken out of jail because they thought the Russians would be pissed off at him, not Park."

"General Namgung?" said Slott, pronouncing the name differently. "The head of People's Army Corp I?"

"Is that around the capital?"

"Yes. It includes Air Force Command One and some security forces as well as a dozen divisions."

"That's my man."

"That's interesting," said Slott. "Because our people in Seoul think Namgung's trying to stop the attack on the South. He may be involved in the coup."

"Our people in Seoul don't know their asses from a hole in the ground," said Ferguson.

"That's your opinion, Ferg," said Slott.

"Based on experience."

"This isn't the time to discuss this," said Parnelles. "Robert, how long can you hold out?"

"Forever," said Ferguson.

"Check in every half hour," said Slott.

"Try every three," said Ferguson. He wanted to save the battery, just in case.

Just in case?

Just in case, because there was no way to trust these guys. No way. No, no, no way.

"Are you *sure* you're all right, Ferg?" said Corrine.

"Hell, no. I'm lying through my teeth," said Ferguson cheerfully, before pressing the End Transmission button.

2

Corrine had just hung up from the conference call and reached for her computer to check her messages when the secure line rang again.

"We may not be able to pick up Ferguson at dusk," said Parnelles when she answered the phone.

"Why not?"

"The North Korean mobilization has reached the critical point: They can launch an attack at any point now. Given that, the failure of a mission might be catastrophic," the CIA director told her. "The decision has to be left to the president."

"I see." Corrine glanced at the clock at the bottom of her computer screen. It was not quite five o'clock; McCarthy had cut short his trip and was due back within another two hours. "I'll bring it up with him."

"Actually, Corrine, I think I should be the one who talks to him about it. Ferguson works for me, and I'd rather be the one making the recommendation."

"Sure," said Corrine. Then she realized why he wanted to do it. "What are you going to tell him?"

"I'm afraid my recommendation at the moment would have to be . . ." Parnelles paused. "I would have to say we should not proceed."

Colonel Van Buren's voice crackled in Rankin's headset,
barely emerging from the static. It was one of the worst
connections Rankin could ever remember.

"We have a location," said Van Buren. "A definite location."

"Hot shit," said Rankin.

"It's Cache Zed. You have your map?"

Rankin unfolded the map across the console in the
Peleliu's secure communications center, studying it as Van
Buren ran down the situation in North Korea. Several divisions were now poised along the DMZ, with additional
units ringing the capital. The coastal highway was a major
north-south route, and Ferguson had already reported
troop movements along it.

"So we'll have to plan accordingly. I'll get with the
ship's captain," added Slott, "but from my calculations it
should take the ship roughly three hours to get into position to launch. We want to time the mission so that you're
crossing land well after nightfall."

"Long time for him to wait," said Rankin. "We could
launch now, use some of the marine helos instead of ours.
They'll get us there and back with plenty of gas to spare."

"No. Washington gets final say on this," said Slott.
"You don't step off until I hear from them."

"Say, Colonel—"

"It's not my decision, Skip. He has a good hiding
place. Ferg told Corrine and Slott he was fine."

"He'd always say that."

The funny thing was, Rankin couldn't stand Ferguson,

didn't like him at all. But Rankin felt as strongly about rescuing him as he would have about his own brother.

Whom, come to think of it, he also couldn't stand.

"I have an MC-130 in the air ready for an emergency mission," said Van Buren. "They can be over the site within an hour. Less. If the word comes, we'll have the teams on the MC-130 drop in, then you go in and pick them up. Set that up with the Marines."

Rankin grunted. He knew it was a plan that would never be implemented, the kind that sounded good in theory but didn't work in real life. An hour would be forever on the ground. By the time Ferguson called for help, he'd be dead.

"What was that, Stephen?" asked Van Buren.

"I got it. Backup plan."

"We'll get him. I'll be aboard the MC-17 before night-fall. I'll check with you."

"Got it."

"We will get him back."

"If Washington approves."

"If Washington approves, yes."

Rankin's noncom training kicked in, and he let the colonel have the last word.

THE HART SENATE OFFICE BUILDING, WASHINGTON, D.C.

"Harry Mangjeol is on the phone, Senator. He says it's urgent, and he won't talk to anyone but you."

Tewilliger looked over at his legislative assistant, who'd stuck his head in the door. The senator really didn't feel like talking to Mangjeol, who would probably ask why he had given the press a "no comment" when asked about the fate of the disarmament treaty when news of the troop movements broke. He'd done it because this was the time to be subtle, to maneuver behind the scenes while the president sweated in front of the cameras. As a rule, constituents didn't understand that.

On the other hand, now was not a good time to blow Mangjeol off.

"When are the aluminum can people coming?" Tewilliger asked the assistant.

"Should have been here five minutes ago," said Hannigan, looking at his watch.

That frosted him—senators kept lobbyists waiting, not the other way around. Especially greedy sons of bitches like Mo and Schmo, Tewilliger's pet names for the two lobbyists who wanted more waivers in the upcoming environmental bill.

"Which line?" Tewilliger asked.

"Two."

"Keep Mo and Schmo outside at least ten minutes before telling me they're here," Tewilliger told his assistant before picking up the phone. "Harry, how the hell are you?"

"Senator, I have important information from a friend in Korea. Very important," said Mangjeol breathlessly. "It is . . . incredible."

"What's that?"

"Kim Jong-Il is to be deposed. A defector will take off tonight with a list of his foreign bank accounts."

He's finally lost it, Tewilliger thought, trying to decide how to deal with him. Sane or not, Mangjeol represented considerable contributions.

"Well, that is . . . *incredible* information," said the senator. "But . . . Well, to act on it . . ."

"I will forward you the e-mail. If you can get it into the right hands."

"Of course I can get it into the right hands," said Tewilliger. Perhaps Mangjeol wasn't insane. Perhaps the e-mail had some small piece of truth in it.

More likely it was part of a complicated phishing scam launched by Chinese pirates.

Then again, it might have some value. He could forward it to the CIA . . .

No, send it directly to McCarthy, or one of his people. Let them take the fall if it was phony.

"I would not believe that it was real," said Mangjeol, "but it does contain specific details, including a location of a secret air base."

"Send it, please," Tewilliger told Mangjeol. "And how are your children?"

THE WHITE HOUSE, WASHINGTON, D.C.

"Ms. Alston, this is Senator Tewilliger. I'm sorry to bother you so late."

Corrine glanced at her watch. It was only a quarter past five.

"Not at all, Senator. How can I help you?"

"As it happens, I may be able to help you. Or, rather, the president. Some important information has come to me and I want to deliver it to Jonathon personally."

"He's not back yet."

"So I heard. This is very important, perhaps time critical. I was wondering if you could meet me in my office."

Corrine hesitated.

"I realize it's an unusual request, but the matter is unusual. It pertains to Korea, which I know the president has been asking you to help him with."

"I can be over in an hour," she told him.

"The sooner the better."

Even though he'd had her rush over, Senator Tewilliger kept Corrine waiting in his outer office nearly fifteen minutes. She spent the time staring at the senator's appointment secretary, a young woman roughly her age, whose long, elaborately painted nails made working the phone an adventure. The senator's legislative assistant, James Hannigan, appeared from the inner office every few minutes to assure her that the senator was "just about ready." Finally, the door to the office opened and two men Corrine recognized as lobbyists for the aluminum industry emerged just ahead of Tewilliger. The senator greeted her in a booming voice, then introduced her to the two lobbyists.

"The president's counsel. I'm sure you know her," said Tewilliger.

Corrine smiled politely and shook the men's hands, convinced the senator had called her over primarily to impress the lobbyists; her presence would suggest he was very close to the president.

The lobbyists gone, Tewilliger ushered her inside, then stepped out to check to see if any important messages had been left while he'd been "in conference." It was an old Washington game, puffing up one's importance, but all it did was antagonize Corrine further.

"Important news," said Tewilliger when he came back in. "I have something that came from unofficial sources."

"OK."

"A North Korean pilot is going to defect in the next twenty-four hours. He'll be in a MiG-29, one of their newest planes. He'll have records with him relating to Kim Jong-Il."

"What sort of records?"

"Financial records." Tewilliger opened his top desk drawer and took a folded piece of paper out. "This is a copy of the e-mail. It's in Korean, unfortunately. I had James make a copy of the file. Apparently you need some sort of special keyboard or letter set to read the characters right or they come out as you see."

"Where exactly did this information come from?"

"A constituent with very high-level contacts over there, business contacts," said the senator. "I don't know much about these things, but I've heard that you can trace e-mail. Supposedly there are map coordinates and actual place names my constituent claims are real."

Corrine glanced at the e-mail header. There was quite a bit of data there, but it was not very difficult to spoof or fake an e-mail address or the path it had taken to its recipient.

"I don't want to sound skeptical . . ." started Corrine.

"But you are."

"I guess I am."

"So am I. As I say, I don't read Korean."

"Have you contacted the CIA?"

"I thought you would prefer to do that," said Tewilliger.

"I will," said Corrine. She rose.

"Ms. Alston, I know the president and I . . . at times we haven't always agreed on policy. The treaty is an example of that. The incident in the North, with the army mobilizing . . . Well, it made me decide I have to oppose the treaty at all costs. But I assure you, what Jon McCarthy and I agree on far surpasses our few disagreements."

"I'm sure the president would agree."

"And with you I have no disagreements," said Tewilliger.

"Thank you, Senator."

Tewilliger got up from behind his desk and took the door as she opened it. "If you ever decide to look for a new boss, come see me," he told her. "I intend to be at this game a long time."

Corrine couldn't think of anything to say, so she only smiled.

6

SEOUL, SOUTH KOREA

"This is a wonderful present, Mr. Park," said Yeop Hu, studying the jeweled hilt. "I am quite honored to receive it."

"It's a small token of friendship." Park nodded to the president.

"We've never been very good friends," admitted South Korea's president. He smiled at his staff members.

"This is true," said Park, "but there is the future, and perhaps we will find our way then."

"Certainly."

The president placed the knife back in its scabbard and returned it to the wooden box Park had presented it in.

"I have something else for you," the billionaire told the politician. "Given the present crisis, it may be of use."

"It's just another bluff by the dictator to show that he is alive," said Yeop. "In a few days, it will blow over."

"Perhaps." Park reached inside his jacket and took out two large envelopes. "A friend asked me to deliver these personally. I do not know what they contain."

"A friend?"

"An important man in the North. General Namgung."

At the mention of the North Korean general, the president reached for one of the ceremonial letter openers on his desk. This disappointed Park; he had hoped the president would use the knife.

One of the envelopes contained detailed orders similar to those that had been carried by the "defector" who'd been shot at the DMZ a few days before. The second was a brief, handwritten letter. The letter stated that the author would do whatever he could to preserve peace between the people of Korea.

"It's not signed," said the president, holding it up for Park to see.

"As I said, I haven't looked at the letters. They were not addressed to me." Park nodded again. "But perhaps the general thought it unwise to put his signature to anything."

The president handed both documents to his chief of staff, directing that they be sent to the National Security Council immediately.

"You know Namgung well?"

"Our families were in business together many years in the past," said Park. "Before the barbarians raped our people in the world war."

The president's mood had deepened considerably. "Let us have lunch," he said. "We can discuss this further."

Park bowed. As they left the room, he shot a glance back toward the ancient knife he had brought as a present. How long would it take the president, he wondered, to learn that the man for whom it had been made, a thirteenth-century traitor to one of the great lords of Korea, had used it to commit suicide after his crime was discovered?

CIA HEADQUARTERS, LANGLEY, VIRGINIA

To get beyond the crisis, Slott knew he had to put his personal feelings aside, but it was difficult, very difficult.

He took a deep breath, then used the secure line to call Corrine Alston.

"This is Corrine."

"The e-mail you sent over, we've translated it," he told her. "It has flight coordinates, not an actual base. But we have a reasonable idea where it would have had to start from."

"It's a real e-mail?"

"It appears so. The course here would take the aircraft to Japan. As it happens, it's almost precisely the course a North Korean defector took a decade ago, bringing his MiG-27 west."

"Did the message come from North Korea?" Corrine asked.

"Ultimately? It's possible. We're not sure."

The National Security Agency had intercepted a similar e-mail to someone in the Japanese consulate in Seoul a few hours ago. Tracing the e-mails' origin was not as easy as people thought, however, since someone who knew what he or she was doing could employ a number of tricks to disguise the true path. There were enough arguments for and against authenticity in this case that the NSA had held off on an official verdict. At the very least, it was an elaborate fake—so elaborate that it had to be taken seriously.

"Can I ask where this came from?" said Slott, trying his best to keep his voice level.

"Gordon Tewilliger got it from a constituent. He called me over to his office about a half hour ago."

"Why you?"

"I don't know. He wanted me to give it to you—to the Agency—and to alert the president. He's opposed to the treaty, though. So I don't know his angle precisely. It's political, obviously."

Slott wasn't convinced that the e-mail had simply dropped into her lap. But there was no point in pursuing it. If Corrine Alston—if the president—was running some sort of backdoor clandestine service, he wasn't in a position to stop it.

"We should share this with the South Koreans and the Japanese."

"By all means."

"Who is it who's defecting?" asked Corrine. "Does it say?"

"It's not just that they're going to defect," explained Slott. "This mentions financial records of the leader. Presumably, those are foreign bank accounts belonging to Kim Jong-Il. That's immensely valuable information. Far more valuable than any aircraft the pilot will take with him."

"That's good."

She didn't sound like someone making an end run around him, thought Slott. That was what was so damn annoying about her. She *seemed* so . . . not naive but upfront. Honest.

The best liars were like that.

"I'm going to attend the National Security Council meeting this evening," said Slott. "There may be more information by then."

"I'll see you there."

"Yup," he said, hanging up.

CHAIN, SOUTH KOREA

The Seven Sisters Medical Treatment Corporation provided diagnostic services to local doctors and hospitals. Patients went there for everything from old-fashioned X rays to elaborate positron emission tomography (PET) scans. Radioactive materials—technically referred to as radiopharmaceuticals—were used in many of the tests, and the facility generated a small but steady stream of waste each week. Special trucks were used to transport the waste to the disposal site.

Thera had no trouble finding this out. She simply joined the flow of patients going in the front door and then, before taking a seat in the large reception area, picked up one of the four-color brochures printed in Korean and English explaining the lab and a few of its more "popular" tests. It even contained a photo of the trucks—Hyundais.

When she was done reading, Thera headed down a back hall where the restrooms were and kept going, passing a number of test suites and arriving at a loading dock at the rear of the building. No one gave her a second look.

Thera slipped down off the loading area and walked around, spotting the two Hyundai transports and looking over the employee cars parked nearby. Then she circled back around to the front of the building, returning to her car to get satellite tracking devices and gamma tabs to put in the trucks.

As she pulled her car around the back, she saw two employees come out on the loading dock for a smoking break. She kept going, passing around the back of the building and following the road to the right, killing time until they were done.

Seven Sisters Medical Treatment Corporation was situated at the front of a commercial park. A long open field sat behind it. Beyond the field, four cement-block buildings were arrayed one after the other. In contrast to the medical testing center, they were old and appeared abandoned, with weeds growing in the lots that surrounded them.

Thera pulled into the second lot to turn around and go back; as she did, she saw there was a large truck parked next to the back of the building. Curious, she continued toward it, realizing as she got closer that it was the same make as the trucks Ferguson had been interested in in Daejeon.

Thera parked at the far end of the lot and got out. The building was definitely abandoned: The rear windows were boarded up, and a pile of scrap wood sat near a rusted steel fire door.

The truck didn't have a license plate, but it looked drivable. The interior was clean, and the gas gauge read full.

The back roll-up door was secured by a combination padlock. Armed with a pen and pad, Thera began working on cracking the combination lock, a ten-gate device only a little more complicated than the locks high school kids used on their gym lockers. She found the gates, then began working through a list of likely combination sequences based on usual lock patterns. It took her about ten minutes to snap the lock open.

The truck was empty. She stuffed the tab near the door the same way Ferguson had, closed it up and returned the lock to its place.

She'd just climbed down when she heard a car approaching. Thera reached beneath her coat for one of her pistols and started to walk back toward her car.

A white sedan pulled alongside her. She resisted the urge to pull the gun.

"*Annyeonghaseyo, manaseo ban-gawoyo,*" yelled a voice from inside the car as the window rolled down.

"Hi, nice to meet you." A pickup line.

Thera glanced at the man sitting in the passenger seat. He looked about twenty. So did the driver.

"*Eodiseo wasseoyo?*" said the kid, asking where she was from.

"Far away," said Thera in Korean.

"You're on your own?"

Thera smirked and resumed walking.

The car stayed alongside her.

"You cute," said the kid, this time using English.

"Yeah," muttered Thera under her breath.

She walked a few more steps, trying to ignore them. The car slowed, and the passenger jumped from the car.

Thera spun around to face him.

"Get lost," she said sharply.

The young man laughed.

"I'm warning you," she told him.

He took a step toward her. Thera, her patience gone and her heart starting to thump, dropped into a combat crouch, pointing her gun at his head.

The man's grin faded. He put up his hands and began backing toward the car.

"That's it," she told him. "Go."

He made a mad dash for the vehicle as his friend began backing up. Once he was inside, the driver spun the car around and sped away.

Thera ran to her car and got in, driving away as deliberately as she could. When she stopped in the city a short time later, her hands started to shake.

She pulled her things out, wiped down the interior and the door, then left the car in the lot, walking several blocks to rent a new one.

Were they kids or security or what?" asked Corrigan when she checked in.

"Probably 'or what.' They seemed pretty young, twenties, like they were cruising and saw somebody they could hit on. Macho shit. You know men."

Corrigan didn't say anything.

"I'll go back tonight and check out the building once it's dark," added Thera. "See if you can find out who owns it."

"Ten bucks says it's Park."

"Probably." Thera looked around the mall where she was sitting.

"We have some good news," said Corrigan. "Ferg's OK."

"He is?"

Thera felt tears coming to her eyes. She brushed them back, took a long breath.

She was sitting on a bench in a park. A little boy and his parents were walking nearby. She waited while they walked to the swings, well out of earshot.

"You there?" asked Corrigan.

"People playing on the swing."

"Can you talk?"

"Go ahead."

"When you were with Park, did he say anything about a General Namgung?" continued Corrigan. "According to Ferguson, they had a secret meeting."

The little boy jumped from the swing, a big smile on his face. Proud of himself, he waved at her. Thera waved back.

"Thera? Are you there?"

"I'm here," she told him. "What general were you talking about?"

"Namgung. I think I have the pronunciation right. He's in charge of all North Korean forces in the capital region."

Hadn't Tak Ch'o mentioned that he worked with him?

"Corrigan, can you hook me into Rankin on the *Peleliu*?"

"Why?"

"Because Ch'o worked with Namgung and did some shielding for air transport."

"The containers the university truck moved!"

"Just get me Rankin."

ABOARD THE USS *PELELIU,* IN THE YELLOW SEA

Jiménez had already finished the morning session with Tak Ch'o and was about to leave when Rankin arrived, fresh off the phone with Thera.

"I have a couple of questions for you," Rankin told the scientist. "If you don't mind."

Ch'o nodded and lay back on his bed. Not only was it more comfortable to rest while he talked, but it was also practical, since the cabin was so small.

"You helped a general named Namgung on a project recently," said Rankin. "He headed the army around Seoul. I wonder if you could tell me about that."

Ch'o glanced at the interviewer, then back at Rankin.

"General *Namgung*," said Ch'o, correcting the American's mispronunciation. "I have worked under his command several times. He is not simply the head of the army around Seoul but an important man in other respects as well. Very influential with the leader."

"Was he involved in the production of nuclear weapons?"

"Not directly. As I said the other day," Ch'o glanced at the interpreter, "my role in the weapons program was extremely limited. My field is primarily dealing with byproducts. Waste."

"You had a way of moving waste so it wouldn't harm people. In airplanes," said Rankin. He knew he needed to prompt Ch'o to fill in the details, but he wasn't sure how to get him to do it.

"The project I was doing with the general involved finding a way to move rods of fuel around the country safely," said Ch'o. "The rods come from reactors. When the operation is stopped and they are removed, first they must cool, of course. After a period of time they can be moved and stored at a facility such as the one where I was working. From there, they would be taken to Russia or somewhere else for processing. The general was interested in doing so in standard jetliners. This would have presented a grave problem without shielding."

"Airliners with passengers?"

"No," said Ch'o. "But there would have been danger to the crews."

Ch'o wasn't telling the entire truth. While the general had mentioned safety as a concern, shielding the rods would also make them nearly impossible to detect. That was the general's real purpose. Namgung had never said that; it was understood.

"These rods were for weapons fuel?" said Jiménez.

"It doesn't exactly work that way," said Ch'o. "Plutonium can be used for weapons, but the danger has nothing to do with that fact. The radiation—"

"So were these used?" asked Jiménez.

"No. The rods are still in storage."

"How do you know?"

"When they are removed from the reactor, they're very hot. They're placed in pools of water. It can take considerable time for them to cool off."

"Weeks?"

"Months. In some cases, years. The rods have been accounted for. The UN, the Chinese, the International Atomic Energy Agency—all of the inspections have certified this."

Rankin remained skeptical. "Maybe some were hidden."

"Plutonium is very expensive and difficult to obtain."

"Would you know of other control rods?" Jiménez asked.

"I might not," admitted Ch'o.

"So you were making containers that could carry hot plutonium?" said Rankin.

"No, the material would have to be cool."

"So wait." It still didn't make sense to Rankin. "When were you doing this?"

"Six months ago. No, perhaps three or four."

"You designed these things. Were they built?"

"I don't know. I gave him the plans."

"Your containers would have allowed you to transport the material without calling attention to it, wouldn't they?" said Jiménez. "In secret, on aircraft that weren't specially modified."

Ch'o nodded.

"Why would you worry about that in North Korea?" said Rankin.

"It was to protect people," said Ch'o, "and, maybe, if there were spies. That is what the general said: to keep them away from spies."

"Yeah," said Rankin. "That's one reason."

10

THE WHITE HOUSE, WASHINGTON, D.C.

"I have always heard that the mice will play while the cat is away, but I did not believe that would apply to the president of the United States and his staff."

McCarthy's rich southern voice jolted Corrine from the paper she was reading; she nearly fell out of her chair.

"Now, relax, dear," said the president, closing the door to her office. "I did not mean to startle you."

"I'm sorry, Jonathon. I didn't realize you'd come back."

"An hour ago. I've been busy." McCarthy sat down in a chair across from her. "And so, I understand, have you."

"Tom Parnelles wants to talk to you," she said, "before the NSC meeting later."

"Mr. Parnelles has already spoken to me," said McCarthy. "About your operative."

"Bob Ferguson."

The president put up his hand. He didn't want to hear any more about the mission than absolutely necessary, and he particularly didn't want to know the name of the man stranded in North Korea.

"We have a plan to get him," said Corrine. "They're going to take off in a few hours, as soon as it's dark."

McCarthy pressed his lips together. Corrine felt a hole open in her stomach.

"I am afraid, dear, that we cannot do that. The life of a single CIA officer, no matter how skilled he may be, cannot justify provoking a war between North and South Korea."

"But—"

"There are no *buts*. It is, unfortunately, my duty to make the decision." McCarthy rose. "I am sorry. It is the way it must be."

Corrine stared at her computer screen.

"You will attend the National Security session, will you not, dear?"

"Now that you're back, I don't—"

"Now that I'm back, I find myself very much in need of the services of my legal counsel."

"Of course, Mr. President. Whatever you want."

11

**NORTH KOREA, SOUTH OF KWAKSAN
ON THE WESTERN COAST**

More and more trucks. This time, Ferguson counted over fifty before he lost track. They were speeding south, hurrying in the direction of the capital . . . or maybe South Korea.

Ferguson dutifully reported what he saw when he called in but didn't bother asking Corrigan what was going on. He figured there wasn't anything Corrigan could tell him that would help him much.

If something truly bad happened—if the North went

ahead and attacked—then they'd come. Then it'd be cool. Or if everybody stepped back, relaxed, then they'd come ahead.

But like this, with everybody moving around, rushing, on high alert but not actually shooting, Slott would hold back. He wouldn't want to be the match that set the shed on fire.

Ferguson knew that. He'd known it when they all talked to him. Now, with all the trucks passing, it was even more obvious.

What he didn't know was what he was going to do next.

He sat down in the bushes as twilight came on, trying to remember how Chaucer had begun the "Pardoneres Tale."

12

ABOARD THE USS *PELELIU*, OFF THE NORTH KOREAN COAST

"What the hell do you mean we're not going?" Rankin slammed his helmet on the chair next to him in the secure communications space. The sailors on the other side of the room jerked around and stared.

"The order is from Parnelles himself," said Van Buren over the secure satellite radio. "We're on Hold."

"Aw, screw that, Colonel. Screw it. We gotta go in."

"We are not, Sergeant. We are standing by until we have further orders."

Sergeant. The chain of command always came up when the shit hit the fan, thought Rankin.

"Stephen?"

"Yeah, all right. We'll stand fucking by," said Rankin. He tossed the microphone down and stalked from the compartment.

13

CHAIN, SOUTH KOREA

Thera stopped the car about a mile down the road from the Seven Sisters Medical Treatment Corporation, parking in the lot of a vast apartment complex. She smiled at a young couple walking toward the high-rise, then removed the bicycle from the rental's trunk. Tucking her hair under a watch cap, she strapped on her backpack, then cycled out of the lot, riding down a small service road in the direction of the business park.

The road ended about forty yards from the parking area. She turned off the macadam and began pedaling across the field. The sun had only just set, but the field was already so dark she could barely see the building she was aiming at. Thera bumped along on the bike, steering between the rocks and scraping against the tall clumps of underbrush.

A chain-link fence separated the field from the parking lot behind the buildings. Thera rode along it until she spotted an opening, then turned, gliding through and bumping down onto the pockmarked asphalt.

She stopped near the pile of discarded wood, not far from the truck, dropping the bike against the pile. It was nearly invisible from five feet away.

Crouching next to the truck, Thera made sure she hadn't been followed. Then she went over to the corner of the building where a large power cable fed into a box and meter. The meter showed that the power was off; she confirmed this with a handheld current meter, the same one she used to detect alarm wiring. Then she checked the rest of the perimeter, making sure she was alone before returning to the back of the building.

The window frames were made of metal, and the plywood covering them had been attached with thick screws. Thera took a large Phillips-head screwdriver from her rucksack and began backing the screws out of the frame closest to the truck. She took out six screws, leaving only the two at the very top, which were hard for her to reach. The wood creaked and split as she pried the board away from the bottom and squeezed underneath.

The glass windows were still intact under the board. Thera smacked her gloved fist and then her elbow against the pane, but it wouldn't shatter. She had to use a glass cutter, and even then it took several minutes to get past the thick outer glass.

The inside pane gave way more easily. Thera made a large hole, then stuck her head through to look around with the help of her night-vision goggles.

Metal studs crisscrossed the vast space. The place smelled as if it were filled with fine metallic dust.

She climbed inside. Though empty, the interior looked in better shape than the outside, clean and neat, the polished concrete floor smooth. Thick canvas tarps covered a cluster of objects of different sizes at the extreme right side of the building.

Choosing one at random, Thera cut away the belt securing the canvas and found a drill press. She reached into her backpack and took out a plastic bag, collecting some of the fillings in the work tray below the table. Then she took a radiation meter and held its wand over the machinery.

The needle didn't move.

She went to the wall, making sure it was the outer one, then began looking around the floor, searching for a trap-door or some other hiding place. But the floor was solid concrete and had been swept so clean that even her great grandmother would have approved.

Wouldn't a shuttered factory like this be filled with dust?

Puzzled, Thera began pulling the tarps off the machines one by one. Most were specialized fabrication tools she was unfamiliar with; she took pictures with the infrared digital camera, just in case.

The shavings in some of the machines were plastic. Thera found a table stacked with thin sheets of metal she thought was lead. Unsure, she took the smallest piece she could find, a narrow strip about a quarter-inch thick and eight inches long.

As she cinched her backpack to go, Thera heard a sharp snap behind her. She spun back in the direction of the sound. In that instant, the lights came on.

14

SOUTH OF KUSŎNG, NORTH KOREA

General Namgung had still not made up his mind which pilot to choose when he arrived at the small airstrip south of Kusŏng. This was uncharacteristic; throughout his career he had decided most important matters literally in seconds. Now, as his most important moment neared, he found it impossible to pick its agent.

Perhaps he needed to look each man in the eye, to feel his grip. Perhaps it was the human connection that he lacked, the spark that would set everything in motion.

It was already in motion, moving across the country. There was grumbling, questions from P'yŏngyang, from the Great Leader himself. The Southerners were slow to react, obviously thinking it was some sort of bluff, but that was just as well.

Several generals had refused to follow his orders, and Namgung knew he might not be able to trust all of the units near the capital. But he had never counted on one hundred percent support in any event. Once the attack was launched, the reactions from the Americans and from the Chinese would propel events. His position would carry him.

Namgung's car stopped in front of a small concrete building. Next to the building, concealed by a large camouflaged net, was a ramp that led to an underground aircraft shelter.

Nearly all of North Korea's air force facilities had underground concrete hangars. This one, however, was unique in that it was occupied by a single plane, a MiG-29 the country had acquired within the past few months, partly with money made available by Park. The aircraft, an improved version of the already formidable fighter-bomber, combined the latest Russian and Western technologies, and was considered superior even by the Americans to all but a handful of fighters. Small and fast, it could avoid the most powerful radars until it was too close to its target to be stopped.

Strapped to its belly was a nuclear device built with the billionaire's help. Park had supplied the plutonium; North Korean scientists working for Namgung had done everything else.

"General, everything is in order," said Lee, saluting as the general approached. "The fuel truck will arrive within ninety minutes, as soon as the satellite passes."

"Very good," said Namgung. "Where are the pilots?"

"Practicing with the simulator, as you ordered. Should I get them?"

Namgung turned back toward the airfield, looking at the dark sky. Clouds obscured the moon. It was perfect.

"Let them practice a little longer," he said.

CHAIN, SOUTH KOREA

Three men stood at the far end of the empty factory.

"Back for fun?" yelled one of them, his English heavily accented.

It was the kid who'd bothered her earlier in the day.

Thera threw herself behind the nearest machine as one of the men began firing a submachine gun. The others yelled at him in Korean to stop wasting his bullets and be careful; they would get in trouble if they damaged the machines.

Thera pulled one of her Glocks out from beneath her coat.

"You remember me from this afternoon?" said the man with the machine gun. "You were very brave when you were the one with the weapon. Let's see how brave you are now."

He fired off another burst.

Thera edged to the side of the machine. They'd have a clear shot at her from where they were if she moved, but staying here didn't make sense; they could move down the side of the building and then attack her from behind the other machines.

She drew her second pistol, took a breath and held it midway. Then she pushed the rest of the air from her lungs and leapt upward, firing twice and taking down the man on her far right.

It took the others two or three seconds to return fire. By that time she had ducked behind the long bending press. Their bullets clinked and clanged as they ricocheted off the heavy machine. Thera scrambled behind it, then rolled to a second tarped hulk nearby.

The two men were cursing bitterly. That was good, she thought; they would react rather than think.

Thera worked her way toward the side of the building where she had come in. When she reached the last machine she slipped one of her guns into her coat pocket and got down on her belly, snaking out from behind the tarp to look for the Koreans.

They weren't where she had left them.

Thera saw something move to her left and jerked back, firing as she ducked behind cover. Her first bullet got the Korean in the chest, where his bulletproof vest caught it, but her second rose all the way to his neck, slicing a hole in his windpipe.

The third went between his eyes. He blasted away with his machine gun as he hit the floor, his death jerk emptying the magazine.

The other man began screaming and firing wildly on the other side of the building, pouring his bullets in the direction of the machine where Thera had first hidden. He ran through the entire clip of his gun, yelling insanely in Korean. When the gun was out of ammo he began to retreat, running up the far side of the building.

Thera jumped to her feet and ran after him. When she was about six feet away she launched herself, landing on his back.

He collapsed. His gun flew across the floor, clattering against the wall. He struggled for a moment, but the fight was out of him; his courage had fled and left him a powerless shell. Thera pounded the side of his head once, then twisted him onto his back, her knees on his arms and her gun in his throat. Tears flowed from his eyes.

"Who are you?" she demanded. "Who?"

He started to answer in Korean.

"English, damn you, or you join your friends."

"We look after the buildings," he said.

"You're security?"

He couldn't understand what she was saying.

"Explain what you do," said Thera.

"We watch. There are cameras in the high-rise. We chase children away, mostly."

"Where are your uniforms?"

"No uniforms; too much attention. Quiet. We must be quiet or no pay."

"Who hired you?"

"Management company." He gave a name in Korean that meant nothing.

"Where'd the electricity come from?" Thera asked.

He didn't understand the question. Thera jumped up and hauled him to his feet.

"The lights," she said. "The power line outside isn't connected."

"Underground. Keys . . . We have keys. Everything quiet. No attention."

"What was this building used for?"

"I don't know."

Thera jabbed her pistol into his throat. "Talk to me or die."

A fresh flood of tears rained down his cheeks. She smelled urine; he'd wet himself.

"I don't know," he said, shaking his head. "No. I don't know."

"The other buildings. What's in them?"

"Nothing."

"Nothing? What did they make here?"

"A box. Big, like a . . . I don't know the word in English. They took it away."

"Use Korean."

He described it in Korean. Thera understood maybe a tenth of the words.

She pushed him against the wall and patted him down quickly. He had another magazine of bullets for his submachine gun and a cell phone; she kicked both across the floor.

"Come," she told him, leading him to her backpack at

the other end of the building. She tied his hands together with plastic-zip handcuffs, then grabbed her sat phone and dialed into The Cube. Lauren was on the other end.

"Get a Korean translator on the line. Ask this guy what he saw in the building. See if it sounds like an airplane container."

"Thera?"

"Do it."

"I'm doing it. I'm doing it."

16

THE WHITE HOUSE, WASHINGTON, D.C.

The National Security Council meeting was scheduled to begin at eight p.m. President McCarthy practically leapt into the room at 7:58, full of energy. The laid-back southern gentleman always yielded to a purposeful commander in a crisis.

"Gentlemen, ladies. I'm glad we're all here." McCarthy's drawl had a decidedly caffeinated flavor to it. "Korea. Update me, if you will."

Verigo Johnson from the CIA began running down the latest intelligence. The key word seemed to be *confusion*; even the North Koreans didn't seem to know what was going on.

The Japanese government had issued a terse though polite "we don't comment on rumors" statement, while at the same time placing its self-defense forces on high alert. The Russians had issued a statement of support for Kim Jong-Il "during his illness"; the Chinese had remained characteristically silent. Behind the scenes, the British were suggesting a coup was underway and had notified the U.S. that two warships would be steaming toward the area and could be called on if necessary.

About halfway through the slides in Johnson's Power-Point presentation, one of Slott's aides came into the room and whispered something in his ear. He grimaced, then looked across at Corrine and motioned with his head toward the door.

She waited a minute after he left, trying to preserve some pretense that she wasn't working with him.

Slott had gone down the hall to the secure communication center and was talking to Thera in South Korea when Corrine got there. The communications specialist on duty had already arranged for her to join the line; all Corrine had to do was pick up the phone.

"The cargo container was lined with lead," Thera was saying. "That's why it was so heavy. It must have gone north when the 727 brought Ferguson north."

"What went north?" asked Corrine.

"The plutonium," explained Thera. "Park had a special container made for his aircraft. We have the scientist who designed it in North Korea, and I've spoken to the people who moved it."

"They must have used it to bring the plutonium south," said Slott.

"No, not south," said Thera. "It *was* south. It went north."

"I doubt that," said Slott. "Park must be buying it from the North Koreans. He wouldn't be *giving* them plutonium."

"Why do you think it went north?" asked Corrine.

"Because the plutonium was at the waste site when I was there, and now it's not. Right? They must have moved it out. Maybe it was in one of those train cars near the tag, and then was removed by the truck that Ferguson saw."

"That just means they moved it to a better hiding place," said Slott. "Giving bomb material to the North would make no sense. They're almost at war."

"Maybe Park thinks he'll somehow benefit if there's an attack on South Korea," said Corrine.

"I don't think so," said Thera. "He's kind of nutty, but not in that way. He collects old Korean relics. He's *really* into history. Really into it."

Corrine glanced up at Slott. "What did Ferguson say about Park? He hates the Japanese."

"Big time," said Thera. "Can't stand them."

"The defector with the dictator's bank data," said Corrine, realizing where the senator's e-mail had come from. "What if that plane were carrying a bomb?"

**NORTH KOREA, SOUTH OF KWAKSAN
ON THE WESTERN COAST**

Ferguson lay in his hiding spot among the rocks, leaning on his elbows as he contemplated the stars. He hadn't slept. He couldn't sleep; his mind spun in a million different directions, just beyond his control.

"We're all going to die," a friend who had pancreatic cancer once told him, "but I've been blessed with the knowledge that it'll be very soon."

"That's because you're a priest," Ferguson had answered. "You see everything as a blessing."

"Aye, but truly it is, because it gives me a chance to do my best until then. Every day."

"Shouldn't we do that anyway?"

"If we did, Ferg, then what in the world would I have to preach about every Sunday? Will you tell me that, lad?"

"Will you tell me that, lad?" said Ferguson now, staring at the night sky. "Will you tell me that?"

The thick clouds refused to answer.

If living meant living like this—shaking from the

cold, exhausted, his mind torn off its pegs—was it worth living?

No.

Why bother?

Ferguson rubbed his eyes. They were like hard marbles in wooden saucers.

The sat phone began to buzz. He grabbed it, held it to his ear expectantly.

"We leaving?" he asked.

"Ferg, this is Corrine Alston. I'm here with Dan Slott."

"Wicked Stepmother," he said, forcing enthusiasm into his voice. "You calling to tell me I'm going to have to walk to China?"

"Ferg, when Park met with the general, was there any talk about a MiG-29?" asked Corrine.

"I didn't hear the conversation," said Ferguson. "Why?"

"We've been told that a MiG pilot is going to defect and fly to Japan with documents saying where Kim Jong-Il has hidden his money. We've located what we think is the airport where he's supposed to be taking off from. It has an unimproved strip."

"Ferg, remember the airstrip A5?" asked Slott.

"More or less."

"It's south of Kusŏng. You looked at it as a possible evac base, but we couldn't be sure if it was inactive."

"Yeah, OK." Ferguson didn't remember it at all.

"It's only about fifteen miles from where you are," said Slott. "The satellite passed over it a few minutes ago, and there was nothing on the strip. But if the aircraft is in an underground hangar, it might be there."

"Why do you think there?"

"We have coordinates that indicate something will take off from that area pretty soon. We're arranging a Global Hawk surveillance flight with ground-penetrating radar, but it's going to take about two hours at least for it to get up and get over there. If you were able to use the bike that's in the cache kit, you'd get there in half the time. You could at least tell us if the runway's clear."

"Yeah." Ferguson got up and started pulling the bike together. "Did you find the plutonium?"

Neither of them answered.

"All righty then. Hook me up with Corrigan so I can get a road map."

18

THE WHITE HOUSE, WASHINGTON, D.C.

The National Security briefing had already broken up by the time Corrine and Slott finished talking with Ferguson. They followed the president and a knot of aides up to the Oval Office. Corrine felt almost sheepish, as if she'd snuck out of class to meet a boyfriend and gotten caught.

Slott felt as if he were in the middle of a painful dream. He still wasn't sure he believed Park and the North Koreans were actually aiming at the Japanese. It was a wild theory but too dangerous to ignore.

Parnelles, who was with the president, saw them in the corridor. The CIA director whispered something to McCarthy, and the president's voice suddenly boomed through the hall.

"I require a few minutes to discuss something with my attorney," McCarthy told the others. "Miss Alston, if you could meet me upstairs please. Tom, why don't you and Dan stand by, and I'll take you right after her. Everyone else, please have a very good dinner."

When they got to the president's office, Corrine insisted that Slott and Parnelles come in and then made Slott say what they had found. McCarthy leaned back in his leather chair, one foot propped against the drawer of the desk.

"It is an *incredible* theory, Mr. Slott. Very incredible," he said when Slott finished.

"It's out there, sir."

"And we're checking it out?"

"We have an officer nearby. A coincidence."

But maybe it wasn't much of a coincidence at all, Slott thought as he said that. Ferguson always managed to get himself in the middle of whatever was going on.

"Lucky for us, Mr. Slott. Can we stop this aircraft?"

"I can try and get it on the ground, Mr. President," Slott said. "I have the Special Forces component of the First Team offshore. I can get them into position to make an attack. With your permission."

McCarthy did not want to accidentally start a war between South and North Korea, but even that paled against the possibility of Japan being attacked with a nuclear weapon.

"If the aircraft is there, do it. In the meantime, alert the air force."

"Jon, if this is a defector," said Parnelles, "we don't necessarily want to shoot him down."

"Better to shoot him down than risk Tokyo being obliterated." McCarthy picked up his phone. "Jess, run and get Larry Stich before he leaves for the Pentagon, would you? And the chairman of the Joint Chiefs. Round him up as well. And the secretary of state and Ms. Manzi. Tell them I have some new developments that require their input."

19

As tired as he was, as dead-dog beat tired as he felt, riding the bike made Ferguson feel incredibly better. It was something to do, a goal. He could turn off the rumbling in his brain and just push down on the pedals, pump up the road Corrigan said would take him directly to the airstrip.

Fifteen miles. That was about an hour's ride at a decent, moderate pace.

I'm going to do it in less, he told himself, pushing. Much less.

Less.

20

Rankin raced into the gym his men were using as a ready room.

"Saddle up! We got a mission, let's go," he shouted through the doorway. "Let's do it. Get aboard the choppers. Come on, let's go."

The men snapped to immediately, grabbing their gear and trotting in the direction of the flight deck.

"We getting Ferguson?" asked Michael Barren, the Special Forces' first sergeant.

"No. We're going to neutralize an air base. The Marines are going to back us up."

"An air base?"

"I'll lay it out in the helicopter. Come on."

21

THE WHITE HOUSE, WASHINGTON, D.C.

Corrine kept a low profile, sitting at the side of the Oval Office and saying absolutely nothing. Reactions to the theory that Park had made or helped make a bomb that would be used in an attack against Japan ranged from incredulous to . . . incredulous. Neither the secretary of state nor the secretary of defense thought it possible. Nor were they willing to accept that the South Korean government—let alone one of its citizens—had been working on a bomb.

"They have done such work before," said Slott, referring to the extraction experiments a decade before. "They only came clean when the International Atomic Energy Agency caught them."

"We can shoot the aircraft down," said Defense Secretary Stich. "They know that. Their airplanes are ancient."

"The North Koreans have purchased at least two new MiG-29s in the past few months," said Parnelles. "Those are formidable aircraft."

"We'll still shoot it down."

"There is at least a theoretical possibility that the aircraft could escape detection," said Parnelles, "once it is in the air."

Slott, impatient to get back to work, tapped his foot as a technical discussion continued about how exactly the aircraft could escape detection and whether the Japanese Self-Defense Force could stop it.

He could tell from the looks he was getting that the others thought he'd lost control of the Agency if not his mind. They were probably thinking of suitable replacements right now.

This was one part of the job he wasn't going to miss, the meetings, the posturing, the backstabbing. Backstabbing, especially.

Slott passed a note to Parnelles saying he wanted to leave. Parnelles nodded. Slott waited for a lull in the conversation, then rose and excused himself, saying he had a few things he had to stay on top of.

"By all means, Daniel. You get back to work," said McCarthy, rising. "We all should. I believe we've discussed this as far as it can be discussed at the moment."

Corrine slipped out as well, ducking down the hall toward her office. Slott, momentarily detained by the chief of staff, followed behind her. She glanced at his face as she went into her office. It looked drawn and tired. Corrine felt as if she needed to say something encouraging to him.

"You're doing a good job," she told him.

"We can't continue this," he snapped.

Corrine stopped and stared at him. The remark seemed almost bizarre, as if they were continuing an affair.

"What do you mean?"

"Never mind," he said, brushing past.

"No. What do you mean?" she insisted, going after him and grabbing his shoulder.

Slott stared at her. She was not quite young enough to be his daughter, but it was close.

"What experience do you have?" he said. "You're a lawyer. You've only worked in Washington."

"If you have some problem with me—"

"You bet I do."

Slott's voice was loud, too loud for the narrow hall. He

glanced over his shoulder; the cabinet members were spilling out of the president's office.

"I don't need this now," he said, turning to go.

"We can work this out."

"Right." He walked away.

Suddenly aware of the people behind her, Corrine clamped her mouth shut and went back to her office.

SOUTHWEST OF KUSŎNG, NORTH KOREA

The engineer who designed Ferguson's bicycle had spent considerable time making it light and easy to take apart. He'd given much less thought to making it easy to pedal and probably no thought at all to making it comfortable.

Ferguson's legs felt as if they would fall off after about five miles. By the eighth, he'd lost all sensation in his lower back. There was barely enough light to see the road in front of him, and though he'd put on extra clothes, he was so cold his bones felt like ice.

But he kept pedaling, and the closer he got to the airstrip—he estimated the distance using his watch—the more confident he felt.

It's delirium, he told himself. Then he started to laugh.

About three guffaws later, the front wheel of the bike hit a pothole, and he found himself flying through the air.

23

Corrine had left her office and was about to set out for
The Cube when Jess Northrup flagged her down in the
parking lot.

"President wants to talk to you," said the assistant to the
chief of staff. "I was calling to you. I guess you didn't hear."

"I'm sorry. I guess I didn't hear," said Corrine.

"Mustang's almost ready," added Northrup as they
walked back inside.

"Still going to give me a ride?"

"Soon as I get an engine."

Y ou are doing a superb job on this, dear," said Mc-
Carthy when she reached his office. The president
had ordered his military aides to wait outside so he could
talk to her alone. "I have a few questions I was hoping
you could answer before I go downstairs to monitor the
situation."

"OK."

"Is Park doing this himself? Or is the government involved?"

"I don't know."

McCarthy ran his fingers through his hair. "I think there
is a strong possibility that the government is helping or at
least turning a blind eye. I would like to know definitively."

"How?"

"If you want to know who all the hens are, you'd best
grab the rooster."

"You want us to get Park?"

"If we don't, I can only assume the South Koreans will. And I would be very surprised if he were able to be candid under such circumstances." The president folded his arms. "The Japanese, for one, will not trust what he says if he is in Korean custody. It would be best for all concerned if he turned up here. A job for Special Demands, if ever there was one," added McCarthy.

"All right," said Corrine. "Dan Slott is pretty upset about the present arrangement."

"Why is that?"

"I think he thinks I'm interfering with his job."

"Are you?"

"No. But—"

She stopped, not sure exactly what she wanted to say.

"Pardon the expression, Miss Alston, but that is a pregnant pause if ever I have heard one."

"You have to admit that the chain of command is confusing," said Corrine. "And I realize that's partly by design, but—"

McCarthy gave her his fox smile. "Are you accusing me of confusing my underlings?"

"I think you try and keep people on their toes."

"I hope so. Don't worry about Mr. Slott. Keep doing what you are doing."

"Who's in charge of the First Team?"

"I am, dear. I am in charge of everyone who works for this government. Their faults are my faults. They can take the credit if they want."

"But as far as operations go—"

"You are my conscience and oversight in matters related to the Office of Special Demands, and the deputy director of operations of the CIA is in charge of Central Intelligence personnel. I see no confusion."

Corrine knew she wasn't going to get more of an answer, and this certainly wasn't the moment to press him anyway.

"Work with him, dear. He's a good man."

"I know that. But I'm not the problem. Sir."

24

SOUTHWEST OF KUSÖNG, NORTH KOREA

Ferguson knew it was going to hurt when he landed.

He seemed to know that forever, flying forward in the blackness toward pain.

He managed to get his right hand up as he landed. This didn't deflect the fall so much as it focused the anguish on the asphalt scraping his palm and forearm raw. He rolled over on the ground, the wind knocked out of him, unable even to scream.

There was no telling how long he might have lain there if he hadn't noticed the faint light of headlights in the distance behind him. He pushed himself to his feet, grabbed the bicycle and dragged it off to the side as the lights rounded the curve behind him and became two distinct cones sweeping the night.

If he'd been in better shape, Ferguson might have leapt onto the back of the fuel truck as it passed, for it lumbered rather than sped. But he was too spent. He had barely enough strength to watch it as it passed.

Thirty yards down the road, the truck's brake lights lit. It stopped, then began moving in reverse. With a groan, Ferguson grabbed for the pistol he'd tucked into the parka's pocket, but the truck had only missed a turn. It took a right, the driver grinding the gears as he went up a winding path.

Ferguson got to his knees, then stood, watching the headlights disappear behind the trees. Corrigan had told him the airport was up about a hundred yards from the roadway, up a hill. There weren't any settlements anywhere nearby.

Was this it already?

He pushed the bicycle into a clump of bushes and started in the direction the truck had taken. Ferguson walked until he came to a chain-link fence topped by barbed wire. His right hand hurt so much that he decided to look for a spot to crawl under rather than use it to pull himself over. Eventually he came to a hole made by a large tree trunk and managed to squeeze underneath.

Threading his way through a clump of young trees, Ferguson found himself at the edge of what he thought at first glance was a farm field. There were lights a few hundred yards away and a small building. It was only when he started walking toward them and dragged his feet across the ground that he was sure he'd found the airstrip.

He backtracked, walking along the perimeter near the fence until he found the road the truck had taken toward the building. As soon as he started down it, however, he caught a glimpse of two shadows moving a short distance away. He stopped, watching as they worked over a third lump. This one barrel-shaped. Fire suddenly erupted from it, and the two men held their hands out to warm themselves.

Can I take them?

I could use one of their uniforms.

Take them.

But if I'm asking the question, then I can't do it. 'Cause if I doubt myself, that's a warning.

Find the plane and call it in. That's most important.

Ferguson slid back in the direction of the fence, circling warily around the sentries. His hand was too mangled and his legs stiff. He couldn't think quickly, and his body felt as if it were moving through mud.

He walked only another seventy or eighty yards before he had to stop and rest. There was definitely a plane there; he could see it in front of the hangar. The truck was nearby and must be refueling it.

What the hell else do I need to know?

Ferguson pulled out the sat phone.

"Corrigan, you awake?" he asked.

"I'm here, Ferg. Where are you?"

"I found your airstrip. There's definitely an airplane here."

"What kind?"

"Some sort of jet."

"Is it a MiG?"

"Hang on, I'll go ask them." Ferguson put the phone down against his leg and shook his head. Then he picked the phone back up. "They say they don't know."

"I guess that was a dumb question, huh?"

"No, Jack, it was a ridiculously dumb question. I'm about seventy-five yards from them, maybe farther. I don't know; my distance judgment's off. They're not using any lights. There's a cube kind of building there, like a bunker. If all of that fits your description, this is the place you're looking for."

"Stand by."

"I am standing."

A moment later, Slott came on the line.

"Ferg?"

"Hey."

"We're sending in a team to take the plane out. Are you OK?"

"I really feel like horseshit to be honest."

Slott sighed, as if the whole weight of the world had now settled on his shoulders.

Ferguson started to laugh. He had to put his arm against his mouth to keep his voice down.

The truck had started to move.

"Hey, when's that team getting here?" he asked.

"Twenty minutes. Why?"

"Too late," he told him, stuffing the phone in his parka as he began to run.

25

CHAIN, SOUTH KOREA

The kid watching the warehouse who'd lost his nerve would be an important witness, but Thera wasn't sure what to do with him. Turning him over to the South Korean security forces didn't make sense for many reasons. For one thing, it was very possible Park was working with the government in some way; handing him to the intelligence agency might be the same as giving him to the billionaire's lackey, Li.

And for another, his two dead comrades would have to be explained, probably ad infinitum.

The only thing Thera could think of to do with him was to take him to Seoul, where she could leave him with the CIA people at the embassy. He sat meekly in the passenger seat, hands cuffed, oblivious as she attempted to pry a little more information out of him.

"I'll put on music if you want," she told him, trying to get him out of his fugue.

The kid continued to stare straight ahead.

Maybe there's something about me that makes men go catatonic, she thought to herself.

She was about an hour out of Seoul when the sat phone rang. It was Corrine Alston.

"Can you talk?" asked Corrine.

"It depends," said Thera. "What's up?"

"We want you to get Park," said Corrine. "Arrest him, offer him protection . . . whatever it takes."

"Protection? He's behind the whole thing."

"Tell him whatever you want, just get him. We don't want the South Koreans dealing with him on their own; they may have been in on it, and will simply use him as a scapegoat. You have to get him before they do."

"I don't know, Corrine."

"It's not a matter for debate."

Right, thought Thera. Dumb ideas never are.

"Do you know where he is?" Thera asked.

"That's your department. Colonel Van Buren is detailing you a Special Forces team."

"I don't think it'll work."

"You have to make it work. It's what the president wants."

Thera glanced at her passenger, still catatonic.

"You don't really know what you're asking," she told Corrine. "It's not going to work."

"Well, try, damn it."

26

SOUTHWEST OF KUSŎNG, NORTH KOREA

The pilots were even the same height.

General Namgung studied Ri Jong-Duk and Lee Ryung, looking first at one, then at the other. The harsh overhead lights in the small underground training room turned each man's face a fiery red.

Ryung, on the right.

Yes. That was it.

"You will take the plane," he told the pilot. "Go."

A broad smile spread across Ryung's face, though he tried to keep it in check. The thirty-three-year-old turned into a teenager again, practically skipping from the room.

Ri Jong-Duk stood stoically, staring straight ahead.

"You, too, have done your duty as a Korean," Namgung said to the pilot. He put his hand on the man's shoulder, feeling sincere compassion. The pilot had done nothing wrong; he had in fact been as brave and courageous as his fellow.

Ri Jong-Duk remained silent.

"You will be accorded a hero's funeral," said the general. He stared into Ri Jong-Duk's eyes. They began to swell.

General Namgung nodded, then turned away. The pilot's stoicism inspired him. It was a propitious omen, a sign that they would succeed.

Very good. He would see the plane off, then drive to P'yŏngyang to begin things.

Namgung was six or seven steps from the flight room when he heard the gunshot signaling that Ri Jong-Dak had done his duty. He quickened his pace, determined to honor the young man's courage with his own actions.

27

SOUTHWEST OF KUSŎNG, NORTH KOREA

Ferguson's lungs felt as if they were collapsing in his chest, compressed by the hard strokes of his legs as he ran across the field. The truck was moving, going off on the road to his right. There were two men near the jet, working on it, illuminated by work lights that made the aircraft seem like a bird of prey hiding in the night. A fat cylinder sat beneath its belly.

Ferguson kept his eyes fixed on the cylinder, which looked more like a fuel tank than the bomb he guessed it must be.

He had the Russian PSM pistol in his left hand; his right couldn't close around the trigger.

He had to get close with that gun, real close. Right next to them.

Shoot them, grab their weapons, screw up the plane somehow.

Step by step.

Go, he told himself. Go, go, go, *go!*

Ferguson was less than thirty yards from the aircraft when he tripped the first time. He felt himself falling and managed to roll onto his left shoulder, curling around and getting back to his feet. The men at the aircraft, consumed by their work, didn't notice.

Go, go, go!

The second time he tripped he was twenty yards away. This time he hit his elbow and lost his pistol.

He couldn't find it at first. The men at the aircraft began shouting.

Ferguson spotted the gun and scooped it up. He was on both knees. He steadied his left hand with his right as best he could and fired.

He missed high, the bullet not even close enough to scare the men pointing at him.

Nothing to do now but go, he told himself, jumping to his feet.

Go!

General Namgung was still in the tunnel from the flight room when he heard the screams.

"An intruder!" he yelled, repeating what the others had said. "Quickly!"

He drew his pistol and began racing toward the airstrip.

The AK-47 sounded like a tin toy to Ferguson, the patter of its bullets the sound a child's mechanical toy made when winding down. He saw the tracers spinning wildly to his left, the soldier's aim thrown off by the shadows from the work lights.

The aircraft's canopy was open and a ladder propped against its side. Two men were racing to the ladder.

Ferguson brought the pistol up and fired at the figures. His bullets missed both.

I'm not that bad a shot, damn it, he thought to himself. He aimed at the lights, got both, and continued running forward.

Pilot Lee Ryung was not sure what was happening, but he knew that he had to do his duty, and his duty now was to board the aircraft. He put his hands on the orange rail of the ladder, pushing away from the crewman trying to help him.

A bullet crashed through the metal hull of the jet a few inches from his head. A soldier ran from the hangar ramp on the other side of the aircraft. The pilot froze for a second as the man began to fire, mistakenly thinking the soldier was shooting at him.

He was so close now there was no way he could miss. Ferguson fired two shots into the face of the man at the base of the ladder and watched him peel off to the side. He leapt past him, raising his gun at the figure descending into the cockpit. He squared his aim and fired.

Nothing happened. The PSM was out of bullets.

General Namgung saw the soldier pull up his rifle as the pilot climbed up the aircraft boarding ladder.

"Don't hit Lee Ryung!" he yelled. "Don't shoot the pilot!"

The soldier stopped. Namgung yelled to the pilot. "Go, go!"

Then he realized the man on the ladder wasn't dressed in flight gear and wasn't in fact the pilot at all.

L ee Ryung slapped the controls, desperate to start the MiG and move it from danger. Then he realized it was too late for that; there was someone on the ladder. He grabbed at his holster, pulling out his service revolver.

Ferguson screamed as he climbed the ladder, pain, anger, and frustration boiling together. He lost his balance, and as he started to slip he threw the last bit of momentum he controlled toward the figure in the cockpit, grabbing at the pilot's helmet.

Something exploded on his left.

A pistol, a big pistol.

Ferguson grabbed for it with his left hand, grappling for the barrel.

It felt like a hot pipe, a hot iron pipe on fire. He pulled it toward the other man, pushing it into his chest as it exploded again.

28

IN THE AIR OVER NORTH KOREA

"They've lost contact with Ferguson," Van Buren told Rankin over the radio.

Before Rankin could reply, the helo pilot pointed at the front of the windscreen.

"Airstrip dead ahead. There's a plane at the far end."

A thin line of tracers arced toward them from the right.

"We're going in!" shouted Rankin. He meant to tell the rest of the team, but in his excitement left the radio channel on the control frequency with Van. "It's hot! LZ is hot!"

"Godspeed," said the colonel.

29

SOUTHWEST OF KUSŎNG, NORTH KOREA

The man on the ladder dove into the cockpit.

Namgung cursed himself for being a fool. He took out his pistol and fired.

It had been so long since he used the weapon that the nose shot up and the bullet flew far from its mark. He fired again, with the same result.

Cursing, he ran toward the ladder, shouting for help.

———

Ferguson pulled the gun from the pilot's hand, bashing the side of the man's head with it, once, twice, a third time before realizing the man was already dead. The bullet the pilot had fired had gone up through his neck and into his brain.

There were more shouts, screams, gunfire. Ferguson was at the center of a roiling tempest, but all he could see was a small circle around him.

Someone was climbing the ladder. Ferguson leaned over and fired the revolver, felt it jerk up in his hand, the bullet sailing far from its intended target.

The plane's the important thing, he told himself.

He put the pistol's nose flat against the biggest screen and fired, then put the rest of the bullets through the panel on the right.

Ducking as the bullet flew past, Namgung lost his balance and slipped down the ladder. He struggled to get his boots back on the rungs, then clambered upward. As he did, the intruder flew over the side of the cockpit.

Namgung reached the cockpit, where the pilot sat upright in his seat.

"Go!" he commanded him. "Start the aircraft and take off! Go!"

Then he saw the blood covering the front of his vest, and realized all was lost.

Ferguson dropped from the MiG's forward cowling, landing on his legs as he planned but immediately pitching forward, rolling in a summersault underneath the plane. He saw two boots in front of him, and grabbed at them, pushing a surprised North Korean soldier to the ground.

The man's assault rifle skittered away. Ferguson dove at it, pulling it to his chest as the Korean recovered and grappled him, a fisherman reeling in an immense catch. But this catch slipped its hook: Ferguson rolled and mashed his mangled right hand onto the trigger of the AK-47.

The gun jerked wildly as the bullets spewed from its nose. Only two or three of the dozen bullets Ferguson fired found their target, but they laced across the North Korean's head, killing him instantly.

There was a second of stillness, of no sound, as if a vacuum had been created beneath Ferguson's body. He felt nothing, not cold or pain, certainly not triumph, nor even despair.

And then the tumult resumed: Helicopter blades whirled in the distance. Guns fired. Someone screamed.

It was Ferguson. He pushed himself out of the dead man's grasp and ran back the way he had come.

Despair overwhelmed General Namgung. His future—Korea's future—sat stone upright in his hands, empty.

"He's escaping!" yelled one of the soldiers.

"Helicopters!" yelled another.

Namgung started down the ladder, moving deliberately. He felt nothing, not anger nor revenge.

The soldier he had stopped from shooting earlier lay on the tarmac a few feet away. Two other soldiers were crouched nearby, firing into the field.

Namgung went to them. He could tell they were firing blind, without a target.

"Bring up more lights so you can see him," he said calmly. He checked his own pistol, making sure it was ready to fire.

Ferguson threw himself down about thirty yards from the strip. He crawled forward, deeper into the darkness. All he had to do was crawl away, just crawl. Rankin and the rest of Van's guys were here now, above, right here, on their way. They'd get the plane and then rescue him.

Or would it be better to die now?

He could stop, stand up, and burn the rest of the magazine, make himself an easy target.

Go out in a blaze of glory.

There was a certain romance in that, a fittingness. People would say he went out the way he wanted to. But the truth was, he didn't want to go out like that. Not now, at least, not here.

There were many things to do, people to see, to talk to.

His dad. Always his dad.

He hunkered down as a fresh wave of bullets flew by, pushing deeper into the darkness.

He's there!" yelled one of the soldiers, pointing at the shadow about forty yards away.

General Namgung grabbed the rifle from the nearby soldier. He would take care of the man himself.

30

IN THE AIR OVER NORTH KOREA

Rankin saw the figures running from the airstrip toward the field.

They must be after Ferguson.

"There," he shouted at the pilot. "I want to go there."

"I thought you wanted the plane."

"There's no one in the cockpit. We get my guy first."

The pilot started to answer, but Rankin didn't hear. He'd already pivoted toward the open door of the helo and put his Uzi on his hip. He steadied the weapon as the aircraft swooped low and began to fire.

31

General Namgung stopped and lowered the nose of his rifle, aiming at the man crawling away.

He showed great courage in attacking us, but now runs like a coward, thought the general.

As he pushed the trigger to fire, he felt the hot wind of hell swirling around him. He glanced up, realizing it was a helicopter.

In the next instant, a half-dozen 9mm parabellum bullets riddled his neck and chest.

Rankin leapt out of the Little Bird as it touched down, running toward the body to the left of the chopper. At first glance, he thought he'd made a mistake; it looked like a Korean.

At second glance, it looked dead.

Ferguson pitched himself onto his back, trying to bring up the AK-47.

Rankin stepped on the gun. Ferguson was so weak he lost his grip on the weapon. He blinked, then realized who was standing there.

"About fuckin' time, Skippy," Ferguson croaked. "You missed all the fun."

32

Corrigan looked up from the console.

"They've got him!" he yelled. "Ferguson is alive! They've got him!"

Tears began to stream from Corrine's eyes.

"Aircraft is under their control," added Corrigan, almost as an afterthought. "We have the bomb. The Marines are inbound!"

Corrine looked down at the communications panel controlling her headset and pushed the button to connect with Slott.

"You heard that, Dan?"

"Yes."

"I think you should be the one to tell the president."

"We should both tell him," he said. "Corrigan?"

There was a light pop in the headphones.

"You're on the line with the White House situation room," said Corrigan.

Corrine waited for Slott to say something.

Slott, waiting for her, remained silent.

"I hope there is nothing wrong with this line," said the president finally.

"Mr. President," said Slott. "The First Team has stopped the aircraft. We are in the process of securing the weapon."

"There *is* a weapon then?"

"Yes, sir."

"Good work, Mr. Slott. How long will it take before the bomb is secured?"

"We're going to use a marine helicopter to airlift it out," said Slott. "We want to bring it to one of our assault ships offshore. It will take a few hours."

"I would imagine that securing that weapon is a tricky thing."

"Yes, sir. One of our people has experience with that," he added, referring to Ferguson. "But, uh, every weapon is different."

"Are the North Koreans in a position to stop us?"

"We don't believe so at this time. We're monitoring the situation closely. There are no units nearby. There's a great deal of confusion in the capital."

"You will tell me the moment the weapon is in our complete control aboard our ship," said McCarthy.

"Yes, sir, I will."

"We will keep a careful watch until then, and do nothing to alert either country."

"I can't guarantee we can keep this a secret," Slott said.

"Then we had best move as quickly as possible," said McCarthy. "Miss Alston, are you on the line?"

"Yes, sir, I am."

"Job well done to you as well."

"Thank you, sir," she said, cringing as she heard Slott click off the line.

33

DAEJEON, SOUTH KOREA

The idea was rather simple; the trick was in its execution. Fortunately, Thera's plan relied heavily on the billionaire's ego, which was commensurate with his wealth.

"I am calling from the BBC," she told Park's official spokesman by phone. "We have heard that the South Korean military has been put on alert because of a possible attack by the North. We would like to arrange an interview with Mr. Park on the situation because of his prominence. His opinion will be of great importance to the business community internationally."

Thera hoped to worm Park's location out of the man or, failing that, to set up a trace on her line when Park came on to be interviewed. But the PR man did even better than she expected: He invited the BBC reporter and camera crew to Park's home at six a.m. for an interview.

"A very complex situation, and Mr. Park can surely shed important light on it," said the aide.

"We'll be there," said Thera.

She punched off the phone. It was half-past two; they were about thirty minutes from the compound.

"You have time to refuel," Thera told the pilot. "I have some calls to make."

34

DAEJEON, SOUTH KOREA

So it was done.

Years of planning and maneuvering. The difficult arrangements with the scientists, the companies, the Northerners, the mobsters and criminals like Manski, so repulsive and yet so necessary—it had all paid off. The plan would be well underway by now. In less than an hour, the people of Korea would have their revenge and be launched on the road to reunion and strength.

Park knew he would not get any credit for it, but credit was never his goal or desire. It was enough to know what had been accomplished.

The billionaire ordinarily had no use for TV, especially the news. But he could not resist the pleasure of seeing the newscasters' response to and coverage of the destruction of Korea's traditional enemy. He went to his office and turned on the small set he kept there, surfing through the channels, though by his calculations it would be at least a half hour before the aircraft would reach Japan.

The half hour passed slowly. Park flipped through the channels, waiting.

Another half hour. He settled on a Japanese station, reasoning that it would carry the news first.

Nothing.

Another half hour. He flipped to CNN. The network was playing a feature about shearing sheep.

Park once more began flipping idly through the channels. There should be news any moment. Any moment.

The phone rang.

Park glanced at the clock on the desk before answering. It was nearly four.

"Something has gone wrong," Li told him. "The Northern troops haven't moved as planned. Namgung is not in the capital. And Tokyo—"

"Yes," said Park, putting down the phone.

35

CIA BUILDING 24-442

"Rankin is aboard the *Peleliu*," Corrigan told Corrine. "The bomb is secure."

Corrine glanced at her watch. It was precisely 2:15 p.m.—a quarter past four in Korea. She punched the line to connect with Slott.

"Give Thera the go-ahead," Slott said.

Corrine nodded to Corrigan.

"Why don't you talk to the president this time?" Slott said. "I'm in the middle of something."

"Sure," said Corrine.

Corrigan made the connection.

"Mr. President, Dan Slott asked me to tell you that the bomb is aboard the *Peleliu*. The First Team is en route to secure Park."

"Well done, dear. We will give your people forty minutes to complete their task, and then I will call Yeop Hu in Seoul. After that, I will share what we know with the American public. It has been a difficult time," added McCarthy, "and I expect a few more difficult moments ahead. But you have all done yeoman's service. Yeoman's service."

"Jonathon, there's one thing you should know about where some of the information came from on this," said Corrine. "There was an e-mail that we think, that I think, came originally from Park or one of his people. It was sent to Senator Tewilliger. He gave it to me, and I gave it to the CIA."

"Gordon was involved in this?"

"Indirectly. And probably unwittingly."

"Well now," said McCarthy, "isn't that a fine, fine twist in the old bull's tail."

"Sir?" Corrine had never heard that expression before.

"Keep that information to yourself a spell, would you, dear?"

"Of course."

"I would imagine it will come out at some point in the future," added McCarthy. "At a much more strategic moment."

DAEJEON, SOUTH KOREA

They did it by the book.

Two teams took the perimeter from the ground, surprising the guards at the main gate and subduing them without resistance. Within seconds, a pair of Marine helicopters swooped in over the grounds, depositing two Special Forces A Teams on the roof of the house. Roughly twenty seconds later, they came in three of the windows.

The lone security officer on duty in the house made the mistake of opening fire at one of the American soldiers. There wasn't enough left of him to fit into a decent-sized garbage bag.

Thera came in behind the point team, racing toward the hallway that led to the residential suite and Park's bedroom. Infrared surveillance of the house had given the assault troops a reasonably good idea of where he was.

"Park, I'm here to help," she yelled as she and the soldiers reached the hallway. "Your government has declared you a criminal. I can offer you asylum."

There was no answer. The plan was for Thera to wait until the Special Forces soldiers with her subdued the billionaire, but she was too juiced with adrenaline to slow down. She reached the door to the room where he'd been at the start of the assault, dropped to her knees, and grabbed a flash-bang stun grenade.

"Park? We know you're in there. Come on. We don't have much time."

She waited a few seconds, pulled the pin out of the grenade, counted to two, and tossed it in the room.

Two soldiers leapt into the room a split second after

the grenade exploded, jumping left and right, securing it before she even got to her feet.

It was empty.

"Shit."

Thera thought for a second, then realized where he must be.

"This way, come on," she yelled to the men, starting back down the hall. She ran through the study, turned right, and sped through the dining room.

The light was on in the museumlike room. Thera waved the others back behind her, slowing to a walk before entering.

"I believed it might be a trick. But of course there was no way to be sure."

Thera froze. Park had dressed himself in one of the ancient sets of armor. He had a long sword in his hands, its jewels glimmering in the light.

"I'm with the American embassy, offering you asylum. Your government considers you an outlaw," said Thera. "They'll be arresting you."

"Do they? Or is that another of the Americans' many lies?"

Park mocked her, even though he suspected that what she said was true, or would be as soon as the Americans explained what had happened. The Korean security force would be ordered to shoot him as he resisted arrest.

He had planned to kill himself before they arrived, but the woman and her soldiers presented a better option.

"I'm with the American embassy," repeated Thera. "I can get you out."

"You were the arms dealer, the one with Manski," said Park, recognizing the red hair beneath the watch cap. "You were both spies, then, both Americans. I was a fool to think he was just a greedy criminal."

"I'm with the embassy," said Thera. "I can get you out. We can give you asylum."

"And what would be your price?"

"No price. Just come."

"You would expect me to explain. You want me to betray my country."

"Your country wants to arrest you."

"The government is not my country. Korea is my country." He raised the sword.

"Don't do it," said Thera. "I'm armed."

Park felt his chest grow warm. All his life he'd had two dreams. The first was to see Korea unified, its ignominy under Japan avenged.

The second was to live the life of a warrior. He could not have the first, but he could achieve the second in this moment. He charged forward with a yell taught to him by his ancestors.

Thera waited until the last moment, then dove to the side, trailing her foot to knock the top-heavy Park off balance. As she dove, she pulled the pistol from her holster.

"Stop!" she yelled at him.

He scrambled upward before she could get to her feet.

"I'll kill you," she warned.

Park smiled and swung the sword down.

Thera fired three times, square into his face. The sword grazed her ear, drawing a trickle of blood and lopping off her hair as it flew to the ground.

"You made it too easy," she told the dead man, pushing him off her chest. "Too damn easy."

EPILOGUE

Find an immortal lady
   And you too will be immortal.

—from "The Seventh Princess,"
traditional Korean song for the dead

1

Senator Gordon Tewilliger smiled for the television cameras as he entered the hallway, heading for the Red Room and the reception. He was only one of the crowd today, but it was a good day nonetheless. He had done well on the weekend talk shows, modestly pointing out that he had foreseen problems like those that had occurred in Korea, problems that necessitated a strong stance by the U.S., not a weasely inaction that couldn't be backed by force. The president needed to negotiate a new arms treaty with teeth. If he didn't, hinted Tewilliger, others would.

"Hey, Senator, you got a second?" said Fred Rosen, a reporter with the *New York Times*.

"For you Fred, anything," said Tewilliger. He hated Rosen, of course, and wouldn't have trusted anything he read in the *Times*. But flattering articles in the *Times* were money in the bank during fund-raising season. And it was always fund-raising season when you were planning to primary a sitting president.

"Just over here," said Rosen, nudging him to the side, away from the others. "I can't go in. Media's barred."

"A shame," said Tewilliger. "Jonathon was never like that in the Senate. He was very open. He's changed a great deal since he became president."

"Yeah." The reporter's mustache twitched. "Listen, I've been hearing some things. Supposedly there was an e-mail that came from this guy named Park trying to throw American forces off."

"What's that?"

"Some sort of information that came through a round-about source about the weapon that was confiscated," said Rosen. "What I heard was that the target was going to be Japan."

"Japan? Preposterous," said Tewilliger.

"Yeah. I also heard . . . This sounds crazy, but I also heard that the weapon may have been made in South Korea, not North Korea like everybody thinks. The administration has been awful dodgy about that."

"Dodgy. Yes." Tewilliger felt sweat starting to run down his neck. "Oh, there is my colleague from Wisconsin," he said, spotting Senator Segriff. "Excuse me, Fred. Senator? Larry?"

've written the letter," Dan Slott told Thomas Parnelles as they queued up to be congratulated by the president for the action in Korea. "I have it with me."

"Now's not the time, Dan. Think about it. Take a few more days."

"I've made up my mind."

"Special Demands is a very special situation. It really stands by itself."

"It won't forever. And even if it does, it's the principle. I have to resign; the president doesn't trust me."

"I'm certain he does."

"I've made up my mind," said Slott. He reached into his jacket pocket and handed Parnelles his letter of resignation just as the president turned to shake his hand.

hera found herself standing alone with Rankin, watching as the CIA and military people were congratulated for finding the weapon in North Korea. The reception was part of an elaborate game, half cover for the First Team and half celebration for the military and Agency personnel who could be acknowledged.

Thera, Rankin, and Ferguson had not been on the original guest list. Corrine Alston, however, had insisted that they be invited to attend, passing them off as nondescript aides to the White House chief of staff.

Rankin hadn't wanted to go. Thera, though, was curious; she'd never been in the White House before, and she convinced him to go.

Ferguson, of course, was always ready to party. He flowed through the crowd as smoothly as if he were working a casino in the Middle East, trolling for information.

And maybe he was.

"Told you it'd be bullshit," said Rankin bitterly. "Look at the stinkin' big shots, getting their handshakes."

"It's not about handshakes, Stephen."

Thera's eyes followed Ferguson across the room as he walked to the bar. He was handsome, and smart and brave. He'd recovered remarkably in the past two weeks, though he still wore a bandage on his wrist. When she'd seen him on the *Peleliu*, he looked like a ghost; now he looked like his old handsome self.

His old handsome self.

I'm in love with him, she realized. How did that happen?

"I need another drink," said Rankin. "Want one?"

Thera started to say that she would get it herself, but then she saw Corrine Alston going to Ferguson, touching his arm.

Something caught in Thera's throat. She turned to Rankin.

"I'll take one if you're getting one," she managed. "I'll be right here."

 know, Ferg."

Ferguson looked at Corrine and smiled.

"You know what? The price of tea in China?"

"I know you're very sick and that you don't want anyone else to know."

For a half of a second—no, less, a half of a half of a half of a second—Ferguson felt the shield he carried before him disintegrate. He was entirely naked, unprotected. Alone, too.

But then he was fine, smiling again as he always did.

"Yeah. In the mind."

"It's cancer, right?"

Ferguson scratched the side of his head and smiled. "Actually, it's an empty hole where my brain once was."

"You're not going to talk about it, are you?"

"If I knew what you were talking about, then I probably wouldn't. But I don't."

"Your secret's safe with me." Corrine tapped his elbow. "OK?"

Ferguson started to make a wisecrack but stopped. "Drink?" he asked instead.

"Sure." Corrine took his arm and he led her to the bar.

Follow Ferg and the First Team into their
next mission in

LARRY BOND'S FIRST TEAM

SOUL OF THE ASSASSIN

LARRY BOND AND JIM DEFELICE

Coming in May 2008 from Forge Books

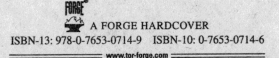

A FORGE HARDCOVER
ISBN-13: 978-0-7653-0714-9   ISBN-10: 0-7653-0714-6
www.tor-forge.com

1

Death had never particularly interested Bob Ferguson as a subject of study. It was a fact in and of itself, without nuance. His religious instruction—Ferguson had gone to parochial schools and a Catholic college—taught him to view death as a necessary passage, but the nuns, brothers, and priests who had instructed him tended to focus on either side of the gateway, rather than death itself.

As a CIA officer assigned to the agency's covert Special Demands team, Ferguson had had a great deal of experience with death; he had often been its agent and provocateur. Still, his relationship was purely professional; he remained neither intrigued nor moved by any aspect of the subject itself. The end of life was simply the end of life. The manner of its coming rarely interested him.

Ferguson's nonplussed expression as the video played on the small screen at the end of the study bothered his host, CIA Director Thomas Parnelles. Unlike Ferguson, death was something Parnelles contemplated a great deal. It bothered him, especially in its most brutal forms, and particularly when it involved someone he knew. The fact that the death on the screen involved both was particularly upsetting; it had happened to a man who worked for him, and required justice, if not vengeance.

Parnelles had known Ferguson for a very long time—

since Ferguson was born, in fact. He had been his father's closest friend, and on more than one occasion served in loco parentis when Ferguson Sr. was out of the country. He assumed because of these things not only that he knew the young man well, but that Ferguson shared his feelings on any matter worthy of having one. So the half-smile on Ferguson's face, the completely unmoved expression that was characteristic of the young man, annoyed Parnelles greatly. He finally reached over and clicked the laptop key to end the video just as it focused on the dead man's battered skull.

Unsure why the video had stopped, Ferguson took a sip of bourbon from the tumbler Parnelles had given him earlier. The liquor burned pleasantly at his throat as it went down.

"Technical problems, General?" Ferguson asked.

"There's not much more," said Parnelles. He flipped off the laptop, momentarily shrouding the study in darkness. When he turned on the light, Ferguson had the exact same expression on his face. "Are you feeling all right, Bobby?"

"Never better."

"North Korea was difficult, I know."

"Change of pace." Ferguson tilted the glass. The bourbon was Johnny Drum Private Stock, a well-aged small batch whiskey more distinctive than such standards as Maker's Mark or Jim Beam. That was one thing about Parnelles—he did not have standard anything.

"Ordinarily, I would tell you to sit down for a while, and take some time off," said Parnelles. "More than the few days you've had. But this is a priority. This is important."

"Not a problem."

"After this, maybe you should take two or three months off. Lay on the beach."

"I'll just get bored." Ferguson leaned forward, stretching his back and neck. "So Michael Dalton was killed in Puys, France, two years ago. Then what happens?"

"Then we spend two years trying to figure out who did it." Parnelles took his own drink from the edge of his desk and walked over to the chair near Ferguson. He told himself he was seeing the younger man's professional distance, nothing more. "We found this video from the bank's surveillance camera. We re-created Dalton's movements. We checked everyone who had stayed in the hotels nearby for up to two weeks before."

"Why was he there?"

"Vacation."

Ferguson smirked.

"No, really, he was taking a vacation," said Parnelles. "This is an out-of-the-way town on the Channel. He liked France, and he'd just spent a year in Asia. So it was different."

"What did the French say about the murder?"

Parnelles settled down in his seat and took a sip of his drink—Scotch—before answering.

"The local police, of course, were incompetent. They believed it was a terrorist attack."

"Just because a car blew up?"

"I really don't know why you're being sarcastic, Robert. You're not taking this seriously."

Ferguson took another sip of the bourbon. Generally Parnelles wasn't quite this worked up. In fact, Ferguson couldn't remember the last time he had briefed him personally on a mission—let alone asked him up to Maine to do so.

"Yes, it did look as if it were the work of terrorists," admitted Parnelles. "But why terrorists would blow up a car at that place and time—of course the police had no answers. A small village on the French coast? Terrorists would never operate there. Clearly, Dalton was the target. We went to the ministry, of course, but they got it into their heads that we were lying."

"About what?"

"That Michael was working, instead of being on vacation."

"Was he?"

"You're being very contrary tonight, Robert. I just told you he wasn't."

Bad publicity about the CIA's secret rendition program had caused a great deal of friction in Europe just prior to Dalton's death. The French believed that the Agency was withholding information about what Dalton had been working on—they thought it involved something in France—and in Parnelles's view had been less than cooperative out of spite.

Ferguson—who admittedly had never cared much for anything French, let alone their spies—knew that the French security service seldom displayed anything approaching alacrity, even when pursuing their own priorities. But he let that observation pass.

"If Dalton was targeted, then something must have happened in Asia," Ferguson told Parnelles. "What was it?"

"Unimportant, Bob. The point is, what I'm getting to—we know who killed him. He was a contract killer known as T Rex."

"Like the dinosaur."

"Exactly. He kills everything in his wake. He's extreme. T Rex."

Actually the name had been used in a text message intercepted by the National Security Agency just before another assassination, this one of a wealthy businessman visiting Lisbon. Ferguson had already seen the information in the text brief of his mission. There had been other "jobs" as well: T Rex had been implicated in the murder of a Thai government minister and a suspected fundraiser for Hezbollah, to name just two. Parnelles ran down the list of known and suspected victims, impressive both in length and variety.

Tired of sitting, Ferguson began bouncing his right leg up and down. His foot was just touching the fringe of a handwoven wool rug Parnelles had retrieved from Iran toward the end of the shah's reign—bad days, Parnelles had said once. It was all he said, ever, on the subject to Ferguson.

"You seem distracted, Bobby." Parnelles glanced at Ferg's foot, tapping on the carpet.

"Foot fell asleep." Ferguson bounded up from the chair. "Can't sit too long."

He did a little jig in front of the chair. "So what's the real story, General? Who is T Rex?"

"We don't know."

"The Israelis hired him, and we can't figure it out?"

"The Israelis *didn't* hire him," said Parnelles. "Hezbollah has a lot of enemies. Including Hezbollah itself."

"So what do you want me to do?"

"Figure out who he is. Apprehend him. Bring him here for trial."

"That's what Slott told me this afternoon." Ferguson glanced at his watch. "Yesterday afternoon."

He got up from the chair and walked around the study. It was as familiar to him as his own condo—more so. He'd played hide-and-seek here as a kid.

Taking T Rex in Italy was sensitive. The agency was still smarting over a well-publicized trial of several of its members, fortunately in abstentia, for the rendition of a suspected terrorist a few years before. The Italian court had found that the man was not a terrorist and had been kidnapped by the CIA, albeit with help from the Italian secret services. The political situation argued for the use of the elite First Team—officially, the Office of Special Demands—a small group of highly trained operatives headed by Ferguson and occasionally assisted by a Special Forces army group.

But the job might have been done by other CIA agents, including a special paramilitary team trained in renditions.

"So when I bring back T Rex," said Ferguson. "What happens? You put him on trial?"

Parnelles frowned.

"If a situation develops where he can't be brought to trial," he said, picking his words very carefully, "that would be something we could all live with."